# SHEEP'S-HEAD AND BABYLON

# SHEEP'S-HEAD AND BABYLON

## AND OTHER STORIES OF YESTERDAY AND TO-DAY

MARJORIE BOWEN

Edited and with an introduction by
Gina R. Collia

Published by Nezu Press
Queensgate House,
48 Queen Street,
Exeter, Devon,
EX4 3SR,
United Kingdom.

This edition published 2025

*Sheep's-Head and Babylon* first published by John Lane the Bodley Head Limited, 1929.



ISBN-13: 978-1-917113-12-0

Cover image: *Angora Goat* by Matthew Grove.

In the interest of preservation, the punctuation and spelling of the original first edition text have been maintained, and the original formatting has been used wherever possible. Only minor publisher errors and spelling inconsistencies have been silently corrected.

# CONTENTS

'Miss Marjorie Bowen'
*The Bystander*, 5 September 1906.

'I have used many names for business purposes, but they were none of them of my choosing and seemed rather to be fastened on me like a series of masks.' - Margaret Campbell, *Myself When Young: By Famous Women of Today*, 1938.

# Margaret Campbell
## The 'Lady with the Hundred Names'
by Gina R. Collia

Margaret Gabrielle Vere Campbell was born into poverty, in a house belonging to an elderly lady named Mrs Cole, on Hayling Island, off the south coast of England, on 1 November 1885.[1] She was the second child of Vere Douglas Campbell (1853–1906) and his wife, Josephine Elizabeth (née Ellis, 1860–1921); Josephine had been pregnant when she married Vere in the summer of 1884, but their first child, Dorothea, had died in infancy in a London lodging house a year before Margaret was born.[2] A third daughter, Phyllis Gertrude Bowen Vere Campbell, was born in the summer of 1890, when Margaret was four years old.[3] Of Irish descent and 'handsome, intelligent, attractive, a giant in stature', Vere was the third son of Dr Hugh Campbell (1823-1902) and his wife, Henrietta (née Johnson, 1826-1912).[4] Josephine was the third daughter of Reverend Charles Bowen Ellis (1821-1887), a West Indies-born Moravian minister, and his first wife, Priscilla (née Bayly, 1829-1879).[5]

Vere and Josephine Campbell's marriage was not a happy one. Vere was an alcoholic who, though he had always been kind to his daughter, disappeared from Margaret's life almost entirely by the time she was five years old.[6] Josephine, to whom Margaret was never close, was prone to 'hysterical ill-humour';[7] she scolded Margaret frequently, regularly made her stand in a corner with her hands on her head, and repeatedly told her that she 'ought never to have been born.'[8] Though Margaret's very early memories were happy ones, as she got older and became more aware of the people around her—of those who had complete power over her—she found that they 'began to be terrifying', and her mother's 'gusts of rage' bewildered and alarmed her.[9]

> 'I heard shouts, quarrels, echoes of scenes—battles or fights, they seemed to me. I was hustled from one room to another, shut in sometimes for hours together, very much afraid and wondering what was happening. Someone would open the door and push in a glass of milk and a slice of bread and butter, and once, I remember, a rag doll, and tell me to be quiet or to "efface myself," or to "run away and play, there's a good girl." '[10]

Margaret received no formal education as a child. Her mother, an aspiring writer and playwright, attempted to teach her to read and write, but each lesson 'exploded in a scene', which only served to increase her frustration and annoyance towards her daughter; five-year-old Margaret was often slapped on the backs of her hands with a hair-brush or shut in a room without any food as a punishment for 'refusing to spell out of obstinacy.'[11] Eventually, Marion Piggott, the family's nurse-cum-housekeeper, who was always referred to as Nana, succeeded where Margaret's own mother had failed. Nana also 'loved to

Josephine Campbell, *Morning Leader*, 1907.

dilate upon murder cases, even taking her charges to see the house where the dark deed was done', inspiring in Margaret an interest in actual murders and celebrated poison cases that 'began to ferment in that young mind of hers' and, many years later, found an outlet in her novels.[12]

During her early years, Margaret had little access to books.[13] Her family moved from one London lodging house to another, to avoid settling debts, and she made use of whatever she could find to read on the current landlady's bookshelf. When the family moved to Kensington, Margaret began to educate herself with books borrowed from the local library, and when, having been evicted for non-payment of rent, they moved again to lodgings on Vauxhall Bridge Road, she began visiting the National Gallery, the British Museum and the South Kensington Museums.[14]

In her teens, Margaret dreamed of becoming a great artist, and one of her mother's friends suggested that her passion for art should be encouraged as there might be money in it. She applied to attend the Royal College of Arts in South Kensington, but she failed the entrance examination.[15] Then, after several more moves to new lodgings to avoid paying yet more creditors, her mother decided that she should attend the Slade School of Fine Art, which she did from 1901.[16] But her work was regarded as poor by her professors, she failed both of the examinations she took whilst there, she was perpetually embarrassed by her mother's failure to pay her tuition fees on time, and she 'began to be aware of the disability of sex.'[17] As a result, she lived in a 'constant state of depression and terror.'[18] She went without food on a daily basis, was embarrassed by the state of her poor clothing, and she felt that every other student was a better artist than she was. Deflated and despairing, she turned to writing and, as there was no money to buy paper, took to scribbling out stories and notes on the backs of her own drawings.[19]

Following several more house moves, Margaret's family took lodgings in a street off Russell Square, and she managed to get some work carrying out research and fact-checking in the British Museum.[20] By that time, she had nearly finished writing a novel and had completed a number of poems and short stories, but her mother, who had failed to secure any interest in her own writing, attempted to persuade her against pursuing a literary career. In an attempt to force her to focus on her painting and drawing, she sent Margaret to Paris, but she failed to provide enough money to pay for lodgings, let alone tuition costs for art school classes.[21] Despite her circumstances—'I was hungrier then than I had ever been'—Margaret enjoyed her time in Paris, visiting museums and galleries and adding to her knowledge of art and history, but she made no progress in her career as an artist and returned to writing.[22]

When she had been in Paris almost a year, Margaret's mother sent for her to return home.[23] Once back in London, she showed some of her writing to her mother; Mrs Campbell's response was to declare it 'hopeless'.[24] This did not, however, prevent her from sending her young daughter's novel, the swashbuckling historical romance *The Viper of Milan,* to an agent. His response was not encouraging: the story was not believable, he disliked the unhappy ending, and it was 'not the kind of thing… that a girl was expected to write.'[25] Her mother suggested that, as she was a girl, she should write a 'pleasant tale', possibly 'something simple', if she wished to be published, but this proved an obstacle for Margaret; the tales she wanted to write were 'often full of dark and sinister shades.'[26] She wrote to escape the world she was forced to exist in, and by writing of dark subjects she managed, to a certain extent, to rid her mind of her own troubles.[27] Margaret's novel went on to be rejected by eleven publishers, and Mrs Campbell suggested that her daughter find an alternative way of making a living.[28] But it was eventually picked up by Alston Rivers Ltd. and published in 1906, when Margaret was twenty years old, and very much to everyone's surprise, not least of all Margaret's, it became a bestseller.[29]

'Miss Marjorie Bowen', *The Tatler*, 12 September 1906.

To avoid possible confusion, as her mother wrote under the name Campbell, *The Viper of Milan* was published under the name Marjorie Bowen, the surname being taken from her grandfather, Charles Bowen Ellis. Margaret later wrote that the decision had not been hers; she had wanted to write under her own name, the pseudonym chosen had been odious to her from the outset, and 'this use of two names unfamiliar and even slightly distasteful to me helped to divorce me from my own work.'[30]

By the end of October 1906, only two months after *The Viper of Milan's* publication, demand for the book was so great that a sixth impression had already been published, and lending libraries were forced to increase their orders for it by the day.[31] And as a result of the success of her first book, 'the literary sensation of the autumn season',[32] Margaret received a cheque for sixty pounds—the money going straight to her mother—and entered into a new contract with the publisher for two more books.[33] Mrs Campbell ceased the little work she had been doing to support herself and her children, Phyllis 'did not believe in work', and Margaret became the family's only breadwinner.[34] However, her income was not quite enough to keep four people, and she found herself 'harnessed to a career of hard work' and forced to 'chase every odd five-pound note in order to keep up with expenses.'[35] Loans had to be repaid, her mother's friends had to be 'helped', and Phyllis wanted singing, dancing and riding lessons; before a year had passed, her earnings had been spent.[36] And nobody was happier for it; in fact, Margaret felt that they were unhappier than they had been before.

Josephine Campbell was bitterly jealous of her daughter's sudden literary success, having failed to achieve any for herself.[37] Critics had questioned why she had bothered to write her novel *The Crime of Keziah Keene*, published in 1889, one calling it 'downright nonsense', another describing it as having 'very little narrative and no plot.'[38] The reviewer for *The Academy* expected it to sink 'into well-deserved oblivion.'[39] And her novel *Ferriby*, published a year after Margaret's first great success, was described as leaving 'an unpleasant taste on the intellectual palate.'[40] Her play *Mizpah Misery*, staged in 1894, was described as 'sorry entertainment', and *The King's Password*, put on in 1900, failed to be 'convincing, satisfying, or even coherent'; it was described by the reviewer for the *Liverpool Mercury* as 'crude', 'artificial', and 'rhapsodically melodramatic', with the occasional carefully-written line 'drowned in verbiage.'[41] After years of trying and failing to make a name for herself, she had 'the galling experience of having to stand aside and be congratulated by foolish tactless people on her "clever daughter".'[42]

Shortly after the publication of *The Viper of Milan*, Margaret's father died; he had been found dead in the street with his wife's address in his pocket.[43] Margaret, with the assistance of her father's brothers, arranged for him to be buried in Kensal Green Cemetery.[44] His wife, though they had been separated for some years, went to pieces and never recovered from her loss, and Margaret, desperate to gain some freedom from her increasingly difficult and volatile mother, returned to Paris.[45] She found that she could write there easily, and she began to make a life for herself, away from the stifling influence of her mother. But Mrs Campbell was not about to let her daughter break away; she followed her to France and insisted she return home.[46]

*The Viper of Milan* was followed quickly by two more novels, both successful and both issued by Alston Rivers, *The Glen o' Weeping* (retitled *The Master of Stair* for the US market), published in 1907, and *The Sword Decides*, which came out in 1908. These were followed by *A Moment's Madness*, which appeared in the Christmas number of *Cassell's Magazine* in 1908, *The Leopard and the Lily*, issued by Doubleday, Page & Co. in 1909, and *Black Magic: The Tale of the Rise and Fall of the Antichrist* published by Alston Rivers in 1909.

Yet no matter how hard Margaret worked, and no matter how much she tried to please them, her family remained unhappy and ungrateful. With more money coming in, though never enough to meet their expenses, they moved to a flat at 55a Maida Vale, near St. John's Wood, the ground floor of which was occupied by the London and Provincial Bank.[47] Margaret found her new home 'extremely gloomy and depressing'; life there was 'untidy, humdrum, and unsatisfactory', and the 'atmosphere was one of constant nervous hysterical storms and tension.'[48] Additionally, the house was haunted, so much so that Mrs Campbell arranged for an expert from the Society for Psychical Research to stay there and investigate while the family escaped to a cottage in Cornwall.[49]

Phyllis Campbell, *The Tatler*, 4 August 1915.

Phyllis and Nana slept in rooms at the top of the Maida Vale house, and it was this top floor that was the focus of the ghostly activity at first; there were groans, footsteps on the stairs, knockings on the doors, and the sound of someone pacing to and fro.[50] Phyllis refused to sleep in her room and moved to the floor below, and the man-of-all-work, a fellow by the name of Frederic Payne, began complaining that the basement was 'overrun by supernatural creatures.'[51] Lights and water taps were switched on and off, windows were flung open, and Margaret's mother, who had begun hearing scufflings and moanings, saw 'a wheel of light whirl down the stairs.'[52] At first, Margaret saw and heard nothing and did not believe in the haunting, but by the time the Society for Psychical Research was contacted she too had begun experiencing ghostly goings on. One evening, when she was alone in the house and the light was beginning to fade, she opened the door of the drawing room and saw 'a gigantic figure, hooded and cloaked, with very square shoulders, passing into the little room on the stairs that had been turned into a bathroom.'[53] Then, not long afterwards, she awoke in the night and felt 'oppressed by a feeling of unreality.'[54]

> 'There seemed an oppression of something intensely evil, an abstraction and yet something in concrete form. As she

lay quite still she saw in the air two objects rather like a pestle and mortar or a bulbous-shaped medicine glass, something with a black body and a long neck, lying in a bowl. They were of a blue colour and seemed to be of thickened glass.'[55]

Margaret was later told that the Maida Vale house had once been a private lunatic asylum, that an 'unchronicled tragedy' had taken place within it, and that after the event the doctor who lived there had moved in a hurry.[56] In truth, the house had been a private nursing home, and the tragedy had been the death of a female patient under the influence of chloroform in December 1902, for which the inquest returned a verdict of 'death from misadventure'.[57]

It was at this time, while her mother, sister and Nana were preoccupied with ghostly goings on, that Margaret met Zefferino Emilio Costanzo (c. 1882-1916), a Sicilian who had lived in London for several years.[58] Her family did not like him, and she liked rather than loved him, but he offered a means of escape; he was going back to Italy and might be there for some years, and he wanted her to go with him. And despite her mother's opposition to the match—she opposed the removal of the family breadwinner—Margaret and Zefferino were married in the October of 1912.[59] Zefferino was given a position with a company that was building a railway in the Carrara district of Lucca, and the following year the couple set out for Italy, taking a furnished house in Lucca Reggio, a two-hour train ride from Florence.[60]

For a time, Margaret was quite content in her new life. She learned to sew and, like her new Italian neighbours, kept hens and pigeons, though hers were not for food; she loathed meat and none was allowed in the house.[61] At the beginning of their married life in Tuscany, the couple lived on Zefferino's income; his wife's earnings continued to support the Campbell family in London. But when the railway in Lucca was completed in 1919, Zefferino lost his position and fell ill as a result, and the couple were forced to live on Margaret's income from writing. In an effort to reduce their outgoings, they moved to Florence and took an apartment in a large farmhouse near Santa Margherita.[62] Their rooms were uncomfortable, and Zefferino, who by then had acquired a constant cough, became increasingly violent-tempered; Margaret felt that all her hopes for a new, different life, away from the petty arguments and miseries of life with her mother, had been crushed. Then, on 4 August 1914, they received the news that England had declared war on Germany.

Margaret and her husband made attempts to get back to England, but their efforts came to nought.[63] The banks restricted withdrawals almost immediately; it was possible to get enough money for basic living expenses but nothing more.[64] Food prices increased, there were riots in Florence, and receiving accurate news from, or sending news to, England was next to impossible. In October, now heavily pregnant, Margaret journeyed with her husband to Sicily to his family home; she grew fond of his father and sister, but she detested the island itself, the way of life there and the disputes that everyone around her seemed to be embroiled in.[65] As she had remained the sole breadwinner of her family in London, she had continued to be productive throughout her marriage—she had produced two or three novels per year since the publication of *The Viper of Milan*—but now she had difficulty acquiring paper to write on or the time in which to use it.[66]

Following the birth of her baby daughter, Giuseppina, on 6 November 1914, Margaret became determined to return to England, and she and Zefferino finally began the long and arduous journey three months later.[67] They arrived in London one wintry day in February 1915, and Margaret found her mother and sister much as she had left them.[68] It soon became apparent that there was no place for Margaret's new family with her old one, so she and her husband moved into a farmhouse above the Kentish marshes, taking old Nana with them, and Zefferino took up poultry farming.[69] But during the cold winter months his health deteriorated.

On 19 May 1915, after a very brief illness, Giuseppina, then only six months old, died, and Zefferino was so affected by the loss of his daughter that his health deteriorated further still.[70] In the hope that milder weather conditions would be beneficial, Margaret arranged for them to move to South Devon.[71] She had continued to write—she was, after all, the only breadwinner for two families now—and was receiving an income which, though not quite as good as it had been before the war, was enough to sustain them. But it was shortly after their arrival in Torquay that she received two life-changing pieces of news: she was pregnant for the second time, and her husband would live no more than six months if he did not return to the warmer climate of his homeland. So, in October Zefferino sailed for home while Margaret remained in Torquay, awaiting the birth of her second child, Michael Birillo Vere, who was born the following January.[72]

One month after Michael's birth, Margaret received bad news from her husband; he was more seriously ill than she had thought, had fallen out with his family in Sicily and moved to Tuscany, and he wanted her to go to him with their baby son.[73] It was, of course, impossible to take a newborn baby on such a journey, so she left Michael in England and travelled to Italy alone. She nursed her husband, with very little help from another soul, until his death. Zefferino died from tuberculosis on 5 November 1916 at the Villa

Margaret in a 'Belle Alliance' dress. *The Sketch*, 10 March 1915.

Ceciale, in the sea town of Forte dei Marmi, in Lucca.[74] Margaret returned to England at the beginning of 1917, to her mother and sister, who still very much disapproved of everything she did, and to the infant son who, after so long a separation, did not recognise her as his mother.[75]

The little family left Torquay and moved to Hampstead Heath, and, in the October of the same year, Margaret entered into her second loveless marriage.[76] Arthur Leonard Long (1886-1983) was aware from the very beginning that his wife did not love him—'her story and her feelings had been fully explained'—but the marriage appears to have been fairly successful; it was a 'singular and pleasing union, to end only with their deaths.'[77] Her second marriage produced two sons—Athelstan Charles Ethelwulf was born on 2 Jan 1919, and Hilary Blaix Winch Vere was born on 24 June of the following year—both of whom, along with their half-brother, Michael, Margaret schooled at home until they were eight years old.[78] As with her first marriage, her second was supported by her writing income, and, as she had done since the publication of her first novel, she remained incredibly productive. In December 1921, Margaret's mother died—'a bitter death that was the direct outcome of her frustrated, unfortunate life'—and 'her sister went away and they saw no more of each other.'[79] From then on, she was no longer weighed down by the troubles and temperaments of her mother and sister, and she was responsible for the support of only her own household.

Articles published in the *Weekly Dispatch* in 1930 and *Sydney Morning Herald* in 1932 give us an insight into Margaret's working methods.[80] She used an ediphone, which she found 'an inspiring helper';[81] considering her prolific output, without it, she explained, 'neither my eyes nor my hands would stand the amount of work'.[82]

Margaret at her Kent home with her three sons: Michael (left), Athelstan (right) and Hilary (centre). *The Graphic*, 3 November 1923.

She narrated her story aloud, 'as though she were reading it from a written page'; once the story was completed, she transcribed it to paper, 'developing and colouring characters and scenes' as she went along.[83] She also took inspiration from listening to music; it was while listening to Beethoven's *Leonore* that the story of *Captain Banner*, a three-act drama written under the pseudonym George R. Preedy, first began to take shape in her mind.[84]

Margaret employed several pseudonyms during her career; in addition to her most well-known pen name, Marjorie Bowen, she wrote as Joseph Shearing, Robert Paye, John Winch and George R. Preedy. These appear to have been adopted to set certain works apart from those issued under the Bowen name, and with Preedy and Shearing there was some effort made to conceal the author's true identity for several years. *The Tatler* reported in 1952 that, a few years earlier, 'these pseudonyms were among the most jealously guarded secrets of the publishing world.'[85]

Margaret explained, many years after Preedy, Shearing, Paye and Winch first appeared in print, 'I became bored with the success of very early years. I felt I was living on another's reputation, so changed was I from the girl who had written "I Will Maintain!".'[86] And it's not terribly surprising that she should attempt to cast off the Bowen pen name for a time; it had been foisted upon her at the beginning of her career, and she had always detested it. 'The name Marjorie Bowen has always annoyed me,' she explained to a reporter in 1931, and she had found it impossible to express her 'second individuality' when using it.[87] In addition to the fact that she very much disliked her first pseudonym, she also felt that, when using it, 'her work was not receiving the close attention of the critics and the public', and that there was still 'a prejudice against women writers.'[88]

> 'When I am writing as George Preedy my whole personality definitely changes. The books I write as George Preedy are no effort whatsoever to me, but those of Marjorie Bowen are difficult and cause trouble.'[89]

Margaret wrote two novels as Robert Paye: *The Devil's Jig*, which appeared in 1930, and *Julia Roseingrave*, published in 1933; the former was still being advertised as an exceptionally successful 'first novel' by a new author when Paye's true identity was revealed in the autumn of 1930.[90] *Idlers' Gate* was published under the name John Winch in 1932, and that author's identity was made public the following year.[91]

The first title written under the name George R. Preedy was *General Crack,* published in 1928. The novel was a bestseller and immediately set the literary world speculating about the true identity of this talented new writer; Arnold Bennett, H. G. Wells, and Rafael Sabatini were all suspects.[92] Preedy was, according to the *Sunday Express*, 'the most retiring author in existence'; all efforts to get in touch with him failed, and appeals for him to reveal himself received no response.[93] He was obviously an expert in eighteenth-century history, and his only rival, according to the same newspaper, was Marjorie Bowen, whom they suggested Mr Preedy should meet.[94] The *Daily News* printed stories by both authors—Preedy's 'A Tune for a Trumpet' and Bowen's 'The Globe of Glass'—just days apart, to 'enable readers to make a comparison for themselves'.[95] It then sent samples of the two authors' handwriting to Dr C. Ainsworth Mitchell for 'microscopical examination', to discover if they were produced by one hand, but the good doctor concluded that there was 'not enough material upon which to base an opinion.'[96]

Speculation continued until the next Preedy novel, *The Rocklitz*, was dramatised in 1931. A reporter spotted Margaret, 'huddled, shyly, in a corner', altering Mr Preedy's script at the Duke of York

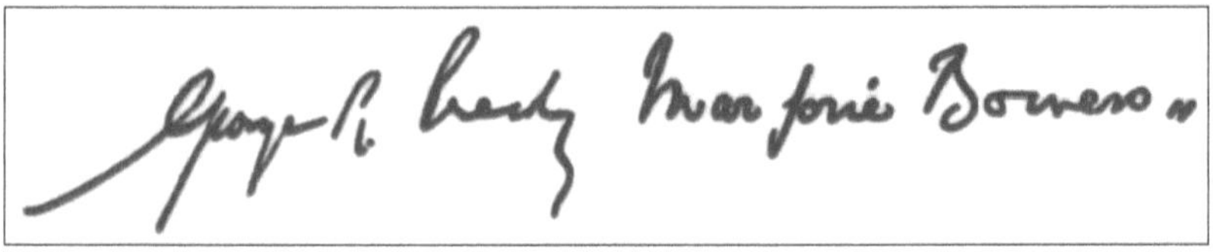

The signatures of George R. Preedy and Marjorie Bowen that were examined by Dr C. Ainsworth Mitchell. *Daily News*, 13 February 1930.

Theatre in London, and the jig was up.[97] 'I was trying to work a hoax,' Margaret explained; 'I wanted to get away from the type of writing done by Marjorie Bowen and to write something different as George Preedy.'[98] Not that this revelation prevented people from continuing to question the Bowen-Preedy connection. The following year, under the heading 'Tales under Two Titles: Bowen-Preedy Riddle Deepens', the *Sunderland Daily Echo* pointed out that, though 'it used to be admitted they they were one and the same person—a Miss Jekyll and a Mr Hyde', *Who's Who* had nonetheless continued to list them as two separate authors, with different biographical details, addresses, and interests.[99]

As Joseph Shearing, Margaret wrote historical novels with a true crime element; these were described as 'evil, sinister, ghostly, strange, baleful, terrible, relentless… and malevolent.'[100] The first Shearing novel, *Forget-me-Not*, was published in 1932, and from the moment of its appearance there was 'a definite and devoted cult of readers of this writer.'[101] Whilst there was much conjecture regarding the author's identity—at first, Mrs. Belloc Lowndes was the prime suspect—it remained a secret for a decade.[102] Joseph Shearing was 'one of the impenetrable mysteries of the day.'[103] It wasn't until 1942, when *Twentieth Century Authors: A Biographical Dictionary of Modern Literature* was going to press, that Margaret finally confessed to the fact that she and Shearing were one and the same person.

In 1939, the autobiography of 'Marjorie Bowen', *The Debate Continues,* was published by William Heinemann under her real name: Margaret Campbell. However, at the time, to make matters more confusing, she was often referred to as Gabrielle Long and Gabrielle Campbell. In 1949, a reviewer suggested that if Lon Chaney was billed as the 'Man With the Hundred Faces', Margaret should likewise be described as the 'Lady With the Hundred Names'.[104] The *Bookseller* considered it necessary to print a glossary of her noms de plume, and the *Evening Despatch* suggested jokingly that it was only a matter of time before Margaret announced she was also 'H. G. Wells, Arnold Bennett, Noel Coward, and Edgar Wallace'.[105] The author herself 'often thought of herself by the name Margaret under which she was baptized, a name borne by many Scotswomen since a royal saint made it popular.'[106]

Margaret achieved a great amount of success during her lifetime; her books sold extremely well for years and several of them were adapted into films and plays: her 1928 George Preedy novel *General Crack* was adapted as the film *General Crack* (1930), starring John Barrymore, her 1939 Shearing novel *Blanche Fury* was adapted as the film *Blanche Fury* (1948), starring Stewart Granger, and another of Shearing's, *For Her to See* (1947), became the film *So Evil My Love* (1948), starring Ray Milland, Ann Todd, and Geraldine Fitzgerald. Margaret was also one of the writers who worked on *Under Capricorn* (1949), the adaptation of Helen Simpson's 1937 novel, directed by Alfred Hitchcock and starring Ingrid Bergman, Joseph Cotton, and Michael Wilding.[107]

Margaret was described as a 'quiet, cultured woman';[108] she was 'a tall, shy, pleasant woman', 'always considerate and punctual for appointments', who, though she made a lot of money from her writing, 'lived modestly' and did 'much of her own housework'.[109] 'There is no vanity in the personality of Marjorie Bowen', wrote the reporter for the *Sydney Morning Herald* in 1932; she was a 'gentle-voiced woman' who was so lacking in self-importance that she answered her own doorbell.[110] Towards the end of her life, she lived quietly in a flat off the King's Road in London, where 'few of her neighbours' knew her 'well enough to point her out and say "That is Marjorie Bowen".'[111] When she was not writing, she had her hobbies; she still enjoyed painting, she was a skilled embroiderer, she particularly liked making dolls, for which she knitted petticoats, and she made many of her own clothes.[112] 'Life without a hobby,' she said, at the Diamond Jubilee Convention of the British Amateur Press Association in 1950, 'would indeed be barren. It is part of the English character to be an amateur and a little eccentric. If we weren't we should cease to be British people.'[113]

In the summer of 1952, Margaret suffered a broken arm.[114] In September, she spent two weeks in Ulster, trying to catch up with work on her novel *The Man with the Scales*, which her publisher had been urging her to finish.[115] She stayed with her friend May Morton, the Irish poetess who in her poem 'Gabrielle', written the previous year, had described Margaret as 'A sword of flame—a mind that probes and flares… A slender willow tree—a form of grace'.[116] With the author herself incapacitated, May took on the task of writing down Margaret's dictation, and the novel was finished while she was in Ireland.[117] It turned out to be the last that Margaret wrote.

On 3 December 1952, Margaret suffered a fall on the parquet floor of her bedroom. She took to her bed and, according to her youngest son, her condition appeared to improve for a while, but on 22 December she collapsed, and she died the following day in St. Charles Hospital, Kensington. She had suffered a haemorrhage due to having fractured her skull during the fall.[118] She was sixty-seven years old. At her death, she left behind more than a hundred and fifty novels and two hundred short stories. She once admitted that she herself was not certain how many books she had written.[119] Sadly, most have never been republished.

# Notes

1 *1939 England and Wales Register* for the date.
With regard to her name: the *England & Wales, Civil Registration Birth Index, 1837-1915* and the *National Probate Calendar* record her name as 'Margaret Gabrielle', while the *England & Wales, Civil Registration Death Index, 1916-2007* and the *1901 England Census* have her down as 'Gabrielle Margaret'. Numerous death notices referred to her as 'Margaret Gabrielle Long'. I have chosen to refer to her by the name she chose in her own autobiography: Margaret.
Name of the cottage's owner, see Margaret Campbell, *The Debate Continues: Being the Autobiography of Marjorie Bowen*. London: William Heinemann Ltd., 1939, p. 1. Mrs Cole was most likely Frances Cole, who lived at 6 Clarendon Road and died in the autumn of 1885, just before Margaret's birth, at the age of 79. *See 1881 England Census.*

2 Marriage: *England & Wales, Civil Registration Marriage Index, 1837-1915.* Dorothea's birth and death: *England & Wales, Civil Registration Death Index, 1837-1915.* Location of Dorothea's birth: Campbell, op. cit., p. 1.

3 Born 1890, died 1982. *England & Wales, Civil Registration Birth Index, 1837-1915*, and *England & Wales, Civil Registration Death Index, 1916-2007.*

4 Description of Margaret's father: Campbell, op. cit., p. 50.
According to the information provided to medical directories at the time, Hugh Campbell studied at Edinburgh and Trinity College, Dublin. So far, I have found no record of him having studied at Trinity College. He passed the necessary examinations at St. Andrews in 1863 (see the *Sun*, 11 May 1863, p. 20).

5 *1871 England Census.*

6 Campbell, op. cit., pp. 7-8.

7 Ibid., p. 9.

8 Ibid., p. 7.

9 Ibid., pp. 2-3.

10 Ibid., p. 8.

11 Ibid., p. 11.

12 *Kensington Post*, 7 June 1947, p. 5. In her comments, Margaret refers to her childhood nurse without naming her, but Nana was her only nurse.

13 Campbell, op. cit., p. 11. Marion Piggot is recorded as the family's housekeeper in the *England Census* for 1901 and 1911.

14 Campbell, op. cit., p. 32.

15 Ibid., p. 42.

16 Ibid., p. 64.

17 Ibid., p. 65.

18 Ibid.

19 Ibid.

20 Ibid., p. 70.

21 Ibid., p. 77.

22 Ibid., p. 79.

23 Ibid., p. 83.

24 Ibid., p. 84.

25 Ibid.

26 Ibid.

27 Ibid., pp. 84-85.

28 Ibid., p. 85.

29 Newspaper reports often claimed that *The Viper of Milan* was published when Margaret was just sixteen or seventeen years old, but when it appeared, in August 1906, she was three months shy of her twenty-first birthday.

30 Campbell, op. cit., p. 91.

31 *Daily News* (London), 19 October 1906, p. 4.

32 *Daily Mirror*, 8 September 1906, p. 5.

33 Campbell, op. cit., p. 93.

34 Ibid., pp. 83 and 94.

35 Ibid., p. 95.

36 Ibd.

37 Ibid., pp. 95-96.

38 *Scottish Leader*, 26 September 1889, p. 2, *Ross Gazette*, 5 February 1890, p. 3, and *The Saturday Review*, 28 September 1889, p. 356.

39 *The Academy*, 19 October 1889, p. 250.

40 *Bath Chronicle*, 5 September 1907, p. 6.

41 *Birmingham Evening Mail*, 13 March 1894, p. 4, and *Morning Post*, 29 May 1900, p. 5, and *Liverpool Mercury*, 22 May 1900, p. 8.

42 Campbell, op. cit., p. 95.

43 Ibid., p. 99.

44 Ibid., and the burial register for Kensal Green Cemetery, London.

45 Campbell, op. cit., p. 99.

46 Ibid., p. 100.

47 *1911 England Census.*

48 Campbell, op. cit., p. 102.

49 Ibid., p. 116.

50 Ibid., p. 106.

51 Ibid., p. 107. Margaret remembers that the man-of-all-work was called Palmer. However, according to the *1911 England Census* his name was Frederic Payne.

52 Ibid.

53 Ibid. p. 116.

54 Ibid. p. 117.

55 Ibid.

56 Ibid. p. 127.

57 *Hastings and St Leonards Observer*, 20 December 1902, p. 2.

58 Campbell, op. cit., p. 118. His name is not given in Margaret's account of her life, *The Debate Continues*; in various other sources it is given as Zeffrino Costanzo, Zefferino Costanzo, Zeffirino Costanzo, and Zeffirine Costanza. In November 1918, Margaret's second husband, Arthur L. Long, wrote to the *New York Herald* to correct a piece about his wife's book, *The Third Estate*, and in that he refers to 'Zefferino Costanzo' (see the *New York Herald*, 17 November 1918, p. 43).

59 *England & Wales, Civil Registration Marriage Index, 1837-1915.*
60 Campbell, op. cit., p. 132.
61 Campbell, op. cit., p. 136.
62 Ibid., p. 151.
63 Ibid., p. 156.
64 Ibid.
65 Ibid., p. 158.
66 Ibid., p. 163.
67 *UK and Ireland, Find a Grave Index, 1300s-Current.*
68 Campbell, op. cit., p. 174.
69 Ibid., p. 175.
70 Ibid. Giuseppina Costanzo was buried in the churchyard of St Mary the Virgin, Stone-cum-Ebony, Ashford, Kent, England.
71 Ibid., p. 182.
72 *England & Wales, Civil Registration Birth Index, 1916-2007.* Full name: birth certificate (registered in Newton Abbot).
73 Campbell, op. cit., p. 188.
74 *England & Wales, National Probate Calendar (Index of Wills and Administrations), 1858-1995.*
75 Campbell, op. cit., p. 288.
76 *England & Wales, Civil Registration Marriage Index, 1916-2005.*
77 Campbell, op. cit., p. 290.
78 Birthdates of her sons: birth certificates, *UK, World War II Allied Prisoners of War, 1939-1945. WO 345*, and *England and Wales, Death Index, 1989-2021.* Schooling: *Sydney Morning Herald*, 27 August 1932, p. 9.
79 Campbell, op. cit., p. 291, and *England & Wales, Civil Registration Death Index, 1916-2007.*
80 *Sydney Morning Herald*, 27 August 1932, p. 9.
81 Ibid. A recording device for oral dictation where sound was recorded on a wax cylinder. The machine marketed by the Edison Records Company was trademarked as the 'Ediphone'.
82 *Weekly Dispatch*, 14 September 1930, p. 1.

83 *Sydney Morning Herald*, 27 August 1932, p. 9.
84 Ibid.
85 *The Tatler*, 13 August 1952, p. 13.
86 E.g.: *Torbay Express and South Devon Echo*, 27 December 1952, p. 5.
87 *Weekly Dispatch*, 1 February 1931, p. 11.
88 *News* (Adelaide, Australia), 3 February 1931, p. 9.
89 *Weekly Dispatch*, 1 February 1931, p. 11.
90 *Weekly Dispatch*, 14 September 1930, p. 1.
91 *Liverpool Daily Post*, 30 September 1933, p. 6.
92 *Weekly Dispatch*, 1 February 1931, p. 1.
93 *Sunday Express*, 9 February 1930, p. 4.
94 Ibid.
95 *Daily News*, 15 February 1930, p. 5.
96 *Daily News*, 13 February 1930, p. 7.
97 *Weekly Dispatch*, 1 February 1931, p. 1, and *Daily News*, 2 February 1931, p. 1.
98 *Daily News*, 2 February 1931, p. 1.
99 *Sunderland Daily Echo and Shipping Gazette*, 10 January 1933, p. 6.
100 Stanley Kunitz and Howard Haycraft, *Twentieth Century Authors: A Biographical Dictionary of Modern Literature*. H. W. Wilson Company, 1942, p. 1272.
101 Ibid.
102 *Daily News*, 3 June 1932, p.4.
103 *Daily News* (London), 19 October 1906, p. 4.
104 *Ireland's Saturday Night*, 26 March 1949, p. 2.
105 *Evening Despatch*, 2 February 1931, p. 6.
106 Campbell, op. cit., p. i.
107 Donald Spoto, *The Dark Side of Genius: The Life of Alfred Hitchcock*. Boston: Little Brown, 1983, p. 309.
108 *Derby Daily Telegraph*, 26 February 1931, p. 4.
109 *Evening Standard*, 27 December 1952, p. 2, and *Belfast News-Letter*, 16 March 1953, p. 3.

110 *Sydney Morning Herald*, 27 August 1932, p. 9.

111 *Evening News*, 10 March 1947, p. 2.

112 *Belfast News-Letter*, 16 March 1953, p. 3.

113 *Bromley & West Kent Mercury*, 22 September 1950, p. 4.

114 *Newcastle Journal*, 4 August 1952, p. 3.

115 *Belfast News-Letter*, 16 March 1953, p. 3.

116 May Morton, 'Gabrielle', in *Sung to the Spinning Wheel*. Quota Press, 1952, p. 18. Though the poetry collection was published in 1952, the poems were written the previous year, see *Belfast News-Letter*, 19 November 1951, p. 3.

117 *Belfast News-Letter*, 16 March 1953, p. 3.

118 *Belfast Telegraph*, 29 December 1952, p. 1.

119 *Evening Standard*, 27 December 1952, p. 2.

# STORIES
# OF YESTERDAY

# SHEEP'S-HEAD AND BABYLON

THE Reverend Zachary Barlas opened the door of the manse and entered with a flagging step.

It was a melancholy day in deep winter, and the wind howled incessantly through the hills, across the moor and beat into the little garden of the manse, (in summer rich with honeysuckle and roses) and on to the unsheltered square walls of the building itself, and up the struggling village street through which the minister had just come with his slow and uneasy walk. It was no earthly trouble that made the Rev. Zachary look haggard and pallid, but prolonged wrestling with spiritual hosts and exhausting struggles with diabolic terrors.

It was indeed only what he had to expect, for he had long been devoting his austere leisure to the writing of a book entitled "The Snares of Satan Exposed," which must certainly be highly displeasing to the Father of Evil, since it so learnedly, succinctly and clearly exposed his traps and wiles, and was a kind of chart or guide to the unwary to avoid the pitfalls set by the legions of the Infernal One.

Long and late had the Rev. Zachary laboured at this work, putting into it a burning zeal, an exalted piety and the fervent outpourings of a devoted heart, and now that his work was nearing completion he felt an exhaustion of the spirit, a feebleness of the body not surprising, for, besides the book into which he had put such passionate ardour, he had toiled ceaselessly in his tiny parish, preaching, exhorting, tending to the sick, the penitent and the sinner, encouraging the worthy, comforting the distressed;

for a holy and fearless man was he, albeit stern and unrelenting.

As he crossed the threshold of the manse the wind sent a dismal sigh through a leafless ash tree that overhung the house, and the minister shivered; the thought of his book lying upstairs, finished save for the last few pages, gave him, however, a sense of chill triumph; he had put through his appointed task, and the Devil had not been able to prevent him. Indeed, he believed that the invisible powers that had been harrying him had given up a vain pursuit, for during several days he had been conscious of a certain calm in the atmosphere in which he moved, an atmosphere hitherto filled with a wild commotion as of spirits battling for his soul.

As he passed down the narrow passage he peeped in at the kitchen, with the yellow sanded floor and the bright pots and pans and the pleasant fire.

On the freshly scrubbed table was the food prepared for his supper: a bundle of herbs, a winter cabbage and a sheep's head.

The minister stood still and gazed at the sheep's head.

It was a drab white colour with great curling horns, a long beard that hung over the edge of the table and slant eyes that appeared still to glow with life.

"Maisie!" cried the minister, and his thin voice failed in his withered throat.

The maid, a big bustling woman with horseshoe shaped mutch on her head, appeared instantly from an inner room, her red hands dripping with fresh cold water.[1]

"Maisie," said the minister, "I no like the look of yon sheep's head. It's ower long in the beard, and ower powerfu' in the horns,

---

[1] Mutch: a close-fitting linen cap.

and unco' cunning in the eyes for the hoose of an honest mon."[2]

"Losh!" cried the old woman, and "Gude save us!" she cried.[3] "What daftlike thing is this? 'Twas the bit wench brought it in, and she'll e'en tak it back."[4]

"It's gey and queerish," added the minister slowly.

"It's a willie goat," said Maisie, sniffing the head; "an unearthly rank smell it has, and it's no the meat for a Christian hoose."

"Boil the pot with a bit of beef," replied the minister, "the thing is no canny."

Slowly he went upstairs, thinking dourly of Tam Todd the butcher who had sent such an unsightly object to the manse, and shuddering as the cleaving wind swept down from the hills and across the bleak moor, curdling the loch and the rivulet into spate and whistling through the crevices in the manse walls.[5] On his neat desk were his neat papers, and he seized on them with lean hands.

"That was an unearthly sign," he muttered; "a Jeroboam among sheep![6] Sheep, did I say? Maybe sae. Maybe sae. But strang is the hand of God! He no let ony sic a mischanter come ower me noo!"[7] Yet he looked round fearfully, prying into every corner of the room and fingering his sharp chin.

---

[2] Unco': strangely. Mon: man.

[3] Losh!: Lord!

[4] Bit: little.

[5] Spate: a torrent of water that bursts its banks.

[6] Jeroboam: first king of the northern Kingdom of Israel who committed the sin of idolatry: 'when he appointed his own priests for the high places and for the goat and calf idols he had made.' (2 Chronicles 11:15)

[7] He'd not let any such misfortune come over me now.

It was very cold in this upper room; the icicles hung on the pane, the madly-fleeing east wind was carrying the first snowflakes past the window.

"There's a fire bleezing awa in the parlour," came Maisie's voice up the narrow stairs, "an' all tosh and comfortable.[8] Wull ye no come down and tak a bit supper?"

"Have ye sent back the deil's heid to the auld carlin that sent it?" demanded the minister.[9]

"It's gone awa," came the screaming reply, "and blessings on it, no the deil, but a willie goat; and dinna fash yersel, I'll get as fine a heid of sheep as ever fed on Cheviot."[10]

"A foolish, doited body," muttered the minister, "do yer no speir the deil's trick through the hands of that puir body Tam Todd?[11] And dinna ye ken the likeness of the Father of Evil when it lies before ye?"

He turned his back again to his desk; neither meal nor fire nor toddy-glass had any attraction for him, save as temptations to be gloriously resisted.

"I maun finish," he said, lovingly taking up his pen, "for the deil's on my tracks.[12] And what needeth man with food when his innards are burnt up with a fervent heat which is the love of the Lord?"

Crouching his limbs together in his rusty black single-breasted

---

[8] Tosh: snug.

[9] Deil's heid: devil's head. Carlin: derogatory term, a worthless person.

[10] Fash: fret. Cheviot: name of the hill-land on the Anglo-Scottish border.

[11] Doited: impaired in intellect. Speir: seek.

[12] Maun: must.

coat, his Cameron breeches, darned stockings and square-toed shoes. propping his meagre face on his hollowed and claw-like hand, Zachary Barlas gazed at the flying storm that leapt past the window and concentrated on his final chapters.

He was writing a vision of Babylon, the City of Sin, the capital of the country called Destruction, circled about by the moat filled with the waters of despair and warmed by the fires of hell.

"Babylon," he wrote, "is not a place, but a state; to be in sin is to be in Babylon; to be in temptation is to be lingering at the gates."

Soaring above the homely vernacular in which he daily expressed himself, the Rev. Zachary launched into the florid and robust diction drawn from the writings of the Covenanters, flushed and glorified by the splendours of the Bible—the Holy Book that lay open at his elbow, and at which he often glanced with a pale but sparkling eye.[13]

As he wrote he forgot the cold, forgot the storm sweeping down from Craigie Saunchie, forgot the disdained comforts of food and warmth below.

"This great city, this glorious city, this rich city, this mighty powerful city, this queen of the earth, with Antichrist, her king and husband, is to be judged by the spirit of life, which ariseth out of the dust of Sion."

Soft the snow thudded on the window, cramped and frozen were the blue fingers of the minister, but unfalteringly flowed the eager words on to the paper.

"Sing, sing, O inhabitant of Sion! Dost thou not perceive the crown of pride going down apace? The decree sealed against her; she cannot escape; yea, she is fallen, she is fallen, she is already

[13] Covenanters: supporters of the Presbyterian Church of Scotland.

taken in the snow; the eye of my life seeth it and rejoiceth over her in the living power."

The minister sank back in his mean chair, his eyes rolled in his head, and he broke into emphatic speech:

" 'Fear God and give glory to Him, for the hour of His judgment is come!' " he cried, adding: "an' ye canna escape! ye canna escape!"

The little room was darkening in the winter twilight; fleeting wind and gathering snow made one commotion outside; the white drift was piling high on the window-sill and blotting the murky panes.

"A beam o' light, O Lord!" prayed the Rev. Zachary, "for the place darkens!"

He rose, but his limbs were stiff and his pace was stumbling; indeed the room seemed to be full of a deep gloom which rendered the objects in it nearly indistinguishable. Whether this was due to the thickening of the storm without or the failing of his own senses the minister did not know. He pulled open the door.

Instead of the mean, shabby staircase of the manse he saw before him a passage of shimmering gold, washed by a pale and unearthly light.

"Babylon!" whispered the Rev. Zachary, and, irritated by this device of the Evil One, he turned to reach the safe harbourage of his chill workroom; but the door had disappeared.

The long gold street was in front and behind him; to his left was a wall of jasper or some translucent material, crowned at intervals with turrets of silver hung with hundreds of little silver bells that clashed gently in an eternal breeze. On the other side tall straight buildings of a milky alabaster rose till they disappeared in the rosy clouds.

There were deep-set windows latticed with ivory and high doors curtained with satin in these houses, and long festoons of roses falling from golden balconies; the air was drowsy with the scents of jasmine, of honeysuckle, of musk, and alive with the sounds of sackbut, dulcimer and zither.[14] The minister felt like a drab insect drawling over a luscious fruit.

Yet he was able to show his contempt for the Devil by walking straight on with no glance to right or left.

"I'll walk clean through yon gaudy show," he said, "and back to my wee bit room."

A door opened with a soft sliding sound and a woman peeped out; a flimsy lawn barely veiled the palpitations of her delicate bosom, long strands of golden hair escaped from a fillet of white roses, and over her polished bare shoulders hung a cloak of royal purple.[15]

"It is far from Drumknockie Manse to Babylon," she said. "Will you not come in and rest?"

So sweet and beguiling was her accent, so delicious the perfume that wafted from the open door, so entrancing the glimpse of the soft couch within and the display of exquisite viands on a table of pure jade, that the Rev. Zachary actually paused.

"I must not eat or rest in Babylon," he muttered. But he fingered his chin and sighed, and many things became dim in his mind.

"Many a holy man has rested here before you," smiled the lady, "and passed on his way much refreshed."

The Rev. Zachary gazed at her dewy lips, her blooming cheeks, her sapphire eyes, and he forgot he was in Babylon.

---

[14] A sackbut is an early trombone. Dulcimers and zithers are stringed musical instruments.

[15] Lawn: lightweight, sheer cloth. Fillet: garland.

His hand went out, wavered and strayed towards the lovely lady's heavy locks.

"I might—rest—a while," he stammered, and stepped on to the threshold. Then he glanced down, dazzled, maybe, by the brightness of the lady's charms; and what did he behold?

A neat little goat's foot—white, it is true, as to hair, and shell-pink as to horn, but indubitably a goat's foot—peeping out under the purple cloak.

And what did he see on the table among the costly meats and delicate drinks?

The sheep's head, with the beard and the horns, leering at him with half-closed eyes.

The Rev. Zachary groaned.

"Sathanas, avaunt!" he cried desperately.[16]

The golden city melted about him; he seemed to pitch into an abyss, and found himself on his hands and knees, sprawling down his own stairs.

"Guid save us!" cried Maisie, running out, "and what cantrips are these?[17] Coming down heid formaist! Losh, but it's a ghaistly sicht!"

The minister sat at the bottom of the stairs and rubbed his elbows.

"Maisie," he mumbled, "I've been to Babylon—it was a maist ungodly sicht! Streets o' gowd, an' a woman——"

"I'll no hear about the woman," retorted Maisie firmly. "If ye've been to Babylon, it's no the women o' that city will be the decent talk for a Christian buddy."

---

[16] "Satan, go away!"

[17] Cantrips: magical spells, mischievous tricks.

The minister rose stiffly from his sitting posture and limped towards the parlour.

"Ye're ower lang at the writing," said the housekeeper, anxiously following him into the light and warmth; "tak a drap and a bite noo."

She pointed to the supper displayed temptingly on the hearth.

But the Rev. Zachary remembered the invitation extended to him recently by a fairer favoured damsel.

"It's no the willie goat?" he asked, glancing at the covered dish.

"The willie goat?" replied Maisie scornfully. "Has na the willie goat gone back to auld Tam Todd?"

"I'm glad," replied the minister. He sank down in the old arm-chair by the cheerful fire and ate his supper with a quiet relish.

He felt great cause for rejoicing. Had he not passed down the very streets of Babylon and returned unscathed? Had he not withstood temptations as successfully as St. Anthony himself (who was but a Papist, after all!) and returned safe and sound to eat his own food by his own fireside? "Surely," he thought, "the Devil has done with me now, and left me in peace." Flushed with a sense of exultation he climbed again to his workroom, and, albeit a little stiff from his fall, he seized his pen with fervour and in a king of delirium of zeal finished the last few pages of his book.

"Auld Mahoun nearly had me that time—I was half-way hame to his cauldron, nae doot," he muttered triumphantly as he tied up the thick pile of manuscript; "and mony hae travelled that road afore me, as the Scarlet Woman herself testified with her soft words and wanton looks."[18]

The wind whirled round the house and cast thuds of snow at the windows and whistled icy breaths through the crevices as

[18] Auld Mahoun: the Devil.

the Rev. Zachary went downstairs to his warm and sheltered, if grim and dour, parlour.

Casting his haggard eyes upwards in self-congratulatory praise, he took down from the shelf that formed his meagre library a big Bible bound in black oak and clasped with silver; he turned over the pages with gaunt fingers and muttered over the familiar passages with which he had often rebuked sin and hurled at the abomination of witchcraft and devilry.

With these forces he had held many a dubious and fierce conflict; on the hills above Drumknockie were the ruins of a Runic temple, well known to be still the abode of unclean spirits, and on the coast not far distant was a wrecked ship, stuck in the quicksands, that had sailed from the haunted coast of Norway, and was still the abode of ghastly spectres; of these things the Rev. Zachary was thinking as he thumbed his Bible and listened to the storm. Yet he felt as secure in his triumph as any of the lonely Covenanters lying in the solitary graves among the hills had felt in their faith.

Had he not actually visited Babylon and rejected it, together with the lure of the Scarlet Woman?

He was totally absorbed in these pleasing reflections when old Maisie opened the door and peeped in, with a look of awed respect for his devotions.

"There's a bit lassie at the door, begging to see you, and saying she's in sair trouble, and has great need of a douce and godly man."[19]

The heart of the pastor swelled with pride; secure as a watcher on the tower of Judah, he ordered the wench to be brought in.[20]

---

19 Sair: sore. Douce: respectable.

20 The watchman who viewed things from an elevated position and warned the people below of coming danger; a symbol of spiritual alertness.

It was always a joy to him to receive penitents and wrestle with crime, sin and folly, and many a redoubtable battle of this kind had been fought out in the dreary little parlour.

"But it's an awfu' night for a lassie to be abroad," he added as another shrieking gust shook the house.

"The lassie," replied Maisie, lowering her voice, "has the snood weel ower her face; but I shouldn't wonder if it were Geordie Murray's daughter, and she'll nae hae far to gang."[21]

The pastor was surprised, for the girl in question lived next door, in one of the better cottages of the village, and was the daughter of a decent shepherd, and but a child in years.

"Aweel, bring her in," he said, and, with the Bible still open on his knee, he waited.

Maisie showed into the parlour a young girl whose maiden snood was drawn well over her face, and whose plaid was huddled closely round her shoulders; her feet were bare, her skirt short, and she carried a bundle wrapped in a white cloth which she at once placed on the table.

The Rev. Zachary saw that his visitor indeed was Jessie Murray, the light-hearted child he had so often seen pulling gowans on the hills and singing at her spinning wheel.[22]

"Oh, I'm in sair trouble," she said, clasping her hands, "sair trouble! What am I brocht to?"

The pastor observed that Jessie, though she had only run a few yards through the storm, was pale and shivering with cold, and drifts of snow already lay in her snood and plaid.

"What for will ye no warm yerself, Jessie Murray?" said the

---

[21] Gang: go, walk.

[22] Gowans: wild white or yellow flowers.

pastor, "and shake the snow frae ye wee plaid? I'm a wearifu' mon to-night, but I'm aye ready for a gude deed."

With a deep sigh the girl took off her plaid, loosened her wet snood, sending showers of auburn curls on to her shoulders, and knelt before the glowing fire.

"Sic a nicht to gang about in!" she said in a low voice, "the snaw drifting, the stars a' put out and a spate in the river, and maybe the Faither o' Lies riding the clouds!"

The tempest had indeed reached a terrific pitch; the shriek of the wind had a human quality, like the screams of tormented voices, and the manse literally quivered on its foundations.

"Preserve us a'!" exclaimed the pastor, gripping the Bible tighter.

"An' dinna ye think it's ower powerfu' for a storm?" whispered Jessie.

"And what wud it be?" demanded the Rev. Zachary. "An'," he added, with a rising voice, "gin it waur the Devil at his tantrums, I'm the maister![23] Sae dinna be frightened."

Thus encouraged, Jessie clasped her hands on her bosom and, crouching nearer to the minister's chair, stammered out her story.

"I'm sair afraid—my father awa'—and I biding in the hoose, when who should come but a bit laddie to the door, through the storm and a', and slippit into my hand——"

She broke off and glanced fearfully at the covered bundle she had placed on the table.

" 'It's the wee meat frae Tam Todd,' says he, and rins awa'—and what is it?"

As she spoke she snatched away the cloth and displayed to

---

[23] Gin it waur: if it was.

the amazed gaze of the minister the sheep's head he had seen on his own kitchen table.

"Sic doings!" he exclaimed. "But be no afeard, lassie—'tis but a willie goat which that miserable creature, Tam Todd, wad pass off as gude Christian meat—gang hame and tak it wi' ye, and think nae mair o't."

"But I'm afeard to take it up!" cried Jessie, "and afeard to gang hame in sic a storm!"

The Rev. Zachary gazed at the head on the table; it was a fearsome sight with the shining curling horns, the drab mottled fur, the long beard and the glinting eyes, and wrath grew in the minister's breast at the impudence of the butcher who persisted in delivering this unsavoury object at the houses of honest folk.

While he was considering the stern terms of rebuke he would administer on the morrow he felt his knees softly clasped and the lassie clinging to him.

"I'm cauld," she murmured, "cauld, cauld, and sair afeard."

The Rev. Zachary looked down at her; he had never remembered that the child was so lovely, so dewy bright, so glowing and soft. As he gazed into the upturned face, the glittering curls falling beside the rounded throat and over the white shoulders, and the delicate bosom swelling beneath the cotton kerchief, the Bible slipped from his knees and crashed unheeded to the floor.

"You're ower lovely for Jessie Murray," he murmured. "But gang awa'—put yon heid in your apron and gang hame."

But the girl did not move; nay, she clung tighter to the minister's knees, and moaned and sobbed while the wind shook and shrilled.

The Rev. Zachary could do nothing but raise her up, and when he had his arms about her she clung like young ivy that has got a hold on a sapling.

The peculiar yet familiar fragrance crept into the pastor's nostrils; the lassie's beauty dazzled him, blotting out the room.

"You're ower bonny for flesh and blood," he muttered faintly.

She twined her arms round his neck; her hair, like a golden net, fell over her shoulders. The storm had ceased, and the peace was beautiful to his tired soul. Gently she drew him to the door, and as she opened it he saw again the long gold streets of Babylon, with the pale hyacinth skies above, the tinkling bells, the festoons of roses.

And now he saw that the girl in his arms wore a chaplet of white roses and a purple robe over her falling lawn.[24]

"It's a long way to Babylon from Drumknockie," she said. "Will you not come in and rest?"

Struggling with the luxurious languor of his senses the minister glanced back into his room and saw the horned head on the table; the lips were moving in a sneer of triumph, and the long wicked eyes shot a gleam of contempt.

With a yell of horror the Rev. Zachary sprang back and snatched at the head; it was in his arms instead of the fair woman; it lay on his bosom like a bride, but his feet were still on the golden streets of Babylon, and he could not find the door into his room. The head had grown a long, dangling body now, and arms that held him fast; a pit opened in the golden street and the Rev. Zachary slipped down . . . down . . . down.

* * * * * *

"Preserve us a'!" exclaimed old Maisie. "What for does the minister need to gang out wi' the nicht like this?"

She sprang out of her little bedroom and into the kitchen,

---

[24] Chaplet: a headdress in the form of a wreath.

and then into the passage; a howl of chilly air had come into the house, then the door was clapped to.

The Rev. Zachary had gone into the darkness; the fire was nearly extinguished on the hearth, the taper was blown out, and the Bible lay on the floor.

"Losh!" cried old Maisie as she picked up the Holy Book, "nae doot he's gang on some errand o' maircy, and may a' gude attend him, but this is no the manner to sarve the blessed Word!"

* * * * * *

They found him frozen stiff in a snowdrift on the way to the hills; dead, with neither coat nor hat, and clasped in his arms the head of the old goat that Tam Todd had hoped would pass for that of a fine Cheviot sheep.

"It's nae wonder," said old Maisie, "that the douce man should gang queer in the head wi' a' that book making an' learning, but, preserve us a'! why should he tak' wi' him the heid o' the willie goat? And he must have creppit into the kitchen maist carefu' and got it frae the basket whaur it were hid biding Tam Todd's lad. It's unco' queer, and maybe the Deil has a hand in't, but I lay the blame o' a gude man's death on Tam Todd."

# A MATRIMONIAL ENTANGLEMENT

LUCIEN confessed, with blushes, that he was in the toils of Madame de la Morilière, and that the description of her, as furnished by the ladies of his acquaintance, "as a puss, a minx, a designing piece," was true enough.

"But I must marry her," he concluded dolefully, "for she has so tangled me in her net that there is no escape."

"Fie, upon such weakness and ungallantry," protested his friend, the Chevalier Lebeuf.[25] "Putting the blame on the lady will not help you to ease your situation!"

"You do not know her tricks——"

"It is their manner to have tricks—what else is there but tricks, after all, poor creatures?"

Lucien was, however, neither consoled nor rebuked.

"You," he declared, "have not to face an angry guardian who has other designs for you, who controls your fortune and has an austere temper!"

"What designs has M. Delaruelle for you, my poor Lucien?"

"Nothing less than a rich heiress," groaned the unhappy youth. "I have seen her and she is the sweetest creature in the world, she makes Madame de la Morilière look like a gipsy, she is submissive to a glance, and with enough money, Adrien, to pay all my debts and yours too——"

"Then marry her and receive the blessing of M. Delaruelle."

"But I am promised to Madame de la Morilière. Cannot you

---

25 Fie: an exclamation of outrage, dismay or disapproval.

understand? And she will by no means let me go."

"I see no reason for the lady's tenacity," smiled the candid friend. "Nay, on reflection, I see three excellent reasons—your titles, honours, and estates."

Lucien flounced, like the pampered, idle, effeminate and vain youth that he was, and declared that the other had neither feeling nor understanding.

But neither his flouncings nor his complaints would help him; he had come up from his château with the purpose of seeing his uncle and guardian, and see him he must, though with such a sorry story on his lips, the more sorry that he had been rescued from an unapproved charmer in Paris and sent to the country to learn wisdom in seclusion, while M. Delaruelle prepared for him an establishment, "worthy," as the phrase went, "of his rank." Lucien was considerably in awe of his uncle who had been rendered, by a disappointment in his youth, harsh and difficult on the subject of feminine allurements, and who, early discovering the pleasures of life to be dusty to his taste, had devoted himself to business and was now a portentous figure in State affairs.

This was another reason for the dislike of Lucien, who thought anything serious tedium and anything difficult boring; keenly did he look forward to the happy day when he should be of age and at liberty to squander his estates, his health and his reputation as he pleased; meanwhile there was this disagreeable moment to be faced, and sulk as he would Lucien must face his uncle.

So he set out in his dove-coloured cabriolet with the glasses up to keep off the November winds, and two lusty hounds to run in front and clear the way, and a coachman with a long whip to lash the stray pedestrians from coming too close, and so arrived at the Hôtel Delaruelle at that very unpleasant time, the twilight of a wet autumn day, but with some state as befitting his rank as a *pair de France*, or so he thought.[26]

His uncle, who from a window had watched his equipage sweep into the forecourt, did not hesitate to express a contrary opinion.

"That coach is absurd for anyone but an opera dancer—and you are most ridiculously over dressed. With all that powder, silk, lace and fal lal you look more like a pet monkey than a man!"

Lucien was not impressed; he never had any respect for the taste of those who disagreed with him and he knew that he was arrayed in the latest fashion and to the admiration of his tailor and barber; in other words, of the people he had paid (or might pay) to set him out like he was.

So he bowed ironically and answered coolly:

"Monseigneur, we cannot all be so immersed in great matters as to be regardless of our appearance, or so intellectual as to be ignorant of the *mode*.[27] *Dieu merci*," he added, impertinently putting up his quizzing glass, "for I declare, my dear uncle, that you cut a very old-fashioned figure."

M. Delaruelle disdained this sally, but it did not improve his temper towards his nephew whom he had disliked ever since he was an odious, spoilt child in a satin frock and silk leading strings, cracking pages on the head with a silver spoon.

"Please do not answer my rebukes till you have the wit to understand them," he replied dryly.

"By that time," said Lucien, making another bow, "I shall be my own master and not need to hear them."

"I have no doubt," answered M. Delaruelle, "that you will ruin

---

[26] *Pair de France*: Peer of France, the highest-ranking of French noblemen.

[27] *Mode*: fashion.

yourself, my dear Lucien, just as soon as you are at liberty to do so; then, as you insinuate, it will be no affair of mine. At present it is, and I, as your guardian, must do my duty by it——"

"Then, pray, monseigneur," asked the frivolous youth, "let that same duty be done as briefly as possible. I find nothing so boring as a grumbling virtue which does good for five minutes and preaches about it for an hour."

"And I," replied his uncle, "find nothing so boring as a mincing young ape who reaches for wit and falls on folly."

After which hopeful beginning the two gentlemen settled to business, the elder bringing out papers and account books and rent rolls, and the younger fetching yawns and sighs and deriving his only consolation from his own sparkling reflection in the only mirror the sober room afforded, near to which he had contrived to place himself.

The room and the person to M. Delaruelle had indeed rather an affectation of plainness; he had been so absorbed in being of service to his country that he had neglected the graces of life, often observing that to be an honest statesman is a full occupation for any man.

What leisure he had over after his scrupulous labours was engaged in securing applause for them; for, as he remarked, it was not for the advantage of the country to have the great and good obscured and the wicked and paltry pushed to the front.

In short, M. Delaruelle had acquired a modicum of that boring quality which has, alas, too frequently given virtue a bad name, and, despite his earnest desire to do good to the unworthy, found that these usually fled his company, leaving him to that of those as dull and as useful as himself.

Having therefore his nephew and (unfortunately) the future

head of his house before him, he did not neglect the opportunity to deliver a homily, under various heads, on all the vices, follies and shortcomings of that disappointing young man.

Seeing that he was thus well in for it, Lucien made a dramatic diversion by relating his entanglement with Madame de la Morilière, even deriving a certain pleasure in the lengthening and blanching of his uncle's face.

"An entanglement! With a widow! Impossible!" cried that gentleman.

"I wish," replied Lucien pettishly, "that it were; but it is not, and you, my dear uncle, must make the worst of it——"

This M. Delaruelle at once proceeded to do, sparing no epithets in his denunciation of Lucien's idiocy.

"And how did this creature find you out?" he concluded. "Where was your tutor and your confessor and your steward that they did not protect you?"

"They were all courting her themselves," replied Lucien, "save M. l'Abbè, and he was occupied in writing a treatise on 'The Perils of Worldly Temptation to the Devout,' which you, no doubt, my dear uncle, will find very edifying."

"Bah!" cried M. Delaruelle, "who is this snake in the grass, and how did she come to be at Château Mailly?"

"She appeared, in a night, in a little farm on the estate; she was attired in mourning and sought, she said, to fly worldly pleasures."

"And you had nothing better to do than to bring them to her notice, I suppose?"

"Absolutely nothing. And that, monseigneur, was your fault—you should have allowed me to remain in Paris."

"And you have promised to marry her?"

"Before witnesses."

M. Delaruelle groaned.

"And I had obtained for you an heiress with a fortune!"

"I regret that myself," admitted Lucien. "I have seen the young lady and approve her—but Madame de la Morilière will be by no means put off——"

"Nonsense," cried M. Delaruelle. "You will return at once to Mailly, seek out this cunning adventuress and repudiate all your engagements to her——"

Lucien smiled.

"You don't know her—to see her is to consider her the most fascinating creature in the world. Only at a distance can I regard her calmly. If I was to see her again I should probably marry her immediately."

"Then," said M. Delaruelle grimly, "I must go."

Lucien was delighted.

"That, of course, would be most suitable; everyone knows how impervious you are, monseigneur, to female charms. And everyone can see," he added in an aside, "how unlikely you are to inspire a tender passion—you are doubly safe."

This was a mere malicious sally, however, for M. Delaruelle was in the prime of life and a handsome man had it not been for a certain cast of rigidity in his face, due to condemning others, and a certain priggishness in his expression, due to a consciousness of his own good qualities.

He did not catch the last part of Lucien's speech and the first flattered him.

"I have had my lesson," he remarked. "As you know, my youth was blighted by the faithlessness of woman."

"And your character soured, most unfortunate——"

"Soured, my dear Lucien! My feet were turned from the way

of folly, my eyes were opened, from a useless fop I became a not unworthy member of the Government. Yes, I really owe a great deal to Terèse. It was," he added reflectively, "a curious case. She was, I may say, in every way my inferior, birth, fortune, talent, character, and yet she jilted me, actually jilted me for a grinning fool with twopence a year!"

"I've heard the tale," said Lucien hastily, fearful of further reminiscences. "Yes, indeed, she must have had no taste whatever. No doubt she has by now heartily repented of her error."

"I believe that she has," replied M. Delaruelle with stern satisfaction. "The last I heard of her, she was living in indigence in Spain."

"Well," said Lucien, rising, "I take it that you, my dear uncle, will settle matters with Madame de la Morilière and leave me free to marry the delicious little heiress."

"I hope," answered his uncle grimly, "that this will be the last trouble that I shall have to take for you——"

"That is unlikely," remarked Lucien with resignation, "for you have, unhappily, a penchant for interfering——"

"Your impertinence is scarcely amusing. I am bound to endure you, Lucien, but do not make my task more disagreeable than it need be. Perhaps, after all, I need not go to Mailly; what could this wretched woman do if we ignored her?"

"Come to Paris and make an *esclandre*; she would relish doing that.[28] She has, also, some notes of mine that I fear you would not call very sensible.

"Very well, then, I must sacrifice myself; my ease, my leisure, my duty to my country, must all, Lucien, be sacrificed to you!"

---

[28] *Esclandre*: scene.

"That," said the ungrateful youth, "is a sad thought, but consider the virtuous glow that will be your reward!"

M. Delaruelle then, in the heaviest of greatcoats and the worst of tempers, set out for Mailly, his nephew's estate; it was that season of the year when the roads were as vile as the weather and the humour of those forced to travel worse than either.

The cold triumphed over fur capes and foot-warmers, over sips of old cognac and pious thoughts; when M. Delaruelle pressed his reddened nose to the carriage window he saw a landscape that appeared to be traced in ashes and vinegar, a sky that looked like iron, and a varied collection of those filthy hovels in which Divine decree had placed the poor.

The inns, expecting no one at this time of the winter, were ill provided with everything save draughts and smoky fires, and M. Delaruelle was obliged to reflect that, plainly as he had lived, he had been a great deal more comfortable that he had supposed.

Water masquerading as soup, an ancient fowl masquerading as capon, wine that turned the stomach instead of raising the spirits, did little to change the mood of M. Delaruelle.

The second day being one of perpetual wind, sleet and floundering of the horses in mud, was a constant (and unnecessary) trial of the Stoic patience that M. Delaruelle under different circumstances had found so easy to employ.

Worse than this, as the darkness came on, the postilion, with the stupidity of his kind, declared that he had lost his way; the road that he had been confidently following had proved to be no road at all, but had run into a track that turned into a gaunt and dreary wood.[29] It was raining heavily and the cold was of a singularly

[29] Postilion: a rider who guides the horses when pulling a coach.

penetrating order; to crown all, M. Delaruelle, on asking for the cognac, discovered that this, by some singular oversight, had been left behind at the last stopping place.

It was an excellent occasion for the exercise of that philosophy that M. Delaruelle had always advocated, but he felt oddly disinclined to profit by it. Dismounting from the carriage into the icy slush he viewed with dismay the barren woods, the rain-slashed prospect, the growing dark, the complete loneliness, and all his intelligence could bring him to no better conclusion than that already arrived at by the postilions, *i.e.*, that they must turn back and endeavour to discover the road to Mailly.

Even this course, however, was far from proving successful; the tempest increased, the lamps flickered in the wind, and the end of the business was the coach in a ditch with a broken wheel.

M. Delaruelle had now to emerge from the comparative shelter of the carriage and survey by the gusty light of the surviving lantern the extent of the damage.

This was not considerable, but it was sufficient; it would be quite impossible to proceed further.

M. Delaruelle therefore took one postilion with him, together with the light, and, leaving the other two men reluctantly in charge of the broken equipage, set out to discover if some shelter might be found.

They were not indeed long before they came upon a neat little house, which, though it was not the kind of dwelling that the statesman usually honoured with his presence, he was, nevertheless, extremely glad to see.

A vigorous knocking brought a pretty little maid to the door; M. Delaruelle, conscious of his draggled appearance, asked pompously if they were on the estates of Monseigneur le Duc de

Mailly, adding that he was no less a person than the Marquis Delaruelle, that nobleman's uncle.

The servant replied respectfully that this was a long way from the Château Mailly, but that she was sure that her mistress, the Baronne, would desire them to take refuge against the inclemency of the weather.

The traveller jumped at the suggestion, explained the accident to the coach, and begged that assistance might be sent to his men and horses.

He was assured that the case would be put before the mistress of the house, and was shown (after being relieved of his dripping coat) into a snug, cosy parlour, where a huge fire burnt on the hearth, a rosy lamp glowed on the table, and a cushioned chair stood invitingly empty.

M. Delaruelle did not hesitate to make use of this, and stretched himself luxuriously before the warm blaze; his returning good humour was helped by the entry of the maid with a tray of cordials and the news that supper was in preparation.

"Evil fortune," remarked M. Delaruelle, who, left alone with the cordials, had carelessly drunk rather more glasses of these excellent liqueurs than he was aware of, "seldom resists the steady fortitude of the lofty minded." And he smiled at the row of bottles with a smile slightly fatuous.

The entry of his hostess brought him in some confusion to his feet.

The lady, who was attired with a nunlike sobriety, a mourning cap with lappets and a housewifely apron, regarded him expectantly.[30]

[30] Lappets: two long strips of material that hang from the top of the cap, down to and over the shoulders.

"Terèse!" he cried.

"Exactly. How nice of you to remember the name!" and she sat down beside him as he sank, astonished, into the great chair.

"What an extraordinary meeting!" he stammered. "I—er—thought you were in Spain——"

"So I was," she said demurely, "but I have returned, a chastened, and, I trust, a better woman."

"Alphonse?" he murmured.

"Dead."

"He would be," said M. Delaruelle. "He was that sort of man."

"A sad error," the widow admitted frankly. "I assure you that if I have wept it was not for his demise, but for my wasted youth."

"That I can believe—and he left you——?"

"A pittance and the memory of a mistake," she sighed.

M. Delaruelle smiled the smile of one justified of himself.

"My dear Terèse! Now I hope that you will confess that you were foolish to cast me off."

Terèse threw up her charming eyes.

"Is there need to confess? And you, Armand, have become a great man!"

"I trust that I have been of some service to my country, and there I will allow you some merit. Had you not early shown me the vanity of earthly affections I might not have been the man I am now."

"I was never," sighed Terèse humbly, "good enough for you, Armand, a little, silly, vain thing!"

"Well, well," he replied generously, "we will not dwell on that. You, no doubt, have paid for your foolishness. Now tell me what you are doing here and how you employ your time?"

"I live in this secluded spot in the retirement suitable to my estate," she said. "I work for the poor and add to my scanty income by fine needlework."

M. Delaruelle approved.

"I am glad that you are of such a turn of mind," he remarked, thinking how plump and comely and neat she still was. "And now perhaps you can help me in a very disagreeable business. Are we near the Château Mailly?"

"No, we are not."

"Dear me, how that fool must have mistaken the road! Well, that simpleton, Lucien, my nephew, has actually entangled himself with a designing female, one Terèse, a widow like yourself, but in character far different."

"Fie, monsieur," protested the lady, casting down her eyes. "I hope that this is a tale that the strictest decorum would permit to be unfolded?"

"Yes, yes, though I admire your caution. Have you heard of a certain Madame de la Morilière?"

"Monsieur, I have. Let my blushes complete my answer."

"Is she—then——?"

"She is. Pray pursue the subject no farther."

"*Mon Dieu!*" cried M. Delaruelle, pouring himself out another glass of cordial. "Is it as bad as that?"

"It is. This reproach to her sex has allured, by the basest of means, all the youths of the neighbourhood, among them your nephew. Let us avert our eyes, Armand, from the degrading spectacle."

"I can't. I've got to rescue the young fool. His marriage is arranged for him——"

"In heaven?"

"No, in Paris, a more definite, if a less reputable locality. I do not remember, Terèse, that you used to be so pious and proper."

"Armand! Have you forgotten my years, my situation? What is there for a woman blighted in her affections, deceived in her marriage, but a retirement given to good works and the most circumspect behaviour?"

"Of course, of course," he agreed hastily. "Now as for this Madame de la Morilière—where does she live?"

"At the very gates of Château Mailly, which she regards as her future residence."

"I must buy her off," sighed M. Delaruelle. "She is, of course, unscrupulous, rapacious, heartless?"

"To the last degree."

"What the devil could Lucien have seen in her?"

"That, Armand, you should be able to answer better than I," replied Terèse demurely. "It is useless to ask a virtuous female of what consist the attractions of the—er—other sort."

"Quite so. But you will have noticed if she is pretty?"

"I always drop my veil when we chance to meet," said Terèse with a shudder.

"Well, well," said M. Delaruelle, resigned, "I must see her myself, that is all. I shall not spare her, I assure you."

"How was it that you left Lucien unprotected so long? I have often wondered."

"How could I guess that in a spot so secluded there would be danger? And you, Terèse, might have warned me!"

"I dare not bring myself to your notice—nor was it an affair in which a female of delicacy could with propriety interfere."

M. Delaruelle regarded his long-lost love with an approval that was not unmingled with amazement. Never, surely, since the days of Luther had there been such a reformation!

Gone were all her wild, roguish tricks, her indiscreet talk, her flighty airs, her careless laugh, the hundred fripperies of her dress, her rouge and powder, her trinkets and laces; she was as demure a piece as the soberest of men could desire.

"Is it possible," thought her former lover, "that this change is due to my precepts? To remorse and regret at my loss?"

Never, surely, had a man ever received such a compliment; and the meek creature seemed to expect no reward; though he observed her glances of shy adoration they were not tempered by hope; she was content to worship from afar the rich prize she had, in her flippant youth, so wantonly flung away.

"I am glad, my dear Terèse," he said, feeling outwardly and inwardly warmed and comforted, "that any recollection of me or of my admonitions should have had this gratifying effect of making you change the mode of life to which I so strongly took exception. I commend your efforts and you may be comforted in your seclusion by the knowledge that your, er—penitence has been appreciated, yes, my dear Terèse, appreciated!"

"How beautifully you speak," she cried, her eyes swimming in tears of gratitude. "Believe me, Armand, never shall I again transgress those rules of decorum the breaking of which cost me, alas, my life's happiness!"

M. Delaruelle had begun by now to forget that it was the lady who had jilted him, and to believe that it was he who had left the lady; this added to his state of spiritual comfort, and when he heard supper announced he smiled with greater amiability than he had shown for years.

The supper was excellent; Terèse had evidently not included the pleasures of the table among the vanities she had renounced, and M. Delaruelle relaxed to that cosy state of sleepy repletion when there is a positive delight in sitting in a warm room with a good meal on the table and listening to the winter wind howling without.

He was beginning to think, with delicious anticipation, of a soft bed, a warming pan, and a tempting breakfast in the distance when Terèse rose and said:

"Now, my dear Armand, I hope that you are sufficiently refreshed to continue your journey."

"Continue my journey!"

"I do not know if you can find the Château Mailly, for it is very dark and stormy and I have no guide to send with you, also I fear you must go on foot as your coach had to be left in the ditch and I have no carriage——"

"But why? Surely I may trespass on your hospitality to the extent of a bed?"

"Fie, Armand, what are you suggesting? Consider my reputation!"

"Consider the night, Terèse—why there is a storm fit to blow one away—icy cold, torrents of rain," cried M. Delaruelle in dismay.

"Armand, you forget yourself—surely it is better that you should expose yourself to—and even perish in—the tempest, than that the rules of decorum should be offended!"

"Rules of decorum!" answered the exasperated gentleman. "You overdo it, Terèse—your good name—and mine—are now above slander——"

"They are not," said the lady firmly. "I am an unprotected female, living alone. What have I if I lose my fair name?"

"And what have I, if I break my neck in a ditch, or catch a mortal chill?"

"A clear conscience," she replied modestly. "Oh, can I believe it possible that he for whose sake I reformed my whole mode of life is now tempting me to a gross indiscretion?"

"Fudge," cried M. Delaruelle, almost rudely. "There is no indiscretion, the storm covers all. Besides, who need be the wiser?"

"A dozen people know you are here—your men, my maids. They have heard us address each other, I fear very imprudently—in the familiar mode—and would it be so difficult for gossip to discover that once we cherished a tender passion for each other?"

These arguments left M. Delaruelle cold.

"It is an indecency," he exclaimed, "to turn a man out a night like this."

"Then what is it," she retorted, "to rob a poor widow of her one possession, her good name? Armand, I will not be compromised because you fear to face a little rain."

"A little rain! *Mon Dieu!* You are altogether too high flown and fantastical, Terèse—I swear I never compromised anyone."

"That I can believe, Armand, but the argument is unaltered. Fie, would you have me spoken of as another Madame de la Morilière!"

"There can be no danger. My hair is grey and yours ought to be," he replied snappishly. "Surely that is our defence?"

" 'Twill but add a touch of ridicule to the *escalandre*," she sighed. "And you may be grey, Armand, though I vow I thought you were powdered, but I, alas, am not yet counted past the period of feminine weakness!"

M. Delaruelle pulled the curtains and tried to look out, but saw only blackness, opened the window and was met by a blast that nearly sent him backwards; a filthy night, there was no doubt of that.

"You will feel odd if my corpse is discovered frozen or drowned or broken by the way," he said morosely.

"I shall feel that you have died in a good cause," she replied. "As one should die whose principal occupation was observing the proprieties. Come, Armand, I will send for your coat, which must be nearly dry, and you will take your staff and set out, trusting in that God who is the sure protector of innocence——"

"I never boasted that manner of innocence," retorted M. Delaruelle, exasperated, "nor was I so presumptuous as to expect Heaven to provide me with a guardian angel——"

"Pray, monsieur," replied the lady primly, "begin, then, to-night to solicit for one, for I doubt whether, without that Divine protection, you will get as far as the Château Mailly."

As she rang the bell to summon the maid, M. Delaruelle groaned; plainly she was inexorable, too rigidly had she learned the lesson that in their mutual youth he had tried in vain to teach her, and he heartily wished that he had left the matrimonial affairs of Lucien to disentangle themselves, as indeed they would now probably have to, for he greatly doubted if he should survive the rigours of the winter storm.

Bitterly he watched while a lantern, his greatcoat and hat (still far from dry) were fetched, and sourly he asked if his men had fared any better than himself?

"They are housed in the stables, long since disused, and, I fear, rat-ridden, but naturally my maids, all chosen for their impeccable characters, refuse to allow them to remain in the house."

When M. Delaruelle reached the door and heard the wind and the rain, felt the cold and saw the dark, he nearly decided to beg permission to share the stables with the postilions, great as that sacrifice of his dignity would be.

Terèse was meanwhile giving him directions as to his road; confused they sounded, nor was the adventure rendered more enticing by her warning that banditti were known to lurk in the woods between her house and the Château Mailly.

At the last moment, however, the lady relented, or rather conceived a brilliant compromise. There was, she said, a summer-house at the end of the garden, known, from the statue of Eros it contained, as the "Temple d'Amour," and there the uninvited guest might spend the night; stone certainly and damp possibly was this refuge, but better perhaps than a journey through the storm.

M. Delaruelle agreed; a straight-faced abigail whose virtue was obviously unassailable by the influence of any god, or temple of love, muffled herself up and, with a martyred air, conducted M. Delaruelle through the wet and cold to the summer-house and there left him with the lantern and the coy deity, who, for the moment, surveyed a barren kingdom.[31]

As soon as he was left alone M. Delaruelle discovered that he had forgotten to ask for pillows and blankets; there was nothing for it but to wrap himself in his damp greatcoat and lie on one of the damp stone seats; wind and rain blew in through the elegant pillars of the open entrance, and shift his position as he would he could by no means become either dry or comfortable; after some hours of this a stiffness and numbness overcame his limbs that made him fear he was seized by a creeping palsy; this was followed by shooting pains that showed he was in the grip of his old enemy—rheumatism.

Sheer fatigue brought him some snatches of uneasy sleep disturbed by nightmares, and when at last the late winter daylight penetrated into the summer-house it was with a cold and sour eye that the shivering M. Delaruelle glanced at the frozen figure of the jaunty Cupid and with a leer of disgust that he thanked him for his icy hospitality.

---

[31] Abigail: a lady's maid.

The storm had abated but even by the light of day the prospect looked desolate; the only cheerful thing in sight was a rosy light in the windows of the house at the end of the garden, the glow of fires that were dissipating the gloom of the winter morning.

M. Delaruelle wished to hide his disordered and discomfited person in retreat, to hasten away to the nearest inn for rest, refreshment and a wheelwright, but the lure of that sparkling, rosy light was too strong; a breakfast and a fire proved irresistible temptations; he moved stiffly towards the house.

The tempting perfume of frothing chocolate came to his nostrils as he approached the parlour window, and, as he passed, he looked in greedily.

There was the breakfast of his desires, the most elegant of equipages set by the most cosy of fires—and there was Terèse presiding at the table in a charming undress, all knots of pink ribbon and falls of blonde lace, in a coquettish cap that made her appear not a day more than twenty-five. So far so good and a pretty enough picture—but Terèse was not alone.

Who was that lounging in the comfortable chair opposite with his toes to the blaze and a smile of lazy self-satisfaction on his face?

No one in the world but Lucien, that miserable "scapegrace."[32]

M. Delaruelle tapped on the window in blind, bewildered fury.

"*Mon Dieu!* " cried Lucien, "it is a ghost!"

"Of a good man," murmured Terèse, daintily serving sugar, "even though he did not die in the Temple of Love!"

Again M. Delaruelle violently rattled at the pane.

Lucien rose languidly and opened the window an inch or so.

---

32 Scapegrace: an incorrigible rascal.

"It is not a ghost, but uncle," he remarked. "We thought you must be dead. You really can't come in, you're far too damp and dirty, monsieur."

"Terèse!" cried M. Delaruelle, his eyes glaring.

"Oh, fie, is she Terèse to you?" exclaimed Lucien. "Occupying a lady's summer-house hardly gives you the right to use her so familiarly."

"Fool," said M. Delaruelle furiously. "What are you doing here?"

"Arguing with you. I was so moped in Paris that I came down here yesterday morning to pay a little visit to Terèse——"

"Terèse," groaned M. Delaruelle.

"I suppose," said Lucien, bored, "you never thought to ask her other name? It is Madame de la Morilière. And now I must close the window. There is a plaguy draught."

He slipped the bolt and drew the curtain, from behind which floated the perfume of chocolate and of laughter.

It was a drab consolation for the man outside to vow that both belonged to a wicked woman.

# THE FOLDING DOORS

A YOUNG man was coming slowly down the wide staircase of a palace in the Rue de Vaugirard. It was, by the new reckoning, the 13th of Brumaire; evening and cold, moonlit and clear; these things being the same by any reckoning, as the young man thought, pausing by the tall window on the landing-place that looked out on to the blue-shadowed, silent street.[33]

There was a ball overhead in the great state rooms, and he could hear the music—violins, flutes and harpsichord—distinctly, though he had closed the door behind him. He was one of the guests, and had the watchful, furtive air of one who has stolen away unperceived and fears that he may be discovered. He seemed now to have stopped with an idea of ascertaining if anyone was abroad, for he leant over the smooth gilt banisters and listened. The great staircase was empty, and empty the vast hall below.

Opposite the landing window was a long mirror with three branched candles before it. The young man turned to this quickly and noiselessly and pulled from the pocket of his coat a strip of gilt-edged paper, folded tightly. He unrolled this and read the message it contained, written in a light pencil:

At half-past ten knock four times on the folding doors. *Do not be late; every moment is one of terror. I am afraid of HIM.*

The last two sentences were underlined, thc last word twice.

The young man looked up and down the stairs, twisted the

---

[33] Brumaire (the month of fog, 22 October to 20 November) was the second month of the French Republican calendar.

paper up, and was about to thrust it into the flame of one of the candles when he caught sight of himself in the tall mirror, and stood starring at the image with the paper held out in his hand.

He saw a figure that to his thinking was that of a mountebank, for it had once been that of the Duc de Jaurès—Citizen Jaurès now—courtier of his one-time Christian Majesty Louis XVI, beheaded recently as Louis Capet in the great square now called by the people the Place de la Révolution.

The people had altered everything, even the person of M. de Jaurès, who wore the classic mode beloved of liberty—the fashion of the directorate of this year one of freedom, hair *à la* Titus, and a black stock swathing the chin.[34] His face was stern and thin, the dark, heavy eyes and black hair accentuating this pallor; his countenance, though sombre in expression, was beautiful by reason of the exquisite lines of the mouth and nostrils, and something elevated and noble in the turn of the head. As he stared at himself a slow colour of terrible shame overspread his paleness; with something like a suppressed shudder he gave the paper to the flame, and scattered the ashes down the stairs.

Then he pulled out the watch hanging from the black watered-silk fob.

It wanted ten minutes to half-past ten. The dance music ceased overhead; in its place came laughter, loud talking, and presently a woman singing in a rapt and excited fashion.

Monsieur de Jaurès paced to and fro on the landing. He loathed these people he mixed with, so like him in dress and appearance, but bourgeois and *canaille* all of them; some butchers of the Terror, some smug deputies, some one-time servants, some soldiers, some

[34] *À la* Titus: a short, layered cut with the hair sweeping towards the crown.

dancers from the opera, some provincials and their wives—all, by the grace of the people, free and equal.[35]

M. de Jaurès, aristocrat by virtue of birth, tradition, temper and qualities, bit his under-lip fiercely to hear these people rioting in this mansion. The late owner, his once dear friend, had been massacred in the prison of La Force a month ago, and the house now belonged to a deputy from Lyons, married to the daughter of a nobleman long since sent to the guillotine.[36]

The note that M. de Jaurès had burnt was from this lady. They had known each other before the rule of chaos, and when the Revolution brought him out of the prison where he had been consigned for a political offence by the late King's ministers, and he had found her, terror-subdued, mistress of a revolutionary salon, the similarity between their positions, the common memories of another world, the sense of kinship amidst a society so alien, so monstrous, so hideous, had grown into a sad but strong love.

She was spared because she had married one of the tyrants and pretended to forget her father's blood; he because he had been a prisoner of the King and affected to subscribe to the new rule of the people. Both had tasted of shame, and together they sought to redeem themselves.

Fired by their mutual sympathy, the horror of what they daily saw around them, the desire to redeem their acquiescence in the overthrow of their order, to redeem, at the risk of death, the lives they should never have consented to save, they had been the instigators of one of the many plots against the Government, the

---

35 *Canaille*: riffraff.

36 Originally a private residence known as the Hôtel de la Force, the prison was used to house political prisoners during the French Revolution.

object of which was to rescue the Austrian Queen from the Temple and the ultimate guillotine.[37]

To-night the intrigue, evolved with skill and secrecy, and materially helped by the knowledge Hortense was enabled to obtain through her husband's position, was to be put into execution, and they were either to fly across the frontier with the rescued Queen or to give up life together, as aristocrats, upon the scaffold.

M. de Jaurès, on the threshold of this hazard, felt that chill, that almost suspension of the faculties which fills the waiting pause before the plunge into violent actions. He was conscious of neither exaltation nor despair, but of a strange sense that time had stopped, or had never been, and that all the events which so oppressed his brain were but pictures that would clear away and reveal at last—reality.

The dance music began again; the noisy music of the People, with its distinct rise and fall. He and Hortense had been present at the opera the night they had played "*Richard Cœur de Lion*," and the audience had risen in a frenzy of devotion at the strains of "*O Richard, O mon roi*."[38]

He recalled the Queen with her children, worshipped and very stately, and Hortense with powdered hair and a hoop festooned with roses; then he thought of the wretched captive in the Temple, and the haggard woman in a Greek gown, with a *filet* through her

---

[37] The Temple, a medieval fortress in Paris which was originally a fortified monastery of the Templars, was used to house royal prisoners during the French Revolution.

[38] "*Richard Cœur de Lion*" (*Richard the Lionheart*), the opéra comique by André Grétry. "*O Richard, O mon roi*" ('Oh Richard, oh my king'), an aria from the aforementioned opera, and a popular rallying song amongst royalists during the French Revolution.

flowing hair, waiting for him downstairs behind the folding doors.[39]

Pacing to and fro, facing now the cold street and bitter night, now his own reflection in the glass, the inner agony of suspense, regret, remorse broke through the dazed control of his overwrought passions. He gave a little sound, caught into the whirl of the dance music unheard, and stepped back sideways against the gleaming white wall, his hand instinctively to his heart.

The next second he was master of himself and wondering wildly what had caused him that sudden utter pang of terror, a terror beyond fear of death or any definition, awful, hideous. He listened, as men will in great dread, and heard what seemed a curious short cry, like the echo of his own, that rose above the dance-beat. He thought it came from the street, and softly opened the window.

Everything was still, but in the distance, where the moonlight fell between two houses, three of the Republican soldiers were dragging a man along, and a girl in a blue gown was following, wringing her hands.

A second, and the little group had passed out of sight. M. de Jaurès closed the window, feeling strangely relieved that his emotion had been caused by such a common thing as the cry of a poor creature following a suspect to the *conciergerie*.[40] He must, unconsciously, have heard her cry before, and this had given him that sensation of terror.

The dance music fell to a softer measure; a clock struck the half hour, and Camille de Jaurès descended to the salon on the next floor.

He entered softly, yet confident of being neither interrupted nor observed.

---

39 *Filet*: fillet, a garland.

40 *Conciergerie*: a courthouse and prison in Paris.

The room was large, with great windows looking on to the street. It had once been painted with flowers, and shepherds asleep with their flocks, and nymphs seated beside fountains, but had lately been painted white from floor to ceiling by a Republican who detested these remnants of aristocracy. White, with stiff wreaths of classic laurel, candles in plain sconces shaded with dead-hued silk, straight grey curtains before the windows, and very little furniture to cumber the polished floor; that little simple, bare-legged and comprising a couch of Grecian shape, covered with striped brocade, such as ladies, dressed in the fashions of the year one of liberty, loved to recline on.

A cold, bare room, with a glimmer from the shaded light like the moon-glow, and with no colour, nor gleam, nor brightness. The wall that faced the window was almost entirely occupied by high, white folding doors with crystal knobs. M. de Jaurès' glance fell at once on these; they led to the private apartments of Hortense, and through them, by the back way across the garden, they were to escape to-night. He advanced, and was about to knock, when one leaf was opened sharply in his face and a man stepped out.

It was Citizen Durosoy, husband of Hortense. M. de Jaurès stepped back; he saw that the room beyond the folding doors was dark, but close where the light penetrated he noticed a fold of soft satin with a pearl border, and an empty white shoe softly rounded to the shape of a foot, lying sideways, as if it had just been taken off. Hortense was there, then, he knew, waiting for him. He straightened himself to meet the unlooked-for-interruption.

He was quite composed as Durosoy closed the doors.

"Your room upstairs is very close," he said, "and I suppose I am not in a festive mood. It is pleasantly cool here."

"Cool!" echoed the Deputy of Lyons. "It seems to me cold,"

he laughed. "Perhaps it is the singing of La Marguerite, which is so bad for the nerves, for my wife has a headache and must lie down in the dark."

M. de Jaurès smiled. He felt such a contempt for this man that it put him absolutely at his ease. The Deputy had been a poor provincial lawyer, to whom the late Jaurès had been kind. He affected to remember this now, and was warmly friendly, even patronizing, to his old patron's son. The aristocrat hated him doubly for it, scorned him that no echo of this hatred seemed ever to awake in his mind; for the Deputy was almost familiar in his manner to M. de Jaurès. He was quiet and modest with everybody.

"I hope my wife is not delicate," he said with an air of anxiety. "I have thought lately that she was in ill-health."

"I have not noticed it," answered the other.

He seated himself on the striped couch and looked carelessly at the grate, where a pale fire burnt. The Deputy crossed to the hearth and stood looking at his guest with an amiable smile. He was a slight man, brown-haired and well-looking, but of a common appearance. He wore a grey cloth coat, with a black sash up under his armpits, and white breeches. This dress and the stiff, long, straggling locks that fell on to his bullion-stitched collar gave him an appearance of gloom and wildness not in keeping with his pleasant countenance.

He stood so long smiling at M. de Jaurès that a feeling of impatience came over the nobleman. He glanced at the pendule clock on the mantelpiece and wondered how long the fool would stay.

"It is unfortunate that you and the Citizeness should both be absent at once," he remarked. He had still the tone of an aristocrat when speaking to Durosoy.

The Deputy held out his right hand.

"I cut my finger with a fruit knife," he answered, "and came down to Hortense to tie it up; but she seemed so to wish to be alone I did not like to press her; her head hurt her so, she said."

A handkerchief was twisted about his hand, and he began to unwind it as he spoke. "Now you are here," he added, "perhaps you could help me tie it up; it really is bleeding damnably."

M. de Jaurès rose slowly. He let his eyes rest for a moment on the folding doors. It was as if he could see Hortense standing the other side in the dark, listening, waiting for her husband to go.

Durosoy held up his bare hand. There was a deep cut on the forefinger, and the blood was running down the palm and staining the close frill of muslin at his wrist.

"A severe wound for a silver knife," remarked M. de Jaurès, taking him by the wrist.

"A steel knife," said the Deputy; "steel as sharp as *La Guillotine*. You see, *mon ami*," and he smiled, "what comes of trying to cut a peach with a steel knife."

M. de Jaurès slowly tore his own handkerchief into strips and carefully bound up the wound. He was wondering the while if Hortense had been delayed by the unexpected visit of her husband; if she was venturing to change her clothes before he finally returned to their guests. By the white shoe he had seen through the folding doors he thought she had done so.

"Thank you, Camille," said the Deputy. He had a trick odious to M. de Jaurès of using Christian names. "It is astonishing how faint the loss of a little blood makes one."

"This from our modern Brutus!" exclaimed M. de Jaurès. That term had been given once, in the Convention, to the Deputy, and the man who despised him dared to quote it ironically, knowing the stupidity of the provincial. As he had expected, the Deputy seemed pleased; he shrugged modestly.

"Oh, one's own blood, you know; not that of other people. I can endure the loss of *that* with great equanimity." He smiled as if he had made a joke, and the aristocrat smiled too, for other reasons. "Will you drink with me—down here? It is, as you say, very close upstairs."

"I fear to detain you, Citizen."

Durosoy rang the bell, then seated himself by the fire.

"No; I am tired of their chatter. I would rather talk with a sensible man like yourself, my dear Camille."

M. de Jaurès did not move from his easy attitude on the brocade couch.

"But we shall disturb the Citizeness," he said. His idea was that, if he could make Durosoy leave with him, he could more or less easily get rid of him upstairs and return.

The Deputy smiled. "Hortense is not so ill. Besides, the doors are thick enough."

M. de Jaurès wondered how thick. Could she hear their talk? Would she understand the delay? His straining ears could catch no sound of her movements.

The Deputy continued in a kind of fatuous self-satisfaction:

"I hope she will be well enough to return soon to the ball. When one has a beautiful wife one likes to show her off."

He paused, put his head on one side and added:

"You do think her beautiful, do you not, Camille?"

M. de Jaurès looked at him coldly. He felt he could afford to endure this man, since in a few moments she would be riding away from his house for ever.

"Naturally, Citizen."

A citizen servant entered, and the Deputy ordered wine.

"I must not stay," said M. de Jaurès. He raised his voice a little that she might hear. "One glass, and I will go back to make my adieux."

Durosoy appeared mildly surprised.

"So early! You cannot have any business this time of night."

The wine was brought in and placed on a thin-legged table by the hearth. M. de Jaurès glanced at the clock. The hand was creeping on towards eleven. His contempt of the Deputy was beginning to change to an impatient hatred of the creature's very presence.

"A matter of mood, not of time," he answered. "I am in no merry-making vein to-night."

The Deputy, pouring out wine, looked at him critically.

"You are too lazy, my friend. You do nothing from one day's end to another—naturally you are wearied. And it is dangerous too."

M. de Jaurès took the glass offered him. "How dangerous?"

Durosoy lifted his common brown eyes. "Those who will not serve the Republic are apt to be considered her enemies."

The young noble smiled.

"Oh, as to that, I am a very good friend to France, but I lack the qualities to be of any use."

He sipped his wine and looked indifferently past the Deputy at the folding doors. His thoughts were: "The time is getting on. How long will a carriage take from here to the Rue du Temple? Half an hour, allowing for the pace we must go and the crowd coming out of the opera."

"No use!" exclaimed the Deputy. "Why, you are a soldier, are you not?"

"Once—that seems a long time ago."

Durosoy laughed and poured out more wine. The tinkling of

the glass on the silver stand had the same thin quality as his voice.

"There is always La Vendée," he said.[41] "The Royalists there are giving us a good deal of trouble."

"I do not fancy going there to be hewn down by a lot of rascals. I leave that to braver men," smiled Jaurès lazily; but his blood burnt with the desire to be with these same Royalists in La Vendée, with his sword drawn against such as this Deputy, whose wine seemed to scorch and choke to-night. When would the man go? The carriage that was waiting at the back might be noticed. The servant in the plot would begin to wonder at the delay; and she, could she hear? She must be undergoing torture—as he was.

"Then there is the revolt in Caen," said the Deputy. "We want good men there."

"I've no fancy to go soldiering."

"You are dull to-night, citizen. Does the business of the Widow Capet interest you? It is to come on this month."

"Ah! The trial?"

"Yes."

"I heard something of it. No, I am not interested."

When would this babbling cease? Ten minutes past eleven, and the rendezvous in the Rue du Temple at twelve.

"Not interested?" echoed the Deputy. "Now, if I might hazard a guess, my friend, I should say that you were rather too interested."

M. de Jaurès looked at him steadily.

"How—too interested?" he asked in accents painfully calm.

"I do not think you would like the Widow Capet to take the same journey to the Place de la Révolution as her husband did."

"Why should I trouble?" answered M. de Jaurès, who for one

---

41 Counter-revolutionary uprisings in the Vendée region of France.

instant had thought himself suspected. He drew his breath a little unevenly; the delay, the suspense was beginning to tell on him, were becoming serious too. He remembered that the hour had been altered at the last moment from one to twelve, and that he had had no opportunity of telling Hortense so. They had to be so careful; there had been so few chances for them to meet at all. Hortense would think they had an hour longer than was the case.

The Deputy was taking his third glass; he seemed to be settled comfortably in his chair. It appeared as if he might maunder on with his idle talk for another hour; and the delay of another hour would be fatal to M. de Jaurès.

"It must seem very strange to you," said the Deputy reflectively, "this year one of liberty."

M. de Jaurès sat forward on the couch. Durosoy had never taken this tone of gravity with him before.

"No stranger to me than to you," he answered. He finished the wine, and set the glass back on the table.

"Well, then, strange to me and to you."

M. de Jaurès laughed; he could not control himself.

"What makes you say that?" he asked.

The Deputy shrugged. "The thought will occur—sitting here in this palace that I used to pass with awe—talking to you whom I used to regard with awe—married to Hortense! Yes, you are right, it is strange to me."

The noble's mouth tightened; a black shame overwhelmed him that he was sitting here listening to this man.

"You," continued the Deputy, "used to know the former owner of this house, did you not?"

M. de Jaurès rose.

"I knew him."

"He was killed at La Force, was he not?"

"I believe so. Why do you recall him?" M. de Jaurès leant against the mantelpiece. The cold, white room, the inane Deputy were fast becoming intolerable. He began to be hideously conscious of two things: the clock, whose hands were coming round slowly to the half-hour, and the folding doors behind which Hortense waited. The interruption, of which he had thought nothing at first, was like to prove fatal. Could he do it in less than half an hour? Merciful God, it was not possible! Some of them were already at the rendezvous—the Queen was ready.

"Let us go back upstairs," he said. "It is, after all, rather doleful here."

"On the contrary, I am very comfortable," smiled the Deputy, crossing his legs.

"You will be missed," said M. de Jaurès. His thoughts were racing furiously. How could he convey to Hortense that the time had been altered—that he could not wait?

The Deputy nodded towards the high ceiling. "Missed? You hear the music? I think they are enjoying themselves."

To abandon her or miss the appointment in the Rue du Temple; to break faith with his friends or with her, to lose all chance of redemption, to jeopardize the Queen's escape, or to forsake Hortense (for success meant that he must be across the frontier, and failure meant death; ether way he was useless to her)—it was fast narrowing to that alternative.

He looked at his face in the large mirror above the mantelpiece, and was almost startled to see how haggard it was above the close cravat and blue striped waistcoat. Surely Durosoy must notice!

The Deputy sat looking into the fire. M. de Jaurès, glancing at him out of furtive eyes, observed that he, too, was pale.

A pause of silence was broken by the shrill chimes of the gilt clock striking the half-hour.

M. de Jaurès could not restrain a start. He must go. He could come back for her if alive; his honour (Heaven help him! he still thought of that) was the pledge to them, his affection to her—she would understand. Perhaps by the servant waiting with the carriage at the back entrance he could convey a message telling her of the changed time.

"You will forgive me," he said with that ease with which breed enabled him to cover his agony, "but I am due at my chambers." He raised his voice for her to hear. "The truth is I have business, important business, to-night. Good evening, Durosoy."

He went towards the door; it would be quick running to make the Rue du Temple in time. Heaven enlighten her as to the cause of his desertion!

"Business?" said the Deputy good-humouredly. "There is no business nowadays but politics or plots. I hope you are not entangled in the latter, my dear Camille."

M. de Jaurès had his hand on the door-knob. "This is private business," he answered, "about my property. I am trying to save some of it."

The Deputy turned in his chair.

"Why, I did not know that your estates were confiscated. Why did you not tell me? I might have helped you."

M. de Jaurès opened the door.

"You are such a busy man, Durosoy. I think I shall manage the affair satisfactorily."

"Monsieur le Duc?"

At that title he turned sharply, and saw the Deputy standing before the fire looking at him.

"Why do you say that?" he asked, and his nostrils widened.

"Forgive me, the expression slipped out. I still think of you as Monsieur le Duc. It is an astonishing thing, but I believe I am still in awe of you, as I used to be in my little office in Lyons." He smiled fatuously, lowered his glance to the floor and shook his head."

"Why did you call me?"

"Well, I wanted to speak to you. Take another glass of wine; it is still early."

"Indeed it is impossible for me to stay. I have an appointment."

"Bah! Make him wait."

"It is a rendezvous that I would rather keep."

"A strange hour for a business appointment. Are you sure it is not a lady that you are anxious to see?"

"Call it a lady, then," said M. de Jaurès, "but believe me that I must go."

He was leaving on that, when the Deputy called after him:

"I entreat you to stay. It is also a lady of whom I wish to speak."

M. de Jaurès turned slowly and closed the door.

"Come," smiled the Deputy, "another glass."

"What have you to say to me, Durosoy?" He felt as if the claw of the devil were on his shoulder, dragging him back into the room; yet every moment—nay, every second—was precious, fast becoming doubly precious.

The Deputy was pouring out the wine. His grey and black figure was illumined by the increasing glow of the fire. He moved bottles and glasses clumsily by reason of the bandaged forefinger of his right hand; behind him the clock showed twenty minutes to twelve.

M. de Jaurès crossed the long room to the hearth.

"What did you wish to say?" he asked. "Nay"—he put the glass aside—"what was it you wished to speak to me of?"

"My wife."

The noble's first thought was "This man is not a fool"; his second, "he suspects"—accompanied with a sense of stupor and confusion.

"You," continued Durosoy, "have known her longer that I have; she was very much admired, was she not, when she was at the court?"

"She was admired, naturally. A strange question! I never knew her well," answered M. de Jaurès. He was sure the fellow suspected, not the plot, but the elopement. He desperately readjusted his plans. He could not leave her now; he must forsake his friends sooner. Had she not said, "I am afraid of *him*."?

"Well, that is all," said the Deputy. "Go and keep your appointment, my friend"—his eyes suddenly gleamed—"and I will finish my wine and presently go and fetch Hortense back to the ball-room."

M. de Jaurès answered his look. "No, I will stay," he said with a kind of cold calm.

"Ah? Now why have you changed your mind?"

"Because you," was the grim reply, "are so amusing."

He was wondering in his anguish why she did not come out. Surely she might have made some diversion with her presence. Yet she had probably changed her gown. Could she hear—could she understand?

The man was playing with him; he might even know of the plot. He must suspect, else why did he remain here, and why did the guests not notice his or her absence if they had not been prepared? It was too late to get to the Rue du Temple now. The governor of the prison was to be abroad for an hour, from twelve to one, and in that time they were to make their attempt. They would make it without him. He could not leave Hortense now. It was certain death ahead of him; he would be denounced to-morrow, and dishonoured, for he had forsaken his friends.

So raced the thoughts of M. de Jaurès, keeping time to the music of the quadrille coming from the room overhead, while he stood impassive by the head of the brocade sofa and gazed at the Deputy, who sipped his wine and blinked into the fire.

Two men went past shouting. When their voices had sunk into the distance the Deputy spoke:

"You are rather imprudent, citizen."

M. de Jaurès was silent; if he had but some manner of weapon he would kill this man—perhaps with his bare hands even. He came a step nearer.

"I see," continued the Deputy, still looking into the fire, "that you have a coronet on this handkerchief. Now, do not you think that very imprudent?"

M. de Jaurès stood arrested. Was this creature, after all, only a fool? He would in any case have killed him; but the days were gone when noblemen wore swords. Besides, the Deputy sat very near the bell, and was a strong man. Traditions, too, were a clog on the young man's passions. He could not use his hands.

"My dear Camille," exclaimed the Deputy, suddenly glancing up, "you look very pale."

The aristocrat, with the instinct of his race, was silent under torment. He gazed at the Deputy straightly.

"Are you going to keep this on your linen?" asked Durosoy, pointing to the coronet on the blood-stained bandage.

"Are you," answered M. de Jaurès, "going to denounce me?"

The Deputy smiled.

"Because of this? Why, no; how absurd!" he laughed. "As if

you, of all men, had not given proof of your love for the people by becoming plain Citizen Jaurès. Not many aristocrats did that."

M. de Jaurès fixed his eyes on the folding doors. It was the one thing that gave him courage to endure, to think of her waiting there, to think that he would share the inevitable end with her; that she would find he had waited.

The quadrille music took on another measure. The clock gave a little whirr and struck twelve. The aristocrat shuddered, but held himself erect. Durosoy suddenly grinned up at him.

"What about your appointment?" he asked.

"I am keeping a more important one," said M. de Jaurès through cold lips.

The Deputy rose.

"Do you not think that I act very well?" he said in a changed tone.

M. de Jaurès smiled superbly.

"My opinion of you in unchanged, monsieur."

He had now no longer anything to gain or lose by adopting the manner of the people. The two men took a step towards the middle of the room, still facing each other.

"Your appointment," repeated Durosoy, "why did you not keep it?"

M. de Jaurès raised his right hand to his heart and retreated a pace backwards. He hardly heard the words; the speaker's presence offended him indescribably; he lowered his eyes in instinctive disgust, withdrawn into his own soul. The attempt in the Rue du Temple had failed or succeeded without him; he had lost the glory of rescuing the Queen, or the glory of being with the aristocrats in La Force. They would justly despise him as a coward and a man of broken faith, but the thing that had induced him to act thus was the thing that rewarded him—the thought of Hortense. Waiting behind the folding doors, she must have heard her fate and his. She knew, perhaps, before he came that Durosoy suspected and their chance was over; she knew now that he had preferred her even to his word, his pledged honour, for even that was gone unless it would be some honour for them to die together. He hoped it would be the guillotine, not butchery in the prison yard—as befell, good Lord—as befell Charles de Maury, with whom he had once eaten and drunk in this very room.

He steadied his reeling senses with a jerking shudder and caught the back of the chair near him. That brute Durosoy was watching him, waiting for him to betray himself, being, no doubt, very sure of both of them—the man before him and the woman behind the folding doors.

M. de Jaunès smiled.

"What are you and I looking at each other like this for, eh?" he asked.

A soldier went past singing "*Ca ira*"; it mingled with the monotonous repeated music of the quadrille.[42]

The coals fell together with a little crash. The Deputy stood in a slack attitude, surveying his victim.

M. de Jaurès laughed.

"We will see," said Durosoy slowly, "if Hortense is recovered from her headache."

He turned towards the folding doors. M. de Jaurès longed for them to open; at least he would have that moment when she came forth and walked straight to him, all disguises over.

The Deputy turned the crystal handle and opened the door a little way; he looked over his shoulder and said one word:

---

[42] "*Ca ira*" was a popular song of the French Revolution.

"Aristocrat!"

"Yes," answered M. de Jaurès, "she and I—both aristocrats."

Durosoy pushed the door a little wider open; his dull, foolish manner was changing to a deep-breathing ferocity.

"The Widow Capet is still in the Temple, aristocrat," he snarled, "and your friends are in La Force by now."

M. de Jaurès kept his head high.

"So you knew," he said softly. "You are a cunning rat, Citizen Durosoy."

The Deputy's eyes were suddenly flushed with blood.

"Hortense must thank you, aristocrat, for breaking your appointment for her——"

M. de Jaurès came nearer. There was darkness beyond the folding doors—the white shoe in the same position, and the fold of pearl-braided satin.

The Deputy suddenly flung the other leaf wide.

"I am a cunning rat, am I not?" he said with a sob of hate. "My wife! My wife!" he cried, pointing to her.

She sat just inside the doors, facing them. There was a long red streak down the bosom of her white bodice, her eyes were fixed and her jaw dropped; across her knee was a knife stained with marks like rust.

The Deputy stood looking at M. de Jaurès.

"You see, I have been cutting peaches with a steel knife."

# THE NECROMANCERS
## A STORY OF TWO CHARLATANS

LAZARILLO de Tolmes was in a dilemma.

It was one which prevented him from taking his noonday repose.

He sat in his white-walled chamber and looked out on to the dusty street blazing with sun, which he could see through the slats of the green blind.

And as he gazed with unseeing eyes he bit his finger-tips and his yellow face was wrinkled with perplexity and chagrin.

He had always lived rather on the edge of things and walked in places where a single mistreading might lead him into danger, but so far he had protected prudently his dubious career and contrived to secure the profits without incurring the perils of his many double dealings.

He passed as a doctor of medicine and even as a professor of Salamanca, but the money that kept up his comfortable home and swelled his private hoard came from other sources than from the practice of his profession.[43]

He was a charlatan and had a large secret sale of lotions, potions and potent drugs for almost any disreputable purpose.

And, further than this, he dabbled in alchemy, in occultism, in charms and in witchcraft.

This was by far the most profitable part of his business and worth the great risk of discovery which would have meant death

---

[43] Salamanca is a prestigious university. It is considered to be the oldest Spanish university in existence.

in the most hideous manner the officers of the Holy Inquisition could devise.

Tolmes had no belief in the arts he practised; he was a mere cheat and his skill consisted in the apt way he could play on the credulity of his patrons and the ingenuity with which he could give a semblance of magic to his tricks.

He employed an old woman, named Camilla, and an unfrocked Franciscan by the name of Father Cheves, and in the sordid kitchen of the former he would exhibit his spells and incantations, raise spectres in the darkened mirror and gaze into the future in slabs of polished jet.

The two instruments of his impostures had always worked well under him, been faithful in the performance of their duties, strict in the keeping of his secret and moderate in their demands for pay, and he had commonly left what he called all the witchcraft foolishness to them while he attended to the more reputable business of perfumes, medicines and potions.

But lately had arisen the serious trouble that kept him brooding at the window and staring into the streets of Madrid at an hour when he was usually comfortably asleep on his couch with a glass of iced sherbet ready for his waking.

A few weeks ago a lady had called upon him and bought some soap and some perfumes.

She was young, handsome and accompanied by a duenna, and in that like many of his clients; she was also masked.[44] This, too, was a common occurrence.

After making her purchases she had lingered and, after much hesitation, stated that she wanted a charm.

[44] Duenna: an older woman acting as a chaperone.

It took Tolmes an hour to wring from her that this was to be a charm to take away the life of her husband.

Tolmes had been startled; never before had such a service been asked of him.

However, the gold the agitated lady showed him soon put him at his ease.

He undertook to do what his fair client asked of him, destroy her husband under the guise of a long lingering illness.

He felt that he was justified in doing this with a clear conscience, since he knew it to be utterly out of his power to inflict any illness on anyone by means of magic.

Hastily revolving a plan of action in his cunning brain, he decided to take as much money as possible and to deceive the lady as long as he was able with juggling tricks and cleverly contrived shows.

And when, finally, he should have to confess that the experiment had been a failure he could always put the blame on refractory spirits, and his client would be afraid to ask him to disgorge his unearned gains.

So Tolmes had settled the question, very comfortably for himself, and so for a few weeks the matter had stood.

The lady had reluctantly disclosed the name of her husband, a court official; old Camilla had hung about his residence to obtain a likeness and an effigy of him had been constructed in hard wax and placed before a slow fire in the witch's kitchen, where it was daily struck with pins which were supposed to hasten the end of the victim.

Tolmes had given no more thought to this mummery, as the lady paid regularly and made no complaint, until a few days ago, when she had visited him, radiant with excitement, to say that her husband was now confined to a bed and was rapidly sinking into great feebleness of mind and body.

He had taken, in amazement and consternation, the necklace she had thrust on him to pay for a continuation of the charm, and that evening had hurried round to old Camilla's kitchen near the river.

What he had seen and heard there had given him a very strange and uncomfortable sensation.

He waited, he watched and judged, and he came to the terrible conclusion that these two miserable tools of his, whom he had always regarded as pitiful tricksters, *had actually got into touch with the unseen world of evil* and were really working a spell that was causing the death of an innocent man.

This was the problem before Lanzarillo de Tolmes: Was he to go on, or was he to draw back? Should he confess his lifelong trickery, disavow his accomplices and return what was now blood money, or should he permit the charm to proceed, the victim to die?

This last meant a large sum of money for him, but he shrank from it, low and mean as he was.

He had meant to cheat, not to murder.

Besides, he was afraid of the consequences, afraid of discovery, afraid of the spirits themselves, which had been raised at his instructions, but which were utterly beyond his control.

The simplest way would have been to stop the incantations and remove the figure from the fire.

But the witch and the wizard would not stop—they defied him.

A handsome reward had been promised them at the successful termination of their experiment, and they were not going to forgo this for any scruples whatever.

He might dismiss them, but he knew well enough that they would go straight to the Inquisition and save themselves by denouncing him.

The problem was acute, and the position perilous and hateful.

Tolmes groaned aloud.

He wished that he had never seen the handsome lady who was so lavish with her gold and who had led him into his terrible dilemma.

Remorse and fear worked equally in his mind—even while he was wondering what to do the life of Don Guzman de Tassis, equerry to the King, was ebbing away.

He rose hastily from his blank contemplation of the street and wiped the drops of perspiration from his forehead.

He would again visit old Camilla and try to bring her to reason.

Never before had he been so imprudent as to go to the witch's kitchen in full daylight, but now he did not care; wrapping his mantle round him he hastened out into the glare of the sun and made his way through the intricate back streets which led to the dwelling of old Camilla.

This worthy passed as a washer and carder of wool, and several baskets of bleached yarn stood about the dirty doorway, and the room that gave on to the street was filled with looms and spinning wheels, carding-frames and shuttles, while hanks of wool, dyed and undyed, hung from the smoky roof.

Tolmes made his way through this, and, descending a steep flight of stairs at the back of the house, went at once into the underground kitchen—or cellar.

The air of this place was foul and smelling of sulphur and several other potent drugs.

It had a concave roof, from which hung a lantern whose powerful light shed a yellow glow round the windowless chamber.

In the centre of the stone floor was a huge diagram in white chalk, an elaborate pattern of signs and figures.

In the centre of this was a brazier, resting on a single foot.

A slow dead-looking fire burnt here, and a thick blue smoke arose and languidly spread abroad.

One side crouched Camilla.

She wore a dark red dress, and her head was tied with a black handkerchief.

On her knees rested a big book with brass clasps; her thin greasy fingers were eagerly turning the pages, and by her side was a porcelain jar from which she continually took handfuls of some aromatic substance and cast it on the flames.

Directly opposite to her sat the ex-monk; his gaze was turned earnestly on the fire, his hands clasped about his knees, which were drawn up almost to his chin.

His wrinkled face, thin, greedy, avaricious, was like that of the hag; each had unkempt grey hair falling over their ears, and each had the same expression of devilish concentration and interest in their task.

Neither looked up at the master when he entered, and he did not look at them, but at the third figure.

It was a life-sized wax model of a cavalier, wearing doublet and hose and a deep lace ruff and coloured in natural hues.

Supported by a rush-bottomed stool, it stood erect behind the fire, and features and limbs were already blurred and wasted by the heat. The face seemed to wear an expression of distress, and the wax had run on the cheeks into the likeness of tears.

Tolmes came to the fourth side of the fire, completing the strange group.

Credulity fought with disbelief as he gazed at these creatures he had so long despised and at all the implements of his former cheating and tricks.

Could devils and spirits really be invoked by these stupid, clumsy means?

Yet that very morning his cautious inquiries had elicited the information that Don Guzman was worse—weaker every hour.

Camilla threw on some spices, and a fragrant odour arose.

She then again consulted her book and whispered something across the brazier to the monk.

Tolmes could bear it no longer.

"This must stop."

Fear lent firmness to his tones.

The old woman glanced disdainfully at him.

The monk began to mutter an incantation under his breath.

Tolmes was disgusted.

"Do you think that you can deceive me?" he cried.

"Do you think that you can deceive us?" answered the Franciscan harshly. "You have no power at all, and now that you see *we* have you are frightened."

Never before had his dependants spoken in such a tone to Tolmes.

Indignation and rage made him pale and stammer.

"Don Guzman is dying!"

Old Camilla looked up, mumbling her lean jaws viciously.

"Well, did not you take money to kill him? Did not you pay us to undertake this experiment, which is being perfectly successful?"

And her wicked eyes glanced disdainfully at the wretched wax figure.

The truth, a stranger indeed to Tolmes, was forced from him by this insolence of his instruments.

"You know well enough, both of you, that it was only jugglery."

"You never said so," sneered Cheves. "You boasted to the lady you could do anything, even raise the dead."

"What is that to you?" cried Tolmes in a rage. "You knew my intention, ruffian that you are!"

"You told us to work a spell on Don Guzman de Tassis," replied the ex-monk doggedly.

"Well, well, let it be now, in the name of Heaven," exclaimed the wretched charlatan.

"Why should we let it be when we are to be paid a hundred ducats apiece on the gentleman's death?" inquired Camilla sourly.

"Because I order you," said Tolmes.

But his power was gone; they only laughed at him, their former servile humility changed to rude defiance.

Tolmes stared at them with rage mingled with awe.

These two figures formerly regarded by him with contempt as grotesque, almost ridiculous, had now become vested with a mystery and terror which rendered them full of dignity and horror.

How had they, miserable creatures that they were, stumbled on any occult secrets?

He could still hardly credit their power, for he had not believed at all in magic; that was why he had played his tricks so contentedly on the borderlands.

The ex-monk rose from his place and spoke:

"Hark ye, our terms are changed now, we shall not take a maravedi less than half of what you get."[45]

"I wash my hands of all of it!" cried Tolmas in a white agitation.

"No, señor, no," replied Cheves, "for you will be useful in getting us clients. Besides," he added, with a leer, "how will you make your noble living?"

Tolmes was silent. Cupidity struggled with fear as he thought of the golden opportunities he was throwing away.

---

[45] Maravedi: a Spanish copper coin of little value.

"Now we are in touch with the Devil," remarked Camilla, "we can certainly make a great deal of money."

"You make it alone," cried the charlatan. "I will earn my money in some honest fashion, not this way."

They laughed in derision.

"You honest?" mocked the hag.

"It will not be so easy for one so long out of practice," said Cheves.

Tolmes glared at them in silent, bitter wrath.

"Besides," said Camilla in a practical tone, as she gazed earnestly into the magic fire, "that you, Señor de Tolmas, are quite in our power now."

"In your power?"

"certainly. First, we could tell all your customers that you are a cheat, and so ruin you; second, we could denounce you to the Inquisition for the death of Don Guzman; third"—she looked up at him—"we could make a wax image of *you*, señor."

Tolmes felt his knees fail beneath him and his heart flutter.

The foul acid atmosphere of the kitchen was like to choke him.

His mouth was hot and dry and his ears buzzed; with helpless eyes he stared at the image of Don Guzman.

"Why does she want her husband murdered?" he asked helplessly.

"One supposes she has found some one better to put in his place," sneered the hag.

"It will be discovered," lamented Tolmes. "It will be discovered and we shall be burnt! And that was a death I always disliked!"

"You disturb the incantation," said Cheves haughtily.

"You will vex the spirit," added Camilla, "and he will do you a mischief."

Tolmes shuddered.

He was silent, meditating many strange things. If he forcibly stopped the business (supposing that he could) he would lose his livelihood; if he let it go on he would lose his soul.

It was difficult, at the moment, to estimate which was of the most consequence.

And then there was his conscience.

For he found that he still possessed one; he was genuinely sorry for Don Guzman and began to hate his wicked wife.

In vain he sought for some means of saving the cavalier without jeopardizing his own safety: his brain, usually so fertile in crafty expedient, was a blank on this matter.

He wished, in his despair, that his insubordinate servants would drop dead before him. He could have found it in his heart to have murdered them.

Bitterly he longed for the old quiet, decent life of chicanery.

Bitterly he cursed the day when he had employed two such ruffians as the wretched Camilla and the ex-monk.

A low chuckle of triumph broke from the hag, and Tolmes, glancing in terror at the image, saw that the head had drooped forward and was melting in a long, thick stream of coloured wax.

Tolmes could bear it no longer.

With a strangled cry he ran out of the hideous cellar, up the dark stairs, through the room full of yarn and out into the street.

It was a relief to be in the warm, clear air and bright sunshine of outer day.

But his terror remained with him.

The horrid sight his eyes could no longer see remained before his mind.

He resolved to give all the money taken from Don Guzman's wife to the poor and to tell her that he would go no further in the matter.

Fired by this new thought he hurried along through the heat towards the square white palace of Don Guzman.

Near the gate he met Don Pasquale de Lormes, a rival charlatan and a fellow whom he much disliked.

Tolmes was hurrying on when the other caught him by the cloak.

"Señor, have you heard the news?"

"What news?"

His tongue seemed to swell in his mouth, he could hardly form the words.

The other charlatan sighed.

"Don Guzman de Tassis is worse."

"Worse?"

Tolmes was reduced to vain repetition of the other's words.

"Much worse."

Tolmes struggled with his terror.

"Why is it such a concern of yours, señor?" he managed to ask.

"Alas, it is a great concern of mine," replied Don Pasquale.

"Why?"

"Because he had just appointed me his physician," was the sad answer.

"Physician!"

Even at this moment Tolmes could not let that pass.

"How did you get the position?" he added contemptuously.

"On my merits," said Don Pasquale meekly; he was ever an unassuming man.

"Well, then, cure him."

So saying, Tolmes tried to pass on; but the other locked his arm in his and drew him under the shade of an ilex tree which hung over the wall of the garden of the Guzman palace.

"I cannot cure him," he said in a confidential and meaning tone.

"Why?"

Tolmes began to tremble.

"Because," said Don Pasquale, still further lowering his voice, "there is magic in it."

"Magic?"

"Nothing less."

"Nonsense!" stammered Tolmes.

"No nonsense at all, my friend. Don Guzman is dying from an incantation."

"Impossible!"

"Not at all—you and I, Don Lazarillo, know well enough that it is not impossible."

But Don Lazarillo was not going to admit that easily.

Don Pasquale would hear none of his protestations, but, locking his arm tighter in his, drew closer to him.

"Dying from an incantation. And I know whose, Don Lazarillo."

The wretched charlatan tried to get away but the other held him tight.

"Do you deny the visit of a certain lady and a duenna—who gave you a necklet of blue stones and red crosses?"

Tolmes groaned in dismay.

"Do you deny that she gave you, besides, a lot of gold and promised you more on the death of Don Guzman?"

Tolmes would have fallen but for the wall behind him.

"And do you deny," continued Don Pasquale, in a low, tense tone, "that the effigy of my unfortunate master is wasting before a slow fire in the kitchen of Doña Camilla, your creature?"

"How did you know?" groaned Tolmes.

"How did I know?" returned the other grandly. "I also am a professor of magic."

Don Lazarillo stared at him in a miserable, abject silence.

"It is my duty," said Don Pasquale, "to denounce you to the Inquisition."

The sallow face of Tolmes turned of a lively, greenish hue.

"How much do you want?" he asked in a queer voice.

"Rather a great deal," replied the other. "You see, when Don Guzman dies I lose a very good place."

"How much?" repeated Don Lazarillo feebly.

Don Pasquale named a sum.

Tolmes shivered; it was half his fortune. With a groan he said so.

"The Inquisition," remarked the other, "will take all, including your skin."

Don Lazarillo wiped the damp from his forehead.

"Very well."

"I will come home with you now," said Don Pasquale cheerfully.

Tolmes could not refuse.

In his comfortable little counting house he signed over to his rival five thousand ducats, which was more than half the proceeds of his long life of work, cheating and pilfering.

And was the provision he had put by for his old age.

As soon as it was dark Don Pasquale came to fetch away the treasure.

"You are a lucky man," he remarked. "I might have been hard hearted."

But Tolmes, who had sat all day motionless, only stared dismally at the yawning mouths of his empty coffers.

All his pity for Don Guzman was now lost in pity for himself and in amazement at that power of magic which he had so long pretended and so long disbelieved in.

As soon as it was completely dark he hurried round to Camilla's kitchen.

The two were still crouching over the fire.

And the wax effigy was now a shapeless mass which was beginning to melt completely away.

"He dies to-night," said Camilla.

"And we had better leave Madrid," said Tolmes sourly.

But his associates were quite out of hand. Even when he told them of Don Pasquale they only smiled.

"We will make a wax figure of him to-morrow," said the ex-monk.

Don Lazarillo was horrified to find that he was inwardly pleased at the idea.

But his elation was short.

"He knows a better magic than you," he said.

"We will see about that," answered Camilla.

Though disconcerted at Don Pasquale's knowledge of their doings, she still stoutly maintained her opinion that she would be able to defeat the rival charlatan on his own grounds.

About the dawn the last drop of wax had melted in the greasy pool on the dirty floor and the untended fire died out.

The two exhausted magicians threw themselves into a corner, and Don Lazarillo staggered home with the weight of murder on his soul.

In the middle of the morning Don Pasquale came to see him.

Tolmes greeted him with a haggard face.

"You need not be frightened," said the other. "Don Guzman is not dead."

"Not dead?"

"No, I cured him, and out of gratitude he has given me a country house and a thousand ducats in gold. In fact, he has been so good to me that I feel I ought to denounce you to the Inquisition for attempting his life, after all."

The unhappy Don Lazarillo groaned.

"You have come for the rest of my money?"

"Well, perhaps. You can keep what Don Guzman's wife gave you," he added. "I have no wish for *that* money."

An hour or so later Don Lazarillo de Tolmes, homeless and penniless save for the money and the necklace of the wicked masked lady, decided to try his fortune elsewhere than in Madrid.

He soon found that his remaining ducats were false and that the necklace was made of glass, but he never discovered that Don Guzman's illness was a colic caused by a mixture of senna and camomile flowers, overripe fig and pepper, administered to him by Don Pasquale, or that the lady and the duenna were servant girls hired by the same personage, but to the end of his dubious career he continued to believe in magic.

As for Doña Camilla and the ex-monk nothing could exceed their disappointment at the sudden recovery of their victim; they spent the rest of their lives trying to discover what had been wrong with the incantation.

## THE POND

SHE looked down at the tawny water, folding her thin hands tightly in her thin lap; the ruddy light of the early morning of autumn cast a soft golden hue over her ungracious figure as she sat on the low stone parapet that edged the pond.

The beech trees of the old park closed in the horizon about her; the sunlight fell between the trunks in patches of rich light on the thick, damp spread of golden leaves.

Leaves lay also on the surface of the untroubled water of the pond, vivid on the darkness, and broken here and there in their brilliant decay by the living brightness of some small green plant.

The woman sat quite still; her small head with the twist of pale hair was not ungraceful, her poise had something of the charm of breed and elegance, but she was dry and fleshless, and her face was such as would inspire fear in little helpless things that might be in her power.

The features were small, the colourless upper lip drawn too sharply back from teeth too white and dry, the chin was feeble in line, the eyes were light and expressed a certain cautious desperation, an intelligent bitterness, that the hesitant lines of the face denied; with her lids down she seemed a very stupid woman, but her unveiled glance was not in the least stupid.

For the rest, she was utterly without charm as she seemed utterly without pretension; the harsh lines of the grey taffeta bodice made no attempt to hide the curveless lines of neck and shoulders, the tight sleeves made no disguise for thin arms and hands with ugly knuckles and wrist bones.

She wore a handsome brooch of pearls on her flat bosom and a quantity of tortoiseshell combs on her flaccid blonde hair; she had the air of one belonging to a sheltered and privileged class, and the hard, reserved expression of a woman to whom nothing had ever happened and who had never stepped outside the limits of the narrowest circles.

Her age might have been anything between forty and fifty, but she had had so little to lose that the passing of her youth made but small difference to her complete unattractiveness.

She was thinking so intently that she did not notice a beautiful collie dog that came running through the birch wood until he was pushing his fine muzzle into her slack hands.

"Good dog," she said with mechanical patronage; he flattered her idea that she was immensely his superior by humbly lifting his beautiful paw to her lap, at which she pushed him away with a cold annoyance that he was too noble to resent.

He lay down near the parapet of the pond, his long coat half gleaming white, half with chestnut colour, shining in the strengthening sun.

Caroline Mordaunt was roused from her deep reflections.

She glanced spitefully at the dog.

"Humphrey's animals are so ill-trained," she said to herself, and flicked away a portion of beech mast the dog's caress had left on her neat gown.

"Go away," she cried aloud; the joyous unconcern of the animal vexed her extremely.

He beat his tail on the ground and eyed her with compassion.

Caroline rose.

"Disobedient," she said.

Her attitude was threatening; the collie generously ignored

her ill-temper and continued to wag his tail, then sprang up with triumphant pleasure as his master came towards the pond.

Brother and sister stood facing each other, for she had advanced to meet him as soon as she was aware of his approach.

"You are out early, Carrie," said Mr. Mordaunt coldly.

"I may suppose," she replied, "that I am at least mistress of my own movements."

Their antagonism was marked; his was disdainful, hers was bitter; in both it was more than passing ill-humour, in both it showed now, under the habitual control of their race and breeding, as something near hate.

"The park is large enough," added Caroline, "we need not cross each other's way."

"No," he said.

Yet neither moved.

He turned to caress his dog as if considering what to say, and she stood erect, waiting, hoping to receive from his words fuel for the fire of jealousy and rage that absorbed her soul. He, too, was angry; he knew that they must speak and he was not afraid of her, but with the habit of his training he paused to choose his speech.

He was full fifteen years younger than she, the only child of his father's second marriage, as she was the only child of the first, and he had none of the ill looks that she had inherited from an invalid mother.

His fair features were a little fine in line, his expression slightly cold, his manner slightly hard and distant, but he was handsome beyond question, and had nothing of the provincial in his dress or manners.

Caroline tightened her lips as she looked at him; his dark gold hair fastened in a club with a black ribbon, the authoritative lines of his profile, the fair cheek, the arched nose, the curved lip, as he bent over his dog, reminded her of his mother, the second Mrs. Mordaunt.

She had loathed the interloper, the fine town lady. Her own mother had been of a better family; Caroline never forgot this.

"Why are you waiting?" she asked. She enjoyed his hesitancy, she knew that he wished to keep his temper and she knew she could make him lose it, yet keep within the bounds of her own control.

He straightened himself to look at her; he was a charming figure in his brown cloth riding-suit against the gold of the beech trees and the gold of the sunshine; she hated him the more for this, and noted with pleasure that he was pale with vexation.

"I was wondering," he said deliberately, "how best I might inform you, Caroline, that I cannot endure this temper of yours."

"And what is the result of this wonderment?" she asked quietly.

Mr. Mordaunt frowned; he had no wish to engage in the usual play by which his sister delighted to confuse and enrage him. He came coldly to the point.

"You might go to town for a while, to Aunt Delia."

"Why?"

"Because you so obviously find Mordaunt Court intolerable," he replied.

"That is not true. It is my home. I could never be happy elsewhere."

"It is also Hetty's home," said Mr. Mordaunt firmly.

Caroline drew a quick breath.

"And I am to make way for Hetty?" she asked. "Are you so entirely befooled and bemused as to turn me out of your house at the command of a parson's daughter?"

He steadied himself by looking down at the affectionate eyes of his dog.

"In my house my wife commands," he said. "For five years you have made her home insufferable to her. In a thousand ways. In those ways that only women understand. I am not aware of all you have done—but Hetty is—she has been very unhappy—but she has not complained——"

"Oh, no," interrupted his sister, "she just cried; it is more effective."

"Caroline, I am speaking very quietly. I must beg you to control your tongue. You have a cruel tongue. I want to speak very quietly. You had better go to London. Hetty is quite—ill after last night. I cannot see her suffer so. You—you humiliate her before the servants, before the child—you are very hard, Caroline."

She was pleased to see that he was breathing deeply; she was sure that neither he nor Hetty had slept after the last scene of last night.

"So this is my sentence of banishment?" she said. "Well, like father, like son, all to the winds for the first piece of pink and white, a shopkeeper's daughter—the daughter of a hedgerow parson; it needs but Harry to grow up and pick his wife from the boards of Drury Lane and the Mordaunts will be finished indeed."

At this insult to his mother and wife Humphrey Mordaunt winced. Truth gave the words a sharp edge, for his mother had been the daughter of a city merchant who carried no arms, and his own marriage was frankly a *mésalliance*, for Hetty was scarcely of gentle blood and had brought him nothing but goodness and beauty.[46]

Caroline could boast sixteen quarterings on the maternal side.[47]

---

[46] *Mésalliance:* A marriage with a person of inferior social rank.

[47] Relating to the number of nobles in previous generations of a person's family. For example, assuming that both parents were of noble blood for the previous four generations, a person would have sixteen quarterings, $2^4 = 16$.

"I am glad," she said, stabbing the silence, "that you are ashamed of these two light women."

The young man flushed darkly.

"My God!" he cried. "I am ashamed to be your kin!"

She smiled grimly to see him roused.

"You are fit," she answered, "to be the husband of that wicked little fool."

Mr. Mordaunt turned aside; he remembered Hetty's anxious words before he left the house: "Don't be unkind with her, don't be harsh. I am only sorry for her, after all."

Yes, Hetty might be sorry, Hetty who had never been angry with anyone in her short life; but he was not; the irritation was too long standing, the anger too deep-seated, the resentment too profound. He considered Hetty's compassion for Caroline as part of hetty's lovable but almost foolish softness, but perhaps it was because Hetty saw more clearly than he into the bitter heart of her sister-in-law.

"You will go to London," he said. He thrust the toe of his boot into the beech mast and did not look at Caroline. "If you care to leave your affairs in my hands I will administer them."

He said this without intention of offence, for it did not occur to him to wound her by reference to her dependency, and she knew it, but she was stung the same as if he had spoken with meaning to insult.

It was another grudge she had against the memory of her father whom she felt had failed her, that he had left her at the mercy of her brother.

"I will not go to London," she said.

"You will not stay in Mordaunt Court," he returned. "Why should you refuse to go to London? There are all your mother's people; they can give you a more diverting life and a better chance of a suitable marriage."

She looked at him with a certain dignity.

"You may spare that," she answered. "I am forty-five and plain and sickly; you know that I have no chance of marriage. And never have had."

"It has not been my fault," returned Mr. Mordaunt, exasperated and thinking of his own desperate efforts to find a match for his sister. "You have had your life in your own hands; no one stood in your way."

He glanced up at her, and the intent look of her small eyes made him vaguely uneasy. She was hateful and yet she was pitiful; suddenly he felt that, and remembered Hetty's plea for mercy; yet he was hardened by the recollection of Hetty's swollen eyes and disfigured face and hysterical sobs as she writhed under the memory of the other woman's tongue.

"You will be happier in London," he said, as if justifying himself. "I will make all suitable provision for you."

"My home is Mordaunt Court," she replied. "And you know it."

"It is also Hetty's home," he returned. "Till I married you were mistress of the place; when I married I—we—wished you to stay, but——" He made a gesture with his fair hands; it was hopeless to try and express in words the utter disaster of the five years that had passed since he had brought Hetty to his house.

And yesterday things had reached a climax: Hetty had lost her control—she had broken down before the servants. Hetty was almost ill. He shuddered at the hatefulness of the whole thing; at all costs it must be stopped.

The sunlight passed the beech boughs now and fell full on her meagre figure and woke a little glitter in the faint blonde of her hair.

"So, because your wife is hysterical," she said, "I am turned out of the house. Did I raise my voice last night or make a scene?"

"You insulted Hetty on her birthday, poor child"—his voice changed; he was very much in love with Hetty—"and you frightened Harry and——"

She interrupted.

"The brat is spoilt."

"I will not have him frightened. Last night was not the first time. You seem to dislike him."

"I do dislike him. He is a hateful child; I have never pretended to think otherwise. Hetty has spoilt him."

He looked at her with an astonishment ingenuous enough; his man's mind could not grasp the motive of her bitterness.

"How you hate Hetty!" he exclaimed.

"She raised her shoulders; she did not trouble to reply. She felt a certain triumph in his startled perception of her feelings.

Mr. Mordaunt glanced away from her down the beautiful vista of golden trees; the collie, restless at the long pause in his walk, was nosing round the moss-splashed silver trunks.

"I must return," he remarked briefly. "You will be ready to depart in two or three days, Caroline."

She was frightened into angry speech; her woman's spite had so long taken advantage of his man's forbearance that she had taken him as weak and his judgments as futile; but in her heart she knew that he was not weak.

"I will not go," she cried. "I will not leave here! This is intolerable. It was you who insulted me last night." Her words came swiftly; her thin voice was roughened with rage. "You gave her the cinnamon diamonds; they were mine, they are mine——"

"They go to the wife of the head of the house," he defended

himself wearily. For five years the Mordaunt diamonds had lain locked in the cellars out of deference to Caroline's jealousy, but in his mind they had been always Hetty's property.

"They were promised me by my mother," said the woman fiercely. "I wore them before you married. They are mine. Part of my marriage portion."

"You have said your marriage is an unlikely event," he returned. "If you do marry you shall not lack jewels. But I will speak no more of this——"

But she was not to be silenced; the wrong and the offence over which she had brooded all night were fuel for the fire of a long rage and hate.

"You are such a fool," she flung at him. "Such a coward. You know the stones are mine, and therefore dare not give them to Hetty, but she cajoled you with her milkmaid coquetry."

"Stop!" he said roughly. "The diamonds have always been Hetty's—as they were my mother's, as they shall be for my son's wife. I showed them to Hetty on her wedding day, but she would not take them because you had worn them and she was fearful to offend; but you had no right to wear them. And you have no right to interfere in my life. And you have no right to insult Hetty and frighten the child. And, by God, you leave Mordaunt Court, if I have to call the servants to turn you out!"

He called the dog sharply and turned on his heel, his young heart hot within him; he felt that he had acted rightly in putting an end to the torture of five years; he considered himself completely justified, but the whole thing was hateful to him; he inwardly raged against circumstance.

The scene of last night stung in the memory; it had been horrible, rather vulgar to his thinking. Women, he reflected, even those who boasted a family of sixteen quarterings, so soon made things vulgar when they were angry.

Caroline had pushed away Harry when he came to show her a thorn in his finger of which he was greatly proud, pushed him so that he had stumbled, and then, because he had touched her foot, she had seized him with ugly vehemence an slapped him again and again.

And Hetty—poor Hetty had lost control too, and been shrill and incoherent and flushed and desperate, and had dragged off the necklace and hurled it down among the wine-glasses and fruit-dishes, and stumbled out of the room clutching the sobbing child. Afterwards she had made him promise to send Caroline away.

"I will not have Harry frightened," she had said between her gusts of dreadful weeping, and her red eyes had shone with a resolution that Mr. Mordaunt respected.

Yes, Caroline must go; her cold fury of yesterday, roused by the sight of the Mordaunt diamonds on Hetty's pretty neck, expressed in a quiet bitterness before which the young couple had been almost defenceless, and ending in her attack on the child, had been but the culmination of a long persecution, a deadly, silent warfare, an unsleeping animosity which had destroyed the peace of Mordaunt Court and poisoned the very air that Hetty breathed.

Mr. Mordaunt had spoken the truth when he had said that Hetty had been fearful to offend; she had been very young, very timid, very eager to propitiate the sister of the husband who she considered had vastly stooped in marrying her, for Hetty greatly undervalued her dowry of goodness and sweetness and beauty and health.

The young bride had been at the feet of the bitter spinster, and Miss Mordaunt had taken full advantage of the weakness of one whom she regarded as a stranger and an interloper. She continued to rule at Mordaunt Court as she had always ruled; she almost ignored Hetty, and the wife found herself continually thwarted, snubbed, even insulted by the sister who was Miss Mordaunt, while she was only Hetty Mathews, who had married above her station.

Mr. Mordaunt, as he strode back towards the house, recalled, in the light of his present resolution, the miseries past as a man suddenly freed might recall his prison.

It was astonishing, he reflected, how long they had endured such an intolerable state of things; astonishing how strong had been the custom and tradition and that false shell of sentiment that they had called family feeling; astonishing how they had supported the tyranny and selfishness of an embittered woman.

He blamed himself for not having ended things sooner; yesterday's scene, and what he had wrung from the distracted Hetty afterwards in the moment of her collapse, told him what his wife had suffered.

Up to yesterday she had been bravely silent; never once had she complained to him, but he could recall her a thousand times as sad, distracted, confused—Hetty trying to disguise tears; Hetty desperately apologetic for some little household oversight; Hetty frightened because of an untidy lock of hair or a rent in her gown; Hetty trying to escape tiptoe into the garden——

And now he was sure it had always been Caroline.

"She must go," he said aloud. "She shall go."

He felt he had been most unjust to Hetty; his sore heart was softened by an unutterable tenderness as he recalled her plea for his sister; she was compassionate even in her own distress.

As he reached the noble terraces that formed the approach to the house a composed Hetty in a white gown came to meet him;

her poor face was carefully powdered, but showed swollen and distorted, for Hetty's tears had been very real.

Her husband kissed her hand.

"She is going, dear," he said rather unsteadily; "And you at last shall be mistress."

"I think it is best," answered Hetty in a low voice; "but we must be kind, for we have everything and she has nothing.

The phrase made no particular impression on Mr. Mordaunt, but it expressed exactly the reflection of Caroline when her brother left her: "everything and nothing."

Nothing indeed now that she was to leave Mordaunt Court.

She returned slowly to the pond and again seated herself on the low stone edge; there was no other seat near, and her legs felt weak. Emotion always made her conscious of her poor health; her throat was dry and her head ached; she smoothed out the pleats of her skirt with shaking hands.

She had no doubt that her brother was in earnest; she saw that she must go.

London represented to her the dreariest of banishment; the relation with whom she would have to make her home was old, infirm and tiresome, and lived excluded from a society that no longer tolerated her acid peevishness.

She was now what Caroline would be in another thirty years.

Miss Mordaunt had many relatives in the capital, but no friends or even acquaintances, and if she had not been able to attract there twenty years ago, it was not likely that she could now. Her mother's noble family, of whom she was so proud, had always civilly ignore one who was useless to them in every way.

To her London was a desert, broken only by the withered oasis of that house in Highgate, always darkened because Aunt

Delia's sight was weak, and always silent because Aunt Delia disliked to be reminded of a world to which she was conscious of no longer belonging.

Mordaunt Court was her home; she really loved the place where she had been born, and which was associated with the timid joys of a sickly childhood and the secret, short dreams of a thwarted youth. And here she was mistress: the servants feared her, the villagers respected her, she ruled them as Hetty never could, had never attempted to; Hetty's personality was not fitted for the position of Squire's lady, and Caroline Mordaunt enjoyed her kingdom.

Besides, she liked to watch her brother and his wife, to keep Hetty in her place, as she called it; to see that she did nothing inconsistent with the rank to which she was not born, nothing to lower the name she was not worthy to bear.

Her tyranny of Hetty had become the object of her life; she had made a fine art of it—and now she must go.

She pictured Mordaunt Court when she had left and Hetty joyous, excited, free at last . . . What foolish, undignified things she would do; once she had said she wanted her rooms painted white with flower wreaths in the French fashion. Caroline's acid contempt had saved the beautiful Tudor oak, but now it would be sacrificed.

That and a thousand similar things. Caroline shuddered; a desperate rebellion shook her, body and soul.

"Why am I like this?" she asked herself. "Why have I nothing? And she everything—even *my* home?"

She looked back over the years and saw herself always sickly, always plain, always disliked, always avoided: her sole weapons against a world that did not want her, her name and her tongue—

she was Caroline Mordaunt, so people had to be civil. She was bitter and unmerciful in her judgments and her comments, and therefore held her own through fear; but she had had nothing out of life—there had seemed a conspiracy to exclude her from everything.

As a child she had been too delicate to join the sports of her age; her sole companion had been an ailing mother, who passed lonely days sighing over a tambour frame and lamenting the absence of the husband who diverted himself in town.[48] As a girl she had been kindly ignored by the mother of Humphrey; her few visits to town had been conspicuous for their ill-success. She had always been glad to return to the place where she was at least a personage; elsewhere she was noting but an unattractive woman.

And then her father had died, and soon after his wife, and Humphrey had gone abroad with his tutor, and she had reigned in Mordaunt Court until the evil day when her brother had married Hetty Mathews.

She set her thin lips; she knew she was face to face with the worst moment of her life, for it would be more terrible than her brother's marriage, this leaving of Mordaunt Court; the first had been like the mere signing of an act of abdication, this was actual dethronement and banishment.

Her rage and jealousy amounted to a genuine agony; she could have thrown up her arms and shrieked aloud to the heavens in her despair.

But the habit of a lifetime kept her restrained.

She knew that there was one sure way by which she might revoke her doom: she could not move her brother, but she could move Hetty; she was quite sure that an appeal to Hetty would not

[48] Tambour frame: an embroidery frame.

be in vain; if she threw herself on Hetty's mercy, Hetty would induce Humphrey to let her remain.

But she would sooner leave than do that; at least she would have the satisfaction of going proudly with a sneer to the last; it would be impossible ever to think of conciliating hetty.

How she hated this woman who had been born to poverty and insignificance, and who had gained wealth and rank, friends, a husband, a child—all that was pleasant—just because she was pretty and knew how to flatter a man.

Now even the shadow of love had crossed Caroline's life, she was not conscious that she had ever desired it; it had always seemed to belong to the world of her enemies, but she had noticed the strength and handsomeness of men, the happiness of lovers, the joy of mothers, with hate and jealousy.

Apart from the rivalry between them, she hated Hetty because she was loved, she hated her for having a child. It had been a grim pleasure to spy on her and make her ashamed of the caresses of the husband who was still her lover.

Once she had discovered them under the apple trees in the autumn and he was kissing Hetty's throat with extraordinary gentleness, on his knees, while she reclined against the tree trunk; within the circle of her arm was her baby.

Caroline had felt curiously sick and weak; she had discovered herself and had had the satisfaction of seeing Hetty's confusion; but now they would be free of the torture of her company. She writhed to think how happy they would be in their freedom . . .

The sun had now risen above the beech trees and was full over the pond and the still figure of the woman.

The wet dead leaves shone on the stagnant surface of the water where five-legged insects plied to and fro; the few broken and withered reeds glistened like ruddy spears, the fresh green of the flags showed verdant above the decay; a tiny plant with succulent foliage and minute white flowers rested lightly on the dark, undisturbed bosom of the pond, which the sunlight could not pierce, but could only touch to murky, tawny gold.

"They will come here and sail paper boats with the boy," thought Caroline dully. She shivered; that night she had not slept, that morning had not eaten; she wanted to return to the house, but her strength did not seem equal to the effort of leaving her place, though her bones were aching from the strain of her position on the hard stone coping.

"I think I am ill," she said to herself. She wondered what would happen if she were taken ill; she would have to stay, and Hetty would nurse her and be kind.

But she was not going to be ill; she did not want Hetty's kindness; she rose with a certain dignity and turned in the direction of the house, but she was really weak and walked with difficulty.

The golden trees against the hazy blue, the silver autumn trunks, the fox-coloured carpet of leaves, the pungent, damp smell of autumn—all this she must leave. As she came within sight of the house (which was near, as the beech wood came up to the last lawn with the cedars) she stopped short in her pain.

She really loved the place.

And now it would be filled with the friends of Hetty, all the creatures that hitherto she had managed to keep at bay; there might even be new servants; there would certainly be new ways.

She became conscious that she was walking quite unsteadily, and rested against one of the last of the beech trees.

Across the lawn and into the wood a little child came running. Caroline looked at him dully; he had his mother's dusky hair, his mother's dark eyes, his mother's frank ways; to Caroline her brother's child never seemed a Mordaunt.

She turned her head to watch him as he trotted through the trees; she remembered what a pleasure it had been to slap him last night and to see Hetty's impotent rage and the spectacle she had made before the servants, tearing off the diamonds with a force that must have broken the clasp.

The diamonds—Caroline trembled to think of them, white and fine they were, set clear with an orange light in the cleft of each, and fastened together by links of gold so fine that they clung close to the neck and flashed loose with every movement. And this for Hetty——

They were hers, *hers*; she was a Mordaunt.

She continued to watch the child.

He had a miniature kite which would not float in the still air; he dragged it contentedly over the beech mast.

It was attached to a long thread of rose-coloured silk.

Caroline suddenly ran after him and overtook him before he was aware of her.

"Where did you get that silk?" she asked.

He was four years of age, and he was frightened, but he put himself into the attitude of a man as he answered:

"Mamma gave it me, ma'am," he replied.

"You lie," said Caroline. "You took it from my work-basket. I told you never to touch my things. You are a wicked boy."

"Harry's mother gave it to Harry," repeated the child, standing his ground bravely; but his little chest was heaving and his lip trembling as he faced his aunt.

"No, she did not," answered Caroline; "of if she did she took it from me—there is no colour like that among her things. It is mine and I want it. I have no other of that shade. Give it me."

"It is mine and I shall keep it," said the child.

His defiant face and the gesture with which he put his hands behind his back, concealing the treasure, roused the woman into a very luxury of rage.

"You have been taught to be rude to me, you naughty, naughty boy!" she cried. She put out her thin hand to seize the silk; he remembered her slaps of the night before and his courage melted into panic; he turned to run back into the house, but she stepped in front of him, and he dodged and ran away through the trees.

Caroline ran after him; she no longer felt weak, but inspired by a terrible strength.

"I am going to punish you, do you hear?" she called after him.

He was sobbing with terror; her spare figure hastening after him was endowed with all the horrors with which his imagination had peopled dark places and long silences, all the dreads that lurked (he somehow knew) in the distant reaches of the world beyond his home.

He kept on running.

She was gaining on him steadily; it was a long time since she had run; the movement went to her head like wine flies to the head of one unused to it; she felt all her pent passions rising, rising, making her crazy.

The child reached the pond. The parapet had been built on purpose to protect him from the water; he dropped against it, panting, crying.

The woman was on him, exultant.

He scrambled up in blind fright and climbed the parapet; Caroline's hands were on him.

"You naughty boy," she kept saying "you naughty boy!"

His little face was livid; in his supreme moment he recalled his father's teachings, who had instilled into him the maxims of a race whose admired virtue was courage.

"I shouldn't have to run away," he sobbed, "only 'cos you're so much bigger than me."

She was shaking him to and fro; the lust of power heated her, the lust of destruction excited her, his softness, his struggles, his cries inflamed all the passions so long repressed—all her hatred, all her bitterness spent itself on the child.

He slipped out of her hands into the water; she leant over eagerly and held him down, chattering like a mad woman; she saw the great circles the dark water made, the disturbed trails of the little green plant with the white flowers—the bubbles.

"You naughty, naughty boy!" she said. "I will give you a lesson."

He so soon ceased to writhe in her grasp that she nearly let go of him, he was so heavy; she was feeling suddenly tired.

With an effort she dragged him up; he fell back once or twice, but at last she got him up over the parapet.

His face was covered with thick green slime, the dead leaves clung in the little crisps of wet hair; in one hand was tightly clutched the paper kite and the skein of rose silk; she noticed that it was stained and spoilt.

She touched him curiously; it was strange that anything could die so easily; she tried to prop him up in a sitting position, to lift him to his feet; she thought of all the dead things she had seen, birds and rabbits, and tried to remember what they had looked like; he couldn't be dead, he was quite warm.

"You may keep the silk," she tried to say, but she couldn't command her voice, "if you are a good boy," she quavered.

He slipped out of her wet hands on to the beech mast; her fingers strayed foolishly over his befouled face.

Like a thread of brilliant light striking into darkness one word penetrated her dazed brain—Murder.

She shrieked at the top of her voice; she snatched up the child and stumbled towards the house; now she scarcely felt his weight.

"Help! Help!" she cried. "Harry has fallen into the pond! Help!"

She had no thought but to get assistance. She was wild with dread and terror.

Her brother and Hetty crossed the lawn; they were already looking for the child when they heard her cries.

They came running towards her, and she thrust her burden into her brother's arms.

"I dragged him out," she said, "but it was too late."

She had no thought of excusing herself, she did not know what they said or did; they seemed two figures of fantasy, thin and unreal beside the intensity of her own action.

She went into the house and up to her room; as she passed the open door of the sitting-room she noticed that the skein of rose-coloured silk was still lying in its place among the neat order of her open work-basket.

"I never knew that Hetty had any of the same shade," she said to herself.

When she reached her chamber she was so tired that she almost crawled to the chair at the foot of the bed, which was the first resting-place that offered.

"If I had had a child of my own," she reflected, "and become used to carrying it, I should not have found him so heavy." Her precise gown was damp and soiled on the bosom, the skirt stained with drippings, the sleeves soaking to the shoulders, for she had plunged her arms into the water to drag up the child.

"I wonder what Humphrey will do?" she thought.

A long time went by and the house was silent.

No one came near her; she sat quite still, gathering her strength.

She had no thought whatever of escaping her fate; like an animal securely trapped she awaited the hand that sooner or later would come to destroy her; the big gallows on the London road suddenly became of interest to her. But Humphrey would never deliver her to that fate, she was of his blood—yet——

Perhaps he would kill her himself. She could imagine that, with Hetty looking on, Hetty who would be different now without a child.

Perhaps they would tell her to destroy herself; it could so easily be done, with any handkerchief——

Or the pond——

That was easy also; she had but to lean over as she had leant that morning and hold her head a little lower and plunge her face beneath the slime and water plants.

"I don't think that he suffered much," she reflected. "If they give me a choice I will choose the pond."

She passed her tongue over her lips and tried to rise, but her limbs were strangely stiff.

"Why should I not go to the pond without waiting for their orders?" she thought.

The sun was now setting and casting red rays into the well-ordered chamber that she had slept in all her life.

The day was nearly over and no one had come near her.

"They have forgotten me," thought Caroline. "I had better go before they remember."

She rose and looked at herself in the glass that had reflected her face every day for so many years.

Her expression was quite composed and stern; she rearranged the thin, limp locks of blonde hair that hung disordered on her thin temples, and she glanced with disgust at her ruined gown.

"But it is not worth while to change it."

With an uneasy step she went towards the door; she was giddy from lack of food; she wondered if she could creep into the dining-room and get a glass of wine before she left the house.

She had to pause a moment before she had strength to open the heavy door.

As she stepped on to the landing she saw her brother and his wife coming up the stairs. She noticed that they were hand in hand and that Hetty had a woollen shawl over her white gown.

Caroline backed into her room, licking her lips; as they entered she still moved away from them, slightly crouching, but facing them; when the wall stopped her retreat she leant against it, glad of the support.

She was surprised to see them so calm; but Hetty's face looked as if it had been beaten, and Humphrey had an expression of utter exhaustion.

Caroline did not flinch.

"Hetty wished to speak to you," said Mr. Mordaunt in a voice distressingly hoarse; he had to clear his throat twice before he could continue. "I have brought her."

He said no more; he placed his shaking hands on Hetty's shoulders and gazed at her as if he implored her to speak.

Hetty was looking at her sister-in-law; she was no longer in the least pretty, Caroline noticed that.

"We are going away," she said quite gently and composedly, "but first I had to speak to you, of course. You see I am calm. I could not sit still to-day. I had to do something. We are going away.

We could not live here now, could we?" She glanced at her husband, who was staring at her in speechless woe.

Caroline tightened her lips, and waited, as many of her house had waited, the descent of the enemy's sword.

The brave, anguished voice of Hetty continued:

"We are going abroad—for a long time. To be away from the pond. I wanted you to know this."

She came forward a little; her face was so disfigured as to be expressionless, battered by grief as from many blows. From the pocket of her gown she drew a long, polished wooden box.

Still Caroline waited, her shoulders raised, her eyes restless; waited for judgment.

Hetty suddenly came up to her and took her gaunt hand.

"Thank you for trying to save him. God bless you for trying to save him," she said. "You never liked me, I know, and it was my fault too; I am so foolish—I must have hurt you—many times—and you tried to save him—see, your dress is still wet—and you carried him to the house—you cried out as if you had been his mother. Thank you, thank you, and forgive me."

She pressed her poor swollen lips to the hard hand she held; Caroline looked swiftly to her brother.

"Forgive us that we did not come sooner," he said faintly. "You have been alone—but I—to-day I have not noticed the passing of the time. You—you—must change your dress, Caroline. I'm afraid you will be ill."

A dusky colour came into Caroline's face; her chest fell with a long breath.

"I don't understand," she said.

"It was the paper boat," the unhappy father explained. "He wanted to sail a paper boat, but Hetty gave him some silk to make a kite instead. And he seemed quite happy on the lawn—but he must have gone to the pond—with the idea of the boat. I always meant to make the parapet higher."

"He climbed," said Caroline; "it was all over in a moment. Just a moment."

She looked at Hetty, who still held her hand, and then she looked at the polished box in Hetty's other hand; she knew it contained the cinnamon diamonds.

And Hetty braced herself for the fulfilment of her task.

"We are so grateful," she said, "please believe that; I—I never understood you. I want you to take these. Yours always. Please."

She held out the box.

"Humphrey wishes it too. Think of them as from—from—Harry."

Caroline's firm fingers closed over the box.

"And when we go away—it will be soon—as soon as——" She stopped. "You will be mistress here—we want that. Both of us. Last night I was unkind. We were going to send you away. And you were willing to give your life for Harry. The doctor said that you might easily have been drowned. Please kiss me. I can't say any more to-night."

Caroline stared at her.

"I don't want to be thanked," she said. "I think I will go to bed now. I am very tired."

The poor mother humbly kissed the hand which she believed had endeavoured to rescue her baby; somehow she managed to strangle the sobs that were tearing her throat, for the parson's daughter had her courage also.

Mr. Mordaunt stood with bowed head.

"I will come and see you in the morning," he said. "I wish to leave everything in your charge."

His wife joined him and they left the room as they had come, hand in hand.

Caroline rang the bell; she felt hungry now and thought with pleasure of food. She glanced at her tea service on the little shelf in the corner. Yes, she would like a cup of tea—and she would change her dress and have a fire in her room.

But first of all she took out the diamonds and, hurrying to the glass, tried them on her throat.

It was good to see them there again—and Hetty was going away and she would be mistress once more.

"As soon as they are gone," she thought with intense satisfaction, "I will take down that hateful partition she put up in the buttery and put back the jam cupboard where it used to be."

# THE TRIUMPH OF MRS. WESTFIELD
## (AT THE PANTHÉON)

"WE are good enough friends," said Mr. Bellamy, "to be able to adjust a matter like this."

Sophia was further angered by this remark, which she received as haughtily as if it had been an impertinence.

"Come," added Mr. Bellamy, "it is mightily foolish for us to quarrel; let us"—he repeated the words which had so subtly annoyed her—"remain friends."

She was shaken now from that well-bred control, that languid indifference which she seldom allowed anything or any person to disturb.

"Friends!" she echoed. "Yes, we have been friends too long. Friends! It is an ugly word, a hateful word, when used between man and woman. Never quote it to me, Mr. Bellamy, for when you do you remind me of my own great folly."

He lifted his straight brown brows, a little surprised, a little pleased at her vehemence.

"It is not my fault it stopped at friendship," he said. "Have you not always very plainly given me to understand that I was but the gallant, the cavalier of a season, who must be ready to dance at your wedding the moment you found one rich enough and fine enough for your taste?"

The words were spoken lightly, but there was an emphasis not unlike a sneer in his tone, and Sophia was silent with humiliated anger and a bitter sense of injustice.

He was all unfair, she thought, for he had spoken but half the truth, and she could not answer him without descending to the level of the shrew or the hysterical schoolgirl, or else dragging the whole situation into tragedy, and she was far too charming and tactful to do any of these things.

Yet she writhed under that terrible sense of unfairness.

It was Mr. Bellamy who had set the standard of their relationship, and she who had followed; it was he who had assumed there was nothing serious in any of it and who had, however, been constantly in attendance on her, that he had effectually kept all pretenders at bay; it was he who had entangled her in this net of friendship, who had kept all his tenderness prudent, all his love-making light, who had bent her to his whims and wishes in her behaviour and deportment, and never allowed her any definite claim on him. For three seasons her women friends had been asking her why she did not marry Jack Bellamy, and Sophia had fenced all manner of evasive replies, while always in her heart the real reason cried aloud: "Because he has never asked me!"

She admitted there was some truth in his last speech. She had been ambitious; she had dreamt of a finer match; she had coquetted with other men; she had not greatly cared to marry at all; she had been content to have his constant attendance. She, too, had played a little with fire.

But the game had been going on now for three years and Sophia Dering was tired.

Tired of town life, of gaiety, of affectation, of the cold language of gallantry, tired of using over again and again the stale weapons of the coquette. Most of her girl friends had married—those who had not were confessed failures—things that had once been delights were now wearinesses. She wanted to be loved, not flattered; to be won, not courted.

And still she found herself playing with Mr. Bellamy the game that had once been so charming and exciting, and now was so dull and unsatisfying.

To-day her discontent had reached a climax. He had objected to a Turkish dress she had worn to a certain masque; she had resented his interference. Their speech had become bitter—she had taunted him with his reputed attendance on Mrs. Westfield, an actress at Drury Lane, and the taunt had covered a real ache in her heart.

He had answered with his usual politeness, his usual lightness, and then had stung her by quoting their friendship. She could not keep the tears from rising in her eyes, and she stared through the red silk fire-screen into the depths of the fire that he might not see her face.

"I am in disgrace," smiled Mr. Bellamy. He sat on the edge of a settee embroidered with red roses and rested his chin on the onyx knob of his handsome malacca cane.

For once she did not throw back a light word which would have been the beginning of a graceful battle of repartee.

She was tired, tired of it all; she felt as if the mask was off and lying in her lap, and that he must at last see her as she was in reality and truth.

He regarded her steadily, and his expression, even if she had been studying it, she would have found, as ever, inscrutable.

Her familiar figure was charming enough to any eyes; she was finely made, tall, long-limbed, dark for an Englishwoman, with hazel eyes an no brightness of colouring anywhere; there was no defect in her to displease the most fastidious, and when her features were in repose, as now, she had a lovely look of grave purity at variance with the gay lightness of her manner.

In her first season she had been a toast, and she was still much admired; then newer beauties had usurped her place, and

Mr. Bellamy had persistently stood between her and the good matches she might have made.

As usual she was dressed in a fashionable gown, vastly becoming; the cream-coloured silk with the black velvet strips, the ruffles of thick lace, the muslin cap on her soft curls, all were carefully chosen to enhance her attractions. She was tired of that too, tired of always dressing to show herself off to the best advantage.

Mr. Bellamy rose.

"I am in such deep disgrace evidently," he said, "that I believe it would be vastly sensible on my part for me to leave."

His tone jarred; she could not restrain a bitter answer.

"Are you going to the green room at Drury Lane?" she asked. "The Westfield will be rehearsing 'Roxanna.' "

He looked amused.

"Perhaps," he answered. "She was diverting, the Westfield. Have you seen her?"

"No," said Sophia, further wounded and angered by the light friendliness of his tone. "What a fool I have been," she thought. "What a fool to so stale myself to him!"

"You must see her in 'Roxanna,' " persisted Mr. Bellamy.

Sophia rose.

"She does not interest me, this actress," was her reply.

He regarded her narrowly; he could not fail to remark that she was deeply angry.

"By heaven!" he cried, "do you pay me the compliment of being jealous of me?"

Sophia laughed.

"We have paid each other enough compliments," she said; "I at least have changed from that."

The truth came to her lips:

"Oh, I am tired, tired!"

"Of me?"

"Of all of it."

"This is a very plain dismissal," said Mr. Bellamy, rather pale and regarding her more seriously than he had done for some long time now.

"Confess that you are glad to be dismissed," she challenged. "Confess that I am wise and kind to end it all this way."

"End what?" he asked.

"Our friendship," she mocked.

Mr. Bellamy looked stormy and vastly handsome with the usual frivolous look gone from his dark face and replaced by real anger, the anger of hurt masculine pride.

"I do not understand," he began with a frown.

"No," said Sophia, resting the tip of one of her long satin shoes on the brass fire-irons, "I suppose not."

"You are trying to anger me," he replied coldly.

"Oh, la," laughed Sophia, "I would not be at that trouble. Let us leave it at a misunderstanding and hasten off to Drury Lane, my good sir, before the Westfield has unlaced and scraped off her paint."

His wrath, feeling round for vent, fell on this mention of the other woman.

"Speak civilly of Mrs. Westfield in my hearing, madam," he said. "She is a good woman, and a generous and a kind——"

At this Sophia blazed.

"You have a mighty courage to praise that raddled doll before an honest gentlewoman!"

Mr. Bellamy was very angry now.

"Raddled doll! Miss Dering," he retorted, "she is a beauty, a beauty, madam, and I'll make her a toast this season, and a belle——"

"And bring her to the Panthéon to make her bow to the great ladies," sneered Sophia, desperate with pain.

"And an honour for them if I did," replied he, red in the face, "for she is as good and honourable as any duchess among you."

"You offend me!" cried Sophia. "You outrage me! I will not hear that creature's name. I despise her. I turn my back on the thought of her, the tawdry piece!"

"I leave you," said Mr. Bellamy furiously. "I take my leave. Many a time, Miss Dering, you have whistled me back, but this time, madam, you will whistle in vain. You have insulted a good woman for whom I have a vast respect. I take my leave, madam, I am gone. I do not return."

With the stiffest of bows he made good his words.

The door clicked after him, then there was a furious sound of the front door banging.

Sophia went to the window and watched his figure, the black cloak flung angrily over his shoulder, his galloned hat crushed on his brow, disappear up the street.

He did not look back.

"I suppose that this is the end," said Sophia. "I am glad, oh, I am glad!" But she was not at all glad; she was desperately and fiercely angry.

She wished that she had not insulted Mrs. Westfield, of whom she knew nothing; she wished that she had not been bitter and angry.

She wished that she had not lost him.

Her mother and her sister came in presently to gossip over a dish of tea; they were full of curiosity over the exit of Jack Bellamy.

"I hope," said Mrs. Dering, "that you will either marry him or dismiss him, my Sophia, for it is quite time that you had an establishment of your own."

"Marry him!" laughed Sophia. "We were only *friends.*"

"Oh, Sophy!" cried the sister, who sighed for Sophia to marry and leave her own path clear, "you know you have been a monstrous coquette with Mr. Bellamy."

"Hold your tongue, miss." said Sophia; "it is no matter of yours."

She went up to her room, tore up a card for Ranelagh that evening and shut herself in, declaring that she had an attack of the vapours.

But she did not go to bed; she paced up and down the little gilt and blue room holding counsel with her own haggard image in the long and oval mirrors.

"What shall I do?" she kept saying. "What shall I do?"

She had brought about the climax for which she had longed; she had ended the game which had grown so stale, and which had irked her to play—but to what purpose?

She wished everything was as it had been an hour ago.

But she had lost him.

"Perhaps he will marry Mrs. Westfield," she thought, and turned so sick that she had to sit down. "Yes, men do marry actresses now; it is even fashionable."

She sat for a while quite ill with humiliated pride and wounded love, hopeless and helpless.

Then suddenly pride stirred within her heart.

She rose and looked at herself in the mirror which hung opposite the brocaded bed.

"Why should I give him up?" she asked herself. "Why should I allow this common woman of the theatre to triumph over me?"

She flushed deeply.

"I will not," she said decidedly. "I will bring him back, indeed I will."

She began to think; she even smiled.

"I will bring him back," she repeated, nodding at her image in the mirror.

—2—

Mr. Bellamy was in the green room at Drury Lane; Fanny Westfield walked slowly up and down the rough floor, a sheet of music in her hand.

She wore a dress of white muslin which fell in billows from her high wait to the ground; her very beautiful fair hair fell in natural curls on to her shoulders.

Mr. Bellamy watched her.

Inside the pocket of his cherry-coloured brocade lay a letter from Sophia Dering—a letter which was intended to heal their quarrel and bring him back to his old allegiance. But Mr. Bellamy had hardened his heart; his mood was wilful and perverse; he did not intend so lightly to return to the thraldom of Miss Dering; he had been very outraged and angered by her abrupt and unreasonable (as he considered it) dismissal, and her letter had not soothed his still smarting pride.

The successful coquette could not easily change her tone and use terms of submission; she had written imperiously, and how was he to know that her heart had beaten painfully and the tears smarted in her eyes while she penned what read so haughtily?

At the present moment Fanny Westfield seemed to him infinitely the more desirable woman of the two; the whimsical half-pity he had felt for her had changed to a deeper interest; it seemed she might catch his heart on the rebound.

He felt a desire to champion her against Sophia Derling, to vex or flaunt the latter lady with the actress whom she so unfairly despised and who was, he thought, in every way her superior.

Fanny Westfield, humming over a little tune from the sheet music in her hand, came to the table and sighed in a tired way, looking down at Mr. Bellamy, who looked up at her.

She was very different from Sophia Derling, and her beauty was so obvious an unusual as to justify that lady's sneers at her commonness of the street, her lure of the stage. Her father had been a candle-snuffer at the theatre, and she herself had helped work a puppet show and danced at Bartholomew Fair; yet she, too, was not without a certain fineness. She was slender and her features were delicate, while a look of ill-health, which slightly marred her loveliness, enhanced her gravity and her refinement.

Mr. Bellamy was sorry for her. She was very successful now, but the memory of what she had been through seemed to remain about her like a cloud over her glory; when she was natural she was sad, and she was always tired.

Her triumphs seemed to bring her little pleasure. Mr. Bellamy thought that the contempt of the women of the great world into which she had climbed stung her more than the homage of the men elated her; she was Fanny Westfield, a toast, a beauty, a genius, but she was also from the gutter, the widow of a strolling player who had drunk himself to death.

"I had best go back to Bartholomew Fair," she said now, putting down her music; and then she told Mr. Bellamy in her changeful actress's voice, with a certain languid indifference, but with a very just emphasis, of a slight she had received from several great ladies who, hearing she was engaged to recite at a coming festival at the Panthéon, had all returned their tickets an annulled their subscriptions.

"So I was told I must not come," smiled Mrs. Westfield.

"Who were the ladies?" asked Mr. Bellamy, very angry. "Was one of them Miss Dering?"

"Miss Sophia Dering, who is the niece of Lady Wartonminster? Yes. She seems to hate me. She was at the theatre the other night, and when I was moving all the others to tears she laughed and, rising up contemptuously, went out of her box with her cavaliers following her."

"Ah," said Mr. Bellamy. "Ah, there are, madam, a good number of such impertinent females who rejoice in such frivolous triumphs, and I should be greatly rejoiced to teach some of them a better charity."

And though he put this sentiment so indefinitely the meaning in his heart was not in the least vague, for he was not thinking of "impertinent females" in general, but of Sophia Dering in particular, for he saw quite clearly that in striking at the actress she was striking at him.

"My dear," he added earnestly, "would you care to go to this festival at the Panthéon—not as an actress to amuse the others, but as a guest?" He rose, dominating her with his height, his strength of purpose, his ardency. "Will you accept of my escort?"

She flushed and brought her hand swiftly to her heart.

"Ah, sir, you mock me! What you suggest is a monstrous impossibility."

"Nay, never—trust to me, say but that you will come, and never doubt that I will protect you."

"But I have no ticket, and there is no one in London would give me one."

"We will enter the Panthéon without tickets," he replied; he took her long, pale hand and looked into her great eyes, which were almost abnormal in their size and brilliancy, "and there will be no woman there prettier or sweeter than Fanny Westfield."

She looked at him as if she was reading his complicated purpose with more clearness than he possessed himself. As if, indeed, she knew him better than he knew himself.

"Oh, Mr. Bellamy," she said, "were you not Sophia Dering's beau?"

He laughed.

"I have been many foolish things—at present I am at your service."

"You make an ill exchange," replied Fanny Westfield, "if you leave Sophia Dering to champion me."

She withdrew her hand and looked at him out of the corner of her eyes.

"If you take me to the Panthéon, Miss Dering will never forgive you."

"I have considered that."

"Have you? You are taking me to pique her, then?"

"Nay," he declared, "you misunderstand me. I am not thinking of Sophia Dering at all."

She smiled and her exquisite face moved nearer to him, like a flower bending forward in the breeze.

"Very well, I will come," she replied. She laughed, as if a spirit of mischief suddenly possessed her frail body; he kissed her hand and drew her nearer towards him.

In that moment he had indeed forgotten Sophia Dering.

Fanny Westfield drew away and glanced at him with a rather searching coquetry.

"It is quite true that I should be mighty pleased to go to the Panthéon," she said, "if only to see how you contrive to force me an entrance. If we get in——"

"We shall get in," declared Mr. Bellamy calmly.

She gravely bowed her head.

"It will be a triumph for me," she finished. "I shall draw all the town and there will be no empty seats at my benefit."

This practical view rather startled Mr. Bellamy. He looked at her earnestly; her face, more free of paint or powder than that of Sophia Dering or any such aristocratic beauty, was extraordinarily pale and delicate looking; an expression of pathos seemed to lurk in her bright, strangely watchful eyes.

"Are you troubling about your benefit?" he asked. "Do *you* fear empty seats?"

"Yes," answered Fanny Westfield. "I am on the wane, sir. I am often ill, and grow dull and unpopular. Miss Mason, at the Haymarket, draws all the beaux now—the town is not merciful, and I have not saved."

For a second her expressive face grew hard and cold, as if she saw ahead an inevitable future of horror and despair; then at once she changed; a delicate gaiety animated her still triumphant loveliness."

"At least I am not yet so faded that I shall show beside you like a ribbon thrice refreshed on a new gown," she said, and Mr. Bellamy, in his piety and admiration and tender compassion, kissed her, leaving a little blush on her cheeks.

When she was alone again she moved slowly to the mirror that hung on the opposite wall next a row of play-bills and looked at her fair reflection, which showed in the dim and greenish clouded glass like drowned beauty under heavy water.

"He has quarrelled with Sophia Dering," she reflected. "I suppose, if I had been anything but Fanny Westfield of Drury Lane, he might have cared for me; nay, he does care for me—but what use is it to either of us?"

She coughed and put her hand to her side where the sharp pain caught her. She realized once more that she was ill, that she would not long be able to fill the parts in which she had hitherto shone, and the colour left her face, and it looked hollow and old and despairing, as it had done when she had spoken of the future to Mr. Bellamy.

But another actress entered the room, a little Irishwoman, all furbelows and flying ribbons and curls, and Mrs. Westfield sparkled and smiled and waved her fine hand.[49]

"Congratulate me!" she exclaimed. "I shall be the talk of the town! My benefit will be a monstrous success! Jack Bellamy is taking me to the next festival at the Panthéon!"

Most of the guests had arrived at the Panthéon, and the entertainment of the evening had already begun with the sweet, thin melody of violins and lutes when a sedan chair was carried under the Doric portico and placed before the circle-flung doors, through which the amber light of candles fell on to the dark street.

The thick gathered crowd moved forward to gain a close view of the new-comer, whose footmen had opened the door of the sedan.

A gentleman who had been walking beside the chair now stepped forward and handed out (very ceremoniously) a lady whose blue silks were like moonlight, and whose diamonds flashed like frozen crystals by moon rays.

A dozen people among the spectators knew her; her name flew from lip to lip.

---

[49] Furbelow: pleated or gathered material, such as a frill or flounce on a woman's skirt.

"It is Fanny Westfield! Mrs. Westfield, the actress!"

Mr. Bellamy handed her up the steps; the sheer orange tawny of her cloak caught and threw back the light, and the soft hue of her gown glimmered between the mellow coloured folds of the velvet mantle.

Her delicate head, crowned with the blonde locks, slightly powdered and gathered in clusters of curls threaded with an amber ribbon, was held high; no look of weakness or ill-health now detracted from the glowing beauty of her face. She wore red and white and a great heart-shaped patch, but so exquisitely was it done that she seemed to bloom with Nature's own tints.[50]

As she stepped into an entrance where the officials stood she slipped back her cloak and stood revealed, a picture to take the breath, in her laces, her silks, he diamonds, her great hoops with the wreaths of yellow roses, all delicate and glowing, so that her beauty seemed enshrined in all that was exquisite and fair and luxurious.

Mr. Bellamy stood behind her; his cloak of white cloth laced with silver fell back to reveal the rose satin of his extravagant ball dress; his face showed rather pale above the black velvet round his throat, but his eyes shone defiantly with audacious recklessness.

The official stepped forward for the tickets, glancing rather doubtfully at the lady.

"There are no tickets required, fellow," said Mr. Bellamy; "this lady's name is a passport anywhere. I pray you announce Mr. Bellamy and Mrs. Westfield."

A look of horror and dismay changed the faces of all as they instinctively closed up to bar the entrance.

---

[50] Patch: an artificial beauty mark.

"Fanny Westfield of Drury Lane," smiled the actress. "Please be so monstrous kind as to permit us to pass."

They found their voices.

"This is incredible! This is an outrage! Only known ladies of great position are admitted here," gasped the master of the ceremonies, who had come breathlessly running up.

"Sir!" thundered Mr. Bellamy, "do you dare to insult the lady I am with?"

The other drew himself up stiffly.

"Sir, I regret to say that you must be intoxicated. I regret to add that if you and your companion do not immediately depart I must use force, sir, force."

Mrs. Westfield unfurled her great chicken-skin fan, which gleamed with the hues of a thousand painted flowers, and smiled with an air of gentle amusement.

"You are very ungallant," she murmured.

"But it makes no difference at all," said Mr. Bellamy. He half turned so as to face the doorway. "Please do not incommode yourself, Mrs. Westfield, madam," he said in a loud voice.

The words were a signal.

With a sudden movement which swept aside the crowd a number of young gallants, admirers of Mrs. Westfield, friends of Mr. Bellamy, and mere gay young men eager for an adventure, ran up the steps and swept off their hats before the lady.

"Gentlemen," cried Mr. Bellamy, "Mrs. Westfield is refused admission to the rooms! But I think she will enter them just the same."

So saying, he drew his sword; every gentleman followed his example, and the entrance hall glittered with bare blades.

"Stand back!" laughed Mr. Bellamy, and with the point of his weapon he drove the furious and frightened master of the ceremonies back against the wall and pinned him there with the sword point lightly against his heart.

The other gentlemen so served the other officials, and Mrs. Westfield swept through an entrance suddenly cleared, whereupon her escort lowered the points of their blades but did not sheath them.

So Fanny Westfield entered the room, where the most exclusive ladies of London were gathered, like a queen with an armed escort behind her.

At the threshold of the ballroom she paused a moment, her fan to her smiling lips and her beautiful eyes challenging the company.

Beside her stood Mr. Bellamy, his drawn sword in his hand.

Some rumours of what was happening had reached the guests; the men, half-angry, half-amused, stood irresolute; the women had swept together in the middle of the shining floor like a group of frightened deer huddling together for protection; the full light of the chandelier was over their silks and laces, and flashed on their jewels and their indignant eyes.

As the intruder, the pariah, the outcast, stepped proudly into their presence, attended by many of the men whom they had imagined at their own service, a shudder ran through the group of ladies, fans fluttered violently, jewels sparkled angrily on fiercely-heaving breasts and little shocked whispers ran from one to another.

But of all those there Sophia Dering was the most bitterly wounded, the most utterly outraged; when she saw Mr. Bellamy standing beside Fanny Westfield she felt as if he had struck her on the face.

The room, the lights, the surprised, amused and angry faces swung before her in a spinning wheel of confusion.

Mrs. Westfield advanced slowly down the shining room.

The ladies began to drift away before her like snowflakes before the sun, for ever retreating in front of her, so that she remained always isolated in the vast empty space of floor.

The men stood apart, silent, watching, feeling that the game was in the women's hands.

Mr. Bellamy followed sternly behind Mrs. Westfield, his drawn sword in his hand, while behind him came the other gallants, waiting for some cue or signal for action.

Mrs. Westfield was paling under her delicate rouge and powder; she stepped lightly but with a slight swaying, as if overwhelmed; more than once her eyes turned to the man behind her as if seeking encouragement and protection.

Never, even on the occasion of her first appearance at Drury Lane, had she felt the nervous tremor that shook her now.

Then suddenly a lady detached herself from the shimmering, glittering group and came forward.

It was Sophia Dering. She was as colourless as her white gauze gown, and her eyes gleamed as if she had a fever.

She came up to Mrs. Westfield and curtsied to the ground, her great hoop of silver brocade spreading about her.

"I am rejoiced to meet you, Mrs. Westfield," she said very gently and sweetly; "I have long been wishing to know you."

She came nearer, holding out her hand wistfully.

Mr. Bellamy stepped forward.

"Ah, sir," said Miss Dering, "this lady is indeed as entrancing off the stage as on the boards, and I congratulate you on being her cavalier."

His composure had suddenly vanished; he blushed and when he tried to speak stammered.

"Let me present you to some other ladies," continued Sophia, gently drawing the actress towards the other guests, who were coming slowly and hesitatingly forward now, impelled by a great curiosity.

Sophia Dering was a power; what she did others could do and need find no shame in, and now she had taken the responsibility of receiving the actress they were quite ready to follow her lead and examine for themselves this mysterious creature who had beguiled away so many of their own gallants.

"I suppose you are going to marry her," she said under her breath, "and she is very beautiful. But might not you have chosen some kinder way of bringing her before me?"

Mr. Bellamy was silent; he hung his head and fingered the steel tassels at his sword hilt (the weapon was now sheathed). He felt rather foolish; Sophia's action had put him in a false position.

And he had no intention of marrying Fanny Westfield.

At this moment the actress looked towards him; she marked Sophia's pale and quivering face, the air of high courage that sustained her, his confusion and distress, and Fanny Westfield sighed as she marked these lovers whom she had separated and brought together again in ways so oblique and strange.

With a graceful little movement she backed from the delicate crowd about her.

"Ladies," she said, raising her lovely voice, "this is not fair—I trespass here—I have no right."

They held their breath, listening with eagerness.

"It was all a wager," continued Fanny Westfield. "I had a wager with Mrs. Graham, who takes the part of confidante in the tragedies, that I would, despite everything, enter the Panthéon to-night, and so—not to weary you—I broke the matter to Mr. Bellamy, who, with the good help of Miss Dering, engaged to win my purse for me."

Every one now looked at Mr. Bellamy and Sophia. So there

had not been a rupture after all; they had been working together all along!

"So these gentlemen engaged to assist me," added the actress; "and here I am, ladies, at the sword's point, and will now go, trusting you are not deeply offended."

There was a gentle murmur of friendliness.

"You can have come by no harm from me," she said with a smile on her lips and tears in her eyes, "in this short time—and those of you who will be charitable I beseech to forgive Mr. Bellamy and Miss Dering and attend my benefit."

She withdrew slowly towards the door, curtseying and smiling and returning the shy salutes of the ladies.

Sophia Dering followed her to the door.

"Why did you say that?" she whispered eagerly. "Why did you connect my name and his? You know I was ignorant of your coming."

The actress looked at her earnestly and rather sadly.

"I said it because he is in love with you, madam, and it is a pity that a poor actress should spoil the happiness of two lovers."

Sophia hardened.

"You take a liberty, madam," she said quietly and turned away.

Mrs. Westfield went home with her escort of gallants to see her to her door; but Sophia Dering would give no private words to Mr. Bellamy.

—4—

Miss Dering retired to a cottage at Hampstead and tended roses.

She was tired of the London season, she said, tired of everything.

As for Mr. Bellamy, he had lost both ladies, and it seemed as if none of his efforts could avail him to capture again either of them. He often came to Hampstead, but he got no further than her garden hedge.

She would come to the gate and speak to him a little, kindly and sadly, but she never asked him within, and she never resumed the old terms they had been on before they quarrelled over Fanny Westfield.

Once he asked her to marry him. She went very pale.

"This is disloyal to Mrs. Westfield," she said, and refused him very coldly and quietly.

But she encouraged no other suitors, and she lived more apart from the world than she had ever done before—so Mr. Bellamy hoped.

He knew now how impossible had been his whimsical fancy for Fanny Westfield, and though tender thoughts and a gentle pity still gilded for him the lovely figure of the actress, his allegiance had returned for ever to Sophia Dering.

And so the spring, which seemed so long and so cold, crept to an end, and the roses Sophia had cherished began to break into bloom beneath the full-blown lilacs and laburnums, and the creeper over the porch was covered with blossom, and the hawthorn was sweet over Hampstead.

Then one day he rode over and spoke to Sophia again.

Her answer was no.

"Is it Fanny Westfield between us?" he asked bitterly.

She said, "Yes."

"And is it always to be so?" cried Mr. Bellamy.

Again Sophia Dering replied "Yes," and turned away.

It was a month later and full summer before he came again.

Sophia Dering was reading under the shade of a little cedar at the foot of the lawn, and this time he left his horse fastened to the staple at the gate and came straight across the grass to where the lady sat.

Sophia rose and looked at him, and something in his face held her silent.

"Are the roses all over?" he asked under his breath.

"Nay, Mr. Bellamy, I still have a-plenty in the pleasance."

"Will you give me some? There are none to be found in town, where it is so hot and dusty."

"Surely," she replied. "Who do you want them for?" she added with a little effort.

"For Fanny Westfield."

Sophia looked away from him.

"She shall have the best in my garden," was her answer. "I am glad that you have come to me for them. Is it her benefit?"

"No."

The muslin ruffles fluttered on Sophia's breast.

"Perhaps—her wedding day?"

"Not that either."

"Simply—your homage?"

"My homage, madam."

They looked at each other for a moment, then her eyes fell.

"I will fetch you the flowers." she said.

"They should be white, madam."

"White?"

She took a step back towards him and there was a strange look on her face.

"White flowers?" she repeated.

"Fanny Westfield in dead," said Mr. Bellamy. "She had been ill for a great while, and last night she fainted on the stage, and shortly afterwards she died."

Sophia could not speak. She sank into the chair and hid her face; then he heard her sobbing, and when he went on his knees beside her she turned and wept on his shoulder.

—5—

Presently they went together into the pleasance to gather white roses, and so for the second time Fanny Westfield brought together the man she loved and the woman whom he loved, and this time they were never more disunited.

# MIRANDA

*THERE are many unexplained things in this tale, and much that I could explain, but will not, leaving it to each to interpret it in your own fashion. And I dare say that each of you, were I to ask when I have finished, would give a different meaning.*

Well, the story begins oddly, I dare say, in Dublin, and in a poor street where there is a mean shop selling soap and candles and dried food. The date is about 1730, and you must imagine the country, the city and the shop as very wretched indeed.

It was kept by a man and his wife and a daughter of the name of O'Sullivan, and the girl's name was Delia, or I call her that. It doesn't seem an Irish name, but to me it has always been Delia.

These people lived in more or less misery, but with a certain decency, and the girl was pretty and lively.

One day an accident occurred in this narrow street; a horse bolted, a coach was overturned, and a lady riding therein was flung across the threshold of the little shop.

I do not know what confusion ensued, but the lady was too injured to be moved, and lay for weeks ill in the best room above the shop. She was French, and spoke little English, and none at all of the city dialect, and the O'Sullivans never quite knew who she was, how she came to be in Dublin, and why her friends did not, as she recovered, come to fetch her away.

She was a lady of birth, and she was visited by grand people who paid the O'Sullivans well for their care, and in particular by one gentleman who was careful to wear a vizard and always came and went in a closed chair.[51]

What the meaning of all this was I don't know—I must leave it to your guesses. What matters is that between the injured lady and Delia there grew up a liking and a friendship, and when the foreigner was at length able to leave the house she wept at parting from Delia, and made her handsome presents in money and in clothes.

She did more than this; she wrote on the fly-leaf of a French prayer-book a name and an address in Paris, and told Delia to write there or come there if ever she was in need of her. Now Delia could neither write nor read, and Paris might as well have been the moon for any chance she had of getting there, but she cherished the little book passionately and brooded a good deal on what might result to her from the help and patronage of this great lady.

But the O'Sullivans never heard of the foreigner again, nor of the masked gentleman, nor of any of the people who used to come to the shop to visit the stranger, and, indeed, they never expected that they should hear of them; they had been well rewarded and were quite content with their good luck.

And as time passed even Delia began to forget, till the whole episode was like the recollection of a fairy-tale told in childhood.

Delia married, married very well, an Englishman with a little money and a business in Belfast, and when he died she married again, more favourably still, a small linen manufacturer. She had one daughter by her first marriage, and when her second husband died this child was about fifteen years old.

---

[51] Vizard: a mask of black velvet for disguise or protection.

Delia was now a well-to-do widow, a little past middle age, energetic, shrewd and ambitious, clever and not as ignorant as she had been, and all these qualities she centred on her one possession, her daughter.

She had taught herself a little book learning, and she had gained much more valuable knowledge than that—a knowledge of men and affairs; but her character had coarsened and her soul was overlaid by the petty preoccupations of worldly success. She was, like so many people of obscure and wretched origin who have prospered, obsessed by social ambition. She had achieved comfort, ease, and even a certain position, but she coveted more than this: she wanted rank, wealth, power, and she thought that through her daughter she could obtain them. She had the girl most carefully trained in every grace and accomplishment, and she looked about for means whereby to satisfy her ambitions; there was a strain of adventuring, reckless blood in her, and, as I have said, much shrewdness and energy.

At this point Mrs. Collum, as she was then, came across the old French prayer-book with the name and address on the fly-leaf.

This she perceived now to be that of a personage so illustrious as to be known, ever to her, as De Choiseul, the power of France.[52]

The writing, so fine and trembling, and already so faded, was: "Madame de Choiseul, Hôtel de Choiseul, France," and Mrs. Collum considered at once how she might turn this to advantage and became obsessed by ambitious hopes when she considered that almost forgotten friendship of two young women above the mean shop in Dublin. She was quick-witted enough to see that

[52] Madame de Choiseul was Louise Honorine, wife of Étienne-François, duke de Choiseul, a French diplomat and statesman.

for herself she could not achieve very much, but for her daughter she might achieve everything.

She consulted with a friend of greater literary skill than herself, and the result was an artful letter to Madame de Choiseul, wherein Mrs. Collum described herself as a widow with a daughter she was desirous of educating in a Parisian convent, and humbly asking for the advice and patronage of Madame de Choiseul in the matter.

With slight delay, and to the incredulous joy of Mrs. Collum (or Delia), the reply came couched in amiable terms, recommending to the two ladies a convent in the Rue de Sèvres and promising countenance and protection in Paris.

You may imagine the excited delight of Delia Collum, the pictures of the future which her ignorant and ambitious fancy drew, the energy she threw into the preparations for this momentous voyage, the boasts to her friends and her own wild dreams.

She was no longer young or handsome, for she had become coarsened by prosperity and roughened by good living, but the daughter was, in a frail, dark style, pretty and of elegant manners.

Her father had christened her Bridget, but the stylish school to which her mother had sent her suggested that this might be changed to Miranda, a fanciful name then in vogue from a version of "The Tempest" that was fashionable.

Mrs. Collum equipped this girl with an expensive wardrobe and every necessity of luxury, and was, by the time that the date of departure drew near, absolutely obsessed by her chimerical ambitions.

You will wonder what all this is leading to. Well, there is a sudden climax to this part of the story. A few days before the arranged sailing Miranda died from an attack of smallpox, exactly as a letter arrived from Madame de Choiseul of future promises and encouragements.

You may imagine the anguish of Delia Collum, in which grief for her only child was mingled with the rage of frustrated ambition—for she saw all her castles in the air dissolve, since what use was it for her, a rough, ageing woman, this chance in Paris?

I could go into much detail in this part of the story, but it is sufficient to say what Mrs. Collum did; there is no need to speculate on what she thought.

At the school where her daughter had been was a little servant, a creature rescued from an obscure and dreadful life, the life of the Dublin slums; this child had no known relations, and paid for the charity which fed and housed her with the hardest of hard work. She had been about three years at the school, and had shown intelligence and refinement and had even caught up some of the graces of the young ladies; she was, too, of a bright Irish beauty and gay in her manners.

Mrs. Collum noticed the little maid, begged her from the school under the excuse of training her for her own service, and took her to Belfast, where she trained her indeed, but not as her servant, but as her daughter.

You will perceive her intention—I need not detain you to dwell on it. She gave the girl six months' rest and good food and care and coaching, and then took her to Paris as her daughter Miranda.

And who was likely to guess the fraud?

Behold the couple, adventuresses both now, lodged in the convent in the Rue de Sèvres, Miranda decked out in the dead girl's wardrobe, and Mrs. Collum staking her fortune on the success of her venture, for she was spending all she possessed.

Madame de Choiseul received them kindly and referred vaguely to her Dublin adventure, which had had to do, she said, with early misfortunes of her sister; she admired Miranda, and was gracious to the mother, and recommended them to friends who were in what she considered their own situation.

To Mrs. Collum's bitter disappointment, she gave no sign of any intention to introduce the strangers into her own great world, which, indeed, would have been unthinkable to Madame de Choiseul, but was the goal of the Irish adventuress who had staked her all on this throw.

Matters hung like this a little until the disgrace of the Duc de Choiseul sent him and his family as exiles to Chanteloup, and all fled, leaving Mrs. Collum and her daughter so-called forgotten and stranded in Paris.[53]

But Mrs. Collum was not of a temper to endure this lightly; she was, besides, desperate, and her money was largely spent; it had gone in futile attempts to emulate the grandeur of a world that utterly ignored her. Therefore she made a bold move; she took Miranda to Amboise and hired a house and servants there.

This offended and irritated Madame de Choiseul, who entirely abandoned her protégé, who would certainly have speedily sunk to despair and ignominy had she not possessed one asset, and that was the beauty of Miranda.

The girl, quick and adaptable, had soon learnt the air with which to set off her charms, had a nice taste in dress, and was in the full lustre of her youth. The defiant and desperate Delia Collum dressed her up and flaunted her in a cabriolet up and down the streets of Amboise, through the forest, and as near the park of Chanteloup as was permitted.

A large number of people had rallied round De Choiseul in

[53] King Louis XV dismissed Choiseul from office in December 1770 and exiled him to his estates at Chanteloup.

his exile, as you will read in your history books, and the pagoda was erected by his friends as an act of homage and respect to the fallen Minister.

There was, indeed, a sort of court at the Château of Chanteloup, which, resplendent with every grandeur, resembled a palace in a fairy-tale whose magic lights glimmer through enchanted trees.

Among all this sumptuous company there was not lacking one at least to be attracted by the charms of Miranda. M. de Montmirail fell romantically in love with her; he was young, elegant, wealthy, a peer of France, and Mrs. Collum clutched frantically at the chance he offered.

She was now launched fully on the tide of deception; she gave herself out as of noble birth, her late father as an officer who had fallen fighting for King James in Clare's Dragoons, her late husband as the owner of vast estates in Ireland, to which Miranda was heiress, and herself as an intimate but secret friend of Madame de Choiseul, between whom and herself she hinted there were important matters.

In this atmosphere she kept her creditors quiet and lured into her acquaintanceship not only M. de Montmirail, but several of his friends.

So far all was well, but Mrs. Collum, for all her luck and cleverness, her lies and inventions, found herself baffled by the rigid caste feeling of the French nobility. Enamoured as M. de Montmirail was, he could scarcely bring himself to marry a foreigner who, as the daughter of a mere Irish landowner, was so greatly his inferior, and all the combined charms and arts of the two women could not bring him to this point.

And, to make matters more difficult for Mrs. Collum, the young gentleman was under the guardianship of a very great gentleman indeed, his uncle, M. de la Pataudière, whose château can still be seen near Chinon.

So affairs remained for several months, and we know nothing of the sentiments of Miranda, nor of the sentiments of M. de la Pataudière, and of M. de Montmirail, only that he was in love, and of Mrs. Collum, only that she was a desperate adventuress.

You may imagine as you please the feelings of the four people until the night when they were finally revealed.

It was about this time of the year when M. de Montmirail at last declared his willingness to marry Miranda—but secretly; he did not dare so affront convention as to do this openly, but he offered this secret marriage, a flight to Paris and subsequent acknowledgement of his wife.

Mrs. Collum had no choice but acceptance; she agreed to bring the girl to the rendezvous and to be a witness at the wedding, but M. de Montmirail had arranged it to take place at the little chapel of Montlouis, where he had already prepared the *curé* and the witnesses.[54]

Now M. de la Pataudière had come several times to see Mrs. Collum and her beautiful daughter in their little house in Amboise, and they lived in terror of his suspicions.

He was not so much older than his nephew, but a man of a different type: a notable soldier, an able diplomat, extremely handsome, rather cold and haughty in his manners—the last man to forgive intrigues, lies or deceptions—a man with a very austere judgment of women.

Even the bold, reckless Mrs. Collum shuddered when she thought of her fate if this proud man discovered the masquerade she was playing.

---

[54] *Curé:* parish priest.

Well, the evening came, a coach drove up to the entrance of the *allée*, and the two women got out and hurried into the shadows of the trees; they wore long-hooded cloaks and masks, such as were the fashion for riding, protecting the complexion and intrigue.[55]

The pagoda rose up dark and clear against a sky paling to a sea green and spangled with the cold glitter of the first stars.

A light appeared and disappeared three times in the window of the first floor; that was the signal that it was safe for them to enter the pagoda.

But the women hesitated and looked round to see if M. de Montmirail had indeed succeeded, as he had promised to succeed, in an attempt to keep the pagoda free of all intruders. It was, indeed, usually quiet here, save on the occasion of a fête or a hunt.

Everything was now very still, the water calm, dazzling, pale, reflecting the new moon which hung between the stars, the trees motionless against that lustrous clarity of the heavens.

The women slipped into the shade of the pillared entrance and listened apprehensively, then ran up the frail stairs to the room on the first floor where the light had shown three times.

M. de Montmirail was waiting for them in the chill, bluish dark; he also wore a long cloak and a mask, and all they could see of him was the glimmer of his pale brocade suit between the dark folds of the mantle, and the flash of the diamonds in the buckle at his neck, and the buckle holding his heavy-powdered curls in place.

"Quick," said Mrs. Collum, who spoke now a very passable French; "I protest my heart shakes me for any minute of delay."

---

[55] *Allée:* a promenade within a formal garden or park, lined on either side with trees or shrubs.

And she could hardly keep anguish from her voice; for her it was this marriage or ruin and shame.

She pushed the girl forward with no over-gentle urge, but Miranda hung back and said, in a resolute voice:

"Madame, I have, before we start for the church, a few words to say to M. de Montmirail."

That gentleman, who had been coming slowly forward—slowly, which Mrs. Collum noticed with terror—stood checked.

"What madness is this?" cried the adventuress. "Let us begone."

"Nay," answered the bridegroom quietly, "there is time enough. A coach waits by the gates, and here we are not likely to be disturbed—so, mademoiselle, if you have something to say—there is time."

"I have something to say, and that of a great urgency," replied Miranda; "and it must be private also. You, madame, must wait for me below."

Mrs. Collum greatly demurred at this, for she did not wish to let the girl out of her sight until she was married to her victim, but there was a passionate insistence about Miranda that she did not dare thwart, and she retired to the room on the ground floor to wait in twilight and impatience.

M. de Montmirail again lit the girandole of candles that he had shown as a signal and placed it on the table of Chinese lacquer.[56]

"No one will see this light," he said, "for there is no one in the forest to-night."

And he did not draw the curtains over the long windows, so

[56] Girandole: a candelabra, usually with six arms that branch out from a central stem.

that they stood there, in that round room, seeing the darkling wood and the paling sky encircling them; for, as you know, there are more windows than wall, and to be in the pagoda is like being in a lighthouse, only instead of waves there are the trees all about, encroaching on the slender building.

The young man said nothing; he remained, a masked figure by the window, obscured in the long mantle.

But Miranda took off her vizard and showed her beautiful face, pale and yet pure in colour and line. I believe she was so beautiful that when you looked at her you could think of nothing else, yet now her beauty was the least thing about her as she spoke.

"Monsieur de Montmirail, I have come here to meet you for our marriage, but there are some things I must say to you first—and quickly, for madame below will have little patience."

She paused just for a second, then spoke in a cold agony:

"Surely you have perceived how you have been enticed and persuaded into this marriage——"

"By your mother."

"By her actively, and by me passively."

He bowed.

"I have perceived it—but——"

"Listen to me. Before you marry me you must know that I am not the daughter of Mrs. Collum. I am a poor foundling of Belfast, a servant—I do not know who my parents were. Nor is she herself what she pretends; we are both impostors—there is no money, and there are no estates—we owe all the tradespeople in Tours. It is your money that is to rescue us from shame and misery."

These dreadful words sounded grimly in the candlelit room of the pagoda, grim and horrible, coming from the lips of this lovely woman in her rich clothes, but the young man did not dispute the truth of them; he gave a great sigh and asked:

"Why do you tell me this?"

"I am sorry," said she bitterly, "to betray that wretched creature, but she has betrayed me by buying my soul when I knew not what a soul was."

"That is not an answer," replied he; "and do you think that I shall marry you now?"

"No. I have saved you and your family from that disgrace and infamy, and I only ask you to allow us to go in peace—for we are without resources—and perhaps you would assist Madame Collum to return to Ireland."

"And what of you? If she discovers that you have betrayed her——"

Miranda shuddered.

"I," she replied wildly, "will go to the convent of Saint Symphorien and ask the nuns to take me in. I can be what I have been—a servant."

Here the young gentleman took off his mask and disclosed that he was not, after all, M. de Montmirail, but M. de la Pataudière, and he stood, with the vizard in his hand, looking at her intently, while Miranda fell back and covered her face.

"M. de Montmirail," said the Duke, "has discovered, mademoiselle, your history, and I hold here"—he touched his breast—"a dossier of Madame Collum's career which we have obtained from Ireland. You have told me nothing that I did not know. This I placed before my nephew to-day, and he—permitted me to take his place here to-night."

Miranda's silence filled the room; she leant against the frame of one of the windows, the dark forest, the clear sky, and the brightening moon behind the drooping figure.

"I think," said M. de la Pataudière, "there will be a *lettre de cachet* out against you and your companion—and that you will be arrested and consigned to prison."[57]

Then Miranda spoke:

"So be it; I have no defence."

M. de la Pataudière came towards her; she had an air of cold indifference to her fate.

"Why did you confess to me?" he asked. "Because you love M. de Montmirail?"

"No," she replied. "Because I love you."

They stood looking at each other—the two people alone in the room in the pagoda. Think what events had gone to bring them there, the girl from the Irish slum and the great French gentleman: the mysterious affair of Madame de Choiseul's visit to Dublin—the story of Delia Collum—all those emotions and incidents and intrigues to bring these two together like this.

"Yes," said Miranda, with the calm of one who has nothing more to lose, "from the moment that you came to our house I loved you, and detested the part I played, and resolved, if my strength permitted, to confess everything. And as this, monsieur, is the last time that I shall see you, give me your pardon."

And she went on her knees before him, being, indeed, no longer able to stand upright.

The magnificent M. de la Pataudière raised her up.

"Rise up, mademoiselle," he replied. "I would not have been here to-night had I not known what you have told me. I intend to save you from your miseries—indeed, I can do no less since your

[57] *Lettre de cachet*: a letter containing a royal warrant for imprisonment without trial.

confession, which it must have gone hard with you to make. As Madame de la Pataudière you will be secure from the past and the future."

*Did he marry her? you may ask.*

*He did. And they lived happy ever after. It was a formal age you must remember.*

# A POSIE FOR FANCHON

FANCHON was ill. Fanchon was, she declared, dying—of boredom, of weariness, of the vapours—nothing diverted her any longer; neither her gleaming green parrot, her long-haired grey monkey, the glossy Nubian page, nor the new silvered and spangled plumes for her hair, nor the rosy velvet slippers with the painted heels for her feet. She languished prostrate on her bed in the finest embroidered lawn and the most coquettish of blue ribbons; none of the offerings so lavishly brought to her bedside amused her, neither the sweetmeats, the fruit, nor the poems; neither the new taffeta of a greenish mauve called "sighs of Venus," neither the diadem entitled the "rainbow," nor silks of a modish colour called "the despair of the opals," nor a "nymph chemise." Nor was she interested in the new wide fichu, which gave the lady the shape of a broad-footed pouter pigeon, nor in the modish casaques which arranged the hair in the shape of a peacock's tail, nor in the last comedy, nor the last jest, nor the last melody from the opera, nor even the latest scandal.[58] Fanchon was languishing, was sick; she was, she declared, dying, and the only people whom she had ever the desire to see were her doctor and her confessor—and this after six months of marriage, six months of Paris, of the most elegant apartments, in the midst of the most charming of society! She appeared no longer to notice the grace and elegance of her apartment, with its draperies of silver moiré and rose-coloured knots, the glass doors of cabinets revealing the most charming groups of porcelain,

[58] Fichu: a small, triangular shawl worn round the shoulders. Casaques: jackets.

the little gilded tables covered by flowered damask, the little dial-faced clock of onyx and alabaster, the two white cats with silver collars tied with violet favours sleeping on watered-satin cushions. What vanity, mortification, passion, disappointment had wrought the fever of which Fanchon was dying? Nobody knew, the physicians least of all. In vain they treated her with stimulants, musk æther, molasses water, Queen of Hungary's drops, Jeffrey's pills. In vain they gave her hay broth and purées of cucumber and chicory; she took the mixtures out of courtesy, but she languished the more.

In the languid morning the maid would dress and powder her ash-blonde hair and arrange it under the elaborate cap of lace and ribbons, would cover her face with white made of egg-shells and Portugal red, would slip over her languid body a delicious little jacket of white satin and swansdown perfumed with amber, and so leave her for the weary day. Fanchon would move no more, not even to complain, and not open her lips even to sigh, as if this slight toilet had exhausted her entire strength.

M. le Chevalier de Châteauroux was in despair; his love for the lady was known all over Paris, nor had she been considered obdurate. But now the gossips believed that they had been wrong in this opinion. If there had been kindness between the lady and her lover, why was she ill, why did she languish and droop, and die of the vapours, of boredom, of melancholy? She had, the gossips thought, nothing to complain of; she had been warmly admired, sought after and popular; the most suitable fruits and flowers that France could provide had been offered her at the delicious little suppers given in her honour, including pears picked in the King's garden. Some people, and they were a fair number, thought that Fanchon was the prettiest and daintiest lady in Paris; she possessed a hundred graces; her eyes were dazzling, her figure exquisite, and her hair—that fashionable blonde which is the colour of ashes coming from burnt gold—was of the prettiest possible; yet all these charms and graces, all this admiration and flattery, all the many attentions she had received could not preserve for Fanchon any interest in life. She had been extinguished as if a gust of wind had passed over her sweetness and left it dead, as the east wind will pass over a bed of frail flowers and leave behind but withered stalks.

M. le Chevalier de Châteauroux was in utter despair. Fanchon had never told him that she loved him, but now he was sure that she did not, and he turned over in his agitated mind the possibility of finding something that would restore her interest in life and love. There must be, somewhere, something—a little trifle, a dainty surprise, a delicate gift, a pleasant and subtle appreciation which would stir the languid pulses of the dying Fanchon. But where was this gift, so delicate, so elegant and delightful, to be found? The search would be long an difficult, as M. le Chevalier de Châteauroux well knew. Fanchon was an extremely wealthy lady and many very clever people had exhausted their brains to give her pleasure, spun out a fertile invention to amuse and please her. She had, in brief, always had everything that money can buy, and it was difficult to think of anything, the Chevalier reflected bitterly, that was at all desirable, that money could not buy . . . .

Exasperated by the difficulty of the situation and his own inability to improve it, the Chevalier, at length, by frantic prayers and many bribes, gained admission to the bedchamber of Fanchon, and fell in a becoming attitude on the bedstep beside her great and gorgeous couch.

Fanchon, at his approach, which had been carefully stage-managed by her maid, showed some faint lingering interest in life by glancing at the large mirror, wreathed with silver garlands, placed so conveniently near; then, with an even deeper languor, fell back on her heaped and downy pillows. Overcome by the sight of this languishing beauty, the Chevalier did a foolish thing. He ventured to ask Fanchon what she would like—a present, a Christmas present, to celebrate the most enchanting season of the winter? Anything that she wished he would get her. Fanchon was too weary even to smile at such an absurdity. Why, any lover should know that the only value in a gift is in its forethought—the surprise!

The Chevalier was forced to depart with no more satisfaction than a not unkindly glance from dark, absent blue eyes that appeared to be gazing into another world than this. As the Chevalier left the chamber of his beloved he already had an inspiration, suggested to him no doubt by the distressing sight of this drooping and expiring loveliness. The last time that Fanchon had spoken to him, she had said:

"You do not love me—nobody loves me—prove to me that you love me."

He believed now that if he could do that she would recover, and he would see her once more, this very winter, arrive at the opera wrapped in a superb and voluptuous mantle, riding in a sledge drawn by gilt dolphins, with an immense muff of Angora goatskins, and a little black velvet hat with three azure ostrich feathers. And he had thought of the gift which would recover the health and spirits of Fanchon, prove to her that he loved her, and return her to the society where she had been so attended and adored. He would give her on Christmas Day a knot of spring flowers—a gift so modest and simple, so costly and so extraordinarily difficult to obtain, would be the fitting symbol of his love and the recovery of Fanchon.

Fanchon lay in her befrilled and befurbelowed bed sipping her hay broth, a cluster of satin ribbons from her bonnet was coquettishly fastened under her chin, she reclined in billows of swansdown, of lawn, of muslin, of satin. The girandoles of candles in the room were shaded with pink silk, for even the robe she wore was not sufficient to disguise the ravages made by her illness. In despair at her continued silence her maid brought out her new frocks for her to see—robes designed by a genius of fantasy and luxury, fluted and striped, trimmed with gold and covered with chenille rosettes, adorned with bouquets of lilac and silver plumes, another with rose-spangled wires of gold, garlands of carnations, then a dress of mosaic satin wreathed with sprays of myrtle. Fanchon took no interest in any of this parade of magnificence. Her lovely little trifle of a face, with the slanting large blue eyes and the tip-tilted nose, which usually was so playful and even roguish with the mischievous smiles of a child, was now peaked and sharp, and even when one of the maids with the last hope of rousing her ventured to tell her she hardly looked pretty at all she did not appear to be affected by the monstrous statement.

Fanchon really wished to die, Fanchon was really tired of life, there could be no doubt about it . . . the giddy, flighty, charming creature, blown about, as it were, by the light breezes of the fashionable moment, suffered from passion or some distress which had overset all her frail life.

"Madame is certainly dying," sighed the maids, whispering together in the ante-chamber. "And what shall we bury her in—blue and silver, do you think? Surely that is the robe that becomes her best. Madame la Comtesse would surely wish to go to her grave in something light and agreeable."

And where, all this time, was the husband? No one had thought of him, though there had been so much solicitation for the lover; he was a poor man, Mons. le Comte de Duras; it had been a great piece of luck for him that with his ancient title he had been able to procure this wealthy wife who was heiress of a farmer-general, and who had really more money than almost any lady in France—aye! a great deal of money, that trifle of a Fanchon!

Now, after six months, Fanchon was dying and her money would return to her father; so, after all, it was poor luck for M. le Comte, though, of course, he had never loved Madame la Comtesse in the way that M. le Chevalier de Châteauroux had loved her—that would be impossible, for he was only her husband. He had always treated Fanchon with the greatest civility, and Fanchon had treated him with cool self-possession; there had been between them always the perfect ease of well-bred company; the bargain had been accurately balanced; Fanchon had had liberty and everything money could buy in Paris, and he had had her fortune. M. le Comte had appeared sufficiently decorously concerned at the illness of Fanchon. He had consulted the doctors, the priests; there were no definite answers to any of his questions—"Madame was languishing, madame was, it might be feared, dying!"

"Of what?"

"Of boredom, of weariness, and distaste of life."

"She has had everything," protested the husband, "everything that a woman could desire—she has been denied nothing. She has been considerably admired."

What possible reply was there to any of this? Fanchon was dying, it seemed, of unhappiness.

M. le Comte considered the situation for several days, and he then paid a formal visit to his wife's chamber, and stood at the end of the great bed with the draped Imperial in the room of

Fanchon, embroidered with flowers, hung with crystal chandeliers and mirrors wreathed with gold and silver.

Fanchon did not even notice his entry; she had now not even the strength to flutter her eyelids towards the mirror. Listless and indifferent she lay beneath the composed glance of her elegant husband.

"Madame, I must ask you a few questions. They tell me that you are dying of weariness, distaste, of lassitude, that you are indolently letting your life flow away, because you have no interest in retaining it . . . ."

Fanchon did not answer. She merely faintly sighed.

"Tell me if you blame me," asked the husband, "tell me what I have done wrong? I have had for six months the care of your fortune and your person."

"And now," murmured Fanchon, with more strength than he thought she had possessed in her devastated condition, "you are about to lose both."

He waved his hand negligently.

"We will not discuss that! I am asking you if I have done anything wrong, if there is any pleasure that you have missed, any excitement that I have not given you, and license you have not sampled, any exquisite delicious hours I have denied you, any toy, frivolity, or amusement I have forbidden you? In brief, have I not been in everything an indulgent husband?"

Fanchon, more faintly now, murmured, "Yes."

"I have kept, I hope, my bargain," he replied, seemingly ill at ease. "You were to come to Paris, you were to have everything that Paris offered."

"And you," murmured the lady, "were to have my fortune—my share of the bargain also has been kept."

"I," he replied, "have made no complaint; neither am I ill, dying of weariness; your state makes me feel that I must have failed in something. Pray tell me what it is," he added, "and I will do my best to repair the omission."

As Fanchon did not answer he pressed the matter. "Is there anything I have not given you—is there anything I have denied you—your cavalier, your Cæsar, your Chevalier de Châteauroux? I have never shown myself so absurd as to be jealous . . . . You had your vivacious, your quicksilver moods; you have danced and gambled and acted, sung, coquetted . . . . "

"Spare me the catalogue," murmured Fanchon. "I have done everything, and I hold you, monseigneur, quite guiltless of any blame for my condition. And now, if you would be so good as to retire and permit me to die in peace, I should be even more grateful to you than I am already."

M. le Comte looked dubiously at the languishing beauty.

"If you would tell me the nature of your complaint," he protested, "I might be able to discover a remedy for it. You have a very large fortune, madame, it is a pity that it should not be employed in restoring you to health."

"But I," sighed Fanchon, "do not wish to be restored.

"You are, then, tired of life?"

"You may, if you will, put it like that."

"You are unhappy?" he insisted.

"You may also, if you wish, put it like that."

"You do not wish to recover?"

Fanchon sighed again for reply.

Her husband, who was a man of some force of character, insisted on endeavouring to discover the deep-seated source of her unhappiness, her malady, her dying condition.

"There is something you wish, but that you have not had?"

Fanchon was silent at first, then she admitted this to be true.

"There is certainly something I have wished for that I have not had," she repeated, "and if I do not get it within the next day or so—well, then, I prefer to die, and cease to be of trouble to anyone."

M. le comte could not forebear a smile at these hypocritical protestations. Fanchon had never cared in the least what trouble she was to anyone; if she had involved the whole world in discomfort it would scarcely have disturbed her coquettish and smiling sweetness.

As her husband was reluctantly and silently leaving the room, Fanchon, languid as she was, roused herself to say:

"Monseigneur, in two days it will be Christmas, and I hope you will exert yourself to procure me a present—probably the last that you will ever be asked to purchase for me."

M. le Comte, to an alarmed household, declared earnestly that Fanchon, M. la Comtesse, was certainly dying, amid all her laces, her swansdown pillows, her satins and her ribbons. Yes, the pale tints of death were creeping over that face, beneath the knot of pale blue ribbons, beneath the cascades of long lace, and the maid forbore to put on the Portugal red and the white made from crushed egg-shell, because of the ghastly contrast these adornments now made to the natural complexion beneath.

But, on the morning of Christmas Day, Fanchon was able to receive her presents, or, at least, some of them . . . . Most of the caskets were left piled in the ante-chamber, on delicate tables of buhl and marqueterie; but Cæsar, the Chevalier de Châteauroux, was admitted into the invalid's bedchamber with his most exquisite gift—a bouquet of spring flowers: violets, hyacinths, tuberose, Provençe roses, lilac—mauve, white, yellow and pink, with delicate trails of greenery—fetched from distant glasshouses, at Heaven alone knew what cost and trouble, brought in on this winter morning and placed with trembling expectation on the bed of Fanchon, and Cæsar, venturing to be indiscreet, leant within the rosy velvet-lined curtains, and murmured:

"You must be convinced by this gift that I love you—if I had not loved you I could not have thought of anything so simple."

Fanchon sighed and permitted the flowers to remain on her pillow.

The doctors, who from the doorway had watched the effect of this charm, murmured together that it had failed, and, if she was not roused, she would hardly last the day. And the maids—Corinne, Musette and Fifine—began softly disputing amongst themselves, between their sobs, what ruffles Madame should wear at the last, and whether, after all, she would look better on her *lit de parade* in the blue and silver, or in her last delicious dress of silver and bronze mohair, trimmed with tufts of ostrich feathers, dyed a citron yellow.[59]

When the other presents had been sorrowfully left at the door of Fanchon's chamber, and M. le Chevalier de Châteauroux had retired in gloomy melancholy at beholding what little effect that fragrant posie of spring flowers, thus miraculously ravished from the bosom of winter, had had on the dying spirit of Fanchon, the husband himself appeared with his present. His also was a posie—but a posie entirely composed of gems. White stars of diamonds, soft petals of sapphires, leaves of hard bright emeralds, buds of opals, bells of pearls, and all bound with a ribbon of pure shimmering gold.

---

[59] *Lit de parade*: lying in state.

Fanchon made an effort to rouse herself to glance at this gift, and those discreetly remaining in the chamber looked at each other with sighs and reproachful glances.

What a banal and ordinary present to bring to Fanchon—Fanchon, the great heiress who had never lacked money with which to indulge her most trifling or foolish caprice! Fanchon, on whom jewels had been showered, who had been wreathed with pearls—shimmering with diamonds, adorned with emeralds and rubies, treading on gold tissues, drinking from gold vessels, all her short life. How tawdry and garish the gift looked beside the simple posie (now beginning to droop in the warm amber-scented air), still resting on the down pillows of Fanchon!

The lady gave the ostentatious gift one fluttering glance, and closed her eyes in a deeper disgust than before.

O shame! O fie! Something that can be ordered from a jeweller's—something that cost no care or thought, something that had been bought with her fortune—that, too, could be turned again into money when she was dead! She roused herself to point out, in a faltering tone, the beauty and delicacy of Cæsar's gift, faded now, as she was faded, amid the muslins and the satins, the swansdowns and the laces.

"It does not please you?" asked the husband coldly.

"You scarcely could have thought much whether it would please me," Fanchon replied wearily. "But what does that matter since you know, and I know, that nothing will please me any more."

"Then what you said a few hours ago about searching for something and dying if you did not get it has come true? You have not discovered what you are looking for . . . . ?"

And Fanchon replied, "No, monseigneur, I have not discovered it; I do not think it worth while for me to go on living any more."

"Your decision rests in your own hands," replied the husband, more coldly still, and with no more than that he left her . . . .

They all left her except Père Bernard, the most discreet, subtle and delicate of priests, who remained to comfort what every one believed to be the last moments of Madame la Comtesse.

He did not, however, begin his discourse by touching on heavenly matters, but dwelt lightly and with a worldly grace on those that belonged to this order of existence. He admired the two gifts that lay on her pillow—the bright, hard, glittering bouquet of gems, and the faded bouquet of unnatural spring flowers.

"I am sorry, madame, that you did not see fit to take a little more kindly to your husband's gift."

"What should I take kindly," asked Fanchon, with a deal more vigour than she had shown when there were others besides the priest in the room, "what cost so little care?"

The priest raised his thin eyebrows and turned down his thin lips:

"You are not, perhaps," he remarked, "quite so clever, my pretty Fanchon, as you might be. You are a very accomplished lady of the world, and no doubt consider yourself very swift and subtle; yet I can conceive that it would be possible for you to be in love with a man and not be able to say so, and for a man to be in love with you and you not be able to discover it."

Fanchon, with a graceful fretfulness, replied that she was far too ill for conundrums.

"The only riddle that I can solve," she said languishingly, "is that which will be answered in the courts of Heaven."

The confessor was heard to murmur something which sounded almost like "courts of a fiddlestick!" but, of course, this could not possibly have been so. He picked up the bouquet of jewels and began admiring the costliness of the material and the fineness of the workmanship.

"Your husband," he remarked dryly, "is a poor man, and to buy these jewels he had to mortgage his last remaining estate in Normandy."

At this Fanchon sat up in bed and, although she had worn no rouge that day, there was a fine colour in her cheeks.

"Of course," she said, "he thinks I am dying, and when I am dead he will be able to sell the jewels again. Do not deceive me, Father, after all there is nothing in the gift."

"You are evidently not better acquainted with the law than you are with the hearts of men," said the good Father, smiling indulgently. "When you are dead, my pretty Fanchon, your jewels will be returned with your dowry and M. le Comte—for indulging you in your whim for a Christmas posie—will find himself even poorer than he was when he married you. He will be reduced, no doubt, to sell his sword and die adventuring in a foreign army on the fields of Flanders, and that will be a pity."

"What?" cried Fanchon, in a voice as clear as her complexion, and with now no trace of illness, fatigue or languor either. "Do you mean to tell me that that is so? That he has spent what is left of his fortune in what he believed was a gift in my dying hour?"

"Precisely so!" smiled the priest, "and I believe that you will find that the affection which bought the gift is a good deal more lasting than the affection which went through that fantastic search for a few poor forced flowers that, I believe, are already faded and their perfume is, my dear Fanchon, not altogether agreeable."

With that he picked up the drooping bouquet of hothouse blooms from the pillow and laid the posie of gems on Fanchon's lap.

At first she sighed, but it was with a sigh full of vigour.

"You might have told me all this long ago."

"You forget," the priest reminded her, "that it is not fashionable for a gentleman to be in love with his wife."

"But it is not," remarked Fanchon, with a lively smile, "forbidden."

"Oh, no, certainly not," replied the good Father, "it is strange, but it is not forbidden. And why did not you yourself say something?"

"You see," said Fanchon, "it is not fashionable for a lady to be in love with her husband."

"It is fashionable," conceded the priest, "for a lady to indulge in any kind of caprice, even that."

"We kept the bargain," reflected Fanchon, "and there was never any mention of love in the bargain, not even if he beggared himself to buy me this . . . . "

"To give your last hours an air of richness and illusion," said the priest; "to make you think that you might wear that posie when you leant on his arm walking up the steps of the opera, when you drove with him in your chaise in the woods of La Bagatelle, when you sat beside him at the suppers in the Palais Royal——"

"Enough! enough!" cried Fanchon. "Tell me, my good Father, if I require rouge or white?"

"Certainly, neither," smiled Père Bernard, "you have blushed most becomingly."

"I swear it is the first time since I came to Paris," protested the lady, "but then the whole affair is so *outré*."[60]

"And the poor Cæsar?" murmured the priest, slyly moving the bouquet of the Chevalier de Châteauroux still further from the lady's bedside.

---

[60] *Outré:* eccentric, bizarre, beyond the bounds of what is considered usual or proper.

"The poor Cæsar," said the lady candidly, "was merely encouraged in case—well you know, dear Father—a suspicion of jealousy——"

"Precisely," agreed the priest.

"He never seemed to care—I never could make him jealous."

"Perhaps he thought it was part of the bargain that he never should be jealous," said Père Bernard, and he put the wilted spring flowers behind his broad back, and Fanchon never noticed that he dropped them into the scented fire as he left the room . . . a waft of perfume, a flutter of flame, and the tender blooms were gone.

Fanchon never noticed. She was too occupied in arranging the curls of that soothing, charming ash-blonde shade beneath the cascades of lace on her brow and in saying:

"My dear Father, pray send my husband to me immediately, that I may thank him for his Christmas gift."

When M. le Comte entered the satin-lined chamber he found her so radiant that he said at once, and with a certain dryness: "I perceive, madame, that you have recovered from your languors."

Fanchon admitted that she had indeed recovered.

"Because I have found what I was searching for," and she held out the little posie of jewels. "You ruined yourself to buy this, I believe——"

"That," he replied haughtily, "is no concern of yours. If it had comforted you for even half an hour I should not have considered myself ruined."

"Comforted me," smiled Fanchon, "not only for half an hour, but for all my life, aye, well, say for a week. You see, *mon ami*, I did not think that you had the least regard for me—it was not in the bargain that you should—and I regretted that so much that I lost interest in everything . . . . In brief, monseigneur, you were so very ungallant as to permit me to be dying of love for you . . . if it became known, your reputation as a man of spirit would suffer—if it is not fashionable to be enamoured of a wife, neither is it modish to allow a lady to languish for your favours."

Seeing that he could not answer for shame and tenderness, Fanchon added lightly, "Monseigneur . . . I will make you a present . . . we will get back that estate in Normandy which I have never seen and which I know is charming, and we will go there together. I am tired of Paris . . . . Love me for ever, eh? Well, say a week . . . "

"You are not then ill?" cried the husband, "you are going to live . . . and to love me . . . for a week . . . ?"

"Eh, monseigneur," sighed Fanchon, with much emphasis, "*what a vast deal of trouble you have put me to!*"

"Just to find out what you knew already," concluded her husband.

# PAT-A-TOO

PAT-A-TOO had many romances in his time, as you all know, but none as delicious as this romance. Those were fine days too, when it was good to be alive.

Pat-a-Too stood on the bridge, the Pont Neuf, near the statue of Henri IV; so old and miserable he was, with his ragged coat and his long white hair and beard, so bent and bowed.

He never could tell where he came from, this old beggar, he was too imbecile; his name, he said, was "Pat-a-Too" and that was all he seemed to know about himself.

He sold broadsheets, but no one bought them save one; but a great many sous were dropped into his palm out of pity for his ragged, wretched looks.

A great deal of fine company passed over the bridge, almost all the fine company in Paris, going to and fro the city and the Palace.

Every evening a lady went past in a gilt coach with scarlet leather linings, and horses trapped in blue bossed with silver; and she always stopped and bought a broadsheet from Pat-a-Too, a poor little love ballad printed on cheap paper that he sold for two sous.

The coach would stop and Pat-a-Too would shamble up to the window, and the compassionate lady would take her sheet, and pay well for it, and say a kind word and drive on.

Sometimes she had companions with her, but most often she was alone.

She was a dark, handsome lady, of a certain robust and sprightly charm, and she was most gorgeously dressed in embroidery velvets and lustred satins and gold laces.

One day she had with her another lady, blonde as a sprig of corn, who was wrapped in a blue silk cardinal and caressed a marmoset which peeped out of her swansdown muff.

As her friend gave her charity to Pat-a-Too this lady remarked:

"What bright eyes that old man has!"

"He is imbecile, my dear. I am so moved towards him that every day I buy a broadsheet."

"What is your name?" asked the blonde lady. She leant from the coach window, and the knot of lilac at her breast perfumed the spring air. "Where do you come from, and why do you stand here?"

To which the old beggar only muttered:

"Pat-a-Too! Pat-a-Too!"

"You see," said the dark lady, who was Madame la Marquise de Courcelles, "he is, poor wretch, idiotic."

She slipped her broadsheet into her velvet bag, but the other lady answered:

"I never saw an idiot with eyes like those."

The old man shuffled back to his place, and the evening clouds, coming up over the river, dimmed them all.

The next time that Madame de Courcelles paused her coach on the Pont Neuf and Pat-a-Too shambled to the window the following curious conversation took place, while the lady made an ado to find some white pieces in her purse.

And it was in whispers.

She said:

"This is becoming too dangerous."

And he:

"No, it is absolutely safe."

But Madame de Courcelles answered:

"That girl yesterday noticed something. Your eyes. I am frightened."

"I will wear spectacles," said Pat-a-Too, and she took his sheet, handing him back several others together with the money, for her jest was to return the beggar his poems to sell again.

Next day Pat-a-Too appeared in horn spectacles with dark glasses, and was more bowed and decrepit than ever as he begged the passers-by for charity.

Presently, through the gay sunshine overhead and the dirt under foot, came tripping along the blonde lady who had ridden in Madame de Courcelles's coach, and that was a strange thing for a high-bred girl to do—to go out alone with never a dame or a page, and plainly attired like a citizen's daughter.

The old man shrank together in the shadow of the plinth of the great statue as she approached, but she stopped directly before him.

"Good day, Pat-a-Too."

Stupidly he whined:

"Pat-a-Too! Pat-a-Too!"

"Why are you wearing spectacles, Pat-a-Too, when your eyes are so bright and clear?"

"Pat-a-Too! Pat-a-Too!" he mumbled.

"Will you sell me one of your broadsheets?" asked the lady and held out daintily a gold coin.

He showed no delight or surprise at this immense sum of money, but tremblingly offered her one of the flimsy sheets.

She took it and read out: "Verses to Chloris on her Buying a Pair of Shoes."

"Why, that is never worth a gold piece," she remarked; she bent low over the beggar, as if she thought he was deaf, and added:

"I want a broadsheet like you sold to Madame de Courcelles."

He whined again:

"Pat-a-Too! Pat-a-Too!"

"You can never take the gold louis with those old ragged gloves on," she said. "Take it, my fine beggar, in your bare hands."

Then Pat-a-Too spoke.

He said in a low voice, full of dignity:

"Mademoiselle, what is a jest to you is life or death to me. the passers-by begin to observe us. I pray you leave me."

With that she ceased her baiting of him and sauntered away.

And soon after Pat-a-Too, groaning, coughing and wheezing, hobbled off too.

But later, when Madame de Courcelles came by for her evening drive, he was in his place.

As she looked for her money he said:

"You are right. It is too dangerous. I cannot come again. But I want a copy of the Treaty."

"I can't get that till to-night," replied Madame de Courcelles, who appeared very agitated. "As this is no longer safe you must come to the Louvre."

"That is to put my head in a trap indeed."

"No," she answered; "come as you are, among the beggars and supplicants in the courtyard, and watch out for a page with a knot of puce-coloured ribbons. To-night, in two hours' time."

She drove on, looking ill and frightened, and Pat-a-Too wandered away off the bridge.

In two hours' time he was among the beggars and supplicants that clustered round the kitchen doors in the further courtyard of the Louvre, and as he was a stranger and seemed imbecile he was rudely jostled and pushed.

It was a lovely evening in spring; the dark mass of the Palace rose against a pale sky of celestial purity in which the cold crescent of the new moon sparkled bright as frost; in the air was a sweet chill that thrilled the blood, and there was a sense of flowers and laughter and love hidden in the gentle oncoming darkness.

The page with the puce ribbons elbowed his way through the crowd pressing round the doors, and sought out the queer old man with his spectacles and ragged gloves.

"Do you sell broadsheets on the Pont Neuf?"

Pat-a-Too muttered "Yes," and the page said:

"My mistress will give you a supper with her own servants. Come inside, old bones."

And the youth, whistling, led the beggar into the Louvre, that sombre, frowning and fatal palace. The King was in Paris, which was a rare thing now, and Pat-a-Too passed many guards and valets in the long back corridors and on the long back staircases.

He had a sensation of getting deeper and deeper into the heart of the building, deeper and deeper into the heart of danger.

The page took him to a lonely ante-chamber which looked on to the river, and which was lit by a single cluster of candles.

By the long window that framed the moon high above the dark shape of Paris stood the blonde lady who had spoken to him on the Pont Neuf.

She looked over her shoulder.

"Pat-a-Too!" she said softly.

"It is Madame de Courcelles's beggar," said the page. "He is to be feasted with her valets."

The lady came at once from the window.

"I am going to Madame de Courcelles's apartments," she said lazily. "The beggar can follow me."

"But no," replied the page, "that were an ill following for you, madame. Surely I will take the idiot to my mistress."

But she went with them, as a radiance in front, for she wore a ball-gown with many diamonds.

When they came to Madame de Courcelles's chambers, she said:

"Boy, go and tell your mistress that I wait to accompany her to the ball, and that the old beggar is here."

As the boy went she stepped quickly up to the crouching figure of Pat-a-Too and said:

"Madame de Courcelles has betrayed you. You have walked into a trap. She is buying her pardon by handing you over."

He straightened his back instantly and showed that he was a magnificent height, towering over the lady.

"Some one has betrayed me," he said coldly, "but I don't know if it is you or she."

"Believe which you prefer—either way you have only a slight chance," she replied haughtily.

"If I believe you," asked Pat-a-Too, "what shall I do? We have only a moment."

"Take this key. Hasten back the way you came, to the room where you met me—this key opens the door in the corner. Lock yourself in there till I come."

Pat-a-Too had a few seconds in which to reflect on this astonishing proposal; all that he could see clearly was that he was trapped, by which woman he did not know.

He had never liked Madame de Courcelles, and he remembered her face early that evening in the coach—a smitten woman.

And lightning quick he saw that, even if she had not betrayed him, she would not be able to save him without discovering herself, since this other woman plainly knew the affair.

So in these few seconds he decided whom to trust his destiny to; yet he raged at his predicament.

"Take off your disguise," whispered the blonde lady, "for, remember, it is an old beggar they will search for."

He slipped away, back down those long corridors. Once he passed a group of valets, who looked at him curiously yet did not interfere with him, since they had seen him go past with Madame de Courcelles's page; and, out of sight of them, he fairly ran, despite his cumbrous clothes, and gained the lonely ante-chamber lit by the solitary cluster of candles, with the long window that framed the icy moon, tranquil above the sombre city.

There were two doors facing each other, each leading to the corridor; the third must be that of the key, thought Pat-a-Too, and he hesitated.

He might be opening it on one of the Ministers, on the King himself!

The King, whose inmost State secrets he had, by means of Madame de Courcelles, been so successful in filching.

Yet certain death there it would be if such were the company awaiting him; it was also certain death to linger about the passages of the Palace.

He tried the key—entered.

Darkness, vaguely dispelled by a crystal lamp.

No one was there.

As his eyes became used to the faint light Pat-a-Too saw that it was a bed-chamber.

A lady's bed-chamber.

He closed the door, locked it and sat down, breathing rather sharply.

She was sincere, then, or she would have hardly sent him here.

And Madame de Courcelles was the traitress.

He raged again in bitter fury against the wretched woman; something had been discovered, and she had been terrified into sacrificing him to save herself.

And what of the other poor devils in the plot—the clerk in the royal cabinet and the clerk to the Minister who supplied Madame de Courcelles with copies of the royal correspondence?

Both silenced for ever by now no doubt.

Pat-a-Too remembered his friend's advice; it was not likely that anyone would know him at once without his disguise; he could flatter himself that it was a very good disguise.

He took off his glasses, wig and beard, his long, heavy patched cloak, his clumsy old gloves, and, rolling these into a bundle, dextrously dropped them out of the window on to a projection of the coping below, where they lodged to rot indefinitely.

Then he stood upright in a shirt fine enough (for he never could bear foul linen) and deerskin breeches; round his waist was a belt, a short sword and a small pistol. He kept on his broken boots, for he had no others, yet he was sorry to defile the delicate apartment with such gutter footwear and kept near the window, on the boards beyond the pale carpet.

With his handkerchief he carefully wiped the paint from his face; but there was not much of this, as he prided himself on disguising his natural face without grease or charcoal.

And meanwhile he was wondering two things: how he was to get a copy of the famous Treaty, that secret document that he had promised to report in full to Holland, and how he was to get out of the Louvre.

Both propositions seemed equally hopeless. Willingly would

he have strangled the life out of the false Madame de Courcelles, strangling her with relish.

Never agin, if he survived (and certainly, he thought, never again if he didn't), would he trust women.

He looked out of the window, wondering if he could drop, leap or climb to freedom that way; he had done perilous things in his time.

But the smooth façade of the Louvre fell flush beneath him, unbroken save for the coping above the next row of windows, where he had thrown his rags.

The pale moon seemed to mock his desperate gaze.

"Oh, fool, fool, to ever enter the trap, to ever set foot in the labyrinth of the Louvre! Never before had he been so incautious, so crazy.

He now searched round the walls for some possible other exit.

There was none.

Pat-a-Too was rather stricken even in this moment by the sight of the lady's dressing-table, with her touching frivolities thereon, and the chair with a silk robe flung across, and the pink brocade curtains looped back from the demure bed, above which hung a holy picture. He surveyed this pretty sanctuary with gratitude not untinged with a certain remorse—and still, perhaps, a certain suspicion.

There was no other door beyond that which he had entered by, and on which he heard now a light tap and the voice of his protectress whispering for admission. He unlocked the door.

She entered, and it was like the moon in person descending, so silver, so white, so radiant she glittered and glimmered in her white satin and diamonds, the pearls on her frosted lace collar and in her pale blonde hair.

She said:

"I have made a feint to leave the ball, saying my flounces are torn. My maids are in the galleries watching the dancing."

Then she went to her dressing-table and lit the candles that stood there in ivory sticks; as the flame spurted from the flint and tinder, and then from one candle to another, she looked at Pat-a-Too.

He was very splendid to behold, with his silver blonde curls, narrow, dark eyes and his clear, candid northern face above his thick northern neck and wide shoulders.

He was what she had thought he was when she had glimpsed his eyes under his wig on the Pont Neuf, the man she had seen in her troubled dreams ever since.

She spoke again across the cluster of tender candle flames.

"Why did you do this?"

Pat-a-Too smiled.

"Can you get me out of the Louvre, mademoiselle?" he asked courteously.

"I do not know," she answered. "*Mon Dieu!* it will be difficult. They are, of course, searching for you throughout the Palace."

Till now Pat-a-Too had still been faintly suspicious of a trap, but there was something in the mournful tone and look of the lady that convinced him of her sincerity.

"Heavens above!" he cried in a burst of fury. "Is it, then, true that woman has betrayed me?"

"It is true, but the first fault is mine. I, indiscreet fool as I was, showed my suspicion of you, and she was so terrified lest I should light on the truth that she disclosed everything to gain her own pardon. She is under arrest now."

Pat-a-Too ground his teeth.

"Perhaps I can save you," said the lady. "They will scarcely search here. And to-night you could slip out in some disguise."

He looked at her curiously.

"Why are you taking such an interest in me?" he asked. "Surely in your eyes I am a traitor and a spy."

She blushed like a summer rose.

"Have you not noticed that I also am English?" she asked. "I am one of the Duchess D'Orleans's women, who came with her from England."

Pat-a-Too, who justly prided himself on the purity of his French accent, was irritated that she should have discovered that he was English.

And Madame D'Orleans and her women were as the French. The lady saw his look, his doubt, his anger, and said:

"Do not think that I am of my mistress's politics—indeed, I know nothing of politics. but desire to help a fellow countryman whom my indiscretion has imperilled."

Pat-a-Too still thought that there was some smell of a trap. but disdained to give any thought further to this aspect of the matter.

He replied:

"I think that it is I who now put *you* in peril. Will you not, for your own sake, get me out of the Louvre?"

They stood facing each other in the window place; on one side of them was the space of the river, the town and the sky, with the moon sailing ever higher in the peerless spring night, and on the other the rich shadows of the sumptuous room, with the tender light of the clustered candles on the dressing-table and the pearly lustre of the crystal lamp. She in the magnificence of her splendour (and the French court then was gorgeous indeed), and he in his shirt and breeches and broken top-boots, and both so young and so comely.

"Oh, Pat-a-Too," she sighed, speaking English now, "have I no place in your memory? Do you not recall an English May in Devon, when we sought privily for violets in the copse? But of course you have forgotten; it is fifteen years ago."

"You know Devon?" he asked sharply. "Fifteen years ago? A child I played with? Why, you are never Margaret Cunning?"

"As surely as you are Edgar Paradyne," she whispered back. "At the farm in the hollow was a white cat, a monstrous beast; they called it 'Pat-a-Too,' and that, I think, gave you your name."

"Truly," smiled Lord Paradyne, "I did from that ancient incident take the name of my disguise."

"Pussy you remembered, but not me!"

"How should I? A little thin maid! And you like a pearl, a lily! And I have been over the world many times since then."

"And seen many fair women. Come, Pat-a-Too, let us sit and talk a little, for here you are safe enough."

She took herself the deep satin chair all embroidered with flowers at the end of the bed, but he remained standing.

They had been neighbours, these two, romped together in the park, round the manor house and the deep woods of Paradyne, then lost sight of each other, as people will, each going the way of their fortunes.

As she had said, he had seen many fair women, and he had forgotten the child of long ago.

But now she returned to him, and with her a flood of sweet memories, profuse and fragrant as blossoms in June.

He turned his face away from her.

"Since I am in the Louvre," he said, "it becomes me to endeavour to obtain a copy of that Treaty—that is my business in hand; that I may by no means neglect."

She was amazed.

"Since Madame de Courcelles has betrayed you, that is impossible."

"Yet," he sighed, "if I return to Holland without that my mission is incomplete."

"Perhaps," said the lady surprisingly, "I could get it for you."

"You!"

"I have some influence. It would be in the Minister's cabinet?"

Pat-a-Too laughed.

"It is not so easy as that, my dear."

She said:

"Give me till midnight."

And left him to his solitary vigil.

The lady returned to the ballroom, where, beneath the glitter of the candelabra, the groups of radiant dancers were discussing in quick whispers the rumours of a plot, of a confession from a certain great lady, and the hunt through the Louvre for the spy so nearly trapped.

Miss Cunning had been the last to see him; he had come with her as far as the door of Madame de Courcelles's apartment, and then suddenly fled; by the time she had raised the alarm he was out of sight down the long, winding corridors.

She had to tell this story again and again—even to the Minister himself. She was greatly in credit because she had been the first, on the bridge, to notice something strange about Pat-a-Too, and so had given the alarm to Madame de Courcelles and frightened her into a confession.

So when she came back they all began to whisper to her over again about the plot and the spy, but she put them all by with a laugh and went to where, in an inner room, the Minister was playing at basset.[61]

He knew that she was coming long before he looked up. and his whole figure tightened, and he looked very earnestly at the cards.

It was some months since he had been paying great court to this lady, but never had he received from her the least favour.

But now she came up, smiling, and leant over the back of his chair.

"Do not rise—go on with your play, but presently, monseigneur, let me know what reward you will give me for discovering the plot."

He laughed.

And she passed on, down the long ballroom, waving the white plumes of her great fan.

It was only a matter of moments before (she had known it would be) he sought her out and asked her the meaning of her whisper.

"What reward do you want, mademoiselle?" he asked eagerly enough, for, hard, dry man as he was, the fair Englishwoman pleased him mightily, beyond reason and common sense.

"How great a reward may I claim?" she smiled.

"The plot is discovered," he said, "but the plotter still evades us."

"But will not long do so," she answered boldly. "The man must be somewhere in the Louvre. And Madame de Courcelles?"

"Is a fool. She has been taken to her country house—under escort."

Miss Cunning did not permit herself to shiver.

"And your two clerks?"

---

[61] Basset: a high-risk gambling game using cards, considered fit only for people of the highest rank, much in vogue amongst the French nobility and responsible for many a bankruptcy.

"Are also disposed of. Comfortably." The great man grinned painfully, for the whole affair had been a grievous blow at his pride and his policy. "But I have had enough of politics for to-night," he added with real weariness and real gallantry. "I hoped you had come to offer me some consolation."

The blue eyes of Margaret Cunning dazzled on him as she replied:

"Perhaps. Monseigneur has been unfortunate, and women dote on misfortune." She thought of Pat-a-Too lonely in her bedroom. She had promised to return before midnight. Less than another hour.

"I hear," she said lightly, "that no woman has ever entered monseigneur's cabinet. Is that true?"

"True."

"Well, I would like to be the first, monseigneur."

The Minister faintly blushed beneath his powder. A rendezvous? A *tête-à-tête?* Was this delicious English rose that had been so long out of reach drooping into his hand at last?

"I should be proud to show you my poor cabinet," he said, with a formalism that disguised his leaping excitement. "But we are in some confusion—my clerks arrested—my secretaries under suspicion—in brief, mademoiselle, should I conduct you there now, we should be alone."

He shot her a straight glance.

"No matter," she said; "we can talk state secrets."

They slipped away through back corridors and secret doors until they reached the great man's cabinet, the repository of the secrets of the statecraft of France.

It was a little room, sumptuous in gilded leather, with a glowing picture of fruit and flowers between the bronze brocade of the long curtains, and a silver lamp held up by cupids garlanded with gems.

Miss Cunning looked at the desk; it was locked, of course.

"What is this Treaty there is so much ado about?" she inquired ingenuously, and he smiled at her innocence, which was by no means feigned, for she knew nothing whatever about politics. "And is it true that there was a copy taken for this spy to steal away with?"

He, pleased beyond what he dare show to have her alone with him, and not venturing as the wary campaigner he was in love, war and business to hasten events, began to talk to her of the Treaty, of the copy. You could talk to her, he felt, for it was like talking to a child; you knew that she understood nothing and would remember nothing of what was said. When she asked to see the famous Treaties he showed them to her at once, unlocking the ormolu desk; he was not conscious of much but her near and dear presence, and the wish (which even these great men will feel) to talk of his humiliation and misfortune, his rage with the wretched Madame de Courcelles, and his vengeance against the spy when this person should fall into his hands.

"There, child," he said, "here is the bit of paper there is so much ado about, and I expect that it looks mighty foolish to you."

At that moment a diamond fell from the laces at Miss Cunning's breast and rolled away under the desk.

The great man who remained upright before kings stooped instantly to this pleasant service and sought for the sparkling jewel, and in that instant Miss Cunning had snatched up the copy of the Treaty and secreted it in her bosom, thrusting it swiftly behind her corsage.

She was reputed in matters of intrigues and politics the most innocent and (the cynics said) the silliest woman about the court, but she was clever enough now.

Her laughter and the rustle of her silks hid her gesture and her movement, and when the Minister turned with the gem she was near the door so that he, following her, had no time to observe his rifled desk.

He had placed the key in the door, meaning, perhaps, to lock her in, and as she stood with her back against it she pulled this out, secretly, and held it in her hand.

She looked so flushed, so radiant, so gay, so lovely that the great man a little lost his presence of mind.

"Will you give me a kiss for my pains?" he said as he tendered the jewel.

With that she swung round, opened the door, fled and locked him in, still standing, like a fool, with the diamond in his hand.

It was a daring stratagem.

She did not know what means he had of getting out or of summoning help—but for at least a few moments he was her prisoner.

She fled like a gleam of moonlight along the corridors to her bed-chamber, and tapped eagerly for Pat-a-Too to admit her. When he did so they faced each other, pale in the moonshine that now was splendid in the room; for he had put out the candles, fearing he might be observed from across the river.

She pulled out the paper, warm from lying over her eager heart, and gave it to him.

"Was this what you wanted? Are you satisfied now?"

In that argent light he read the document and saw that it was what he sought.

"How much peril have you gone through to secure this?" he demanded.

"Oh, Pat-a-Too, I have only a little fooled a man who is in love with me!"

"Fooled?" He frowned.

"Yes. Inasmuch as I have not paid him—by even a kiss."

"Perhaps the payment is still to come. How will you account to him for this turn?"

"I will trust to my wits, Pat-a-Too"—her smile trembled a little—"but first I have to think how to get you out of the Louvre."

"First I have to think how to thank you, Margaret of Margarets."

He touched her shoulders, he turned her towards him; in that moment they hated politics and intrigues and courts and all the world, and cared only for each other and for youth.

Their eyes were soft with infinite regrets; the moonlight veiled them, a silver melancholy, their feet set on such different ways.

He thought:

"How sweet to take her with me! But how impossible!"

She thought:

"How sweet to go with him! But how impossible!"

Then, gravely, they kissed.

"Pat-a-Too, perhaps some other day—we shall be more fortunate."

"Margaret—some other day!"

Ah, the pity!

So much to come between, so much to interfere with love!

Reluctantly they drew apart, and she hastened to a great press in the wall and drew out a woman's cardinal of crimson, fur lined, a heavy garment in which she bade Pat-a-Too wrap himself.

Miss Cunning was tall, and the garment came to Pat-a-Too's feet, but the trouble was his boots, and they were both so young that they fell laughing at his large feet in the broken boots beneath the rich coat. Yet this defect seemed like to ruin everything, and Miss Cunning, for all her courage, paled a little, for she had no other disguise at hand.

And at any moment now her maids might be coming up from the dancing, or the great man might have missed his copy of the Treaty and be sending after her.

Pat-a-Too said:

"It must be done boldly. No one here knows my face. I will pass out and risk a challenge."

"That were well enough if you had the attire. But so, without a coat or hat, and those arms—and the boots!"

"But where can I find other clothes?" he asked. "Time presses."

"Time presses indeed," she replied. "Now, if I have any wit, I must show it. We are not far from the little back door by which you entered. You would know the way?"

"Yes." He was too experienced at this kind of adventure not to notice these things.

"But I know a quicker, past the apartments of His Highness's gentlemen. They are all at the ball, or searching for Pat-a-Too, the grotesque beggar-man." For, you see, not even Madame de Courcelles could give an account of what he was like without his disguise, for she had never seen him without his mummery.

They kisses again, still sadly, and with a sigh for the wastage of the sweet spring night and the tender moonlight and the silver silence of the sumptuous chamber, and then crept out into the corridors, hand in hand, like two children.

She led him round the corner, past the doors of His Majesty's suite; one of these was ajar, and showed an empty room.

This part of the palace had been well searched for Pat-a-Too and was now deserted, but at the end of the corridor Miss

Cunning could see a sentry and a group of valets.

She thrust Pat-a-Too inside the half-open door with a prayer on her lips.

"Seize what clothes you can; rifle the wardrobe and hasten!"

In two minutes he was out again. He had thrust on the first coat to his hand in the press, a blonde peruke he had seen on a stand, a pair of riding boots; these garments, though ill-fitting, passed well enough, and the full curls of the wig came generously over his face.[62]

Miss Cunning was as pale as her gown by now; she knew the extreme peril that they ran, the risk that any moment threatened them—the risk of discovery and death.

They came up courageously towards the soldier and the valets, and she began to laugh and jest bravely so that her companion, in answering her raillery, might keep his face turned to her.

To their surprise the men not only drew back, but bowed respectfully, and the soldier saluted.

Out of their sight on the stairs Miss Cunning clung to him with muffed laughter.

"They took you for His Highness; that was His Highness's room you entered!"

They were so young they could laugh even now, with peril so near, with all their good fortune edged with danger.

At the privy door he had no longer any need of her guidance, and she let him go.

The sentries here made no ado of his passing; they were used to many escapades of royalty, and Pat-a-Too had something of the figure and bearing of the Prince.

---

62 Peruke: a man's wig.

She watched him saunter across the moonlight in the courtyard, and then lost to sight in the shadow of the outer gate.

Miss Cunning went back to the ballroom in time for the *danse aux flambeaux*, which she danced with eyes as bright as the torch she held.[63]

Those were the gallant days when people did wonderful things for love and policy.

It might be thought that the Minister, on discovering her trick and imposture, would have crushed her at once, but here she was saved by her simplicity. He never associated such a shallow coquette with the loss of the copy of the Treaty—and more than one of his spies whispered to him that she had been seen with His Highness!

A shallow coquette! Under powerful protection.

The Minister left her alone, in love and hate.

You might have thought too that Margaret Cunning and Pat-a-Too would never meet again, but it is true that they did, in a certain Devon church, two years hence, and Lady Paradyne took home with her in the bridal coach an aged farm cat, the sole descendant of a certain other Pat-a-Too.

---

[63] *Danse aux flambeaux:* a dance by flaming torchlight.

# STORIES OF TO-DAY

# "CROWD—WITH FLAGS"

MERCIA'S most exalted moods were but the intensifications of her disposition; she could no more think grossly than she could move heavily; she received a pure pleasure, rapt and unconscious from the swift grace of her own movements and from the austere purity of her own mind.

She liked her own poverty, clean, rigid, bracing, her own work, hard, severe, noble, her own youth, healthy, lovely, strong, liked even her own isolation, both shy and proud from the usual delights of the young.

She was, of course, often considered hard; virtue always seems hard to the feeble and the uneasy, and it was true that she was more in love with ideals than with humanity, there was something cold in her detachment from the trivial and the foolish, the fond and the sentimental.

She paused at the corner of the park where a bouquet of great trees stood at the edge of the ordered, railed grass; behind these trees the clouds rose, plume on plume, dense, opal coloured into the faint blue of that unfathomable distance which is our nearest image of eternity; Mercia had looked at these trees, these clouds, this blue, and then down at the crowd which tramped and straggled past.

A crowd with flags.

The young student in her well brushed, shabby clothes, so careless and yet so sure of herself, watched them curiously.

She did not know who they were, nor what they were doing; on this chill noble day of spring they seemed impersonal, symbolic of humanity, struggling forwards, against a background of remote sky, in the face of a cold wind, with these soiled, fluttering flags inscribed with odd signs and devices.

"How odd," thought Mercia, "that would look to anyone gazing down from above—that crowd of miserable looking people carrying rags on poles."

She went home.

Home to Mercia was an upper part in a decayed side street, above a fruiterer's shop—a few rooms neither elegant nor convenient but which had a grand air because they were in the charge of an intelligent and loving woman; Mrs. Graham was that uncommon creature, a housekeeper who is neither worried nor fussy, a home maker who is neither narrow nor stupid; with very little assistance she cleaned, polished, cooked, served, and yet always had a leisured manner, an open, sympathetic mind; the simplicity of the white room concealed the poverty, an exquisite management had long since taken the sting out of the lack of pence; she contrived their limited means with a grace that eliminated the sordid from their lives.

Mercia was a student of chemistry, James a student of architecture; they worked in the same college; James, who was a year younger, would soon leave to enter an architect's office.

Their lives were epics of work, of enthusiasm, of dreams of achievement—of this more than of fame.

To Mercia they seemed not three but four; to her, the father, six years dead, was always of the company.

This wise, tender, brilliant man, the physician who had toiled so hard and earned so little, had bequeathed a memory that refreshed the lives of his children.

He had died of over work, leaving by reason of the most

strenuous effort, the most patient self denial, sufficient means to provide for his three dependents.

Since then strenuous effort, patient self denial had been Mrs. Graham's portion too; the children had accepted this earnest, austere atmosphere, tinged with beautiful thoughts, as the cold rain clouds are tinged with the arc that holds every conceivable colour, as their heritage; but Mercia had responded with the deeper passion; her soul became a shrine for all difficult, lovely things.

She possessed either talent or genius for her work, which, it was too early to decide, but of the strength of her intelligence and the splendour of her endeavour there could be no doubt.

Mrs. Graham had set the table when Mercia returned; the high room was full of clear light, the white china gleamed with polished reflections; the loaf, the fruit, the jug of milk had each a fragrant look; beneath an old soft mezzotint of a great grandfather in judge's robes, James sat over a book; his profile was massive, noble; he was slightly awkward and his shabbiness, though so decent, so clean, was more noticeable than the shabbiness of Mercia.

Mrs. Graham was standing by the window; she had an open letter in her hand and gazed through the thin white muslin curtains she had so often washed and mended.

She had been grand and graceful, like Mercia; her face was now hollowed, her full locks were colourless; she looked more severe than either of her children knew her to be. Mercia wondered at the letter in her mother's hand.

Their correspondence was so meagre, so obvious; there was never any occasion to ponder over a letter.

They kept out of debt as proudly as they kept out of friendships; they avoided obligation as they avoided extravagance; they had come to London as strangers and after six years they were still strangers.

Mrs. Graham turned and looked deliberately at her daughter.

There was something rare about this glance; Mercia sensed uneasiness, appeal in her mother's eyes; she had never seen either there before.

"It is a wonderful day," she said.

"Is it?" asked Mrs. Graham wistfully. "A wonderful day?"

Mercia was instantly aware of a double meaning in this timid remark; she answered quickly:

"The sky is lovely, so clear—it seems as if you could see that cold rain has just fallen through it, gorgeous clouds too, so prodigal, like a triumph—and that kind of little wind that makes your flesh quiver."

"I haven't been out," said Mrs. Graham; she folded up the letter and placed it inside the big lexicon on top of the overcrowded bookcase.

Mercia had seen that it was a long letter; many pages of a fine handwriting, a heavy, stamped address in a violet blue; an alien letter.

Something had happened.

News had arrived.

"They sat down to their meal; above the mended clear curtains they could still see the clouds climbing above the rigid lines of the dirty stucco fronts of the houses opposite.

"I saw a crowd with flags," said Mercia suddenly, "they looked—funny."

James agreed that they were funny, those people. No one knew what they wanted, they didn't know themselves.

"And yet they go about with flags, trying to explain."

"Poor things," said Mrs. Graham. She poured the milk and cut the bread and butter as if she had never had to calculate the price of anything; you would never have associated her with any kind of economy.

"I don't know who they were," said Mercia. "Just a crowd with flags."

She looked past her mother at the big lexicon on top of the bookshelf; her brooding, rather sombre grey eyes, were hostile.

Something strange had entered into their lives; her mother was moved, nervous, restless; that letter, that alien letter.

She looked at James.

He was unconscious, undisturbed; he had not noticed the letter, the reading of the letter, the effect of the letter.

This did not surprise Mercia; she had already observed the bluntness of masculine perceptions in these fine-drawn matters.

She was glad when James had gone to his lecture and she and her mother were clearing the table.

She hoped that now Mrs. Graham would speak about her news.

But there was nothing but general remarks not so serene as usual.

The two grand-looking women carefully put away the remnants of the food in the meagre larder, washed the scanty china in cold water, rearranged the chairs and table.

It was cold; had they not long since been used to regard every comfort as a luxury they would have had a fire; as it was they shivered without noticing how chilly the bare room was.

Mrs. Graham brought out what has been so much extolled and so much ridiculed but which can hardly fail to survive as long as poverty and pride continue to exist together—a basket of mending.

She sat down to this with a leisured air that robbed the task of sordidness.

Mercia, whose nature was of the very essence of candour, asked quietly:

"Mother, what was that letter?"

Mrs. Graham did not look up from the cuff of James's shirt.

"I hoped you'd ask that."

"It was important, then?"

"Rather important, yes."

It was queer to think that anything important could happen to them that was not the result of their own efforts or actions; Mercia, so long trained in utter independence, complete self reliance, was amazed.

"A relation?" she asked.

"No, dear. We have no relations who are likely to write to us."

"So I thought."

To gain time, perhaps, Mrs. Graham explained what Mercia already knew.

"We are strangely solitary in that sense, Mercia, our few relations have gone such different ways."

"Who, then, is the letter from?" asked the girl.

"From an old friend—some one whom I knew before I married."

Mercia gazed intently at her mother's bent profile, so fine, so worn.

"Are you glad to hear from—to get that letter?"

Mrs. Graham was silent.

"I believe you are," added Mercia; her low tone held accusation.

"I don't know," replied the mother. "I was shocked—startled— "

She dropped her work and looked bravely at Mercia.

"It is from a man who wanted to marry me—twenty-three years ago——"

"What happened?" asked Mercia.

"That is so difficult to tell, yet I want you to know—it concerns you too."

"Mother, do you really want me to know? Is there any need?"

"There is, dear. Because I've got to decide."

She carefully picked up her work again. "You've got to help me decide," she said in a low tone.

Mercia was pale in the pale twilight.

"He—this man," added Mrs. Graham, "wants me to marry him now."

"Mother!"

Mrs. Graham lifted defensive eyes.

"Wait—you've got to hear the whole story. It's so silly, *really*, to keep these things secret, they're bound to come out some time."

"But need they?" asked Mercia coldly and sternly, and yet desperately too, repelling this intrusion into their lives. "Tear that letter up and forget about it——"

Mrs. Graham answered with more decision than she had yet shown.

"No—I can't do that. You must be considered. And then there's James. James must know too."

"Why?" demanded Mercia like a challenge.

Mrs. Graham said:

"Mr. Fenton is a very rich man."

"Whatever should that have to do with it?"

Mrs. Graham smiled wistfully.

"It's no use pretending, Mercia, that that isn't very important—that it doesn't weigh on me."

"I don't understand."

The mother took several small stitches before she answered.

"I want to tell you everything so that you will understand," she said at last. "When I was a young girl, about your age, I was engaged to Mr. Fenton. And very much in love with him. There was a good deal of opposition both sides because I was expected to marry a man with position and money—my people were proud and struggling hard to keep up appearances—and he, too, was penniless, a very brilliant young engineer, and he wanted money too, and influence to help him in his career. So you see, Mercia, we had every one against us."

The girl did not speak.

Without looking up the mother continued:

"We were reckless, indiscreet, we insisted on an engagement, we rather flaunted the situation, we became very conspicuous, always about together—every one, save our own people, rather championing us."

Mrs. Graham snipped her thread and added quietly:

"Then his mother got round him—he jilted me, married a rich woman and went to India."

"Oh!" exclaimed Mercia; a thin colour flushed into her grave face.

"It was only a small place—a little country town—you can imagine that it was rather terrible for me, Mercia."

"And yet—after all these years, he writes to you!"

Mrs. Graham ignored that.

"Soon after I married your father. He knew the whole story—and he married me."

Mercia glowed with triumphant love; her father's memory, always radiant, became further glorified.

"And I never heard of Mr. Fenton until to-day, when I got his letter. He is in a big position now, has made a great deal of money. His wife is dead a long time ago and he had no children."

"And he wants to marry you, now, after all," breathed Mercia.

"He wants to make amends. He says he has heard about us,

kept in touch with us through a friend in London; he knows about you and James."

"We've been spied on, then?"

"Oh, Mercia, I shouldn't call it that!" Mrs. Graham's voice quivered a little at last. "One must be tolerant."

"One should not be, could not be, over such an action as that!"

Mercia rose, and mechanically switched on the electric light; the bleached flood of whiteness filled the bare pale room.

"There was his point of view," replied Mrs. Graham quietly. "He was very ambitious. I dare say we should not have been happy, I have long ceased to feel any bitterness about him——"

Mercia remained standing.

"Why are we discussing this?" she asked nervously. "There is nothing to be said really."

"I think there is. Mr. Fenton wants heirs for his fortune, he could make life very different for you and James. I'm bound to consider that."

"Not for me, not for one moment for me."

Mrs. Graham looked up.

"Mercia, don't be hard. He is in poor health and very lonely. And it's only ignorance that despises money—opportunity."

"We can make our own opportunities," replied Mercia passionately. "Father left us independent—he wanted us to work."

"But it is poverty."

"You never said so before."

"There was no use in saying so before."

"Father lived in poverty."

"But he worried about you," said Mrs. Graham, looking up now with tears in her tired eyes, "he could hardly endure to leave us with so little. I am sure, if he had known of this—he would have been glad, relieved, thankful. There can be no question of disloyalty—a sick, ageing man——"

Her voice trailed away, she bent closer over her work.

"No question of disloyalty!" echoed Mercia. She checked her scorn and added, with cold constraint, "Of course you are free to do exactly as you wish, but for myself I refuse, refuse, refuse——"

"There's James," replied Mrs. Graham with a touch of obstinacy. "James must be given his choice."

"It will be the same as mine."

"James is ambitious—he must sometimes, often, feel the pinch, so must you, Mercia, for all your brave talk."

"Have we ever complained? Have you ever seen us discouraged or downcast?"

"You've been wonderful," replied Mrs. Graham wistfully, "but it is a hard life."

"A fine life," said Mercia. "What is there we need that we haven't got? And the struggle is nearly over for you, mother. James and I will both soon be independent, we shall get work, useful, well-paid work—we shall succeed, in an honourable kind of way—and you will have enough money then, Father's honest money, for leisure and the things you like——"

Mrs. Graham dropped her sewing on her knee and was silent.

Mercia approached her with a sudden, passionate movement.

"Mother—what could you do that would bring you the happiness this brings you? Keeping this place for us—to come home to all of us, carrying on, as Father would have liked."

Her voice broke and she turned away as abruptly, as passionately as she had advanced.

"Yes, you are right," said Mrs. Graham faintly, humbly, "my place is here."

"It can never be anywhere else," replied Mercia. "Oh, mother, let us forget all about it—tear up that letter, lose even the address."

"We must ask James," murmured Mrs. Graham, "that is only fair. Mr. Fenton particularly mentions James—it would mean more to James than to any of us."

Mercia's rigid sense of justice admitted that the question must be put to James, but it was, she said, a mere ugly formality. James would answer as she had answered and then they would forget the whole thing.

Two quiet, pallid women put the question before James when the boy returned from his lecture.

Mrs. Graham would have found it difficult to tell him the pitiful story, but Mercia related the tale with a cold delicacy that made it impersonal.

James flushed several times during the narration; he had a candid, pure skin that showed the blood easily.

"Is it George Fenton, the great engineer?" he asked once.

"Yes," said Mrs. Graham.

"Then it's Sir George—he got a knighthood last year."

"I hadn't heard." The mother spoke painfully. "It doesn't make any difference——"

The boy looked from one to the other shyly.

"He's very rich, isn't he?"

"I always heard so—he says himself that he is a very wealthy man."

"He wants to make me and Mercia his heirs?"

"Yes."

"Oh, why go over it?" asked Mercia impatiently. "Isn't it clear, James?"

"Yes. But it's startling. Such an utter surprise."

The boy's eyes sparkled as he spoke.

Mercia said sharply:

"There isn't any need to discuss it, is there?"

She was offended because James didn't instantly end the horrible matter, as she had called it, with indignation and scorn.

"I thought that you wanted it discussed." The boy looked shyly at his mother.

"So I did. I want you to think it over—but Mercia has made up her mind so completely she hates to hear anything more about it."

James appeared absorbed in earnest reflections.

"A man like that—a lot of money—it hardly seems possible," he murmured. "Why I was only thinking as I came along—how wonderful it would be if I could get that Exhibition—forty pounds a year for three years——"

"And so it would," broke in Mercia eagerly, "far more wonderful than any money you could get any other way——"

The boy still looked abstracted, hesitant.

"But what," he replied, "is forty pounds a year compared to a chance like this?"

"You haven't ever wanted money, never missed it!" cried Mercia hotly.

Mrs. Graham said quietly:

"Don't goad him, dear, he has a right to his own decision."

But Mercia repeated passionately:

"You've never missed not having money!"

"I don't know," said James slowly. "One put it out of one's mind, didn't dare to think about it."

Mrs. Graham caught her breath.

"Ah, I thought so. You've been afraid to speak, even to think, about our poverty?"

"I suppose one—just shut it away," admitted James reluctantly.

"But it is no use pretending——"

He paused. Mrs. Graham said quickly:

"I don't want you to pretend."

"Well, then, I'd *like* to have money—I think it would be marvellous—there's a lot of things one could do. It's no good pretending that money only buys horrible things, it buys beautiful things as well."

"You've thought about it?" said Mrs. Graham gently. "Well, here is a chance. Mr. Fenton, Sir George, is willing to adopt you—a chance."

The boy's blond, candid face glowed.

"Mother, can't we take it?"

Mercia did not allow her mother to answer.

"You're not thinking, James," she said impetuously. "It is a monstrous sacrifice you are asking of Mother, a frightful insult to Father—to get this money, these chances, for you, she's got to marry this man she hasn't seen for over twenty years, old, sick——"

"Lonely and sad too," added Mrs. Graham. "And as for your father——"

"Leave Father," said Mercia painfully.

James had looked from one woman to another, flushing, uneasy.

"If you put it like that," he muttered awkwardly.

His sister was ashamed for him; he seemed to her to have failed miserably when the right thing was so obvious and easy; he had done the wrong thing.

"You haven't thought about it," she urged. "You didn't mean what you said—why, you spoke as if you'd been hating our life here!"

"Perhaps," said Mrs. Graham, "he has hated it—everyone can't be as strong as you, Mercia, it would be only natural if James had found it very hard——"

Encouraged by his mother's sympathy the boy said defiantly:

"You couldn't call it easy, could you? I made up my mind not to squeal when I didn't see a way out, but now this chance comes along——"

"You've every right to take it," added Mrs. Graham.

"Not at the expense of our dignity, of Father's memory," cried Mercia passionately. "Why, it would make a mockery of the whole thing, scrap all our effort—all our endeavour, all our dreams, surely you wouldn't put it into the power of this stranger to buy our very souls—for that's what it comes to——"

"There are other ways of looking at it," said James stubbornly. "You're a bit hard."

Mercia turned on him angrily.

"That's always said of people who stick to their principles, if you don't take the easy way out you get hated—very well, I am hard. I'll never give in to putting a money value on this home, on our life, on our hopes—to just selling it all—for money!"

"It's for Mother to decide," replied the boy sullenly.

"How *can* there be any decision? Don't you see how repulsive the whole thing is?"

"No, I don't." James was defiant now. "I think that it would be a fine thing even for Mother. She's still young, and she's had a pretty rough time—I don't see why she shouldn't have a little ease and pleasure—it's silly to run down money." He began to speak quickly, passionately. "What is the alternative? Suppose we don't make successes? Don't get jobs even?"

"We shall, we shall!" cried Mercia.

"I'm not so sure. I haven't dared to think lately about how overcrowded everything is—and how hard for those who haven't got influence—I've woken up in the night, shuddering—seeing myself tramping the streets, looking for work——"

Mrs. Graham had listened intently to her children's hot contention; now she spoke:

"I've had those nightmares too, James. I've known for years that if rents or taxes or food got even a little higher we couldn't make it. For there is nothing we could cut out."

"That's it," said James sombrely, "nothing we could cut out. Not a holiday, a book, a theatre ticket, smokes—clothes all cut out long ago."

"I've thanked God on my knees," added Mrs. Graham, "that we had no illness—one illness would have sunk us."

"There would always have been something that I could do," said Mercia grandly.

"You've only just left off being a child," replied Mrs. Graham tenderly. "There wasn't anything an untrained woman and two children could do."

"Well, we pulled through"—the girl's bitter voice quivered now—"and I at least have been happy, haven't you?"

She demanded this, almost savagely, of the other two.

Both were silent.

Mercia added, in a panic:

"Has it all been a pretence, then?'

Mrs. Graham answered quickly:

"No, no, not a pretence. But to live like that, on the edge of things, wondering if you can do it."

"We did do it," said Mercia desperately, "and we were happy. Why did this man come along to spoil everything?"

"I don't see why anything should be spoilt," flung out James.

He rose from his narrow chair and left the room.

They heard his own door close.

Mercia turned instantly to her mother.

"There are things I can't say in front of James. Mother, you *can't*. Think how this man humiliated you. Think of Father, how he found you humiliated and in despair and rescued you—you *must* be loyal to him——"

Mrs. Graham shrank from this fierce pleading.

"Your father was so good, so wise, he understood everything," she murmured in a tired, sobbing voice. "He would have been very grateful for any good fortune for you and James."

"Not this good fortune."

"Mercia, when he was dying he reproached himself bitterly for leaving us with such scanty means—'I'd not any right to marry,' he said, 'but I counted on health and strength.' "

"He would not have married," said Mercia quietly, "if he had not found you in such distress."

"How do you know that?" asked Mrs. Graham, startled.

"I guess, knowing Father. He sacrificed his own peace of mind to you. He rescued you by a marriage he knew was improvident, even reckless, he took on that burden against his own principles, his own wisdom, and it killed him. Can't you be loyal to his memory?"

Mrs. Graham, her hands dropped in her lap, stared at her daughter.

Her daughter! This cold, pitiless young woman, so pale and noble, seemed alien to her in every way; hardly human even, an abstract Fate or Virtue.

"I've got to think of James," she replied faintly. "You heard what he said——"

"James is young, healthy, educated," said the quiet, menacing voice, "James can take his chance. There is no need for you to sacrifice yourself to James."

No answer.

"But I suppose," added Mercia, "that is what you intend to do."

Mrs. Graham spoke now, slowly:

"I suppose I might get behind that—sacrificing myself for James."

"Get behind?"

"Yes, but I want to be honest with you, Mercia," said Mrs. Graham faintly, wistfully. "You at least deserve that."

"Haven't we been honest, all this while?"

The mother moved wearily.

"You have, and James, I think, though there was one thing that James did not speak of—there's a girl he'd like to marry some day——"

"James!"

"Why not? He's over twenty. A fellow student, of course—he told me some time ago——"

"So you and James have secrets together!" cried Mercia in bitter surprise.

"You're so hard, Mercia, and it seemed so hopeless, James didn't want you to know. I ought not to have told you now but I thought that it would explain James's attitude to you."

A weary little pause of silence fell; both women moved restlessly; the white glare of the electric light seemed horrible; there was no escape in that unshaded light, in that bare plain room, from themselves, from each other.

They seemed in prison.

Mrs. Graham drooped in her chin, her thin hand over her thin face.

Mercia remained rigid, walking about, pausing here and there, but always, as she had been from the first, rigid.

"What did you mean about being honest with me, mother?"

"I meant I didn't want to pretend that I was tempted—because of James."

"You *are* tempted?"

"Yes, Mercia."

"You want to marry this man?"

Mrs. Graham pressed her hand closer over her eyes.

"I'm tired of poverty, afraid of it—I do want some ease, some comfort, some pleasure. It does tempt me, Mercia——"

The girl looked with wonder at the bent grey head.

"It would be wonderful to see James successful, happily married, to be able to spend money, to travel, to have pretty things——"

"Does that really tempt you?"

"It does. I was, I dare say you would never guess it, but I was a very frivolous, pleasure-loving girl—that part of me has been repressed all these years."

"It's all been a pretence, then, our happiness?"

"If you like to call it a pretence, Mercia," continued Mrs. Graham faintly. "I was never anything like the heroine you thought I was. As James said, I tried not to squeal——"

"But you hated it really?" put in the daughter's pitiless voice.

The mother responded to this by a colder tone.

"If you like to put it that way, Mercia. I never bothered you with this before. I did what I could. Now there is this chance to get away—I'd like to take it—not only for James's sake, for my own."

Mercia moved up and down the room with a bitter restlessness.

"You could never have cared for Father," she accused the drooping figure in the shabby chair. "You were just frightened I suppose and clutched at him, and then you had to go on pretending."

"Mercia, don't you think those are awful things for you to say to me?"

"I dare say, oh, I dare say! But if we don't get the truth now, where are we? In darkness."

"Oh, no, Mercia, don't look at it like that, do be tolerant——"

"I've said I can't be tolerant—about this."

The girl paused by the window; so sick and shaken by the storms and shocks of the last few hours that she could hardly control herself; for the first time in her serene life she knew what it was to feel the body overwhelmed by the misfortune of the soul.

Even the sharp agony of her father's death had been a noble, even an enthusiastic pain, the resolve to live as he would have wished, to travel successfully the thorny, narrow path he had left her on, had gilded her loss with exaltation.

But now there was no such compensation; this was a mere sordid collapse of what had seemed a lovely edifice; a stranger's breath had blown down the walls of her sanctified palace, showing the foundations to have been of sand, a stranger's breath had quenched the light on the altar in the Holy of Holies, showing that gleam to have been a common rush dip, not the glory of the sacred fire.

Her mother had been pretending, James had been pretending, just making the best of conditions they loathed.

Mrs. Graham turned, dropped her hand and gazed at her daughter's tortured face.

"You've always judged us too much by yourself, Mercia," she said gently, "by your own dreams. And, after all," she added timidly, "perhaps it was easier for you, with this great idealism you have, than it was for James and me—with our worldly souls."

"You were pretending," accused Mercia bitterly.

"Don't you think life is more difficult for those who have to pretend?"

Mrs. Graham rose; the discussion had become intolerable; nothing, of course, had been made lighter, nor clearer, nor easier by all this exchange of bitter words, so guarded, so low, so horrible.

Both the women were exhausted, both realised the helplessness of further speech, yet both knew that the essential things remained unsaid.

The words that would have justified one to the other remained locked in the heart of each.

"You're tired," said Mercia, "better go to bed. Perhaps in the morning—but I don't suppose that's much use, everything will be the same in the morning."

Mrs. Graham went to the door and paused there without answering.

"I shall stay here," continued the girl. "I shall go on living, just like this, just as I promised Father——"

"All alone, Mercia?"

"It seems I've been alone. All this time. Except for Father."

Mrs. Graham had one more thing to say.

"You're doing all this for love. Well, you might forgive us—James has got his girl, and I—George Fenton was the man I always loved—not my husband."

The girl turned and stared at her with eyes of fearful amaze.

"There was a desperate reason for my marriage as you seemed to guess. My husband was all that was fine and chivalrous and good and wise. But I always loved the other man and he knew it."

Mercia's stiff lips moved, but she did not speak, nor did Mrs. Graham seem to want any words of hers now.

"So I am being loyal too," she added. "After all these years of punishment, of penitence, I've a right to go where I've always been loyal in my soul."

"Punishment, penitence!" muttered Mercia.

"Do you think that it was anything? Living with a man who had sacrificed himself for you, who knew all about you, how small and weak you were, how you were crying out after the other one who had treated you so shamefully?"

"How could you have ever married—feeling that?" whispered Mercia.

"I was frightened. Silly. And a coward. My husband was a doctor. I first met him as a patient."

Mercia stared, stared at her mother's face which was like ashes, so faint, so grey, so lifeless.

"Why do you say 'my husband'?" asked the girl.

Mrs. Graham answered:

"I've got something to show you," and left the room.

Mercia remained at the window.

A crowd with flags.

The memory of that motley hoard trailing round the Park assailed her misery—that random procession with floating rags on which were inscribed their symbols, their hopes, their delusions! They were all of them the same, pressing forward aimlessly, eagerly, carrying banners inscribed with lies.

She as well as the others—she even more blindly than the others.

Her mother had been tramping doggedly towards a letter that had come, James had trudged towards love and success which would be his, but she, with Chimera on her banner, had chased Chimers and walked headlong into a pit.

A crowd with flags.

Mrs. Graham came back into the room; she held a photograph against her breast; Mercia could read the photographer's name, in long gilt letters on a shiny background.

"This is George Fenton's portrait," said Mrs. Graham. "I wanted you to see that I've had it, all these years."

She paused, peered into her daughter's face across the room.

"I had an impulse to show it to you—I don't think I will."

Mercia smiled in her exceeding pain

"I know. It's too like me. Never mind."

"I thought," supplicated Mrs. Graham, "it might make you come with us—where you belong——"

Mercia shook her head.

"It doesn't make any difference. You didn't love—Dr. Graham—I did. He got that out of it, anyhow."

A crowd with flags; a medley pressing on in a confusion with tattered banners inscribed with lies and delusions.

And sometimes the glittering truth.

"I loved him, anyhow."

# THE CAREFUL YOUTH
## A NEW VERSION OF THE INDUSTRIOUS AND IDLE APPRENTICE

ROBERT Dacre was glad that his name *was* Robert Dacre; it sounded well, and it looked well when written down. It was a little piece of good luck, and he could congratulate himself that there were, in his own opinion, at least, several little bits of good luck about his person and his character. He was nice-looking, for instance, and every one admitted that he was nice-mannered; he had been successful at school, though more with the masters than with the boys, and he had never given any trouble at home. No one could have ventured to call him a prig, or effeminate, for he had a fine, manly appearance; and it was really very fortunate and gratifying to think he had been so well-favoured by the gods and so much appreciated by his fellow-mortals.

He had no vices. He thought vices silly, and always had his eye on the consequences. No doubt he was not very gifted, and he certainly was not very rich; so far he had had to work quite hard for a humble livelihood, but he felt confident that fortune would smile on him—and before very long. He was such a universal favourite, and every one had so many kind words for him and so many pleasant prophecies as to his future.

His home life had been rather arid; his mother had married again, and though there was no question of the justice and kindness of his stepfather, still it rather (as Robert put it to himself) " 'loosened things out.' You didn't feel there was so very much call to a home where you had a stepfather, and no brothers or sisters." He was rather glad of that too; he had seen too many other fellows hampered, sometimes almost ruined, by the calls of some insistent affection of mother or father, or brother or sister. After all, if you looked at it in a level-headed sort of way, it was better to be quite free of all that sort of thing. In his case, now, he had nothing to worry about but himself. Sentiment apart (and sentiment, of course, was really all nonsense), who could deny that that was a very satisfactory state of affairs?

Robert could spend all his spare time and all his spare cash, not on enjoying himself, as more vulgar youths under these felicitous circumstances might have done, but on improving himself. He was an articled pupil in the office of a quite influential engineer, and had nearly finished the three years of his training. He lodged with some very quiet, genteel sort of people; he went to evening classes and lectures, and was always extremely careful to buy the right sort of clothes and cultivate the right sort of accent—not in a self-conscious sort of way, but carelessly and as if these things were his by right; and of course they were not really quite his by right, for Robert belonged for precisely that class where attempts at self-improvement may be taken as presumption by the really superior people who do not need to improve themselves, since they belong to a society where all faults are forgiven.

Robert didn't.

He really owed all his present advantages to himself, and of course that is rather unforgivable in the eyes of a good many of just those kind of people whose acquaintance Robert wished to cultivate.

His fellow pupils and the clerks in the office looked up to him with rather sulky, envious deference, but Robert was very careful not to allow this to turn his head or fill him with undue arrogance. He reminded himself, with commendable prudence, that one should never rely on the admiration of one's inferiors.

Cautious as he was, however, he permitted himself to be elated by the very gratifying notice of Mr. Forter, the engineer in whose office he worked. Mr. Forter really seemed to think a good deal of him, and Robert exerted himself strenuously to deserve this happy turn of fortune.

It had been the same at school: he always seemed to have the luck to attract the approbation of those older and wiser than himself; he didn't quite know how he did it, and he hoped it wouldn't make him stuffy or smug; but of course it was a very useful asset, and he cultivated it with extreme diligence. Mr. Forter was a precise sort of man—a widower, and very well-off. He read the classics and was meticulous in his person. He belonged to one or two or those clubs which always seemed to Robert the very zenith of correctness and exclusiveness, and he appeared to passionately appreciate prudence and industry in youth. He considered the times in which he lived almost unspeakably degenerate, and every symptom of disorder and folly which he perceived (and the daily papers in which he indulged took good care that many such symptoms should be brought to his notice) called forth from him measured but bitter condemnation.

In the face of this very pronounced attitude on the part of Mr. Forter, Robert rather wondered how Elsie Wylie got into the office; for she certainly was very typical of the frivolity of the times against which Mr. Forter was always using his decorous invective. But then, perhaps (Robert argued) Mr. Forter didn't notice Elsie at all. To him she was just part of her machine. She contrived somehow—a miracle it seemed to Robert—to be a good typist, and perhaps that was all that Mr. Forter demanded. Perhaps he was able to overlook the blatant flimsiness of Elsie in the blatant solidity of the machine behind which she sat.

Robert couldn't. He was in the office too much and sat too near to Elsie too often.

Elsie was about nineteen, and common; common in just the same sort of way as Robert would have been if he hadn't been so prudent and careful.

Elsie was neither prudent not careful; she was just exactly as common as she had always been meant to be. She was also extremely pretty—"like a chocolate box," Robert would say to himself. For Robert rather dealt in *clichés*, despite the evening classes and the lectures on English literature that he so sedulously attended. And yet, when you came to argue the matter out in a logical manner, didn't they always put the most charming of faces on chocolate boxes? And wouldn't most girls be simply delighted to look exactly like those sirens who smiled out between the bows of ribbon in the confectioners' shops?

Elsie was fair. Her shingled locks were beginning to grow.[64] She had copied the very newest fashion out of the picture page of one of the evening papers, and underneath an imitation tortoiseshell comb genuine golden curls were twisted upwards in quite an entrancing manner. Elsie had blue eyes—quite unstrained, unshadowed blue eyes—and most delicious features, and a charming colouring of cream and roses, thought Robert, dropping into *clichés* again; and yet he really could think of no other words that so exactly expressed Elsie's fragrant loveliness.

She had no sense, and the worst of taste. She bought far too many cheap hats; but she knew how to drag them on at a most becoming angle. She also wore pearls that you can buy by the yard; but there's no doubt that they looked very delightful round her charming throat.

---

64 A shingle cut is a very short bobbed hairstyle.

Elsie went to all the dances and "movies"—hideous word to Robert—that she could afford, or to which she could induce anyone to take her. She always had a trashy novel in her bag; she used a quite unnecessary lipstick and experimented in the less expensive perfumes. Robert was convinced that she didn't go to night clubs purely through lack of opportunity, and on one regrettable occasion, when he chanced into the same teashop, he had seen her drinking ginger-ale at four o'clock in the afternoon with an air as if she raised a cocktail. Robert, who knew it was a great mistake to be "superior," gave Elsie her good points and tried to be tolerant towards her defects. The girl seemed kind-hearted, and she certainly enjoyed herself. An atmosphere of happiness and pleasure surrounded the shallowness of Elsie. She did her job not only efficiently, but cheerfully. She kept her cigarettes and chocolates dutifully out of the office. Robert wished she could have kept her own provoking person out of the office. There was no doubt that she disturbed him. And of course it was quite ridiculous for a youth like Robert to be disturbed by a girl like Elsie; especially just now, when Mr. Forter was taking so much notice of him—even asking him down to his place on the river where he stayed in the spring, and introducing him to his daughter and heiress, Winifred.

Robert had thought a great deal about Winifred even before he had met her. A promising youth who has been commended by his master can hardly help thinking about that master's daughter. Wasn't it a very, very old story—the industrious apprentice and the rich master's charming child? Only—as so often and so unfortunately happens—real life was not quite so pleasant as the romance.

Winifred Forter was not charming. She was too tall, wore glasses and had a Degree in Domestic Science. Like Robert himself, she had done all she could to improve her natural abilities; but, unlike Robert, she had scorned to improve her natural appearance. While his thick locks showed a becoming permanent wave, Winifred Forter had cropped hers into her neck and let them hang. She represented, however, all that towards which Robert had striven so persistently and so laboriously: culture, leisure, easy means. She had travelled; she could ride, manage a boat, swim, play tennis excellently. She had graceful manners and a fund of intelligent conversation. What a pity that she was not as pretty as Elsie, and what a pity that he had to be sorry that she wasn't as pretty as Elsie! The worse pity of the two, that he, on the plane to which he had raised himself, should ever have noticed that Winifred Forter did not possess cheap and superficial attractions! He reminded himself continuously that beauty is but skin deep, and was annoyed that the reflection would always follow, without his own volition, that the skin is very important, and if you get as deep as that it's about as deep as you often need to get; especially in a girl!

His pride became more and more gratified by the continued kindness of the Forters. Robert tried to persuade himself that Winifred was really not so plain: if it hadn't been for that drab whiteness of her complexion and those rather ashy-looking eyes behind the glasses, the lightness of her hair that was rather the tint of dead grass—well, she might have been quite a presentable young woman; and Robert, the more frequently that he was a visitor at that charming house at Maidenhead, tried to persuade himself, with a certain fierce determination, that not only *might* she be a presentable young woman, but she actually *was* so; for as that very gratifying spring unfolded itself he was convinced that she favoured him, and that her father wished her to favour him.

"What an excellent match it would be!" thought Robert. He would inherit the fortune and the business; a well-planned, easy, honourable career straight ahead of him. At one step he would have moved into competence, and those upper circles which he had always gazed at with longing and envious eyes. He was really very fortunate—almost as fortunate, he reminded himself, as he deserved to be. One didn't want to be priggish or conceited, but after all he was really a very good-looking, amiable young man, industrious and clever, without a single vice, and he had taken a very great deal of pains with himself. Even with all her financial advantages, Winifred Forter wasn't exactly the kind of girl that a young man like himself would be liable to lose his head over. She might, he reminded himself, consider herself almost as lucky as he considered himself. Of course nothing was settled yet. They had been to tennis parties and tea parties together, and up the river, and to lectures; and her father had smiled on these proceedings. Robert's work was really very good, and Mr. Forter declared that a really steady, domesticated young man of presentable appearance and courteous manners was extremely difficult, in these wretched, decayed days, to find. In one genial moment he had even hinted quite broadly that he would not be ill-pleased to see Robert, after he had served a sufficient apprenticeship in work and love, installed as his partner and son-in-law.

Meanwhile Robert had a great deal of clerical work to do, and was bound to see rather too much of Elsie. To keep this young woman in her place—for she was, in her free way, a great deal too familiar—Robert contrived casually to remark on the frequency of his visits to the Forters.

This move did not seem to have much effect.

"I've seen her," smiled Elsie, and made no further comment.

Robert, exasperated, could not resist handing Elsie marked copies of papers and magazines in which a retired clergyman, making a good deal of money out of journalism, lamented the decadence of modern femininity and pointed out the horrors of short skirts, open blouses, cropped hair, jazz and the loss of the chaperone.

What impression this made on Elsie he did not know, for she offered no comment whatever; but one day, after he had laid silently on her typewriter a peculiarly pungent article entitled "Modern Jezebels," she asked him if he would take her out to a dance that evening, as her young man, she added casually, had "fallen through."

Robert stifled a temptation to reply "Fallen through what?" and pleaded, with correct courtesy, a prior engagement.

"Going to a lecture?" asked Elsie.

And Robert smiled in a manner that he strove to render compassionate, as if the impertinence of Elsie were really beneath his notice.

It was a lovely spring, even in London. There was hardly a street that was not adorned by packed baskets of flowers, in the arms of hawkers or standing on the kerbs. The parks were misty with young green, and sharp with the new fragrance of the bells of daffodil and hyacinth.

Elsie always had violets by her typewriter, and sometimes violets at her breast. There were flowers in the Forters' drawing-room too; but they were brought in from a conservatory and were somehow different. Robert vaguely felt the spring to be out of tune with his affair with the Forters—an *obbligato* that did not fit with the melody.[65] Could it be the plainness of Winifred that was wrong? She said she disliked the spring, and preferred the autumn, and

---

[65] *Obbligato:* an essential but subordinate instrumental part of a piece of music that must not be omitted.

complained of the long, bleak, lightish evenings, which Robert could not help feeling full of a beckoning wind and an enticing perfume.

One evening he happened to come into the office to fetch some drawings just as Elsie was locking up her typewriter. He paused beside her without being able in the least to help it. She wore a hat and a dress of a colour that he had always found peculiarly seductive—a pale lily-of-the-valley green—and a quite absurd grey silk coat; but in that twilight, with the dewy violets in her hand, she could hardly have looked more entrancing if she had been exquisitely gowned in the most expensive materials. The cheapness of her attire did not matter in the least—not even to Robert, sedulously cultivated as was his taste. Why must he think to himself "I've nothing to do this evening"? Of course he'd something to do! Wasn't there always work—self-improvement—study? He lingered and hesitated. One ought to be sorry for Elsie; poor little thing, what was going to be the end of her? No one would marry her, of course: inefficient, untrained, silly, good for nothing but to amuse herself and thump a typewriter.

"Lovely evening," she remarked, looking up.

Yes, it was a lovely evening. He had noticed that himself. Such a pellucid sky above the darkness of the houses! Such a crystal slip of moon rising above the straight lines of the chimney pots! Such an odour of the spring, and the streets so deliciously filled with twilight shadows!

"You don't seem in a hurry," smiled Elsie.

And he said stiffly:

"Are you doing anything to-night?"

"I don't know yet," she replied pertly. "Is that your way of asking me out, Mr. Dacre?"

"We might go somewhere," said Robert, thinking instantly

that after all no one need ever know; and after all it was part of life, wasn't it, even for the best of young men, just occasionally to amuse themselves with girls like Elsie? No wild oats, of course, but just a cautious surveying of the ground where they might possibly have been sown . . . the "movies," as she called them, for instance, or a dance hall, or——

"Let's go to the pictures!" Elsie interrupted his thoughts perfectly casually, as if there was nothing in such an episode. "I haven't seen 'Flaming Hearts' yet; we might go there. I don't suppose it's up to much, but it passes the time."

Robert wanted to say how utterly he scorned such places.

"There's a dance-room there too," said Elsie, "and you can get supper. Let's go—it'll be fun!" And she gave the young man a look which plainly showed him that she found him desirable. Such a different look from the glances with which Winifred Forter had told him she did not regard him with disfavour!

"All right," he said stiffly; and he was at once involved in a picture of the cinema house; the warm, yellowish dark; the smoke; the smell of the disinfectants—sweetish, strong; the sense of dust and perfume; the muggy heat; and the voluptuous pictures—embraces, kisses, clinging arms, pressing hands, human bodies viewed from all possible angles—beautiful, seductive, always making love . . . that had been *his* impression of the cinema the few times he had been. There was no doubt that there was a sort of heady effect about it, and with Elsie beside him—Elsie in her thin silks, with her violets wilting in the heat, and those little yellow curls at the nape of her neck, and her blue eyes; Elsie with her white fingers busy with a box of chocolates, happy, graceful, yielding . . . What a cheap temptation for a young man like Robert to be assailed with! Go home and study!

The girl's eyes forbade this withdrawal. He yielded, as many have yielded before, out of a fear of looking a fool in the eyes of an inferior. Already she seemed to mock him as much as to say, "You don't dare!" And that was enough for Robert. They found themselves in the street together, and Elsie did not disguise her gratification and her admiration of her handsome cavalier.

Of course she soon proved herself even more distressingly ignorant and stupid than he had thought she was. Yet there was a certain native shrewdness about her that prevented him from setting her down as altogether a fool. He shuddered to think of the fate in store for the man who would be infatuated enough to marry Elsie.

He spoke of the Forters rather mechanically. He said what extraordinarily nice people they were, and how extraordinarily kind they had been to him; how charming and cultured Winifred was. Elsie cut in cheerfully and said yes, old Forter wasn't a bad sort if you took him in the right way, and as for Winifred, she dared say she couldn't help her face, poor girl!

Robert said stiffly that Miss Forter had considerable charm, and Elsie said well, yes, she supposed that was what you *did* say about people when you couldn't say anything else kind! The Imperial, which was showing "Flaming Hearts," proved to be a much more gorgeous affair than Robert had ever imagined. It all might be—and no doubt was—in the very worst of taste, and yet he could not deny that it was imposing and effective: so many gilt pillars, so many vast mirrors, so many clustering lights and so many pretty girls, haughty and aloof in grotesque uniforms, selling programmes, and such a very loud and harmonious orchestra; and then, such comfortable seats, and such an air of being a patron, of having paid for the best and having got it . . .

Elsie accepted chocolates as a matter of course. He noticed that, in contradiction to all the medical articles he had ever read, despite her smoking and sweet-eating her teeth were remarkably good.

As soon as the sumptuous lights went down the couple in front at once passed their arms round each other's waists, and Robert wondered if he should do the same with Elsie; but no doubt the other two were engaged, or going to be . . . and he blushed at the effrontery of his own thoughts. Good gracious, if he wasn't careful he would find himself really involved! He must cling firmly to his principles and the thought of the future in store for him with the Forters.

He had heard Winifred Forter speak of the cinema passion as "a manifestation of the pleasure-loving tendency of the age," and he must remember it in that light. He secretly thought, however, that the film shown was, despite its absurd title, extremely good. Of the beauty of the female stars there could be no doubt, although in the close-ups their paint was rather plain.

Elsie kept up a running fire of acute and slightly contemptuous criticisms, yet she was obviously enjoying herself. In the interval she had ices, and criticized all the other girls whom she could perceive through the smoky atmosphere with good nature but penetration.

After the film was over she suggested dancing, and Robert didn't know how to dance. And his efforts to appear unashamed of this fact made him rather disagreeable. He would certainly have liked very much to dance with Elsie; he couldn't imagine ever wanting to dance with Winifred—and there seemed something wrong there somehow. Was it altogether wise, he put to his slightly muddled brain, to want to marry a woman with whom you didn't want to dance? He tried to steady himself by the anchor labelled "Intellectual Affinity." He would be bored with Elsie in a week, and surely it must be the devil who was whispering to him that it would be a good first week—a rather worth-while week!

He had noticed that she was one of the prettiest girls there, and a good many other young men were glancing at her: cheap, common young men of course . . . Robert Dacre felt a dreadful cheapness and commonness himself to-night, exactly as if this were where he belonged—a sort of "coming-home" feeling. How genial and pleasant everything was after those dull evenings studying in his own room, attending classes or lectures, or spent in the arid company of Winifred!

They went to look at the dancing despite his protests; and he hated vehemently all the other youths who were able to sail with such a negligent air across the polished floor, carelessly holding some adoring girl. Elsie would have looked like that at him if he had been able to dance with her . . . . She was just the right height too; they would have been quite the handsomest couple in the room. And he resolved that he would have dancing lessons on the morrow. After all, as a man of the world—and he hoped that quite soon he could call himself a man of the world—he ought to know how to dance; and it didn't look difficult either.

Winifred Forter had always smiled wearily when dancing was mentioned, and Robert caught himself in the ungenerous thought that perhaps this was because she was by no means sure of partners.

They left at last, and Elsie said that it had been a pleasant evening. He thought this was, in the circumstances, very kind of her, and he stopped and bought her flowers from an old woman standing by the station who had still a huge basket of red and cream-coloured roses.

He had never been so extravagant with flowers before, for he had not thought it "quite the thing" to give floral offerings to

Winifred Forter; but he bought shillingsworths now of these stiff foreign roses with the long stems, and felt a remarkable pleasure in putting them into Elsie's pretty arms.

She accepted the charming gift without embarrassment. He saw her home, and on the doorstep she said: "Good night, and thank you!" quite frankly.

Robert went home wondering.

The morning brought discretion, of course; but for several days he slackened in his attentions to Winifred Forter. Somehow he couldn't bring himself to go down to see her, or to meet her in town. Even when Mr. Forter began to look rather dry and glacial still Robert couldn't quite bring himself. He meant to in the end, of course; he meant to seize this golden opportunity. But he was content to let it dangle within his reach just a little longer. After all, he was sure of Winifred. He had, of course, his ready excuses: he was studying hard, he had had to visit relations. Meanwhile he was taking surreptitious dancing lessons, and occasionally escorting Elsie out in the evenings; occasionally, for she did not seem free very often.

Once he asked her to kiss him, but she replied placidly: "Well, I don't suppose it would hurt either of us," and without passion, allowed him to kiss her. "It's all very well for her," he thought grimly. "I dare say she's used to it; but if one isn't——" He drew back from the abyss of temptation.

He intended on the next Saturday to call on Winifred Forter with flowers and excuses. He ventured on the flowers now, for his brief but vivid experiences with Elsie had given him more confidence in his dealings with women. These were not blooms bought in the street, of course, but really expensive flowers from a florist. Rather silly to take them to her when she grew them herself, but still he felt it was the right gesture; and, laden with his frail exotics, he presented himself in the pleasant drawing-room of the riverside house determined to devote himself, in the immediate future at least, exclusively to Winifred Forter, and not, in the immediate future at least, take Else out again.

Winifred was playing cards with a lean and hungry-looking young man who cut an odious figure, Robert thought, in flannels, and was, he knew, a University Extension Lecturer whose acquaintance they had mutually made a few months ago. Robert did not admire him as much as he had once done, and did not think with the same enthusiasm of the hobby they had once shared—that for prehistoric remains.

Winifred received him coldly, though she was gratified by the gift of the flowers. Though it was so early in the year she had contrived to become unpleasantly sunburnt. She was that kind of girl. And her tennis frock was too short and too skimpy, and made her appear as if she had more joints than is usual in the human anatomy. Elsie, now, seemed put together by curves, not by hinges! Still, Robert reminded himself sharply, he must not think of these stupid comparisons. He decided he had better quench his wandering thoughts by an instant proposal to Winifred Forter.

He did not have an immediate opportunity, however, for the other young man lingered and monopolized both Winifred and the conversation.

Winifred devoted herself to this raw-boned fellow with such enthusiasm that Robert began almost to suspect that spies had been at work. Yet, of course, that was impossible; Elsie and Winifred moved in such different worlds that at no possible point could they touch; and, conscious of his immense superiority over this unattractive rival, he patiently bided his time: but in vain. When the young man, replete with tea and admiration, at length left,

Winifred remarked—not without a flash of malice—that she was engaged to him, and "quite the happiest girl in the world"; and didn't Mr. Dacre think he was delightful?

Pride enabled Robert to bear this shattering blow with some equanimity. He told himself that never had she looked plainer. He was quite sure that, if she had known he was going to propose marriage, she would have allowed him to do so for the mere gratification of her vanity; and he congratulated himself on this escape. Of course on his return to London his sense of defeat was bitter in his mind—a big loss too. That abominable, scrawny wretch would come into the Forter fortune; things wouldn't be quite so easy for him, Robert Dacre, as he had hoped they might be. But there was Elsie . . . . Of course he couldn't marry Elsie; he'd have to marry a woman who could help him along—an intelligent woman with a little money; but meanwhile he might "go about" with Elsie. Winifred had no call on him now, he thought viciously; and he needn't be so careful not to offend Mr. Forter's old-fashioned susceptibilities. Already Robert had begun to call them "old-fashioned."

He regretted the money he had spent on the flowers for Winifred, and wished he had laid it out for Elsie, and he began to dream fatuously that perhaps, with time and goodwill, one might educate and polish Elsie—subdue her cheapness and commonness.

He called at her modest home on the Sunday, but she was out. He felt a pang of jealousy.

On Monday morning she was at her place with an even more than usually large bunch of violets beside her typewriter.

For the first time he wondered if she bought these violets for herself, or if he had one (or perhaps several) rivals. She certainly went out a good deal; but then they said nowadays this didn't mean anything to girls.

When he stopped to speak to her he found, to his amazement, that she knew of Winifred Forter's engagement.

"I hope," she said frankly, "it isn't because you've been taking me out. You never know with that sort, do you? I certainly thought you had a good chance there; and I hope I haven't spoiled it," she added with a friendly smile.

Robert hated this, but laughed airily, and suggested that they should go out somewhere that evening with as casual an air as he could command.

Elsie fluttered a hand on which showed a big diamond.

"I can't go out with you any more," she said candidly. "I'm engaged now—'the happiest girl in the world': isn't that what one ought to say? I want to finish my week's work here, and then—goodbye to girlie!"

"You're engaged too?" asked Robert with a sinking heart.

"Yes—didn't you see it coming on?" she smiled. "He's been paying me a lot of attention, though he liked to keep it quiet. These are his violets I always have here. A pretty thought, wasn't it?" said the wretched girl, with a sentimental look. "Last night we settled it all, and he spoke to Mother and Father. He's taking me to the Riviera and buying me lots of pretty clothes; and, now that Winifred's going to get married, it won't matter—we shall be all to ourselves. Of course he's a bit old, but I always said he was a good sort if you knew how to manage him."

"To whom are you referring?" asked Robert icily.

"Why, to Mr. Forter, of course!" said Elsie, tossing her head. "A girl's got her value nowadays, I can tell you. Fooling about is all very well, but I want to settle down."

Robert passed into the next room. He felt that he understood very little of human character and human motives. Mr. Forter and that little fool! She to enjoy the fortune that he had worked for, that he, with all his industry and fortune, deserved, and after all that Mr. Forter had said too . . .

Robert felt that something was very wrong somewhere.

# THE WALL

ELISA and her mother hated the wall; it was a symbol of oppression and cruelty—indeed, of all the misfortunes of their lives.

It blocked out light and air and came so close to the back of the house that there was only space for a tiny court, so sunless that nothing would grow there.

The front of the house had always been dark, for it looked on to the street, and the house opposite was only an arm's breadth away, and so since the wall had been built the whole dwelling was in perpetual shadow.

There had been once gardens, olive slopes, and stretches of maize and rice, peach and almond trees and a low pergola of vines to be seen from the back windows of the house of the Pesetti. All this had been sold to an American firm, who had swept away everything to establish a stonemason's yard, and who had raised the great wall to shut out the untidy row of little houses that made such a poor background for the statuary.

The Pesetti had not reckoned on the wall when they sold the land, but they could do nothing but console themselves with the thought that they had made a proviso that they might buy back the land whenever they wished. To Elisa and her mother this was the golden prospect that kept them patient and even cheerful in their hopeless poverty—this prospect of the day when they would buy back the land, pull down the wall and let daylight into their lives again.

When Antonio Pesetti had died, revealing the ruin of his affairs, the two men most concerned, Ercole, his son, and Araldo

Giacosa, who was betrothed to Elisa, had gone to America to seek their fortune. Both knew something of farming, and were confident of returning in a very short time with sufficient funds to re-establish the Pesetti family. The proceeds of the sale of the land paid off most of the debts, the bottom of the little house was let off as a barber's shop, and mother and daughter lived in the three dark rooms overhead.

They earned their living by fine needlework and lace-making, supplying several shops in Viareggio, and even Florence, with the beautiful embroideries so eagerly bought by the foreign visitors.

Journeys to Viareggio in the tram with a parcel of work were the only breaks in the monotony of their eventless lives; the letters from the Argentine the only excitement.

At first Elisa had suffered in a way that seemed to her incredible: the postponement of her wedding, the departure of her lover, the ruin symbolized by the wall at which she stared out, stared daily—the bitterness of these things was not to be expressed in words.

She was twenty years old, and she wanted to die; but her mother's resignation, her mother's hope, piety and courage had supported her, and finally brought her to the same mood, agonized but quiescent, and shot with gleams of breathless hope. Of course the men would not be away long; fortunes were quickly made in the Argentine. The first letters home were full of ardour and certain success; they would come back in a year—at most two—and the wall would be pulled down . . . .

Ercole's room was kept ready for him; it was the large one overlooking the street. He would not care, even for a night, his mother said, to sleep in the shadow of the wall.

Every day his room was swept and dusted and made ready; there were so many instances of men returning unexpectedly from

America—coming from Leghorn without even a day's notice. The best furniture had been sold with the land, but the most decent of what remained was arranged in the chamber of Ercole.

There was an iron bedstead with three painted pictures of Alpine scenes in three medallions at the top, with home-bleached sheets and a large white-thread crochet quilt mounted over yellow satin; a string mat, stamped with an elephant, in red and green, on the tiled floor; a marble topped table by the bed; a chest of drawers and two Austrian bent-wood chairs. On the walls hung two prints of Garibaldi and a German lithograph of the Madonna in crude colours, after no known painter. Every morning Elisa put fresh water in the bottle on the side table, dusted the candle and the match-box in the tin stick, and every *festa*, when she returned from Mass, she brought in a gaudy little vase packed with odd flowers and set it on the chest of drawers.[66]

To look after this room was the pleasantest of the occupations of these two women; it seemed to bring that delightful home-coming so much nearer, to make the return of good fortune clear and certain. When Elisa smoothed the pillow and the turned-over sheet, when she sent the clear water babbling into the bottle, when she placed her little bouquet on the varnished top of the cheap chest of drawers, she was conscious of a sensation of almost positive happiness. At Eastertide, after the priest had blessed the room, the mother fastened up the strip of blessed palm above the bedstead and felt the place sanctified. But it was only a small portion of the day that they could spend in this pleasant manner; their lives were passed at the back in the shadow of the wall.

In one room they slept, kept their few clothes and the relics

---

[66] *Festa:* a festival or feast day.

saved from happy times; in the other they cooked and fed and worked.

There were two hard chairs and a table, a small desk, two *scaldin* and a little cooking stove, a shelf of pots and pans, a looking-glass, a work table and a long coffer for the sewing materials, a glass-fronted cupboard, a few framed photographs and little coloured cards of saints given away on *festa*.[67]

The women needed to sit very near the window to work, so completely did the wall shadow the room; the lamp had to be lit very early in the evening, and in the winter in the mornings, while they sat over the embroidery sipping their first cup of coffee.

They were glad when they could draw the shabby curtains and shut out the wall; better the thick yellow glow of the little lamp than the murky light that the wall would allow to filter into the room.

The slavery of this constant needlework was the salvation of the two women, for it provided a source of endless interest. Elisa began to design her own patterns, tracing them with a lead pencil direct on to the cambric or linen.

There were the designs in the monthly women's papers, and those given them by the ladies at the shops in Viareggio, and Elisa took pleasure in all of them, but most in those of her own invention. She learnt every variety of stitch and pattern, and her earnings became as high as it was possible for them to be in this field of labour; yet they were never sufficient to lift her existence from the dull and well-ordered poverty. The mother began to suffer with cramp in her hands, and often could not work at all; but even their all-united efforts brought in but a few francs a week. The barber's rent just paid the taxes on the house and the weekly offering to the church, and perhaps the bunch of flowers for the chamber of Ercole.

---

[67] *Scaldin*: scaldini, earthenware braziers.

They had no friends; gradually it became that they had no acquaintances. Though they knew every one in the little town by sight and by name their life was too self-centred, too absorbed in inner interests, for them to have anything to give or to receive from outsiders.

So the existence of these two women became one of complete isolation in the midst of friendly neighbours and the even life of the little town. Days, weeks, months, years became one like another; there was nothing to mark the passage of time but the change of season. The letters from the Argentine came regularly; they were always full of hope, but hope deferred; there was always some good reason why it was useless to think of an immediate return. It took longer than one thought to accumulate a fortune, and what was the use of a home-coming without? Meanwhile they were doing well and saving . . . . They might send good news any moment. "What more can you expect?" asked the mother placidly.

And after a time Elisa began to feel placid too—even happy.

Yes, in this curious confined existence there was even happiness—a thousand little pleasures, keen and delightful.

The cup of hot coffee in the morning, the preparing of the tasty midday meal, the soups in winter, the salads in summer, the journeys into Viareggio, that long tram ride between the sea and the mountains, the glimpse of the shops and cafés in the big town, the evenings round the cheerful lamp, the Sundays listening to the comfortable words of the priest, with perhaps a walk up through the olive groves in the afternoon, or down to the sea at Fiumetto.

And there were always the long soothing talks and discussions that gave a delightful sense of preparation for something wonderful . . . . What they would do when the men returned, when the wall was pulled down . . . . The house would be painted, the barber turned out, the garden, the vineyard replanted. This would be the town house, and then they would buy a farm in the *pianura* and perhaps build a cottage at Fiumetto, like all the well-to-do people of Pietrasanta.[68]

The letters from America always provided cheerful food for their discussions; the two men were really doing very well, and hoped soon to have saved enough to buy a little *estancia* of their own, which they would work up and sell for enough money to bring them home triumphant.[69] Elisa was making her *corredo;* already it filled every drawer in the little bedroom: sheets, pillow cases, coverlets, towels, added to whenever there was a spare franc, all worked with "E" and "A" for Elisa and Araldo, surrounded by a spray of violets.[70]

She did this embroidery when she could snatch a moment from her paid labours; her mother sewed the buttonholes and tapes and made slowly an elaborate crochet quilt with thread as fine as a spider's web. "The longer Araldo stays away the finer the *corredo* will be," was the jest between them.

Every year Elisa became happier. For one thing, she enjoyed more and more the dictates of King Custom; for another, did not every year bring her nearer to the end of her waiting?

She was just as pretty as she had ever been; she was sure of that, for she would often look in the little glass above the work coffer. Yes, her hair was just as dark and thick, her eyes just as bright, her skin just as clear. He would find no change in her any

---

68 *Pianura:* lowlands.

69 *Estancia:* a horse or cattle ranch.

70 *Corredo:* trousseau.

more than she found any in the suit of *turchino* and high buttoned boots she kept so carefully cherished.[71] She had worn them on that momentous day when she had gone with her mother as far as Pisa to see Araldo and her brother off on their journey.

In those day-dreams which were her chief joy she often saw those two kind, eager faces, those two strong, alert figures; they wove themselves into the patterns of her embroideries—as knights pursuing the dragons in the "Point de Venice"; as hunters and men-at-arms in the "Richelieu work"; as the riders on dolphins and the courtiers and shepherds in the *filet* that was so difficult and so tedious.

After a while it was not these figures that interested her so much as the other details of the design—the garlands of flowers, the baskets of fruit, the sprays of foliage, the curling arabesques.

These led her fancy down strange and delicious paths that the wall could not block out: to cool caves of white coral beneath the green sea, to forests full of ferns and violets, to castles on high hills with banners over the portals, to boats floating on purple lakes, to orchards laden with magnificent fruit, and lofty trees where birds sang perpetually; all these things and more did she find in the delicate scrolls and twists of her frail embroideries.

It was hateful to lift one's eyes from these day-dreams and to see the wall blotting out light and air and filling the room with shadow . . . . Better to sit all day till one's shoulders ached and one's arms were stiff, and hardly look up at all till the blinds were drawn and the lamp lit. One day her eyes began to hurt and the work to become quite blurred; she had to go to the hospital.

"You are working in a half-light," the doctor told her. "You must rest your eyes for a while at least."

[71] *Turchino:* deep blue.

But she had to work all the harder to pay for the pair of glasses that he ordered.

The mother was doing less and less now; she would busy herself with the *risotto* and the *minestrone*, with sweeping and cleaning Ercole's room and turning over the white piles of the *corredo.*

"You should use that front room instead of blinding yourself at the back as you do," the barber told her.

"And my son? He might return any moment, even unawares like Silvestro Picci did, and what am I to say if he finds that his room isn't ready?"

"But he is away such a long time, your son."

"He will soon be back now, and then we shall pull the wall down and the whole house will be light."

The yard behind the house was not used now; the firm had another nearer the marble quarries, and trade not being very good there were not enough workmen for this; empty it remained, therefore, saving for blocks of marble and some half-finished statues, and the two women were no loner annoyed by the sound of sawing and hammering, shouting and laughing from behind the hated wall. But the wall itself was still there, unchanged, shutting out the sun and the mountains, making a deep shadow in the two little rooms.

"I begin to forget what the view was," said the mother.

"You will soon see it again," smiled the daughter. "See how Araldo writes—the *estancia* is paying well."

The letters did not come now as frequently as formerly, but neither of them noticed that, for they were not looking out for them so eagerly—and somehow it aroused no comment that there was less and less to say.

And so, though the letters were fewer and shorter, they always seemed frequent enough and long enough and wholly satisfying. There came one bad winter—the mother was ill a good deal, there was quite a lot of money needed for medicines and food, charcoal was dear and less was paid for the embroideries. The big needlework schools, the shops said, were beginning to supply piece-work at a very low price, and the foreigners wanted to spend less every year. So with all diligence and care and economy it was only just possible to manage.

Yet Elisa was happy; the day-dreams were so persistent, so clear; the future so assured, so pleasant to brood over.

What could be easier than to sit down with one's back to the window and the wall and to lose oneself in the fantasies of the intricate design—flowers, shells, trees, birds—that grew beneath the unflagging needle?

Then the joy of taking out the *corredo*, sheet after sheet, neatly folded in a pile and tied in two places with pink tape: chemises and night-gowns and petticoats in sets, adorned with hand-made lace and stitching.

It was a curious sight to see in the poor, bare chamber the lengths of fine cambric and hand-woven lawn, and beautiful luxurious garments wrought with so much patient skill . . . . Often Elisa had in her hands a piece of work worth many pounds, and of such fragile richness that only the very wealthy could buy it . . . . Always white was this work; neither mother nor daughter ever touched colour, and when the *corrido* was put out and the shop-work was lying over chairs and tables, the dim-lit room looked as if it was filled with snow, shadowed drifts of delicate snow.

This hard winter there was much snow without; it lay on the top of the wall, and a little fell into the narrow courtyard; the room was darker even than usual, and Elisa had to sit very near the window indeed when she was doing her difficult *appliqué* and drawn work, or the "seeding" and "sparring," in which she had to use a needle so fine and so minutely count the threads of the cambric that her eyes watered behind the glasses that she now perpetually wore.

When she looked up to rest she saw nothing but the wall—that dull, blank brick wall that stood so close to the window that she could nearly touch it with her outstretched hand. The hateful wall: symbol of all the disaster of her life.

Yet what did it matter?

In the design she was bending over was a creature like a winged griffin, twisting in and out of the knots and lilies. Could not one mount between his pinions and fly away to wonderful places—valleys and mountains of fairy lands, shores where the white birds flew out to sea, castles where knights with the face of Araldo kept watch? . . .

"Next spring, when the boys come back and the wall is pulled down——" said the mother.

Elisa dropped her work into her lap; the twilight was gathering; a smell of coffee came from the little pot leaning on the charcoal embers. These cups of coffee were beginning to have all the joy of a luxury; it cost nearly a halfpenny for the two of them now.

"We will move the kitchen downstairs; this is really very inconvenient," she added.

"Yes, I think they are certain to come in the spring," replied Elisa cheerfully, "and we shall be able to buy the land back for less now, as the yard is no longer used."

She had made the same remark a great many times, but the older woman did not seem to remember this.

"Yes, they will surely be here by *Pasqua*, and we will go to meet them at Pisa.[72] Your *turchino* is still good, and so is the pair of boots."

"But you will need a new black dress, mother."

"No; this will do very well turned about and pressed—and I have my silk handkerchief put away, and the watch and chain Ercole gave me. *Pasqua* will be a nice time for them to come."

"The *corredo* is quite ready," said Elisa. She was still half in her dreams; she saw herself, very young and beautiful, wearing splendid clothes, receiving her lover in a castle by the sea—not a sea like that at Fiumetto, but one all pearl-flecked with waves that broke on the shore in thin lines of gold.

The winter passed almost without letters. What did that matter when everything—all the waiting, all the hope deferred, all the yearning, all the poverty, everything, even the shadow of the wall—would be over by Easter?

For of this both the women remained firmly convinced.

One morning in January Elisa stood in the chilly, disused front chamber, arranging with cold fingers a posy of cyclamen on the shiny top of the chest of drawers, when her mother came into the room with an open letter in her hand.

"It is from Ercole," she said; "he is coming back, as we knew, by *Pasqua*, and he sends five thousand francs to buy the wall."

"To buy the wall, to pull the wall down," said Elisa.

The two women turned over the letter and the foreign money draft; they did not say very much to one another; habit was so strong with them that they went through the daily duties as usual, and it was only in the afternoon that they went to the bank.

With the thousand-franc notes clasped tightly in the shabby purse which was their sole treasury, the two women went to the notary.

---

[72] *Pasqua:* Easter.

He was to buy back the land for them, and the wall; they put all the money down in front of him on the worn desk.

"It is nearly double what we were paid," said Elisa.

"But the value of land has increased," said the notary pleasantly. "My father sold that *terrene* for you twenty years ago."[73]

"Twenty years ago," repeated Elisa; she had never heard the period of their waiting put into those two words yet.

"Do what you can for us," said the mother, "as long as you can buy the wall—I do not want my son to come home and find the shadow of that in the house."

"And then we shall be having a wedding, eh?" smiled the notary when he had promised to do his best.

"Ah, yes," said the women together. Araldo had not written for a long time, but both felt that letters were no longer necessary.

A few more days of suspense and the notary came round to the darkened house with very pleasant news, as he considered. The American company wanted a high figure; it would cost them a good deal to even clear the yard, but in consideration of their promise to resell they were willing to take the wall down and allow a good strip of ground, large enough for a fair-sized garden; this for a moderate sum. The notary had a good deal of money to return.

"It really does not matter as long as we have the wall down," said the mother. "It would be a long time before we were able to do anything with the land, as it has been uncultivated for years—and Ercole means to buy a farm in Pianura."

So it was settled satisfactorily, and the good news sent out to Ercole. Another letter followed that with the money. He wrote very cheerfully; he had sold the *estancia* for a large sum and his

---

73 *Terrene:* land.

stock fetched good prices. He would be with them soon after *Pasqua.* He added that he was bringing home a wife.

This gave a strange shock to the two women. They felt that it altered, even distorted, everything, and yet it was only natural, they told themselves.

"After all, it is twenty years," said Elisa. She now took a good many occasions to say this; the two words seemed to stick in her memory.

The wall was being demolished; workmen who had been children when it was put up were gaily pulling it down. It did not take very long.

"It will be ready long before *Pasqua,*" said the mother.

Elisa went on with her sewing—for the *corredo*, since there was now no need to work for the shops.

There was so much noise and so much dust from the demolition of the wall that she sat in the front room now, being very careful not to disturb anything nor drop any threads.

One day she carried her sewing into the back room in order to prepare the noonday meal.

On the threshold she paused. The wall had gone from the level of the window, through which showed the gleam of sky and mountain and the marble in the mason's yard.

It was a day of dazzling sunshine; the whole atmosphere was quivering with light. Elisa looked round the room.

It looked incredibly shabby and dirty: there were stains on walls and floor that she had never noticed before—dust and cobwebs on the pots and in the corners. She glanced down at her gown; that too was stained and faded. She went to the mirror and looked at her face. The radiant sunlight showed the cracks in the joints of the frame, the defects in the glass; it showed Elisa herself wrinkled, uncared for, streaks of grey in the greasy hair, the eyes red and swollen, the throat lean, the tucker of the bodice soiled.

Why, how many things had she grown careless about while day-dreaming? . . . Twenty years . . . If she had married Araldo before he went away she might be going to her daughter's wedding now.

She picked up some of the garments of her *corredo* that lay on the coffer beneath the mirror and shook them out of the pink paper.

There were missed stitches she had never noticed before . . . mother had bungled the button-holes . . . . Of course they had never been able to see properly working in those half-lights.

"Never been able to see properly," said Elisa.

She looked at the embroidery she was now working on, that had been the source of so many delightful day-dreams. Gone were the castles, the oceans and orchards; the bright light of the sun dispersed these fancies and showed it was just linen and thread that she held, worked with a pattern full of flaws, that had often gone awry.

Outside the workmen whistled at their task, and brick by brick the wall was demolished; the fine dust danced up and made motes in the sunshine; there was a sharp scent of young green things in the cold air.

The mother came labouring up the stairs. Elisa heard her, and stood still, and glanced at her almost furtively as she entered the room.

What an old woman she was, with watery eyes magnified behind the thick glasses!

She stood blinking in the radiant light; she carried eggs and coffee and an open letter in her red *faggotta*.[74]

[74] *Faggotta:* bundle.

"The wall is down," said Elisa

"We must have some one to clean the place," answered the mother. She spoke uncertainly.

"Another letter?"

"Yes. Oh, yes, they gave it to me on the piazza—from Ercole. What a noise these workmen make!"

"They are young," said Elisa shivering. "It looks—a poor place now, doesn't it, mother?"

"We must buy some new furniture," said the old woman vaguely.

"Some things one cannot buy, mother."

"And there is your *turchino*, Elisa, and the boots. I must tell you, I looked at them this morning before I went out; there is the moth in the stuff and in the lining of the boots."

"I shall never wear them, mother. They were made for a young woman—and Araldo."

"There is news about him here." She waved the letter in the light. "He isn't coming back—not yet. Ercole is bringing a message."

"I know. He is married of course—it is all clear. As if he could wait twenty years—it was all dreams—always. Look at me—look at everything falling to pieces; look at the *corredo*—yellow and rotten. He won't come back at all."

The old woman sat down and folded up the letter.

"I would read to you what he says, but this light hurts my eyes."

Elisa came to the table, shrinking in the sunlight like a guilty thing.

"Mother," she said eagerly, "do you think we have enough money left to build up the wall again?"

# THE PRESCRIPTION

JOHN Cuming collected ghost stories; he always declared that this was the best that he knew, although it was partially second-hand and contained a mystery that had no reasonable solution, while most really good ghost stories allow of a plausible explanation, even if it is one as feeble as a dream, excusing all; or a hallucination or a crude deception. Cuming told the story rather well. The first part of it at least had come under his own observation and been carefully noted by him in the flat green book which he kept for the record of all curious cases of this sort. He was a shrewd and a trained observer; he honestly restrained his love of drama from leading him into embellishing facts. Cuming told the story to us all on the most suitable occasion—Christmas Eve—and prefaced it with a little homily.

"You all know the good old saw—'The more it changes the more it is the same thing'—and I should like you to notice that this extremely up-to-date ultra-modern ghost story is really almost exactly the same as one that might have puzzled Babylonian or Assyrian sages.[75] I can give you the first start of the tale in my own words, but the second part will have to be in the words of some one else. They were, however, most carefully and scrupulously taken down. As for the conclusion, I must leave you to draw that for yourselves—each according to your own mood, fancy and temperament; it may be that you will all think of the same solution, it may be that you will each think of a different one,

---

[75] Old saw: an old saying.

and it may be that every one will be left wondering."

Having thus enjoyed himself by whetting our curiosity, Cuming settled himself down comfortably in his deep arm-chair and unfolded his tale.

"It was about five years ago. I don't wish to be exact with time, and of course I shall alter names—that's one of the first rules of the game, isn't it? Well, whenever it was, I was the guest of a—Mrs. Janey we will call her—who was, to some extent, a friend of mine; an intelligent, lively, rather bustling sort of woman who had the knack of gathering interesting people about her. She had lately taken a new house in Buckinghamshire. It stood in the grounds of one of those large estates which are now so frequently being broken up. She was very pleased with the house, which was quite new and had only been finished about a year, and seemed, according to her own rather excited imagination, in every way desirable. I don't want to emphasize anything about the house except that it *was* new and did stand on the verge, as it were, of this large old estate, which had belonged to one of those notable English families now extinct and completely forgotten. I am no antiquarian or connoisseur in architecture, and the rather blatant modernity of the house did not offend me. I was able to appreciate its comfort and to enjoy what Mrs. Janey rather maddeningly called 'the old-world gardens,' which were really a section of the larger gardens of the vanished mansion which had once commanded this domain. Mrs. Janey, I should tell you, knew nothing about the neighbourhood nor anyone who lived there, except that for the first it was very convenient for town and for the second she believed that they were all '*nice*' people, not likely to bother one. I was slightly disappointed with the crowd she had gathered together at Christmas. They were all people whom either I knew too well or whom I didn't wish to know at all, and at first the party showed signs of being extremely flat. Mrs. Janey seemed to perceive this too, and with rather nervous haste produced, on Christmas Eve, a trump card in the way of amusement—a professional medium, called Mrs. Mahogany, because that could not possibly have been her name. Some of us 'believed in,' as the saying goes, mediums, and some didn't; but we were all willing to be diverted by the experiment. Mrs. Janey continually lamented that a certain Dr. Dilke would not be present. He was going to be one of the party, but had been detained in town and would not reach Verrall, which was the name of the house, until later, and the medium, it seemed, could not stay; for she, being a personage in great demand, must go on to a further engagement. I, of course, like every one else possessed of an intelligent curiosity and a certain amount of leisure, had been to mediums before. I had been slightly impressed, slightly disgusted, and very much bewildered, and on the whole had decided to let the matter alone, considering that I really preferred the more direct and old-fashioned method of getting in touch with what we used to call 'the Unseen.' This sitting in the great new house seemed rather banal. I could understand in some haunted old manor that a clairvoyant, or a clairaudient, or a trance-medium might have found something interesting to say, but what was she going to get out of Mrs. Janey's bright, brilliant and comfortable dwelling?

"Mrs. Mahogany was a nondescript sort of woman—neither young nor old, neither clever nor stupid, neither dark nor fair, placid, and not in the least self-conscious. After an extremely good luncheon (it was a gloomy, stormy afternoon) we all sat down in a circle in the cheerful drawing-room; the curtains were pulled across the dreary prospect of grey sky and grey landscape, and we had merely the light of the fire. We sat quite close together in order to increase 'the power,' as Mrs. Mahogany said, and the medium sat in the middle, with no special precautions against trickery; but we all knew that trickery would have been really impossible, and we were quite prepared to be tremendously impressed and startled if any manifestations took place. I think we all felt rather foolish, as we did not know each other very well, sitting round there, staring at this very ordinary, rather common, stout little woman, who kept nervously pulling a little tippet of grey wool over her shoulders, closing her eyes and muttering, while she twisted her fingers together. When we had sat silent for about ten minutes Mrs. Janey announced in a rather raw whisper that the medium had gone into a trance. 'Beautifully,' she added. I thought that Mrs. Mahogany did not look at all beautiful. Her communication began with a lot of rambling talk which had no point at all, and a good deal of generalization under which I think we all became a little restive. There was too much of various spirits who had all sorts of ordinary names, just regular Toms, Dicks and Harrys of the spirit world, floating round behind us, their arms full of flowers and their mouths full of goodwill—all rather pointless. And though, occasionally, a Tom, a Dick, or a Harry was identified by some of us, it wasn't very convincing and, what was worse, not very interesting. We got, however, our surprise and our shock, because Mrs. Mahogany began suddenly to writhe into ugly contortions and called out in a loud voice, quite different from the one she had hitherto used:

" 'Murder!'

"This word gave us all a little thrill, and we leant forward eagerly to hear what further she had to say. With every sign of distress and horror Mrs. Mahogany began to speak:

" 'He's murdered her. Oh, how dreadful. Look at him! Can't somebody stop him? It's so near here too. He tried to save her. He was sorry, you know. Oh, how dreadful! Look at him—he's borne it as long as he can, and now he's murdered her! I see him mixing it in a glass. Oh, isn't it awful that no one could have saved her—and he was so terribly remorseful afterwards. Oh, how dreadful! how horrible!'

"She ended in a whimpering of fright and horror, and Mrs. Janey, who seemed an adept at this sort of thing, leant forward and asked eagerly:

" 'Can't you get the name—can't you find out who it is? Why do you get that here?'

" 'I don't know,' muttered the medium; 'it's somewhere near here—a house, an old dark house, and there are curtains of mauve velvet—do you call it mauve?—a kind of blue-red at the windows. There's a garden outside with a fish-pond and you go through a low doorway and down stone steps.'

" 'It isn't near here,' said Mrs. Janey decidedly, 'all the houses are new.'

" 'The house is near here,' persisted the medium. 'I am walking through it now; I can see the room, I can see that poor, poor woman, and a glass of milk——'

" 'I wish you'd get the name,' insisted Mrs. Janey, and she cast a look, as I thought not without suspicion, round the circle. 'You can't be getting this from my house, you know, Mrs. Mahogany,' she added decidedly, 'it must be given out by some one here—something they've read or seen, you know,' she said, to reassure us that our characters were not in dispute.

"But the medium replied drowsily, 'No, it's somewhere near here. I see a light dress covered with small roses. If he could have got help he would have gone for it, but there was no one; so all his remorse was useless . . . . '

"No further urging would induce the medium to say more; soon afterwards she came out of the trance, and all of us, I think, felt that she had made rather a stupid blunder by introducing this vague piece of melodrama, and if it was, as we suspected, a cheap attempt to give a ghostly and mysterious atmosphere to Christmas Eve, it was a failure.

"When Mrs. Mahogany, blinking round her, said brightly, 'Well, here I am again! I wonder if I said anything that interested you?' we all replied rather coldly, 'Of course it has been most interesting, but there hasn't been anything definite.' And I think that even Mrs. Janey felt that the sitting had been rather a disappointment, and she suggested that if the weather was really too horrible to venture out of doors we should sit round the fire and tell old-fashioned ghost stories. 'The kind,' she said brightly, 'that are about bones and chairs and shrouds. I really think that is the most thrilling kind after all!' Then, with some embarrassment, and when Mrs. Mahogany had left the room, she suggested that not one of us should say anything about what the medium had said in her trance.

" 'It really was rather absurd,' said our hostess, 'and it would make me look a little foolish if it got about; you know some people think these mediums are absolute fakes, and anyhow the whole thing, I am afraid, was quite stupid. She must have got her contacts mixed. There is no old house about here and never has been since the original Verrall was pulled down, and that's a good fifty years ago, I believe, from what the estate agent told me; and as for a murder, I never heard the shadow of any such story.'

"We all agreed not to mention what the medium had said, and did this with the more heartiness as we were, not any one of us, impressed. The feeling was rather that Mrs. Mahogany had been obliged to say something, and had said that . . . .

"Well," said Cuming comfortably, "that is the first part of my story, and I dare say you'll think it's dull enough. Now we come to the second part.

"Latish that evening Dr. Dilke arrived. He was not in any way a remarkable man, just an ordinary successful physician, and I refuse to say that he was suffering from overwork or nervous strain; you know, that is so often put into this kind of story as a sort of excuse for what happens afterwards. On the contrary, Dr. Dilke seemed to be in the most robust of health and the most cheerful frame of mind, and quite prepared to make the most of his brief holiday. The car that fetched him from the station was taking Mrs. Mahogany away, and the doctor and the medium met for just a moment in the hall. Mrs. Janey did not trouble to introduce them, but without waiting for this Mrs. Mahogany turned to the doctor and, looking at him fixedly, said, 'You're very psychic, aren't you?' And upon that Mrs. Janey was forced to say hastily: 'This is Mrs. Mahogany, Dr. Dilke, the famous medium.'

"The physician was indifferently impressed: 'I really don't know,' he answered, smiling. 'I have never gone in for that sort of thing. I shouldn't think I am what you call "psychic" really, I have a hard scientific training, and that rather knocks the bottom out of fantasies.'

" 'Well, you are, you know,' said Mrs. Mahogany. 'I felt it at once; I shouldn't be at all surprised if you had some strange experiences one of these days.'

"Mrs. Mahogany left the house and was duly driven away to the station. I want to make the point very clear that she and Dr. Dilke did not meet again and that they held no communication except those few words in the hall spoken in the presence of Mrs. Janey. Of course Dr. Dilke got twitted a good deal about what the medium had said; it made quite a topic of conversation during dinner and after dinner, and we all had queer little ghost stories or incidents of what we considered 'psychic' experiences to trot out and discuss. Dr. Dilke remained civil, amused, but entirely unconvinced. He had what he called a material, or physical, or medical explanation for almost everything that we said, and, apart from all these explanations, he added, with some justice, that human credulity was such that there was always some one who would accept and embellish anything, however wild, unlikely or grotesque it was.

" 'I should rather like to hear what you would say if such an experience happened to you,' Mrs. Janey challenged him; 'whether you use the ancient terms of "ghost," "witches," "black magic," and so on, or whether you speak in modern terms like "medium," "clairvoyance," "psychic contacts," and all the rest of it; well, it seems one is in a bit of a tangle, anyhow, and if any queer thing ever happens to you——'

"Dr. Dilke broke in pleasantly: 'Well, if it ever does I will let you know all about it, and I dare say I shall have an explanation to add at the end of the tale.'

"When we all met again the next morning we rather hoped that Dr. Dilke *would* have something to tell us—some odd experience that might have befallen him in the night, new as the house was and banal as was his bedroom. He told us, of course, that he had passed a perfectly good night.

"We most of us went to the morning service in the small church that had once been the chapel belonging to the demolished mansion, and which had some rather curious monuments inside and in the churchyard. As I went in I noticed a mortuary chapel with niches for the coffins to be stood upright, now whitewashed and used as a sacristy. The monuments and mural tablets were mostly to the memory of members of the family of Verrall—the Verralls of Verrall Hall, who appeared to have been people of little interest or distinction. Dr. Dilke sat beside me, and I, having nothing better to do through the more familiar and monotonous portions of the service, found myself idly looking at the mural tablet beyond him. This was a large slab of black marble deeply cut with a very worn Latin inscription which I found, unconsciously, I was spelling out. The stone, it seemed, commemorated a woman who had been, of course, the possessor of all the virtues; her name was Philadelphia Carwithen, and I rather pleasantly sampled the flavour of that ancient name—Philadelphia. Then I noticed a smaller inscription at the bottom of the slab, which indicated that the lady's husband also rested in the vault; he had died suddenly about six months after her—of grief at her loss, no doubt, I thought, scenting out a pretty romance.

"As we walked home across the frost-bitten fields and icy lanes Dr. Dilke, who walked beside me, as he had sat beside me in church, began to complain of cold; he said he believed that he had caught a chill. I was rather amused to hear this old-womanish expression on the lips of so distinguished a physician, and I told him that I had been taught in my more enlightened days that there was no such thing as 'catching a chill.' To my surprise he did not laugh at this, but said:

" 'Oh, yes, there is, and I believe I've got it—I keep on shivering; I think it was that slab of black stone I was sitting next. It was as cold as ice, for I touched it, and it seemed to me exuding moisture—some of that old stone does, you know; it's always, as it were, sweating; and I felt exactly as if I were sitting next a slab of ice from which a cold wind was blowing; it was really as if it penetrated my flesh.'

"He looked pale, and I thought how disagreeable it would be for us all, and particularly for Mrs. Janey, if the good man was to be taken ill in the midst of her already not too successful Christmas party. Dr. Dilke seemed, too, in that ill-humour which so often presages an illness; he was quite peevish about the church and the service, and the fact that he had been asked to go there.

" 'These places are nothing but charnel-houses after all,' he said fretfully; 'one sits there among all those rotting bones, with that damp marble at one's side . . . '

"It is supposed to give you 'atmosphere,' I said. The atmosphere of an old-fashioned Christmas . . . . Did you notice who your black stone was erected 'to the memory of'? I asked, and the doctor replied that he had not.

"They were to a woman—a young women, I took it, and her husband: 'Philadelphia Carwithen,' I noticed that, and of course there was a long eulogy of her virtues, and then underneath it just said that he had died a few months afterwards. As far as I could see it was the only example of that name in the church—all the rest were Verralls. I suppose they were strangers here.

" 'What was the date?' asked the doctor, and I replied that really I had not been able to make it out, for where the Roman figures came the stone had been very worn.

"The day ambled along somehow, with games, diversions, and plenty of good food and drink, and towards the evening we began to feel a little more satisfied with each other and our hostess. Only Dr. Dilke remained a little peevish and apart, and this was remarkable in one who was obviously of a robust temperament and an even temper. He still continued to talk of a 'chill,' and I did notice that he shuddered once or twice, and continually sat near the large fire which Mrs. Janey had rather laboriously arranged in imitation of what she would call 'the good old times.'

"That evening, the evening of Christmas Day, there was no talk whatever of ghosts or psychic matters; our discussions were entirely topical and of mundane affairs, in which Dr. Dilke, who seemed to have recovered his spirits, took his part with ability and agreeableness. When it was time to break up I asked him, half in jest, about his mysterious chill, and he looked at me with some surprise and appeared to have forgotten that he had ever said he had got such a thing; the impression, whatever it was, which he had received in the church had evidently been effaced from his mind. I wish to make that quite clear.

"The next morning Dr. Dilke appeared very late at the breakfast table, and when he did so his looks were matter for hints and comment; he was pale, distracted, troubled, untidy in his dress, absent in his manner, and I, at least, instantly recalled what he had said yesterday, and feared he was sickening for some illness.

"On Mrs. Janey putting to him some direct question as to his looks and manners, so strange and so troubled, he replied rather abruptly, 'Well, I don't know what you can expect from a fellow who's been up all night. I thought I came down here for a rest.'

"We all looked at him as he dropped into his place and began to drink his coffee with eager gusto; I noticed that he continually shivered. There was something about this astounding statement and his curious appearance which held us all discreetly silent. We waited for further developments before committing ourselves; even Mrs. Janey, whom I had never thought of as tactful, contrived to say casually:

" 'Up all night, doctor. Couldn't you sleep then? I'm so sorry if your bed wasn't comfortable.' "

" 'The bed was all right,' he answered, 'that made me the more sorry to leave it. Haven't you got a local doctor who can take the local cases?' he added.

" 'Why, of course we have; there's Dr. Armstrong and Dr. Fraser—I made sure about that before I came here.'

" 'Well, then,' demanded Dr. Dilke angrily, 'why on earth couldn't one of them have gone last night?'

"Mrs. Janey looked at me helplessly, and I, obeying her glance, took up the matter.

"What do you mean, doctor? Do you mean that you were called out of your bed last night to attend a case? I asked deliberately.

" 'Of course I was—I only got back with the dawn.'

"Here Mrs. Janey could not forbear breaking in.

" 'But, whoever could it have been? I know nobody about here yet, at least, only one or two people by name, and they would not be aware that you were here. And how did you get out of the house? It's locked every night.'

"Then the doctor gave his story in rather, I must confess, a confused fashion, and yet with an earnest conviction that he was speaking the simple truth. It was broken up a good deal by ejaculations and comments from the rest of us, but I give it you here shorn of all that and exactly as I put it down in my notebook afterwards.

" 'I was woken up by a tap at the door. I was instantly wide awake and I said "Come in." I thought immediately that probably some one in the house was ill—a doctor, you know, is always ready for these emergencies. The door opened at once and a man entered holding a small ordinary storm-lantern. I noticed nothing peculiar about the man. He had a dark greatcoat on, and appeared extremely anxious. "I am sorry to disturb you," he said at once, "but there is a young woman dangerously ill. I want you to come and see her." I, somehow, did not think of arguing or of suggesting that there were other medical men in the neighbourhood, or of asking how it was he knew of my presence at Verrall. I dressed myself quickly and accompanied him out of the house. He opened the front door without any trouble, and it did not occur to me to ask him how it was he had obtained either admission or egress. There was a small carriage outside the door, such a one as you may still see in isolated country places, but such a one as I was certainly surprised to see here. I could not very well make out either the horse or the driver for, though the moon was high in the heavens, it was frequently obscured by clouds. I got into the carriage and noticed, as I have often noticed before in these ancient vehicles, a most repulsive smell of decay and damp. My companion got in beside me. He did not speak a word during the whole of the journey, which was, I have the impression, extremely long, and yet I could not say how long. I had also the sense that he was in the greatest trouble, anguish, and almost despair; I do not know why I did not question him. I should tell you that he had drawn down the blinds of the carriage and we travelled in darkness, yet I was perfectly aware of his presence and seemed to see him in his heavy greatcoat turned up round his chin, his black hair low on his forehead, and his anxious, furtive dark eyes. I think I may have gone to sleep in the carriage, I was tired and cold. I was aware, however, when it stopped, and of my companion opening the door and helping me out. We went through a garden, down some steps and past a fishpond; I could see by the moonlight the silver and gold shapes of fishes slipping in and out of the black water. We entered the house by a side-door—I remember that very distinctly—and went up what seemed to be some secret or seldom-used stairs, and into a bedroom. I was by now quite alert, as one is when one gets into the presence of the patient, and I said to myself, "What a fool I've been, I've brought nothing with me"; and I tried to remember, but could not quite do so, whether or not I had brought anything with me—my cases and so on—to Verrall. The room was very badly lit, but a certain illumination, I could not say whether it came from any artificial light within the room or merely from the moonlight through the open window, draped with mauve velvet curtains, fell on the bed, and there I saw my patient. She was a young woman who, I surmised, would have been, when in health, of considerable though coarse charm. She was now in great suffering, twisted and contorted with agony, and in her struggles of anguish had pulled and torn the bed-clothes into a heap. I noticed that she wore a dress of some light material spotted with small roses, and it occurred to me at once that she had been taken ill during the daytime and must have lain thus in great pain for many hours, and I turned with some reproach to the man who had fetched me and demanded why help had not been sought sooner. For answer he wrung his hands—a gesture that I do not remember having noticed in any human being before; one hears a great deal of hands being wrung, but one does not so often see it. This man, I remember distinctly, wrung his hands, and muttered, "Do what you can for her—do what you can!" I feared that this would be very little. I endeavoured to make an examination of the patient, but owing to her half-delirious struggles this was very difficult; she was, however, I thought, likely to die, and of what malady I could not determine. There was a table nearby on which lay some papers—one I took to be a will—and a glass in which there had been milk. I do not remember seeing anything else in the room—the light was so bad. I endeavoured to question the man, whom I took to be the husband, but without success. He merely repeated his monotonous appeal to me to save her. Then I was aware of a sound outside the room—of a woman laughing, perpetually and shrilly laughing. "Pray stop that," I cried to the man; "who have you got in the house—a lunatic?" But he took no notice of my appeal, merely repeating his own hushed lamentations. The sick woman appeared to hear that demoniacal laughter outside, and, raising herself on one elbow, said, "You have destroyed me and you may well laugh!"

" 'I sat down at the table on which were the papers and the glass half full of milk, and wrote a prescription on a sheet torn out of my notebook. The man snatched it eagerly. "I don't know when and where you can get that made up," I said, "but it's the only hope." At this he seemed wishful for me to depart, as wishful as he had been for me to come. "That's all I want," he said. He took me by the arm and led me out of the house by the same back stairs. As I descended I still heard those two dreadful sounds—the thin laughter of the woman I had not seen, and the groans, becoming every moment fainter, of the young woman whom I had seen. The carriage was waiting for me and I was driven back by the same way I had come. When I reached the house and my room I saw the dawn just breaking. I rested till I heard the breakfast gong. I suppose some time had gone by since I returned to the house, but I wasn't quite aware of it; all through the night I had rather lost the sense of time.'

"When Dr. Dilke had finished his narrative, which I give here baldly—but, I hope, to the point—we all glanced at each other rather uncomfortably, for who was to tell a man like Dr. Dilke that he had been suffering from a severe hallucination? It was, of course, quite impossible that he could have left the house and gone through the peculiar scene he had described, and it seemed extraordinary that he could for a moment have believed that he had done so. What was even more remarkable was that so many points of his story agreed with what the medium, Mrs. Mahogany, had said in her trance. We recognized the frock with the roses, the mauve velvet curtains, the glass of milk, the man who had fetched Dr. Dilke sounded like the murderer, and the unfortunate woman writhing on the bed sounded like the victim; but how had the doctor got hold of these particulars? We all knew that he had not spoken to Mrs. Mahogany and each suspected the other of having told him what the medium had said, and that this having wrought on his mind he had the dream, vision, or hallucination he had just described to us. I must add that this was found afterwards to be wholly false; we were all reliable people and there was not a shadow of doubt we had all kept out counsel about Mrs. Mahogany. In fact, none of us had been alone with Dr. Dilke the previous day for more than a moment or so save myself, who had walked with him home from the church, when we had certainly spoken of nothing except the black stone in the church and the chill which he had said emanated from it . . . . Well, to put the matter as briefly as possible, and to leave out a great deal of amazement and wonder, explanation and so on, we will come to the point when Dr. Dilke was finally persuaded that he had not left Verrall all the night. When his story was taken to pieces and put before him, as it were, in the raw, he himself recognized many absurdities; how could the man have come straight to his bedroom? How could he have left the house?—the doors were locked every night, there was no doubt about that. Where did the carriage come from and where was the house to which he had been taken? And who could possibly have known of his presence in the neighbourhood? Had not, too, the scene in the house to which he was taken all the resemblance of a nightmare? Who was it laughing in the other room? What was the mysterious illness that was destroying the young woman? Who was the black-browed man who had fetched him? And, in these days of telephone and motor cars, people didn't go out in old-fashioned one-horse carriages to fetch doctors from miles away in the case of dangerous illness.

"Dr. Dilke was finally silenced, uneasy, but not convinced. I could see that he disliked intensely the idea that he had been the victim of an hallucination, and that he equally intensely regretted the impulse which had made him relate his extraordinary adventure of the night. I could only conclude that he must have done so while still, to an extent, under the influence of his delusion, which had been so strong that never for a moment had he questioned the reality of it. Though he was forced at last to allow us to put the whole thing down as a most remarkable dream, I could see that he did not intend to let the matter rest there, and later in the day (out of good manners we had eventually ceased discussing the story) he asked me if I would accompany him on some investigation in the neighbourhood.

" 'I think I should know the house,' he said, 'even though I saw it in the dark. I was impressed by the fish-pond and the low doorway through which I had to stoop in order to pass without knocking my head.'

"I did not tell him that Mrs. Mahogany had also mentioned a fish-pond and a low door.

"We made the excuse of some old brasses we wished to discover in a nearby church to take my car and go out that afternoon on an investigation of the neighbourhood in the hope of discovering Dr. Dilke's dream house.

"We covered a good deal of distance and spent a good deal of time without any success at all, and the short day was already darkening when we came upon a row of almshouses in which, for no reason at all that I could discern, Dr. Dilke showed an interest and insisted on stopping before them. He pointed out an inscription cut in the centre gable, which said that these had been built by a certain Richard Carwithen in memory of Philadelphia, his wife.

"The people whose tablet you sat next in the church, I remarked.

" 'Yes,' murmured Dr. Dilke, 'when I felt the chill,' and he added, 'when I *first* felt the chill. You see the date is 1830. That would be about right.'

"We stopped in the little village, which was a good many miles from Verrall, and after some tedious delays because everything was shut up for the holidays we did discover an old man who was willing to tell us something about the almshouses, though there was nothing much to be said about them. They had been founded by a certain Mr. Richard Carwithen with his wife's fortune. He had been a poor man, a kind of adventurer, our informant thought, who had married a wealthy woman; they had not been at all happy. There had been quarrels and disputes, and a separation (at least, so the gossip went, as his father had told it to him) finally, the Carwithens had taken a house here in the village of Sunford—a large house it was, and it still stood. The Carwithens weren't buried in the village though, but at Verrall, she had been a Verrall by birth—perhaps that's why they came to this neighbourhood—it was the name of a great family in those days you know . . . . There was another woman in the old story, as it went, and she got hold of Mr. Carwithen and was for making him put his wife aside; and so, perhaps, he would have done, but the poor lady died suddenly, and there was some talk about it, having the other woman in the house at the time, and it being so convenient for both of them . . . . But he didn't marry the other woman, because he died six months after his wife . . . . By his will he left all his wife's money to found these almshouses.

"Dr. Dilke asked if he could see the house where the Carwithens had lived.

" 'It belongs to a London gentleman,' the old man said, 'who never comes here. It's going to be pulled down and the land sold in building lots; why, it's been locked up these ten years or more. I don't suppose it's been inhabited since—no, not for a hundred years.'

" 'Well, I'm looking for a house round about here. I don't mind spending a little money on repairs if that house is in the market.'

"The old man didn't know whether it was in the market or not, but kept repeating that the property was to be sold and broken up for building lots.

"I won't bother you with all the delays and arguments, but merely tell you that we did finally discover the lodge-keeper of the estate, who gave us the key. It was not such a very large estate, nothing to be compared to Verrall, but had been, in its time, of some pretension. Builders' boards had already been raised along the high road frontage. There were some fine old trees, black and bare, in a little park. As we turned in through the rusty gates and motored towards the house it was nearly dark, but we had our electric torches and the powerful head-lamps of the car. Dr. Dilke made no comment on what we had found, but he reconstructed the story of the Carwithens whose names were on that black stone in Verrall church.

" 'They were quarrelling over money, he was trying to get her to sign a will in his favour; she had some little sickness perhaps—brought on probably by rage—he had got the other woman in the house remember. I expect he was no good. There was some sort of poison about—perhaps for a face wash, perhaps as a drug.[76] He put it in the milk and gave it to her.'

"Here I interrupted: How do you know it was in the milk?

"The doctor did not reply to this. I had now swung the car round to the front of the ancient mansion—a poor, pretentious place, sinister in the half-darkness.

" 'And then, when he had done it,' continued Dr. Dilke, mounting the steps of the house, 'he repented most horribly; he wanted to fly for a doctor to get some antidote for the poison with the idea in his head that if he could have got help he could have saved her himself. The other woman kept on laughing. He couldn't forgive that—that she could laugh at a moment like that! He couldn't get help. He couldn't find a doctor. His wife died. No one suspected foul play—they seldom did in those days as long as the people were respectable, you must remember the state in which medical knowledge was in 1830. He couldn't marry the other woman, and he couldn't touch the money; he left it all to found the almshouses; then he died himself, six months afterwards, leaving instructions that his name should be added on that black stone. I dare say he died by his own hand. Probably he loved her through it all, you know—it was only the money, that cursed money, a fortune just within his grasp, but which he couldn't take!'

"A pretty romance, I suggested as we entered the house; I am sure there is a three-volume novel in it of what Mrs. Janey would call 'the good old-fashioned' sort.

"To this Dr. Dilke answered: 'Suppose the miserable man can't rest? Supposing he is still searching for a doctor?'

---

[76] Beauty products at the time sometimes contained poisonous ingredients, such as arsenic.

"We passed from one room to another of the dismal, dusty, dismantled house. Dr. Dilke opened a damaged shutter which concealed one of the windows at the back, and pointed out in the waning light a decayed garden with stone steps and a fish-pond—dry now, of course, but certainly once a fish-pond; and a low gateway, to pass through which a man of his height would have had to stoop. We could just discern this in the twilight. He made no comment. We went upstairs."

Here Cuming paused dramatically to give us the full flavour of the final part of the story. He reminded us, rather unnecessarily, for somehow he had convinced us, that it was all perfectly true.

"I am not romancing; I won't answer for what Dr. Dilke said or did, or his adventure of the night before, or the story of the Carwithens as he constructed it, but *this* is actually what happened . . . . We went upstairs by the wide main stairs. Dr. Dilke searched about for and found a door which opened on to the back stairs, and then he said: 'This must be the room.' It was entirely devoid of any furniture, and stained with damp, the walls stripped of panelling and cheaply covered with decayed paper, peeling and in parts fallen.

" 'What's this?' said Dr. Dilke.

"He picked up a scrap of paper that showed vivid on the dusty floor and handed it to me. It was a prescription. He took out his notebook and showed me the page where this fitted in.

" 'This page I tore out last night when I wrote that prescription in this room. The bed was just there, and there was the table on which were the papers and the glass of milk.'

"But you couldn't have been here last night, I protested feebly, the locked doors—the whole thing! . . .

"Dr. Dilke said nothing. After a while neither did I. Let's get out of the place, I said. Then another thought struck me. What is your prescription? I asked.

"He said, 'A very uncommon kind of prescription, a very desperate sort of prescription, one that I've never written before, nor I hope shall again—an antidote for severe arsenic poisoning.'

"I leave you" smiled Cuming, "to your various attitudes of incredulity or explanation."

## MRS. HOPETON AT THE FLOWER SHOW

MRS. Hopeton was so bogged in civilization that when she sat on the grass she felt more like a tramp than a dryad; but, since she could not find a man-made seat and her feet ached dismally, she timidly sat on the little slope behind the big trees a little away from the immense crowd.

She was thinking that it had been very kind of Mrs. Lemoine to send her a ticket for the first day (the important, fashionable, Royal day) of the great Flower Show, that it was beautiful weather, and that she was enjoying herself very much; but she was very hot, tired and uncomfortable, and if she had done what she really wanted to do she would have gone home at once.

But Mrs. Hopeton never did do what she really wanted to do; she had got out of the way of even knowing what she wanted. Her clothes were all wrong. She was a slave to shop windows; she bought odd things that took her fancy, driftage of cheap fashion. Her high-heeled patent leather shoes seemed to burn into her feet, her hat was hard and heavy, her dress dragged at the arms and neck, and she had brought a heavy coat in case it rained that galled an arm laden with handbag and parasol.

She was not in the least vain, as her wisps of hair and shining face witnessed, and she was merely uncomfortable through ignorance of how to make herself comfortable.

She smiled vaguely in case some acquaintance should see her and think she was not enjoying herself, which would seem like a reflection on Mrs. Lemoine.

But no one did see her; no one in that huge press of people

took any notice of her, and presently she thought that she ought to go back to the tents.

That she ought to walk through the tents, one after another, squeezing and pushing past the exhibits, like every one else was doing.

Wonderful how many people there were!

Royalty had been there this morning, in coolness and leisure, and now all these hot people were crowding over the track of Royalty to admire what Royalty had admired and to buy what Royalty had bought, and if possible to descry some eminent person, perhaps even some one with a title, to whom they might be well known enough to pass a word with. Mrs. Hopeton had no such ambition; she felt that she was very lucky to be there at all. Of course if Eric had been with her he would have known a great many people; he was very popular, and when she was out with him he was continually being stopped and spoken to. Mrs. Hopeton, who wanted nothing for herself, wanted the whole world for Eric, her only son.

Eric was always in the front of her mind; everything else was in the back. The young man seemed to her beautiful, noble, grand and yet touching; in him, from the first moment he was put into her arms, she had found her God.

And now she was in an inner agony about Eric, without daring to disclose to anyone her distress.

Eric was in love, and the girl would have none of him.

This had hit Mrs. Hopeton in the bitterest way; it was terrible to realize that the time had come when he would leave her for another woman, and it was terrible to realize that her peerless boy, the result of all her love, her care, her sacrifice, her money, should be rejected by an ordinary young woman.

Of course she had been very careful not to allow Eric to see that she had guessed his secret—she had the almost crazy English reserve on the matter of emotion to the full, and so had he—but she had gone with him, step by step, in all the distresses of his hopeless passion. And she was now able to think of little else, and even that little in only a desultory, vague fashion.

She pushed rather mechanically into the vast tent, which several people, with that odd admiration of size that is so general, remarked was the largest in the world.

The sun on the canvas gave an intense heat, accentuated by the perfumes of all the flowers, of all the women; the little air that passed through the door was eagerly used up by human beings and plants. Mrs. Hopeton soon felt dizzy in this heat, in this crowd, in this vitiated atmosphere, and in this noise; for every one was talking at once, either in business-like tones to the salesman, or with light cries of delight and wonder.

The flowers were perfection; that one word, "perfection," kept occurring to Mrs. Hopeton.

The blooms trailed and flowed and massed and blazed in every ingenuity of shape and tint behind their trade cards and their gilt-lettered awards; through the exhausted air came the moist odour of exotic ferns, the luscious scent of roses, the sickly perfume of lilies.

Mrs. Hopeton pushed on a pace at a time, high hats, chiffon dresses, hands holding glossy catalogues surrounding her; the flowers were mere glimpses in between the bodies of the crowd.

She became so giddy that she decided to push out at the next entrance; but that was a long distance off, so she edged her way into the next tent in the hope of more air, and there, by the orchid stand, she saw Eunice Brent, the girl that Eric loved.

Mrs. Hopeton pushed away; she felt an impulse of dislike that touched hatred; she could hardly have borne to have spoken to the girl.

Between the heads of other people she peered at Miss Brent as if she was an enemy in ambush.

The girl was like the orchids—rare, haughty, exquisite; her thin gown of faintest yellow blended with the creamy lustre of her skin, her pale rosy hat, with graceful ribbons, threw a warm shadow over her rich hair; the meshes of a golden bag showed between her long fingers. She was talking with composed aloofness to a man whom Mrs. Hopeton instantly loathed as a possible rival to Eric.

Like the orchids, yes—flawless, amazing, hateful. Mrs. Hopeton remembered to have heard that these overbred prize blooms, the epitome of graces of shape, texture and hue, were sterile.

It seemed to her that Miss Brent, so without blemish, or timidity, or hesitation, was sterile too, without any of those warm, erring, dear qualities that go to help life (and living) on.

When she withered there would be an end of her, as there would be an end of the orchid; she also would leave nothing behind but the catalogue of her perfections.

She saw Mrs. Hopeton, bowed coolly and turned away; they were nothing but acquaintances. Eric had never seemed to want his mother to assist in the conquest of Miss Brent; he had even kept the two women apart.

Mrs. Hopeton had always been glad of this. "I could never have helped him," she thought; "I dislike her too much."

Now the poor mother tried to get away from the orchid stall. "How dare she make Eric love her and not love him? She isn't good enough; no one is good enough for Eric."

How endless the vista of the tent seemed, how she was hemmed in on all sides by the chattering hordes, the banks of flowers, the hot yellow canvas!

Too many flowers—flowers over everything: flowers of silk, of muslin, of shells, of feathers, of precious stones, of ivory, of gold and silver, on women's hats, dresses, bags and parasols; all sorts of flowers and distortions of flowers, and grotesques of flowers.

Mrs. Hopeton felt overwhelmed by these endless blossoms, these bowers and garlands of drooping blooms, these rich spikes, these rigid flags, these gaudy bells and streaked cups, these balls of packed flowerets, these single chalices. Why were there so many kinds of flowers?

They seemed to menace and assail her, one after another, with their vivid completeness—flawless, all flawless, like a regiment of Eunice Brents, disdaining her, disdaining Eric.

Even the vegetables were arranged in faultless bouquets, exquisite globes untouched by an insect, glossy leaves, rosy spheres that seem never to have been in the earth; and the immaculate fruit, of monstrous dimensions, had the hard, pale lividness of coloured wax.

Mrs. Hopeton fought into the open air. The crowd was dense on the walks, about the stalls where garden implements and furniture were sold; the dust clung to her shoes and dress, the sun glared on the tight silk and gauze ruffles of parasols; through the tall trees came the music of the Guards playing to those fortunate enough to secure seats and ices in the tea enclosure.

Mrs. Hopeton saw Eunice Brent again—just ahead of her, with a group of friends.

The girl seemed neither hot nor dusty nor tired; she stood

erect, cool and indifferent; every one in the group seemed to defer to her. She held a delicate sunshade carelessly; the light streaming through it gave her a peach-like glow from head to foot.

Mrs. Hopeton, loathing her, hurried by on her aching feet, but she could not resist looking back at that disdainful lovely, unconquerable figure. And Miss Brent was looking at her, quite intently, but with unsmiling eyes.

Mrs. Hopeton took this as a rebuke; the girl did not wish to be troubled, even by a look, by the rejected lover's mother. Mrs. Hopeton's hot cheeks became more flushed; she walked blindly, and was buffeted by newcomers from the entrance gates.

She was miserably tired when she reached home, and agitated from her encounter with Miss Brent, but she tried to be cheerful when she saw Eric in the long chair by the window. He had only come back to change, she knew, for he was going out to dinner, but he had an idle moment and was sitting easily with a book.

Mrs. Hopeton asked him rather breathlessly if he had had tea.

"Oh, yes—ages ago."

She sat down, overcome by her thoughts, and Eric, looking at her pleasantly, remarked that she seemed tired.

"A little. I've been to the Flower Show."

"Didn't you enjoy it?"

"Oh, yes—but there were too many flowers," she answered stupidly.

Eric was always kind to this sort of remark.

"I know—a sort of orgy. I wonder why people go. It isn't much fun really."

She gazed at him with deep yearning. He was so gallant, so cheerful. Had he given up all hope? Received the final dismissal?

From Miss Brent's look she thought so, but she must find out.

"I saw Miss Brent," she said as quietly as possible.

"Which Miss Brent?"

He spoke as if he knew hundreds of Miss Brents and was indifferent to all of them.

"Eunice Brent."

"Oh, yes." The boy's reserve was unfaltering.

"You haven't seen her lately?" Mrs. Hopeton forced herself to say.

"No—not for a while." Then he added casually: "I've got into another set; somehow, we don't often meet."

So it was over! Mrs. Hopeton's anger flamed up against the girl. How she had encouraged him! At one time they had always been together. If that was flirtation, what was love?

She ventured to glance at him. He was certainly pale, and though he was looking down at his book he was not reading. How she longed for him to confide in her, to be able to tell him how vain, worthless and detestable, how unworthy of him she thought Eunice Brent, how sure she was that a pearl of a maiden was waiting for him somewhere!

But he would not speak, and she could not. He seemed so desirable to her in his slim grace, in his blond radiance, so healthy, modest and brilliant, first in everything he undertook, amiable and vivid, with those odd light eyes, set rather far apart, the colour of Malaga grapes, and a bloom on his skin over a golden dust of freckles.

His family was good; he had money; he had done "splendidly" at Oxford and was reading for the Bar. Mrs. Hopeton was passionately sure that he was going to be a great man. And yet all his beauty and grandeur, this vivid promise, had been rejected by a cold girl like Miss Brent.

He seemed to the watching love of his mother to be so innocent, virtuous in a strong and noble fashion, while Miss Brent was sly and mean and cunning—a maiden without maidenhood—and it was anguish to consider how she had had the power to wound him. Mrs. Hopeton could hardly keep her secret gaze from the pure lines of his firm face; she loved him for the gold glint in his stiff hair and for the precise curves of his generous lips as if these had been due to some effort of his own.

He spoke without looking up.

"By the by, I shan't be back to-night; I'm going away for a few days with the Eckersleys—Marlow, you know."

She knew; she understood at once. He was hiding himself from her (surely he knew that she knew!), from his usual world, among these new acquaintances, who would be unaware of his tragedy.

She said, as casual as he:

"Of course—that will be pleasant—it's so hot in town now."

He answered:

"You ought to get away too—or have some one here—I hate leaving you."

And he looked up with a sudden pleasant smile.

Her heart overflowed with gratitude. That he should think of her in the moment of his agony!

"Why, I'm happy here," she answered with as much quiet as she could command herself; and she added in her thoughts: "And so I was happy until we met Eunice Brent."

He rose and went out easily. How intensely she admired his self-control! She was proud of him, rejoiced in him and yearned in a fury of pity over his hurt, dwelt in a fury of anger on the inflictor of that hurt.

She was relieved when he had gone. He had taken his suitcase with him; he was motoring down to Marlow after dinner. She understood that he wanted to get away at once from even her tactfulness; she was glad that he was free even from her love; men, she thought, wanted freedom even from love.

She ate her lonely dinner thinking of nothing but her son; the little house was his shrine, and when he was away memories of him filled the emptiness.

Mrs. Hopeton was not as dowdy in her house as she was in her clothes; she had been trained to look after a home if she had not been trained to look after herself, and she had two excellent servants, knit to her by her kindness and courtesy; everything was very comfortable and well bred and easy, and she was always so thankful that she was well enough off to give Eric such a pleasant home.

She thought about him as he had been as a baby, as a little boy, to her so extraordinarily beautiful, with a gleaming white body which she had tended and nourished and trained with such reverence and care, and an innocent, brilliant mind which she had so diligently filled with all that was noble and fine, so that when he had left her care his body had seemed impervious to disease, and his mind to anything that was base or mean. At least he had never had an illness nor done a contemptible action.

And his taste was so sure, so lofty—at least Eunice Brent was beautiful and well bred. How much worse if he had broken his heart over a painted barmaid as she believed some boys did!

She remembered now, when he was about six, he had stood by her knee in a railway carriage, motionless, and then the warm little hand had touched her cheek and the radiant little face had looked up, and the boy's voice had whispered:

"Mamma, don't you think that's a wery handsome lady over there?"

And she had looked and been proud to see that it *was* a

handsome lady (proud, though, rather like Eunice Brent; a lady who seemed to disdain her company and her own rather shabby clothes), and had agreed eagerly:

"Yes, daring, a very handsome lady."

"I like her," he had said, and gazed at the dark, cold beauty till they had had to leave the carriage.

She recalled that incident so poignantly, and the tears smarted in her eyes. She had been able to get most things for him, but not his "handsome lady." How cheerfully she would have died if that could have prevented any woman from hurting him!

The evening was warm and all the windows were open on to the square; the lilac dusk was lovely above the dark trees, and charming the room with a rosy gold lamplight, but Mrs. Hopeton sat with the tears on her face, very lonely.

With the last post a letter.

As she lifted it from the salver she knew at once it was from Eunice Brent.

Ochre-coloured envelope, a tiny E. B. on the flap, addressed so clearly to Eric and marked "Urgent."

Even when the servant had gone Mrs. Hopeton sat still with the letter on her lap.

*The* letter!

How often a few weeks ago, when the first coolness seemed to have come between him and Eunice Brent, had he asked restlessly about letters—and never been satisfied with any that came!

She had never written before.

And now her letter lay on Mrs. Hopeton's lap, marked "Urgent."

She trembled with delight; the girl had relented, surely relented!

Otherwise she would not have written openly like this, with her initials on the envelope and marked "Urgent."

The whole house seemed beautified by that letter, which might be full of love and tenderness, which surely was full of love and tenderness!

Mrs. Hopeton was passionately thankful that she would be the means of giving her son this great pleasure, that she could put it into his hands, saying, "Here is something for you," as once she had put a toy or a longed-for gift, and watch his face as he broke the seals.

Then she recalled that he was away and that she could not have this joy, for she must forward the letter.

And then she recalled also that she did not know the address of Eric's friends nor even where or with whom he had been dining.

She was careless about such things and had a bad memory, and, besides, she had always shrunk from asking about Eric's engagements—though to-night she would have asked his address if she had not been overwhelmed by their mutual secret emotion and fearful of any speech.

The Eckersleys, Marlow—would that reach him?

She dare not risk the precious message. She tried the telephone, but "trunks" could not tell her of any such name with a telephone number at Marlow.

She felt cut off. Her instinct was to start at once for Marlow and search till she found Eric, but she checked this impulse, as she had checked so many others, because it would make Eric look foolish. Even if she went down to-morrow it would be a conspicuous thing to do, and attract too much attention to him, to her and to the letter.

Besides, he might be back to-morrow; he never stayed away more than a day or two; he was over eager, over keen on his work for long holidays.

Mrs. Hopeton resigned herself to a sleepless, excited night.

She wrapped the letter in a pale pink handkerchief and put it under her pillow. Often in the night her hand touched it, and again she was reminded of the days when he was little and she had awakened during the dawn to see the shape of packages for him (Christmas or birthday presents) on the table by the bed, and had touched them happily, thinking of his future pleasure.

There was no message from Eric in the morning, and Mrs. Hopeton found the day long and tedious.

She kept saying to herself, "It's come, darling; she's written; I've got a letter for you," with an intensity that she felt must reach him. By the afternoon she had telephoned to one or two friends of his whom she thought might know the Eckersleys' address, but in vain.

Then love wrought on her timidity (as indeed love had often wrought before) to do a very bold thing.

She telephoned to Eunice Brent, risking a snub or rebuke. At the sound of the girl's cold voice she shivered with repulsion, but she said bravely:

"Mrs. Hopeton speaking. There's a letter here—for Eric. I think, I believe—that it is from you."

"I wrote yesterday."

"Oh, yes." Mrs. Hopeton became confused. "I thought—that is—Eric is away——"

"Away?"

The cool voice gave her no help; she floundered on:

"You marked it 'Important'—I mean 'Urgent'—and I don't know his address.

"Oh!" (Impossible to gauge Miss Brent's feelings!) "How strange!"

"Yes, it's very stupid. He's with some people called Eckersley at Marlow. You don't know them?"

"No, they're not friends of mine."

"I can't trace them. I'm so sorry about your letter."

"Thank you. But don't worry; please keep it till he comes back."

Mrs. Hopeton was rebuked by the chill of this; she felt childish, futile.

"I only thought I'd let you know," she faltered, "in case it was rather important and you were expecting an answer."

A pause, and then the proud voice said:

"Thank you, Mrs. Hopeton. I was expecting an answer. It is rather important. Will you give it to him when he comes back?"

The anxious mother's hopes revived eagerly.

"Oh, that? Of course. I'm keeping it carefully. I only wanted to explain——"

"That's all right. Thank you again. Good-bye."

Miss Brent rang off.

Mrs. Hopeton was jubilant. She was looking for a reply. It was important!

A message of hope at last; perhaps a message of acceptance of Eric.

Then a wave of dislike, almost of hatred, overcame Mrs. Hopeton.

How galling to think that haughty creature had the happiness of Eric in her power! How dryly she had spoken just now; almost with disdain. How terrible to have to be grateful to her for any kindness!

She was thankful for the mercy of this proud girl, but she could not help loathing her. It was bitterly hard to have to accept this cold largess, and yet how thankful she was to have it to offer to Eric!

The evening of that day he returned, and she was without words with which to greet him.

It seemed to her so difficult to assail his admirable control even with good news.

She kept fingering the treasured letter inside her bag, full of a sense of drama, of expectation, but also of confusion and fear.

At last she produced it, schooled into indifferency by his gay reserve.

"This came while you were away. I couldn't forward it; I didn't know your address."

She could not look at him while he received it; when she did glance round it was in his pocket.

He said, with admirable calm, that he was going out.

Of course—to that girl—of course.

He left the room.

Mrs. Hopeton trembled. Wouldn't he take her into his confidence now? Wouldn't he tell her his good news? Didn't she deserve that? But she braced herself to passivity; only when he came to say good night she said:

"Where are you going?"

"Don't you remember?" he smiled. "It's the Johnstons' party——"

Mrs. Hopeton was stricken. He wasn't going, then, to Eunice Brent!

"I remember," she murmured.

When he had gone she wondered if Eunice Brent was to be at the Johnstons. Perhaps that was the appointment. She rang up the Brents' house and asked if the girl was in.

No; she had gone to the theatre.

So she wasn't meeting Eric to-night.

Mrs. Hopeton felt an anguish of disappointment. That letter which she had treasured so, which she had given him with such delight, which had seemed to fill the whole house with the perfume of love, was it after all but a delusion?

A final rejection, perhaps, a gesture of cruel coquetry. Mrs. Hopeton's hostility towards the girl increased bitterly; she loathed her; a gust of rage possessed her soul when she thought of the detestable creature who had picked up Eric to break him so ruthlessly.

She thought of her son ruined, driven from his work, hurled into despair, perhaps into drink by this refused passion. She had vague, horrible ideas of what men did under the effects of unrequited love; her innocence glimpsed at unnameable dark places where Eric might now be forced to tread. She felt herself growing ill from these thoughts and the kind servants looking at her with sympathy.

"He seems to me so wonderful," she kept saying to herself, "and yet this ordinary girl despises him."

She thought of her own brief married life. She had brought such boundless goodwill, patience and devotion to her marriage that, if her husband had lived, she would have made a success of it, and she had been an exemplary widow; but she could not, looking back, think that her husband had been half so wonderful as Eric, and yet she had been so honoured and glad to marry him!

What did women expect nowadays, what did they expect?

Mrs. Hopeton passed another miserable night and stayed late in bed; when she came down Eric had gone out, and she was relieved.

It was a cloudy, chill day. That afternoon she brought out her winter coat again and went out, went, on some obscure impulse, to the Flower Show. You could get in for a shilling now, and the flowers were being sold cheap in masses, in sheaves, in armfuls; the immaculate beauty of three days ago, that then you must not touch, you could now buy for a few pence.

The huge tents looked forlorn; the grey clouds were low over the big trees that shivered in an unpleasant little wind; everything was slightly damaged, despoiled, neglected; carts were taking away the trade exhibits; tired men and women were packing up their wares behind the stalls.

Mrs. Hopeton went to the orchid stand; the chill, perfect blooms she remembered were now wilted, stained with brown, drooping, some snapped off and prostrate.

A universal decay after so much pride; everywhere falling flowers, the ground strewn with petals, the air tainted by dying perfumes, and outside the tents the sunless day, the unkind wind, the restless trees that seemed ill at ease.

Mrs. Hopeton hurried home. Eric was still out.

She was quite unnerved; she thought (though, indeed, it was usual for him to be out at this hour) of him lashed into desperation, thought of even his suicide. She tried to control this panic, and she went upstairs and looked into his room to reassure herself by the sight of all his familiar things.

There were several papers on a desk by the window, and among them she at once descried the ochre-coloured letter, open, flung down as if of no importance.

Mrs. Hopeton, trembling, approached this desk; never had she ever read his letters or gone through his pockets, even when he was a schoolboy, but her gaze went to this letter now.

There was the signature "Eunice," written it seemed with a failing hand. Mrs. Hopeton's glance travelled over one or two sentences, and then she moved aside and sat down heavily on one of the easy chairs she had provided for Eric's comfort.

For a second her face, her whole attitude was blank; then she rose again and with quivering hands seized the largest book she could see and placed it over the letter so that it was concealed utterly.

Then she sat down again, shivering.

She had received a great shock, the most poignant shock of her life.

The letter, even what she had read of it, made it vividly clear that Eric had won and abandoned the girl, that she and not he was in despair.

What Mrs. Hopeton had thought his reserve of passionate emotion was merely indifference. He no longer cared about Eunice Brent; he had left carelessly on his desk her sad appeal and gone off gaily to his work and his pleasure.

Mrs. Hopeton had never thought in terms of sex, nor had there been any complications in her simple code; the Laws of Man suited her completely; but now she was stirred with horror, with wonder, with shame and by an odd sense of being really awakened for the first time in her life.

She had not been mistaken in the charm of Eric. He was the dominant male who inherits the earth; the first girl he had wooed had been his victim. But how absolutely she had been mistaken in the character of Eric; she, who had been so sure of every detail of his heart and mind, had been grotesquely deceived in him for weeks past.

Mrs. Hopeton tried to adjust all this in her shaken soul. Her first sensation was one that amazed her own conscience. It was that of triumph. Eric was hers again, she would not have to give him up to another woman; and she was avenged on this girl who had been so hostile to her, who had made her suffer so. Yes, the girl, and not she, was the wretched supplicant for the favours of Eric.

She felt secure, enthroned, while the rival who had been her torment for weeks, for months, was cast out and despised.

Rightly too; she had been "cheap" and "easy," the unforgivable feminine crime in the eyes of Mrs. Hopeton, who had always contemptuously blamed any woman who had made it possible for any man to humiliate her. She had the odd hardness of the virtuous and the untempted under all her good nature and tolerance.

She did not wish to read the letter through. She was afraid of it; shame and pain were in it, not love or tenderness as she had thought, not even romance; the affair had become sordid, horrible.

She hurried downstairs, and recalled how she had come up struggling with a fearful dread of Eric's suicide.

She could be quite at ease about him now.

If anyone—Eunice Brent—not Eric.

This thought pulled her up. What would the girl do?

Eric would not answer that letter, nor the next.

Mrs. Hopeton's thoughts turned to Eric. How she had exalted him!

Not so grand, so noble, so innocent after all, but a rather alien creature. Recalling his face, she thought she saw a sinister look in the calm features; those greenish eyes were oddly placid. How could he have sat there so still when she had asked him about Eunice Brent!

Not her baby now, not her little boy, but a man.

A man she did not know.

She was bewildered by her own feeling towards this beloved son—a feeling of hostility, the deep secret hostility of the sexes.

Not her boy, but a man.

Her knowledge of men was most superficial, but she had

always unconsciously avoided and dreaded them, and she had never considered Eric as one of these formidable masters of the world towards whom she had always felt that faint antagonism.

Eric, in ceasing to be her baby boy, had become involved in that antagonism.

She saw herself as a fool to trouble any more about Eric; he would get all he wanted always.

It was the girl who was in need of help, the girl who had no mother, the girl who had been undone, while Eric was scatheless.

Mrs. Hopeton remembered the orchids at the Flower Show, so bruised and broken, going cheap after all their pride.

And she remembered the unsmiling look the girl had given her, a look that she had grossly misinterpreted. For surely that had been a look, not of disdain, but of appeal?

She remembered too that quiet voice on the telephone: "Yes, it is rather important." "Yes, I am expecting an answer."

Though the whole of Mrs. Hopeton's innocent, simple life had been filled first by girlish futility, and then by love for her son, there was something in her stronger than this futility and this love.

She was, in the beautiful sense of the word, good, in the lofty meaning of the phrase, "a virtuous woman," and goodness and virtue being even stronger than the power of maternal love, she veered from the thing she adored to the thing she hated.

Of course Mrs. Hopeton was not aware of this; she merely felt feeble, confused and what she would have called "upset."

But this inner emotion within her, roused for the first time in her life, drove her into an action that she seemed to perform without her own volition.

She went to her room, put on her ill-shaped coat, her uncomfortable hat, and, looking very insignificant and dowdy, very flustered and red of face, she went out on her heroic errand.

Direct to the opulent house of Eunice Brent—her enemy until an hour ago.

Miss Brent was in, but could see no one. Would she leave a message?

Mrs. Hopeton showed a boldness she had never displayed before in all her life.

"Miss Brent will see me, I'm sure. Will you tell her, please, that I am here?"

She sat in the grand, fashionable room waiting, so absorbed in her thought that she did not feel, as at any other time she would have felt, at all nervous or embarrassed.

Yes, Miss Brent would see her. Mrs. Hopeton went upstairs still communing with her heart.

Eunice Brent sat alone in a small, rich room. As Mrs. Hopeton entered the girl turned on her the look she had turned on her at the Flower Show—a still, deep look.

Mrs. Hopeton came and sat down beside her. How could she ever have hated this poor child?

Eunice Brent was wilted like the orchids, pale, heavy-eyed, all her pride, all her grandeur gone.

"I always wanted a daughter," said Mrs. Hopeton, smiling. "I should have been very glad if she had been like you. I dare say we should have got on very well together and had a lot of fun."

"You know?" whispered Eunice without altering her imploring gaze.

"Yes."

"He didn't tell you?"

"No—I guessed." The evasion came spontaneously; never could she have told the girl of that carelessly tossed aside letter.

"Is he going to answer my letter?"

Mrs. Hopeton put her arms round the girl with a glory of pity and comfort.

"I don't know. I don't know him. I thought I did. I thought I'd made him, in a way—that he was mine. Now I've lost him too."

Eunice, at the warm kindness of clasp and voice, broke into an anguish of tears long bitterly repressed.

"I can't bear it, I can't bear it! O God, how differently I dreamed it!"

She was tormented by sobs in the other woman's arms.

"So did I," said Mrs. Hopeton, half-weeping too, clasping her closer.

"You can't help me," came the muffled voice, "no one can help me."

Mrs. Hopeton's tears fell on the bowed radiant head.

"I'd give him to you if I could. But he isn't mine now. Not anyone's—you'll understand that?"

"I know, I know——" The girl held her convulsively. "I loved him too much—I couldn't hold him."

"I also loved him too much," said Mrs. Hopeton passionately. "I thought of nothing but him, and now he's gone. Don't cry so, dear, don't cry—a woman can always help a woman—I'll stand by you."

"Oh, I've been lonely—and—*afraid!*"

Mrs. Hopeton kissed her in the way she would never again kiss Eric; they clung together in an understanding stronger than any understanding between man and woman, stronger even than that between mother and son.

"I'd like to go away," said Mrs. Hopeton tenderly. "We might go away together, you and I—alone."

It was her renunciation of Eric, her salutation to something that was more to her than Eric.

# FALSE PRETENCES

AT once she saw the fur coat. There were never very many fur coats hanging up in the dressing-room of Betty's club; the members who had them generally wore them to show they'd got them, and also because the heating arrangements weren't of the best. It was a progressive club, and scorned both effeminate finery and mannish comfort; judging by the cooking there must have been a lot of Stoics among the members. Betty wasn't a Stoic; her "poverty, not her will consented" when she became a member of that club.

Now she stared at the fur coat—beaver with an orange-blue shot lining and really well *cut;* not the kind to make you look as if you wanted a stand and a string and a place in a Christmas bazaar.

And Betty felt so particularly shabby. She had that brave threadbare look of one whom winter has caught in a "between season" suit; the strip of fur round her neck was common or roof cat, her hat "passed," but only because Betty was pretty and knew how to wear her things. She had to, for she was an actress, not at all successful, and beginning to regard looking-glasses with a rather restive eagerness; for though she was intellectual and played in "high-brow" productions, she had no wish to show this in her face.

Linda came in.

"Looking at the fur coat?" she said. "Mine."

"You've sold your soul?" questioned Betty.

"My dear! It's *real* fur! I got it on tick."

"But Linda, the price?" murmured Betty.

"Never mind. They gave me credit. And I've got a job."

She was pallid, and her eyes gleamed. Linda was a journalist, and the dramatic habit and the "human touch" had become second nature to her. Betty, who played those very modern misery parts where you shuffle and mutter, was always afraid of catching melodrama from Linda.

"Come into lunch," she added, "and I'll talk."

"Can't we go somewhere else, if you've a job?" said Betty wistfully. You see, she had seen the menu, displayed like a doleful warning in the hall on the board where dusty notices claimed about thirty umbrellas "taken by mistake."

As they sat in the crowded little restaurant between a spinster chrysanthemum about as fresh as the suet in the meat pie served by a waitress who had just been given "notice" by a manageress who had just received it, and watched by a purple-haired cashier in an open box who was brooding over a possible action against the committee, Linda unfolded her story.

"I've got a job as society reporter on 'The Blue Moon.' "

"Oh, Linda!"

"Isn't it wonderful? I begin next week. Lots of frocks—the entrée everywhere! Such a chance!"

They had a bottle of club claret to celebrate.

"Next week I'll be drinking wine," said Linda.

Animated by this atmosphere of success, Betty began to unfold her excitement.

"Simon Kettlewell asked me out to tea to-day. I believe he's going to give me a big part."

"Oh, Betty!"

"Isn't it wonderful? He's so serious—he never does these things without a meaning."

Linda said:

"Isn't it wonderful? I'll write you up."

And Betty:

"You're wonderful. I believe he's in love with me; he's been paying me a lot of attention."

Linda was as enthusiastic as possible. Of course there is nothing so boring as hearing about some one else's love affair—except having none of your own.

And Linda simply couldn't help thinking that, if the great Kettlewell was as susceptible as all that, it was a pity she hadn't met him herself. But then Betty was getting to that stage, poor darling, when she *had* to be mean about you meeting her men.

So Linda said, with great sweetness:

"How wonderful!"

They had coffee in the lounge, so called because the chairs were so uncomfortable you preferred to lean against them instead of sitting in them.

"If only I wasn't so shabby!" sighed Betty. "It puts a man off so."

Linda sparkled.

"I'll lend you the fur coat."

"Oh, Linda!"

"I mean it. I shan't want it to-day. You can look in on your way home. I'll be here about six."

"I'll never forget this," said Betty solemnly, with the air of one whose rememberings would soon be worth a good deal.

Linda watched her snuggle into the fur coat. It really hid all deficiencies; even the hat shone with a reflected glory. Betty felt confident, assured, superb.

Linda was a real *friend*. They would have kissed if it hadn't been for the lipstick.

Betty, from the vantage point of that fur coat, found the drabbish November streets a pleasant place. Until the hour of her appointment she walked about enjoying the vicarious delight of gazing in at the shop windows and thinking of the big thrill of walking into—oh, all of them, one after another, and ordering things. "To my account—Mrs. Simon Kettlewell—please."

She wondered quite how much money he'd got. He'd been able to afford two divorces, anyhow. He was a quiet, serious sort of man, and Betty was afraid he was looking for an "ideal." Of course you always had to pretend to be something, but the bother of pretending to be an ideal was that you had no model to imitate; you just had to try and think what he liked and then embody it in an effective way. Both his wives had been different. Well, it was no use worrying; thank Heaven, they all liked you to *listen*. "A few timid questions about himself," thought Betty, "will fill up any awkward pauses."

As she entered the White Park Hotel Betty felt her spirits rise. The coat was so *right*. What taste Linda had!

Every other woman there had a fur coat; that is what made Betty feel so comfortable. But the difference with Betty was that she kept hers on, though it was overheated; with a pleading shiver she accused the room of draughts as she greeted Kettlewell, already waiting.

"I'll keep my coat on."

He hadn't recognized her at once, for he had been thinking:

"The poor girl will look different from every one who comes in."

He knew her clothes by heart. He had often pictured her mending and brushing them: tacking on little collars, pulling about little bits of feathers and things, poor, dear child. But this coat was an alien.

"Didn't know you at first."

"How unkind!" murmured Betty, distracted by a sight of herself in one of those gigantic glasses that as it were double your money's worth.

"Women all the same nowadays. Sort of uniform."

"Hope I'm not quite the same," smiled Betty, sitting down and flicking out the fur coat to show the gleam of the brocade.

"You're not."

She brightened, rather mechanically, for his tone was not tender. He ordered tea with that air of hostility so many Englishmen show at any mention of food; a sort of suspicious defiance of what they expect (and generally get) foisted on to them.

Betty, haunted by the ghost of the club lunch, would have liked something substantial, but had to be vague and feminine. Kettlewell seemed sullen. He was thinking:

"What frauds they all are! I thought she was so different, a really hard-working, sweet, honest little woman, and she turns up in a thing like that! Cost all of what she earns in a year."

He found his tea bitter, cold, sour, strong, expensive, and said so.

"It's a mercy he's got so much money," thought Betty. "We shan't have to have many meals together."

Aloud she praised his good judgment and the courage with which he condemned the atrocity of the tea.

"But tea's only an excuse, isn't it?"

"A very poor excuse," he replied. He was wondering what the fur coat had cost. He had a pretty fair idea of the price of most things, including women, but he had considered Betty an exception. Now he began to think that her value was exactly the value of the fur coat.

What a fool!

What a couple of fools!

He had meant to make her his leading lady and his wife.

He had experienced an infantile and almost holy joy in the thought of buying her things after her long self-denial. She would have been a rich, an adored, a famous woman—and she had let some idiot buy her a fur coat!

Just like all the others!

He hated fur coats. This one didn't suit her, anyhow; she lost all distinction, all "difference"; she was like something from one of those houses in Hampstead with greenhouses and "at home" days.

And what taste the fellow had! He loathed that gaudy lining, anyway.

The tea was bitter indeed. And flavourless the silly cakes.

What was she saying?

He hadn't heard, and didn't care.

Betty was cheerful; she saw that he was struggling with some unusual emotion, and felt the great moment was arriving.

Their divan was quite lonely (the "White Park" rather specialized in discreet loneliness; what they lost in floor space they gained in the type of client too absorbed to notice the bills); there was a dance tune being played somewhere near; everything was appropriate, including the rose-coloured shade on the lamp by Betty's elbow.

Kettlewell looked sombre.

Then he actually pulled out his watch and looked at it.

Betty felt a wave of fright.

Heavens! was the man merely absent-minded or really a dud?

" 'Fraid I must be getting on," he said. "Rehearsal at six at the Climax. By the by, I've decided on May Carlyon for next season's lead. Thought you'd be interested.

They both left.

Betty had a taxi home because she was too exhausted to walk. She'd employed enough tact to run a Church Congress in the Kettlewell affair, and this was the end of it—May Carlyon! who acted like a schoolgirl at a breaking-up party, and off the stage behaved as if she had served the drinks in a cabaret in the war zone. May Carlyon!

"I've mistaken his type all this time," moaned Betty. "As if any woman could do what May does."

She had a headache, she was hot with rage; the taxi was blocked again and again; she forgot it was Linda's coat she was pushing off and thrusting back in the stuffy obscurity of the cab.

She paid the man with a half-crown that meant more to her evidently than it did to him, for her reluctance to part with it was scarcely more marked than his to accept it. Her club wasn't in the same neighbourhood as the "White Park."

She rushed to find Linda, to tell Linda how shamefully she'd been used.

Linda was in the "rest room," huddled on a couch.

"Don't speak to me!" she snapped when she saw Betty. "The 'Blue Moon' rang me up as soon as you were gone and asked me to go over——"

"Well?"

"Well, I went, in *your* coat and bit of cat, and they turned me down at once. Mistaken my personality, they said, or some such rot—thought I ought to have bucked up by now! If only I'd kept the fur coat!"

Betty sat down and stared.

"Wonder if they'll take that coat back," added Linda bitterly. "Where is it?"

Betty gazed at herself. She was without it, clothed only in her limp black coat.

"Heavens! I've left it in the taxi!"

# AN APPOINTMENT WITH STIFFKEY

THE light had been put out on the stairs. Usually, when he returned late to spend the night in his rooms, he found it burning. Now he had to make his way slowly, striking matches as he went up the old, dingy enclosed stairs. It was a long time since he had spent a night in this house, and he did not greatly care about doing so. It was an ancient inconvenient residence, hidden away in a small square which had been half demolished, and was hemmed in on either side by massive modern buildings. Only when, as now, the young man had been detained so late at a dance that he had missed the last train to his home in the country, did he resort to this expedient of spending the night in this makeshift fashion. Roger Hoby knew that he would be alone in the house, with a great many other empty houses to right and left of him, and there was something in this silence more oppressive than the silence of the open country—so many buildings round him, so busy and crowded in the day, at night so empty and silent; and he blamed the caretaker, who had not left the old-fashioned gas (for there was no electric light in the house) burning on the stairs. So heavy was the sense of oppression on him that he decided the next night he had to pass in town would be in an hotel.

He found his own door, opened it and entered the suite of chambers he occupied on the second floor, lit the gas in the first room and passed into the second, which he used as his architect's office.

It was a hateful, raw, cold and foggy night, and Roger Hoby was shuddering and shivering from having passed through the bitter, bleak streets and the damp cold of the dark stairway. He was therefore pleasantly amazed when he felt the warmth that met him as he opened the second door and saw the room, full of all his own familiar and pleasant possessions, brightly illuminated by the glow of a large fire. As he had not been there since the afternoon he wondered who could have made up such a large fire to last until this late hour. The caretaker was seldom in the building after six. Even as Hoby wondered he noticed that some one was sitting in the large arm-chair drawn up by the fireplace—a man whose dark shape appeared to be one with that of the chair and was outlined against the bright blaze of the coals.

"Hullo!" cried Hoby, considerably startled, and not without an odd creep of fear in his heart, and more than ordinary amazement.

The figure did not move. One hand was hanging over the edge of the arm-chair, and Hoby noticed that it was a peculiar-shaped hand with long splay-ended fingers. Roger Hoby, advancing with a considerable effort of will, almost laughed aloud with relief when he saw that the man whom he had seen sitting before the fire was Durant Loveday, who occupied the rooms above his own. He was a person with whom Hoby had no more than the most casual acquaintance, and for whom he did not greatly care. It was more than odd to find him sitting there at this hour, yet not quite so odd as Hoby thought it would have been to find a total stranger by his fire.

"Oh, it's you," said Loveday, and he seemed as relieved to see Hoby as Hoby had been to see him. He had not been asleep; only holding himself very still and quiet in the deep chair.

"What do you want?" asked Roger Hoby. "I didn't know you ever spent the night here. How did you get in?"

"I don't ever spend the night here," replied Durant Loveday

quickly. "This is the first time I have ever been here late. But then, you see, I have an appointment."

"An appointment here at this hour?"

"Yes, it sounds peculiar, doesn't it?"

Roger Hoby thought it sounded very peculiar. He wondered that he had never noticed before that Loveday had such ugly splayed fingers. But then he had never given him more than the most cursory glance on the stairs or in the street. He knew nothing at all about the fellow, and he never liked the thin dry face, the eyes that were too pale, too deeply-cut and deeply-set. All he knew of Loveday was that he also was an architect and appeared to have an income independent of his work, which amounted to very little as far as Hoby knew.

"Well, you didn't make an appointment here, I suppose?" said Hoby, warming himself before the fire which his uninvited guest had kept so generously piled with coal.

"No; it was because I decided not to keep my appointment that I came here," replied the other. "Some one was coming back for me, but I didn't want to see him."

"How did you get in?"

"I slipped in before your clerk went. I hid, and he went and left me locked in."

"Did he?" thought Hoby.

"I'm glad you've come back," said Loveday in a confidential tone, leaning forward from the arm-chair. "I've been here for hours; I am glad of your company. I kept on piling up the fire to make a bright light, but still I am glad of your company."

"Well, I can't keep you company," replied Hoby; "I want to go to bed. It must be two o'clock."

Loveday put up his hand; his thick finger-ends travelled over his thin lips, and those pale deep-set eyes gazed at Hoby with an expression that the young man had never seen in a human face before—one of absolute terror.

"Why, you're afraid!" cried Hoby involuntarily.

"I've got an appointment," muttered Loveday, "at half-past two."

Hoby went to his cupboard and set out the whisky and soda. "Look here," he said in a voice he tried to make as practical as possible, "you'd better tell me what this is all about. You seem to have lost your nerve a bit, have't you? What are you doing here really—hiding?"

"There's some one coming back to see me at half-past two," cried Loveday, "whom I have been avoiding for years."

"Then why on earth," asked Hoby, "did you make an appointment with him in such a place, and at such an hour?"

"He forced me," said Loveday, his voice falling to a whimper, "he forced me to it. You don't know what power he's got over me. I met him in the street, and then in a restaurant, but that wouldn't do. He would come here at half-past two. I didn't make the appointment; he did. He told me, 'Half-past two to-day, and I'll be there.' He came and went without saying anything except 'I'll be back at half-past two to-night.' "

"How is he going to get in?" asked Hoby. "I closed the door behind me."

"He forced me to give him the pass-key," said loveday. "He'll get in all right. But"—his voice dropped to an accent of cunning—"he'll go upstairs to the offices overhead, he won't think of looking for me here; and I'm locked in, aren't I?"

"Yes, I shut the door," said Hoby doubtfully. He took a drink and gave one to Loveday, who, however, refused it. "You had better tell me what it's all about, hadn't you?"

"It would be a very long story," grinned Loveday; "there's a great deal in it; in fact, there's everything in it." Then, seeing that Hoby had taken up some matches, he cried out: "Don't light the gas; he'll know there's somebody here then, and he might try to get in."

"But he can't," replied Hoby briefly, "and we're two to one if he does."

"You don't know Stiffkey," said Loveday, still with a grin.

Hoby put down the box of matches. The room was really sufficiently illuminated by the fire, and it occurred to him that if anyone did come they would judge by firelight as easily as by gaslight that the room was occupied. He did not, however, mention this to Loveday. He had come to his own conclusions about him, the usual conclusions that the ordinary man comes to when faced with anything peculiar or extraordinary—he thought that Loveday was ill or out of his mind.

"Well," he remarked soothingly, "you can have a shakedown here all night if you like.[77] I sleep in the other room. There's a sofa there too, if you would like it."

But Loveday said no, he preferred to sit by the fire. He looked at the clock on the mantelpiece, which now showed ten minutes past two.

No one will come of course, thought Roger Hoby; the man's been badly scared by something, and this is the way it's taken him. He imagines an appointment with an enemy, but no one would come to such a place and at such a time. Observing again that snarl of terror on Loveday's face he was, however, himself slightly affected by fear, and said: "You had better really tell me

[77] Shakedown: a makeshift bed.

something of what it's about if you want me to stand by you in this, you know."

"I robbed Stiffkey," confessed Loveday, "years ago, when we were in Africa. He entrusted me with something of his to sell—stones—and I brought them over to England and gave them to a jeweller to value, and then I told him that the jeweller had absconded with them. Of course, I had sold them and kept the money. That was the beginning of better times for me. I thought Stiffkey had died in Africa; I didn't hear from him for years . . . . Hush! what was that?" He paused to listen, and Hoby listened too, but there was no sound in the empty house.

"It sounds a pretty rotten sort of trick," said Hoby, drinking his whisky and soda. "I wonder you care to talk about it."

"There are other things," said Loveday. "We were great enemies, but for years I haven't seen him, I haven't thought about him, until I met him just the other day, and he insisted on this appointment—'to settle scores,' he said. I offered him money—a great deal of money—but he said money wouldn't pay for all those years. Hush! I do think that's his step on the stairs."

"It isn't," said Hoby impatiently; "there is no sound of anything. It's *too* silent." He went to the window. "The fog is quite thick," he added.

"He'll find his way through the fog all right," answered Loveday faintly. "He means to have his vengeance."

"Vengeance?" repeated Hoby. "Do you think he'll come here to revenge himself on you?"

"Of course," said Loveday, huddling himself together; "he always said he'd get me in the end."

"Well, I shouldn't have met him in this place and at this time of night," replied Hoby, trying to speak with more confidence than he felt. He also found himself straining his ears to catch the possible sound of a footstep on the stairs, a rap, or a voice at the door.

"He would come," whimpered Loveday. "It's his own fault; he would come, nothing else would do for him; and I was in his power wasn't I? 'I'll come back,' he said, 'at half-past two.' "

Roger Hoby shuddered and drew nearer to the fire. He didn't want to go to bed, after all; he thought he'd prefer to sit up with Loveday; not to leave him, anyhow, until half-past two. The clock now showed twenty minutes past that hour. The fog had drifted into the low room, thickening the firelight. Loveday leaned forward to pile on more coal, but Hoby restrained him. "The place is too hot already."

"I'm cold," whimpered Loveday, "cold."

Hoby had no compassion for him. He had never liked the man, who, on his own showing, deserved no friendship or respect from anyone—a thief, a traitor and a coward. No, Hoby had no compassion for him, but he was drawn to him by a stronger link than compassion—that of terror. He was infected by the fear that Loveday gave out—fear that was so definite that it seemed another personality in the room, and one that had laid its grip on Hoby, who was seized by this terror that had seized Loveday, and shuddering and dreading—whoever it was—this Stiffkey, who was coming at half-past two. So strongly and suddenly did this terror overwhelm him that he made an impulsive movement towards the clock to stop the hands. Loveday, watching him, grinned. "I thought of that," he said; "but it's no use, there are other clocks outside."

"Look here," said Hoby roughly, trying to keep up his own courage, "this is all nonsense, you know; you're imagining the whole thing; nobody's coming, and even if they did——"

Loveday interrupted, more by his movement and his clutch on the arm of the chair and the look on his face than by anything he said, though he did mutter for the third time, "Hush!"

"It sounds like the front door," said Hoby, "opening and closing."

"Can't you hear?" whispered Loveday. "There's some one coming up the stairs."

"No, I can't," said Hoby roughly.

The clock on the mantelpiece struck half-past two.

"Warmth! warmth!" cried Loveday; "I want to get warmth." He pulled his chair up to the fire, so closely it seemed that he must scorch.

Hoby went into the outer room and listened. That shivering man was afraid of murder. There certainly was some one coming up the stairs, slowly and deliberately, as if unhindered by the dark. Hoby moved by some unaccountable impulse of dread, saw that his own door was secure, and then returned to where Loveday crouched lower and lower over the fire. Hoby could still hear the footsteps, slow and deliberate. Had Stiffkey come with purpose of murder? Hoby looked round—he did not know why—for a weapon, and picked up a heavy stone paperweight, which had been carelessly placed on the chimneypiece to hold down a few odd papers beside the clock. He found it was wet. He dropped it and, holding his fingers into the firelight, saw they were red."

"What's this—blood?" cried Hoby.

Loveday began to laugh. "Do you hear a footstep? Half-past two—exactly to his appointment."

Hoby could hear the footsteps. They had passed the door now. He could hear them overhead, tramping to and fro. He had struck a match and was staring at the chimneypiece. The papers underneath the paperweight were splashed and spluttered with red.

A thin dark line was running down the wall. Hoby, looking up, saw it was coming from a patch on the plastered ceiling, exactly where it met the wall—a patch that seemed to be spreading as he looked. Loveday's room was exactly overhead. The footsteps were exactly overhead, by the dark patch on the plaster.

"Up in your room," whispered Hoby, dropping the flaring match.

"Stiffkey," grinned Loveday, staring, "Stiffkey."

"And who else?" whispered Hoby.

"Only Stiffkey," said Loveday.

The steps were again crossing the room overhead and coming down the stairs. The two men listened, bending closer together, Loveday further and further leaning towards the fire. The footsteps paused at the outer door, and there was a sharp rap.

"I won't let him in," whispered Hoby.

"It doesn't matter whether you do or not," whimpered Loveday; "the door is open."

"No, I shut the door."

But even as the young man spoke he felt a draught of cold outer air. The door, which he was certain he had closed, stood open on the black staircase. The sound of footsteps had departed, in the direction of Loveday, but he saw no one. Then he heard Loveday from behind him give a gurgle and a shriek of incredible anguish, and he did not dare go back to the fire. He knew that it was useless to do so, that Loveday was dead.

It was quite a long time before he was able to return to the room, light the gas and stare at Loveday, rigid in his chair, beneath that red patch on the ceiling.

Hoby had known that he would be there alone.

The fog was now so thick that even with the gaslight everything looked dim, monstrous and misshapen.

Torn by a fearful curiosity, Roger Hoby went up into Loveday's chambers. They were not locked. Hoby, striking matches, found what he had expected to find—a dead man lying by the wainscot, who had been battered to death by the poker which lay beside him, and whose blood was slowly soaking between the ceiling and the wall. His watch was staring on the floor beside him; it had stopped at half-past two, which must have been the hour when Loveday murdered him.

The appointment was for half-past two, but in the afternoon, not in the night . . . He had said he would return . . .

But who was the other? Who had Loveday waited for all those hours, first upstairs, and then hiding down in Hoby's room? Stiffkey, returning to keep his second appointment the next time the clock was at half-past two?

# THE USUAL THING

THE great scientist had finished his lecture: "an epoch-making lecture" the newspapers would call it in the articles that, carried all over the world, would make his name even more famous than it was to-day; Richard Crighton, one of *the* names of all time.

While they were all discussing him, all excited, all seeing in these discoveries, inventions, or, as Crighton called them, "condensations of eternal verities," the ultimate realization of their own personal dreams of progress, goodness, ambition or money, the man himself went away, very tired, taking only one with him, a young Frenchman whose work closely pursued his own, had even breasted it, might in time surpass it. Crighton liked this man for his intelligence, his industry and his serene adoration; common adulation had long since disgusted the lofty genius of Richard Crighton, but he could still savour the admiration of one quite—well, nearly his intellectual equal, only lesser than he by the difference in years and the knowledge the years bring.

The two men sat silent, each gazing in the tall clear flames on the straight plain hearth, that burnt with the bright serenity of the fires rising from some sacrifice on an altar.

The room was, of course, severe, ordered with a keen economy of beauty rare to the west.

There was one picture, a Claude Lorraine (but Crighton called him Gellée), one bronze, an early Florentine David, and one bowl of flowers, branches of forced white lilac, each with a dull grey lacquer wall apart—on the wall with the fireplace nothing but two fantastic andirons cast by Cellini.

Plain grey curtains shut out the London March night. For the rest, simplest of chairs and tables and a large, untidy desk; no secretaries came into this room.

A "queer" room, people said; not many saw it, fewer liked it; even the young Frenchman who sat there to-night rather resented the Claude Lorraine—what did a taste so fine-drawn, so weary of mere beauty, so precise and over-trained, want with this fairy landscape?

The men neither smoked nor drank; one was too tired, the other too excited, and neither cared for habit.

"Of course, it is quite wonderful," said Dessalle in his excellent English. "The pinnacle, the pinnacle!"

"For me?" asked Crighton quietly.

"Naturally. You are one of—them—now. Archimedes, Galileo, Newton, Faraday—it's—well, there is nothing like it—can be nothing like. Even you—must feel that?"

"I don't know," said the great man slowly. "I think it seems rather flat."

"Flat?"

"Or flavourless. Like something you have sucked the taste out of——"

"Ah, you have had always too much success."

"Dessalle, what *do* we mean by this—success?"

The Frenchman smiled queerly.

"You want to analyse—even that?"

"No, no—again, a Mumbo Jumbo word, analyse! The thing I mean is just the thing that always escapes . . . analysis."

"Just?"

"Why Psyche missed in the dark—what Pandora shut the lid on—the side of the apple Adam *didn't* bite—a few grains of 'unknown matter' at the bottom of your crucible!"

"Not much unknown to you, professor, at the bottom of your crucible; but I see what you mean, of course. You can teach the Universe how to spin, but you cannot control your own heartbeats."

Crighton smiled; he leant forward in the spare-looking but supremely comfortable chair; the subdued glow of the electric bulbs concealed somewhere in the cornice showed his heavy yet fallen figure, the bearded face, fine, yet physically a ruin, his precise, expressionless evening clothes, the dead-black, the glazed white, the heavily veined pale hands.

"Right as usual, Dessalle," he said; his tired voice was almost sad. "Heart, or conscience—that is what I mean, I suppose."

The alert Frenchman caught at a word in the sentence that seemed to him peculiarly grotesque.

"Conscience! That cannot concern you, professor. The most generous of men, the most just and kind——"

Crighton checked him with a lift of the tired hand.

"You always admired me, Dessalle. Well, well!" The faded, strained eyes flashed a second behind the spectacles. "Who paid for your training, Dessalle?"

So direct was this suddenly personal question that the younger man almost flushed.

"My people, sir."

"Ah! . . . They were—are—well to do?"

"Wealthy, you might say, professor. Where are you leading me?"

"Nowhere. My mind rambles. Tired, Dessalle. Wealthy! They spent a lot of money on you?"

"I'm afraid . . . a great deal, sir."

"Expensive training! Expensive experiments! Travel! Leisure! Books! Yes, a great deal—a great deal of money."

Crighton spoke thoughtfully, gazing into the fire, springing straightly up, as from a poured libation.

"You do not earn much money now, Dessalle?"

"Not a great deal, sir."

"You will. As I have done. A great deal of money. You are not forty yet? And well on the road."

"Thank you, sir. But I never much wanted money."

"Money!" repeated the old man. "You speak with an emphasis of contempt——"

"Not contempt."

"You do, you do—because you have always had it. And were able to forget it, eh?"

"That—perhaps."

"Now, supposing you had been poor, conscious of your powers, knowing what you needed to cultivate them—with no one to help you; only capable of earning a small wage by hard, distasteful work . . . well, you would have found yourself thinking a great deal about money, Dessalle."

The Frenchman's lean face showed concentrated and keen in expression.

"Yes," he admitted.

"And what would you, so young, so ambitious, so sure of yourself, so desperate, have done to obtain that money?" demanded the great man.

"Almost anything, I suppose, sir."

"*Almost* anything! We come to the bottom of the crucible, Dessalle, the small residue in our tubes of 'unknown material.' *Almost* anything!"

"Well, one would not care for a career founded on fraud, or wrong, or lies, or any kind of thievery or trickery——"

"Are you sure?" asked Crighton quickly. "Or are you just repeating the usual thing?"

"The usual thing?"

"What we are expected to say to these questions; I mean—the answers dictated by tradition, convention!"

"I do not know, sir," replied Dessalle slowly. "I have never been tried. One takes so much for granted——"

"Wealthy people do," came the rather harsh interruption.

"And I have always, I think, believed—in tradition," finished the Frenchman with a touch of stiffness.

"But you've never been tempted?"

"Tempted, professor?"

Crighton smiled at the intonation.

"Oh, not crudely. We can most of us keep our hands out of each other's pockets. But—well—there are degrees—it's like a man priding himself on his disdain for a flashy street-walker. *She* does not tempt you, of course, but there may be a woman somewhere who could make you do something you would rather not."

The Frenchman very slightly shrugged.

"Of course. Nevertheless, I should hope to withstand your 'one in a million' woman as successfully as the poor prostitute."

"Ah, Dessalle, Dessalle!" sighed Crighton. "Listen to what I am going to tell you. I want to tell *some one*. It is at the bottom of everything with me."

"The usual thing, again?"

"You mean—Love? How curious the word sounds. Cheapened till we are ashamed to use it, eh? Made common as dirt, vulgar as town mud! Romance! Love!"

His glance just flickered, in a pause of silence, to the Claude Lorraine, cunningly lit by hidden lamps to show the golden distance, the gleaming river, the ethereal clouds.

"Exquisite," said Dessalle respectfully. "This room has made me discontented with every picture gallery and museum in Europe."

"That is not what you meant to say," smiled Crighton.

"Yes, professor. Not what I thought, perhaps."

"And that?"

"I always thought that picture out of place," conceded the Frenchman.

"Yes. A fairy-tale slipped into a treatise on molecules! Never mind. I want to show you something."

Dessalle made no further attempt to change the subject; he had wanted to talk "shop," but he knew when it was useless to induce Crighton to do this, and there was something too reverential in his attitude towards the older man to permit him to endeavour to lead the conversation.

Besides, he was becoming interested.

With a slow, rather awkward movement Crighton turned in his chair and opened a drawer in the little slender table that stood beside him, and held the untouched decanters, the unopened cabinet of cigars.

From this drawer, with clumsy hands that slightly trembled (Dessalle reminded himself that the great man was old, old) he drew out a small box.

Dessalle knew it at once for one of those cheap affairs of unstained wood, crudely carved and sold to "tourists" in every Swiss town. It was locked; Crighton actually had the tiny key on his watch-chain, and fumbled with it slowly.

Dessalle was interested.

"It does not look fifty years old—nearly?" smiled the great man. "They make them just the same now. But they were more uncommon then. And more expensive. This cost—ten francs. A lot of money to me then . . . a lot of money to a very poor young man."

The last words impressed the Frenchman with a quick sense of queerness, but, being subtle, he did not say, "You were poor, then?" but:

"*You* bought it, professor?"

"Nearly fifty years ago. At—a little village at the foot of the Alps. You remember *Julie?*"[78]

Dessalle smiled.

"Yes. But I should not have thought you would, professor."

"It was a favourite book with me then. I think I took it for 'light literature'! Well, well." He had the box unlocked now.

Inside—a ring, a letter, a flat and withered flower, star-shaped.

"Very much the usual thing," smiled Crighton.

Dessalle took out his cigarette case; the love story of Richard Crighton! How poignant . . . and how utterly trivial . . . an old man dwelling on a half-century-old romance . . . rather dreadful. To Dessalle it was almost like a first horrible touch of senility . . . as if Crighton had begun to talk of his first breeches or the attack of measles he had had at six . . . almost.

"I am not going to be garrulous," smiled the great man, with a humorous look at the other's cigarette.

"Garrulous!" repeated Dessalle. "The word is an affront——"

He was sincere, yet what had been in his own mind save what this word expressed? Crighton looked at his treasures and lifted them out, one by one.

[78] *Julie ou la nouvelle Héloïse* (*Julie or the New Heloise*), an epistolary novel by Jean-Jacques Rousseau. Published in 1761, its original title was *Lettres de deux amans, habitans d'une petite ville au pied des Alpes* (*Letters From Two Lovers, Living in a Small Town at the Foot of the Alps*).

First, the ring, that just circled the top of his little finger, "cheap" as the box from which it came, made when "artificial" stones were so crudely done, glass coloured red and white that gave out not one flicker of light, but stared dull and blank from the thick setting.

Second, the flower: edelweiss (*of course*, thought Dessalle), looking like heavy flannel, dried and flat, dirty white, dingy green, a touch of withered gold.

Third, the letter, a buff envelope, the mauve stamp with the old Queen's head, the thin postmark—the address in a careful hand to:

Richard Crighton Esquire,
88 Blomfield Street,
Mary le Bone.

No letters after the name . . . and what an address . . . fifty years ago . . .

"I just want you to see this picture," said the great man, putting the three objects back into the box, which he held open on his lounging knee. "A young man, myself, very poor, very friendly, very ambitious, at the end of his little resources, forced to give up all his dreams—which were—well, not so wild—and take a job, they would say now, at—a soap factory, shall we call it? A small salary, continuous work, no time, no money, no heart *for what he wants to do*, what he thinks, God help him, he *ought to do*."

"He was right, sir."

"Wait, Dessalle. I see him in this little village—he had got away to think it out; Switzerland was a bit of an adventure in those days, almost like Rousseau saw it—it was his last assertion of liberty. He was really at the end of things . . . and going back to the . . . soap factory."

"Was there no way, sir?"

"None. He had tried everything. It was all so much more difficult then. People were very comfortable. And blind. They did not really want—scientists. Discovery seemed, well, a little blasphemous. You weren't encouraged. No one was looking out for you. They—they honestly thought you would do better in—in the soap factory."

Dessalle pressed out his cigarette and sat still.

"I see this young fellow, myself, a likely young fellow, I suppose . . . and, my God! how much in earnest . . . coming across those fields at the foot of the Alps, and a girl with him, a funny little dark girl—not—no, I do not think you would call her pretty. She was not anything else, either, not distinguished, nor clever, nor wealthy—just a little English governess in one of the better families of the place. She wore this ring. She had not, ever, I think, very good taste. I have forgotten the dress. I remember the hat—with plaid ribbons. She was carrying this box—she had admired it so much that the young man had asked her to keep it—he had only bought it himself because he was sorry for the peasant who made it, and sold so few."

The quiet voice, weary with the long lecture, dropped a second.

Dessalle glanced almost furtively at the Claude Lorraine.

"So I see them" continued the great man, "going side by side. And soon—another picture. The girl—dying. Some quick infection—some carelessness—and the funny little dark girl is dying. In the deal-boarded, white-curtained Swiss bedroom. Her—employers—are kind. She has asked for the young man, and he is allowed to sit beside her. It is too early for flowers, but he brings the little spray of edelweiss, not knowing why, and she tries to kiss it. She will not let him leave her. And when she is delirious, which is often, she says, 'Richard, Richard!' The doctor is sorry. They are all sorry. They did not know that she had—a romance, they call it. They thought her plain, not interesting. Every one is sympathetic—kind—sorry. They telegraphed to England, which still seemed rather a wonderful thing to do—and the only relative comes—an aunt, very affectionate, very tremulous, rather—fine—no, not the word—noble, I think; something noble about this agitated, plain, elderly woman."

Crighton was silent a second; he had the indrawn look of one who sees pictures of his own making that blot out actuality.

"Almost as soon as the aunt arrives the girl dies—this box, this flower on the pillow, the young man—so close—that his face was the last thing she saw. Well! It is over . . . there is the funeral, the comments—the aunt goes back to England in her black crepe dress—and presently the young man goes too—back to the soap factory."

"Wretched," murmured Dessalle. "Wretched!"

"Wretched! Poor devil! Now—another picture. It is just a few days before he takes up his new post, and he is in his common little room, dark, rather dirty and uncomfortable, I think, though he did not notice that then—and he means to burn his books and never dream of them again—the books that could only whet his appetite. There is the fire in a heavy grate, and the books ready. When—the post. A letter. This letter."

Dessalle felt a curious pang; he wished the old man would stop.

"From the aunt of the funny little dark girl—by the same post a parcel, with the edelweiss, the box, the cheap ring she had always worn. This is the letter. She had written to the Swiss hotel for my address. Listen." Slowly he drew a single sheet of paper out of the buff envelope and read aloud:

DEAR MR. CRIGHTON,

Mary had no time to tell me of you, and afterwards I saw you did not feel you could speak of it. But I understood. How much she loved you! I send you her ring—your betrothal ring I guess it to be—the mountain flower and the box she treasured so. Also, what will surprise you very much, a cheque for three hundred pounds. Mary's little fortune that I had charge of—it was for her dowry, or, if she never married, to set her up in a little school. Now it seems so naturally yours that I can hardly think you need telling so. I heard you were not rich and wished to study—medicine, was it? Mary can help you, perhaps, with this money, as she will, I know, by the memory of her love. She would have been your wife, remember.

Crighton folded the letter away without a word of comment.

"A pathetic idyll, sir," remarked Dessalle gently.

"I took the money," said Crighton, closing the box. "I never went to the soap factory. I meant to pay it back, but the woman died soon after. That money was the foundation of everything for me."

"Rather beautiful, sir—I do not see what there should be to question in it. She would have been so pleased——"

As Dessalle spoke he recalled that the great man had never married.

"How pleased and proud she would have been," he added warmly.

"Do you think so?" asked Crighton slowly, falling sunken into the chair and replacing the box carefully on the little table. "I wonder. Did she care for me—or was it the delirium? The usual thing?"

"I do not follow you, sir."

"I took the money," said Crighton again, not heeding him. "There was your delicate temptation! I took it. Lie, fraud, cheat—well, what do you say now, Dessalle? Those are my foundations—the ambitious grab, the swift, unscrupulous seizing of advantage, the absence of honour, of rectitude! The usual thing!"

"I have not got it clear, sir."

"No? I'll tell you. I do not know if that girl loved me—but I did not love her——"

"Ah!" Dessalle looked again at the Claude Lorraine.

"I was not betrothed to her—I did not know her name—I met her in the fields three days before she died . . . for the first time. She spoke to me casually—about the way; I offered her the box to put some winter mosses in, her hands were so full—that was all. She must have known my name, for she sent for me when she was ill. And every one thought we were lovers. It did not seem possible to undeceive them. Or worth while. The girl was dead. And I took her money."

Dessalle dropped his glance from the golden picture. The flames had died down on the heath now, peaceful as an offering accepted, a sacrifice completed. Crighton put the Swiss box back into the drawer of the table.

"Think it over," he said in a very tired voice. "Think it over. I only know . . . I haven't told you . . . there was a lock of her hair . . . with the other things . . . . I had to burn that . . . "

# ALL THE SAME PRICE

SEATON was a cold, hard man who had been amazingly successful; he was applauded and encouraged beyond his merits, and only the grace of a clever manner saved him the blatant offences of vanity and coxcombry.

In his heart he delighted to think how dominant and triumphant he was; with his lips he smiled away flatteries. Now he was on holiday, lazy, content, compassionate to all those poor devils who were not John Seaton.

The women talked, aware of him, but not addressing him. He lounged in a canvas chair, allowing himself the taciturnity of the great man preoccupied, even in his leisure, with vast designs. The women were showing off; when Seaton was listening women usually did show off.

There were four of them, delicate creatures to look at, seated on the lawn on pale cushions, smoking negligently.

Marcia said:

"He is so narrow-minded; he can't understand how a woman can pay twenty, ten or even five pounds for a hat."

She spoke of Lord Loving, a fellow guest and the butt of their conversation.

"When he was young," answered Pamela, "there must have been a lot of women who wondered how he could pay—whatever he did—for port wine, ballet dancers and a private hansom."

"My dear," protested Sylvia, "he doesn't go so far back as that!"

But Pamela thought that he did—quite.

Elizabeth said it was so stupid of men to be surprised at

women getting what they really liked now they could earn the money to pay the bill.

"Didn't they always get what they really liked?" murmured Sylvia.

"Not without paying for it," Marcia was sure. "You had to please some man for your expensive hats, and the man despised you for it."

"If you were his wife?" queried Elizabeth demurely.

"Oh, then you never did please him—enough to get the hats," smiled Marcia.

"Surely—sometimes husbands were generous?"

Elizabeth answered the question of Sylvia's asking.

"The price of peace, not possession, was all a husband conceded—a poor thing, Sylvia!"

But Sylvia said they weren't to be cynical; she was sure there were plenty of devoted wives even nowadays.

"There are," said Marcia; "I've seen them."

Seaton spoke from the shady background, as they had all known that, sooner or later, he would speak.

"Whether they buy their own hats or not men find women very—amusing."

This was rude, of course. Seaton had a licence to be rude; he stressed the word "amusing."

The four gave him glances of varying depth and brightness.

"You don't think," he added lazily, "that women have really altered, do you? We used to pet them for playing the harp or making potpourri; now we pet them for writing indecent books in their 'teens and running town councils when they're too old to run anything else. It's equally amusing for us."

"Do you really think that is what we are out for?" purred Marcia; "the men's petting?'

"Of course," mocked Seaton, half closing his eyes in the pleasant shadows.

All four laughed, disdain masking excitement. They were all young and pretty, sweetly dressed and enjoying a summer day, a very luxurious summer day.

"Believe me," continued Seaton, clasping his hands behind his head, "to a man a woman's either adorable or funny; the very clever independent ones are generally the funniest."

Elizabeth said that showed how stupid men were, poor souls; women found them neither adorable nor funny, but just pathetic.

"They don't." replied Seaton; "they find them—just men."

Marcia refused to take him seriously. Did he mean that a man never considered a woman save according to her charm, her desirability?

"Of course," he assented.

"And nowadays—all the things that women *do*," protested Pamela.

"Just stunts," smiled Seaton, "like piano playing and fainting fits and sampler work; just gestures to attract attention."

Marcia shrugged her shoulders; the conversation was becoming acrid; she thought that if the others had gone she, alone with Seaton, could have given it a pleasanter tone.

But the others were lounging comfortably, with no intention of leaving.

"You're trying to be clever," said Elizabeth; "but we're not a bit angry, Mr. Seaton."

"Of course not," he agreed; "you're flattered, every one of you."

"At the mere notice of a man!" mocked Pamela.

He smiled as if in assent.

"What would you like to say?" challenged Marcia.

He closed his eyes, still smiling. The women controlled their tempers; there was no one so conspicuous as Seaton in the house party, but there were others, and what could one do worth while, four of one sex together?

They drifted away across the costly lawn—lovely frocks like sweet peas, silvery voices, delicate steps.

Seaton opened his eyes to look after them. How easily he could marry any one of them! Marcia, the rich widow, standing in the autumn for her husband's seat in Parliament; Pamela, an earl's daughter, studying economics; Elizabeth, the successful medical student; Sylvia, eighteen, lovely, who meant to go on the Stock Exchange—all well-born, alluring women, all the same price now as a thousand years ago, as a thousand years hence.

Marriage. He might have any one of them by lifting up his finger. Didn't they know that he knew that?

It was very pleasant to play with the admiration of the women; his great success had brought him no more delightful diversion—one's pick of exquisite women.

But there were so many of them.

Without moving from his idle attitude he reviewed these four. Marcia, so cool, so superb—she would sink her "career" in his with a very passion of abnegation, the very lap spaniel type; that he could see in her wistful brown eyes, that implored while her tongue spoke sharply.

Pamela, who affected a demure aspect, was extremely vain and quick tempered; there would be fun in breaking her in.

Elizabeth was ambitious; she'd want to shine.

Sylvia, poor child, so aggressive and smart, was really in love with him in the crudest schoolgirl fashion.

Seaton did not prefer one to another; he had almost decided to marry one of them. Why?

Well, brilliant, conspicuous men always did get married before marriage made them look old or a "back number." To marry after fifty was to draw attention to one's age.

Seaton was not nearly fifty, but one must be quite on the safe side. To appear as a handsome, alert bridegroom was a good advertisement; to lead a fresh young woman up to the lilies on the altar looking yourself bald and frayed (how one came out, anyhow, in those Press snaps!) was to invite ridicule.

He would be in the government next year, and then one wanted a wife for the social side of things. Yes, he must get married, though it seemed a pity to give up the marvellous asset of his bachelorhood. Still, he consoled himself, matrimony need not interfere with his success with women. On the contrary.

A fifth woman came across the lawn. Seaton loathed her frock—white—ready made—sale price. He knew too much about women's clothes for his own peace of mind; he was constantly being worried by some sartorial detail.

This was Betty Powell, companion "chauffeuse" to that atrocious old woman, Mrs. Crighton. She came over sometimes to play tennis and fag; he'd seen her, too, driving the dark blue limousine about the narrow lanes while the yellow crone and her puffy dogs dozed behind the plate glass windows.

She did not perceive him until she was close to him; then she blushed becomingly, a delicate tint of red mounting to her forehead in confusion.

Flattered by her hesitant awe, the great man exerted himself to be agreeable.

"Every one has abandoned me, Miss Powell; do stay and talk."

The blush was deeper.

"I am surprised that you should remember my name, Mr. Seaton."

"Why surprised?" He had risen with a deference wholly assumed. (After all, masculine deference to women usually is.)

She said, in embarrassment, still with a hot colour and ill-chosen words, that she was going home by the short cut—the side gate.

"Don't. Stay and talk."

She recovered something of her equanimity and eyed the great man, with a modest entreaty for his compassion. What could she talk to him about? She knew nothing; no one could be more unlettered.

"The most interesting subjects a man and woman can discuss," said Seaton suavely, "require no learning."

Of course he had said that before, and it had never failed of effect. Miss Powell was disarmed; she seated herself on one of the cushions in the tremulous shadow.

Seaton appraised her. He could, by dint of practice, discount the annoying clothes. After all, modern dress was pretty frank; it wasn't difficult to get a fair idea of the best and worst of things.

A lovely woman, this, with long elegant limbs and grace in every movement; she made those other four look mannered. Why couldn't she do better for herself than old Mrs. Crighton?

She must be a fool.

Lovely women so often were.

And did it matter?

Folly was sometimes not so stupid as cleverness.

He began to talk, to "draw her out." She had a perfect profile, a delicious throat, a charming bust—a really beautiful creature, and one docile to a flutter of his eyelid.

Not a sophisticated, willing victim like the other four, but breathlessly submissive in ingenuous surrender, overwhelmed that he should talk to her, abashed that he had noticed her; and Seaton now told himself that he had noticed her a good deal lately—rather more than he had realized.

He said didn't she find it dull here—with Mrs. Crighton?

And she said, dull? One didn't have to think about that.

"But what do you do all day?"

She was not able to say. There were the dogs; Mrs. Crighton liked to be read to; walks and driving the car.

Seaton marvelled that some women allowed themselves to be entrapped like this. Why didn't this girl strike out for herself?

Stupid, of course.

Her next remark confirmed this opinion.

"I can't really do anything but drive a car and look after the dogs."

Well bred, though. He liked her voice and her manners.

"You're wasted here," he assured her, with a warm look.

She was blushingly candid.

"Well, I never could find anything better. I was very glad to get the place, really."

"You haven't looked about. There are such chances for women nowadays, aren't there?"

"I don't know. I believe I would have liked to have lived a hundred years ago and been looked after."

He believed she would—the darling!

"Day dreaming, eh?" he smiled.

"Yes, I do a lot of that in the evenings—and taking walks with the dogs."

"You haven't any friends?"

"People are very kind," she said evasively. Seaton knew what she meant: as long as she was sufficiently humble she was allowed, on sufferance, on the fringe of what society the place afforded—not often up to the great house where she was now.

Marcia was coming towards them. Miss Powell rose at once, timidly said good-bye and almost ran away.

Frightened, thought Seaton. He could guess (as near as a man ever can) how terrible women can be one to another, and he felt a more generous emotion than was usual to him towards the companion "chauffeuse" (horrible word!).

Marcia had seen her; Marcia saw most things. Marcia hoped that he had been bored, and her eyes were hard.

"It's rather awkward; the girl runs about here and doesn't quite know——"

He answered, with the deliberate purpose of annoying Marcia:

"A delicious creature—such a rare type. I was sorry that you frightened her away."

Marcia could do nothing but laugh. He knew Miss Powell would not be asked again, but that did not matter to Seaton.

Marcia began to talk of the charades they would have to-night, and the new band from town. The great man pretended to go to sleep.

He had now a direct interest in Miss Powell; it was worth while encouraging her if only to vex the other egregious women.

All the same price!

If the others were ready to surrender at mention of the word "marriage," what of the poor companion?

Seaton's pride and vanity were both elated at the thought of what a god, a very Jove, he would appear to Miss Powell if he were to offer her marriage. What a sensation such a match must make (successful men must think in terms of success); far more of a sensation than any marriage in his own set! Nothing was so popular as a love match, and when there was no money in the case people thought there must be love; and he was rather playing for popularity just now.

Yes, it would be the *beau geste*, the Prince and the beggar maid—Cinderella. The common crowd would rapturously applaud, and his own set would be—well, stimulated.

Seaton began by thinking like this in ironic self-mockery, but after twenty-four hours' reflection he was rather in love with the idea.

Indeed he could almost have persuaded himself that he was rather in love with Betty Powell.

He had quite cleverly arranged to meet her when she was giving the obese dogs their airing.

The lanes were hung with clematis and bryony, and coronals of honeysuckle decked the pretty blue of the soft sky; a charming place, this narrow lane, and the girl wholly in place against the sweet background.

Her cheap gown was not so obtrusive now; a faded pink, of simple cut, it did very well.

It would be a fresh sensation to a man to whom most sensations were stale to make splendid presents to this simple creature.

Seaton could imagine her with a string of pearls in her hand, looking at him with incoherent gratitude.

He remarked on the beauty of the weather and the attractiveness of the walk.

Miss Powell said:

"I get a little tired of it, you know."

He supposed she did. He looked at her critically.

A really lovely woman.

"But you must not think that I am discontented," she added, with a blush of confusion at having ventured to voice an opinion.

There was tennis at the great house. Seaton loathed tennis, which showed off the attractions of the younger men. He proposed a visit to Clympton; tea at the old inn.

He liked to think he was great enough to do unconventional things. She was dazzled. (He reflected that she ought to have been.)

"But how could I?" she faltered. "Mrs. Crighton is in bed to-day, and when I've exercised the dogs I've got to get a prescription made up——"

"Don't they make up prescriptions at Clympton?"

"Oh, yet—but——"

"I'm sure you'll give me a lift," smiled Seaton in his most masterful manner. "I'll be at the corner in half an hour, by the sign post."

He was. The rosy Miss Powell, trembling with excitement, came up in the little two-seater that did Mrs. Crighton's odd jobs.

Seaton took the wheel; she surrendered it gladly. She really disliked driving, she said; she was always nervous.

"I knew," he said, "that you were that kind of woman."

And then she became surprisingly bold, for, glancing at him directly, she asked:

"I wonder, Mr. Seaton, if you do know what kind of woman I am?"

"The kind that I admire," he said gallantly, feeling more thrilled than his years and experience warranted.

"Then I wonder——" She checked herself, adorably troubled.

"You were going to ask me something?" Seaton guessed.

"Oh, no!" Her awe was genuine. "I should not dare."

The little car took the road gaily; a very attractive road it seemed to Seaton, and one that led him a long way from the cynical silly talk of those other women.

Life was like that; it wasn't logical or all of a piece, it began an episode like a smart farce and ended it as a serious drama. Or a love romance?

How pleasant to think that he, the famous John Seaton, could, if he wished, afford a love romance!

Clympton proved the most coquettish of small towns; the chemist had bow windows, the inn hollyhocks and beehives in the gardens. The day continued as blue as a forget-me-not.

They had their tea in the garden; such a different garden from that of the great house, where now quite a lot of important people would be wondering what had become of Seaton.

He allowed himself to drift further into love in this sweet and simple atmosphere, and he read in her startled eyes overwhelmed rapture at his obvious homage.

She was persuaded to tell him what she had wanted to ask him in the car.

"It was only, Mr. Seaton—that I would like to get to London—if you should possibly hear of a job——"

She paused, silenced by her own effrontery.

"I dare say I might," he assured her gravely.

Tears came into her candid eyes as she thanked him. They lingered till it was well into the afternoon before they started home.

There would be a hue and cry by now no doubt. Seaton did not know if women could ever be compromised nowadays, but he thought that old Mrs. Crighton would contrive to make it unpleasant for Betty Powell.

The great man now was, or had persuaded himself that he was, in love with the lovely nobody, and fully intended to indulge himself and vex all his acquaintances and make a "sensation" by marrying the lovely nobody.

These thoughts occupied him most of the drive home. He dwelt maliciously on the approaching discomfiture of the superb Marcia and those other three cocksure girls; he was sick of the crowd of them when there were Betty Powells about.

They separated at Mrs. Crighton's door. The companion felt guilty about the medicine; she ran the car into the drive with a hunted air.

"She'll get into disgrace," smiled Seaton; "but I'll make it up to her."

He went up leisurely to the great house, hoping that his absence would have been fully commented upon.

At the imposing gates of the mansion a red-faced young man asked him the way to Mrs. Crighton's house. He was a very ordinary young man indeed, and must have been applying for some sort of place, and Seaton felt outraged both by the confidence of the stranger's address and the thought that these were the people Betty Powell did have and would have to associate with while she remained in servitude.

He replied with a dignity which only provoked a slight grin from the coarse young stranger, and turned into the grandiose drive feeling like a knight-errant who was about to rescue a maiden from a dragon.

The first person he met was Marcia, trailing a glittering shawl in the dusk of the chestnut avenue.

Seaton began posing at once, taking on an air of abstraction, and even gloom.

She said: "Did you run away from all the lion hunters?"

"My dear Marcia, where should I go if I fled from lion hunters."

"To Clympton, perhaps?"

He preserved his famous composure.

"I was seen there?"

"Naturally." Marcia was pleasant. "Elizabeth——"

"Ah, she was in Clympton this afternoon?" parried Seaton.

"She was. You didn't see her? But dear Elizabeth has a trained observation."

"Most women have, from their cradles."

How long the avenue seemed, and how pervading, almost unescapable was the personality of Marcia!

"Poor Miss Powell, it must have been a great day for her. I rather admire her, don't you? She is just like one of those bunches of wild flowers you see stuck in a jam pot at the local show."

A true jest is a poor jest; the comparison stung. Never mind, before they reached the end of the avenue he would demolish Marcia with the news of his engagement.

He began to work himself up to this point by a good deal of rather ponderous talk; he got into his "after dinner" speech stride. If she had been listening-in she would have clicked him off; as it was she planned future revenge.

Marcia also had something to say before they reached the end of the chestnut avenue. She walked very slowly.

Seaton was maintaining the beauty of love matches, the sanctity of simplicity, the joys of home life, the ugliness of modernity; all this was really his stock-in-trade, and, spurred on by the thought of one woman and the presence of another, he delivered what, liberally blue pencilled, would have been an accepted article for one of the more boring Sunday papers.

Marcia knew his climax, and resolved to spare him. She interrupted:

"Betty Powell wants a job in town."

"I know." Seaton, swelling with his own virtue, was grandiose. "And *I* will find her one——"

Marcia hurried in to his rescue. "How nice for her! She's engaged to be married, poor thing, to a kind of motor-shop person. He's coming down for this week-end; Mrs. Crighton relented and said he might come. The inn, of course; but a visit to the poor child permitted! It's *like* you to help them."

She spoke at length to give him a chance of recovery. The dark helped.

He answered. He remembered the red-faced, impudent young man. His voice lost some of its boom, but relief at his great escape helped to steady him. His vanity unscathed, what else mattered?

"Yes"—he managed to take up her cue—"I was considering helping them. She rather pestered me, of course."

"I understand," said Marcia quickly, as if this was an apology. "I've always understood how"—her voice quivered—"*big* you are."

"Sentimental, you mean!" Her compliment was balm. "It gets in my way, Marcia, sometimes."

She came closer. "The warm, generous heart! I must look after you."

His hour had struck. It was as easy as throwing a noose round a man who had scrambled, half drowned, out of a swamp; gasping with the horror of his escape the victim was hauled away. By the time they left the avenue Marcia was planning her wedding dress—widow's white—oyster pink.

"All the same price," she thought as she glanced up at her imposing capture; "*patience and a little flattery.*"

THE END

www.ingramcontent.com/pod-product-compliance
Lightning Source LLC
Chambersburg PA
CBHW020932310726
48980CB00007B/742/J

* 9 7 8 1 9 1 7 1 1 3 1 2 0 *